ANOTHER MESS...?
SORRY, MY BAD!

YASUNARI NAGATOSHI

I'm no good at keeping things tidy and in order. Even when I do get around to cleaning, the mess comes back before I realize it. If only my cat could clean up for me when that happens...

ZOMBIE BOY'S METAMORPHOSIS COLLECTION

ANT ZOMBIE-BOY

AAGH.
SUGAR

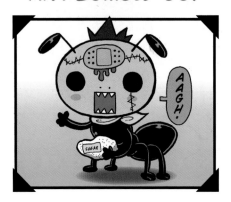

Just like real ants, they move as a group and carry things to their anthill. They cause all sorts of trouble by stealing not only food but also manga magazines, appliances like TVs, refrigerators, and laundry machines, and even big things like cars. If you see them, be careful they don't steal anything from you.

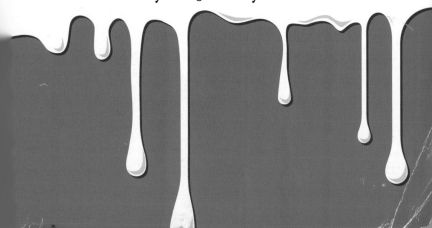

ZO ZO ZOMBIE

VOL. 4

VROOM
AGH!

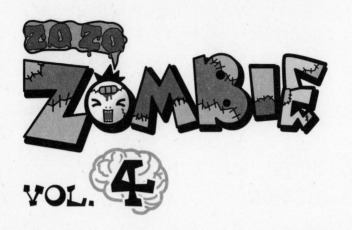

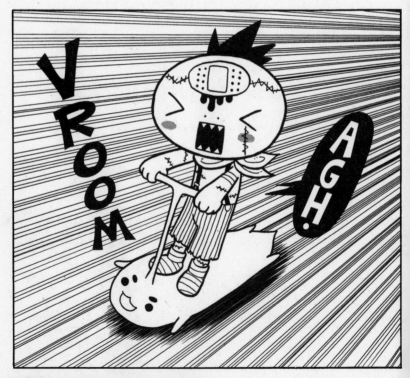

YASUNARI NAGATOSHI

CONTENTS

MANGA

AAGH!

BANDAGES!!

TABLE OF

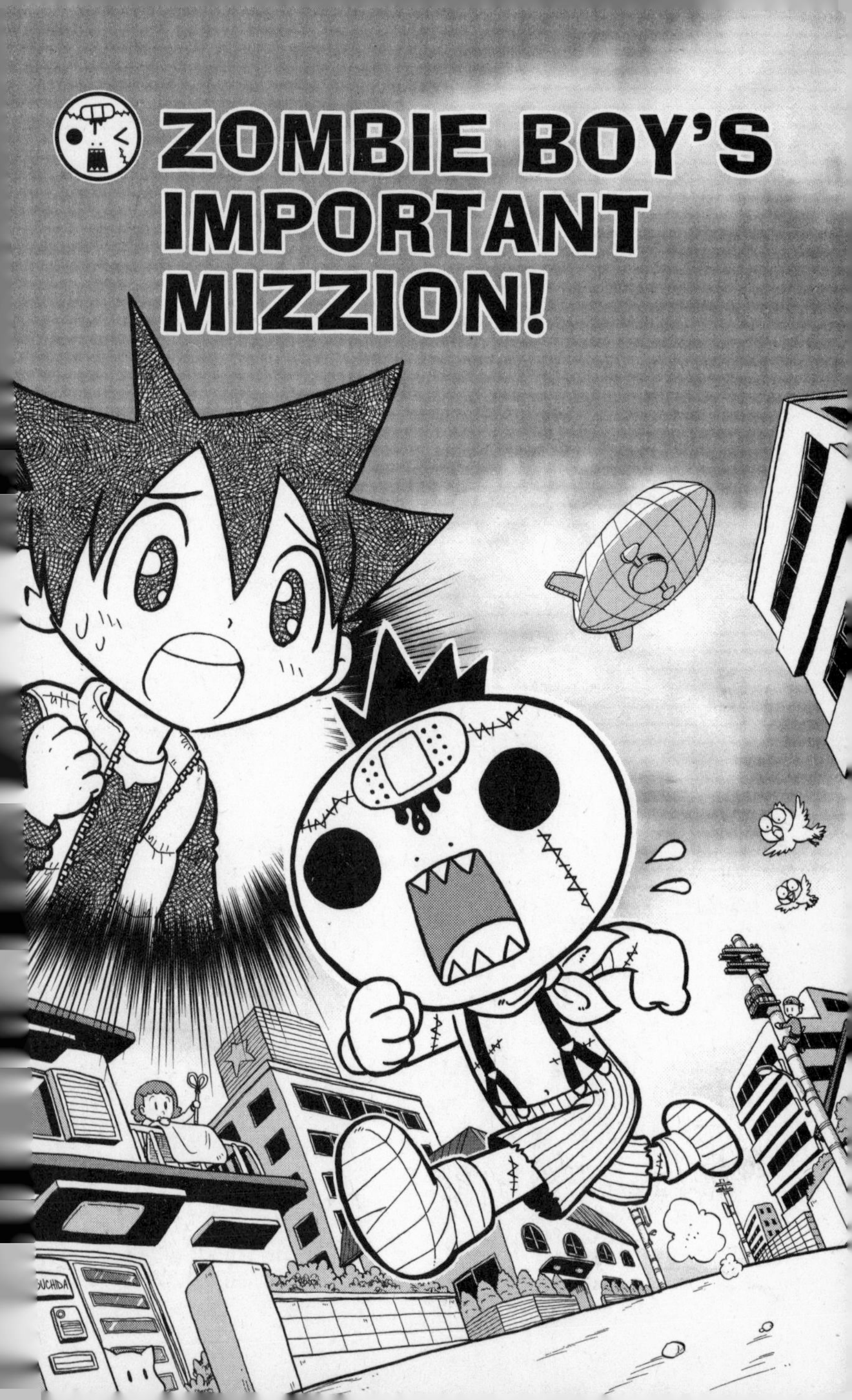
ZOMBIE BOY'S
IMPORTANT
MIZZION!

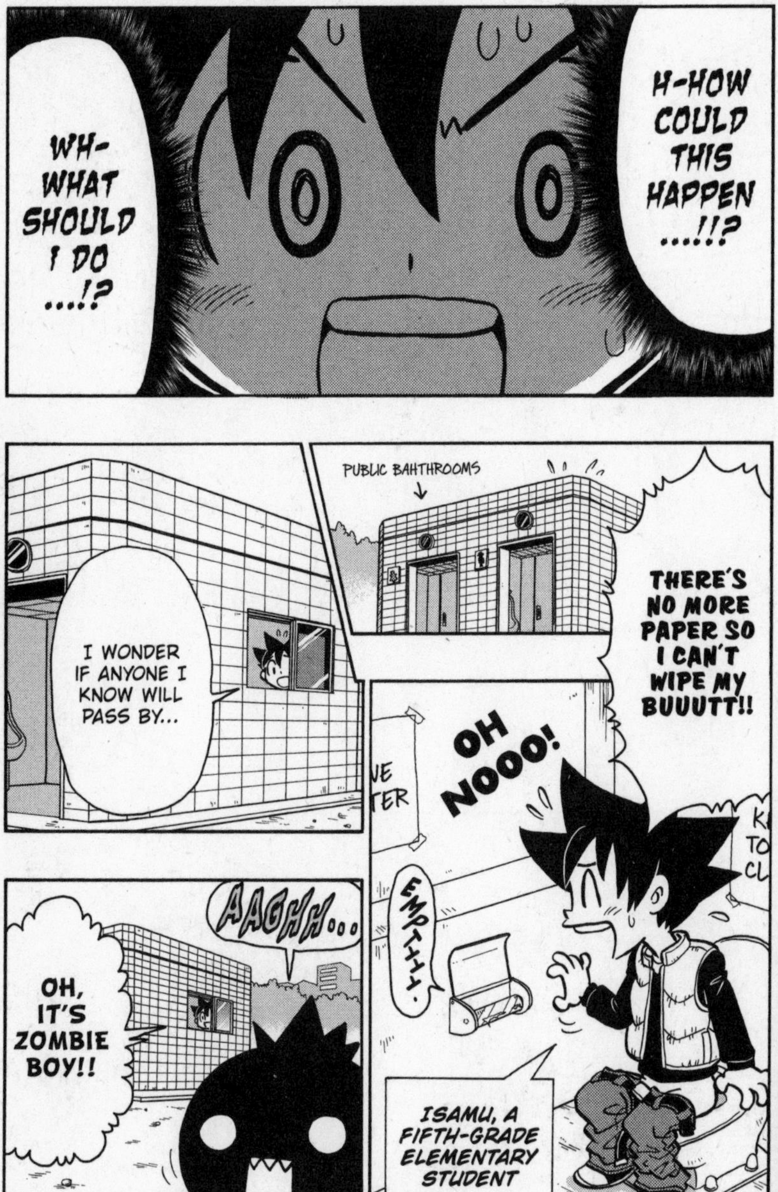

H-HOW COULD THIS HAPPEN ....!!?
WH-WHAT SHOULD I DO ...!?
PUBLIC BAHTHROOMS
THERE'S NO MORE PAPER SO I CAN'T WIPE MY BUUUTT!!
OH NOOO!
EMPTYYYY.
ISAMU, A FIFTH-GRADE ELEMENTARY STUDENT
I WONDER IF ANYONE I KNOW WILL PASS BY...
AAGHH...
OH, IT'S ZOMBIE BOY!!

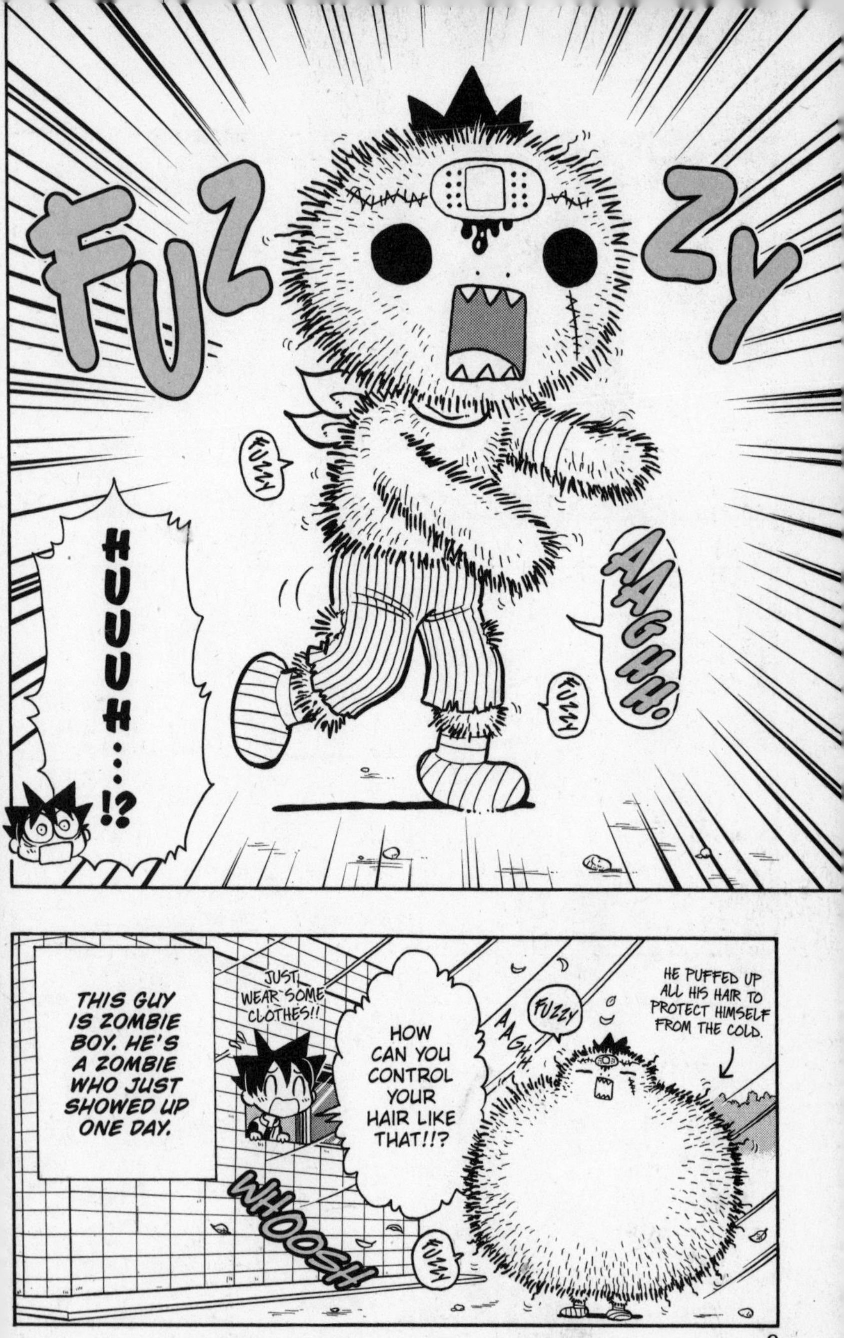
FUZZY
AAGHH.
FUZZY
FUZZY
HUUUUH...!?
HE PUFFED UP ALL HIS HAIR TO PROTECT HIMSELF FROM THE COLD.
FUZZY
AAGHH
HOW CAN YOU CONTROL YOUR HAIR LIKE THAT!!?
JUST WEAR SOME CLOTHES!!
THIS GUY IS ZOMBIE BOY. HE'S A ZOMBIE WHO JUST SHOWED UP ONE DAY.
WHOOSH
FUZZY

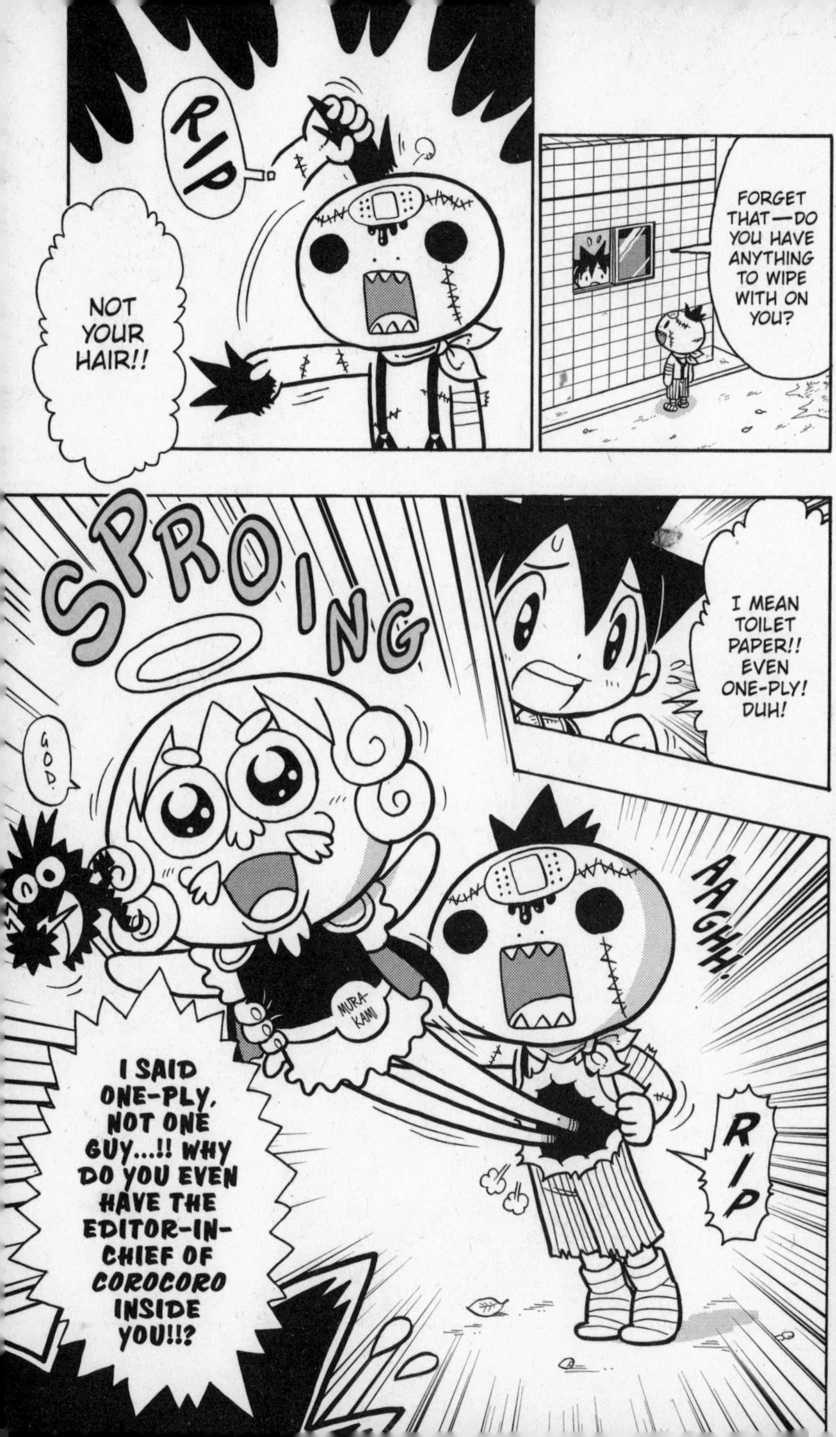
FORGET THAT—DO YOU HAVE ANYTHING TO WIPE WITH ON YOU?
RIP
NOT YOUR HAIR!!
I MEAN TOILET PAPER!! EVEN ONE-PLY! DUH!
SPROING
AAGHH.
RIP
GOD.
MURA-KAMI
I SAID ONE-PLY, NOT ONE GUY...!! WHY DO YOU EVEN HAVE THE EDITOR-IN-CHIEF OF COROCORO INSIDE YOU!!?

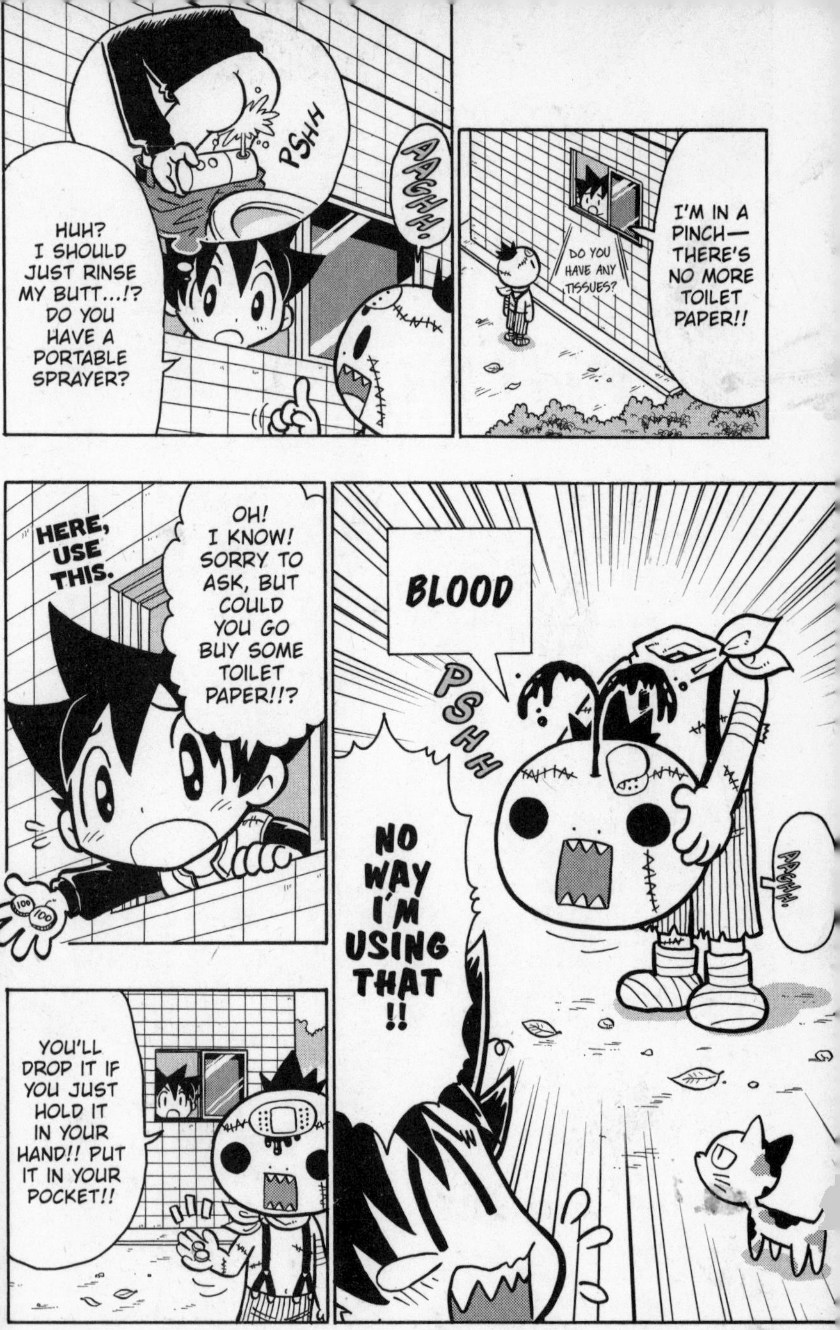
I'M IN A PINCH—THERE'S NO MORE TOILET PAPER!!
DO YOU HAVE ANY TISSUES?
PSHH
AAGHH.
HUH? I SHOULD JUST RINSE MY BUTT...!? DO YOU HAVE A PORTABLE SPRAYER?
BLOOD
PSHH
AAGHH.
NO WAY I'M USING THAT!!
OH! I KNOW! SORRY TO ASK, BUT COULD YOU GO BUY SOME TOILET PAPER!!?
HERE, USE THIS.
100
100
YOU'LL DROP IT IF YOU JUST HOLD IT IN YOUR HAND!! PUT IT IN YOUR POCKET!!

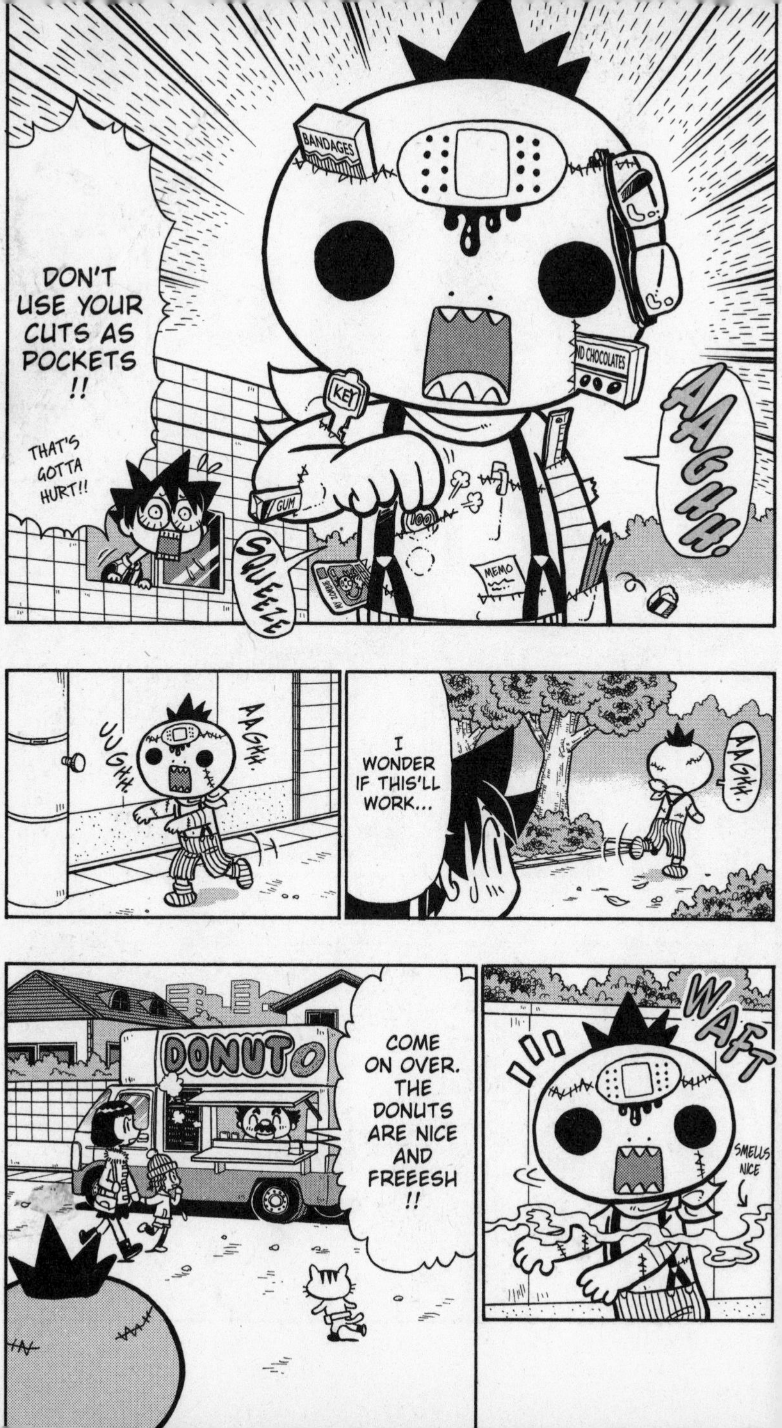
AAGHH!
BANDAGES
ND CHOCOLATES
KEY
DON'T USE YOUR CUTS AS POCKETS!!
THAT'S GOTTA HURT!!
GUM
MEMO
SQUEEZE
AAGHH.
I WONDER IF THIS'LL WORK...
AAGHH.
UUGHH.
WAFT
SMELLS NICE
COME ON OVER. THE DONUTS ARE NICE AND FREEESH!!
DONUTO

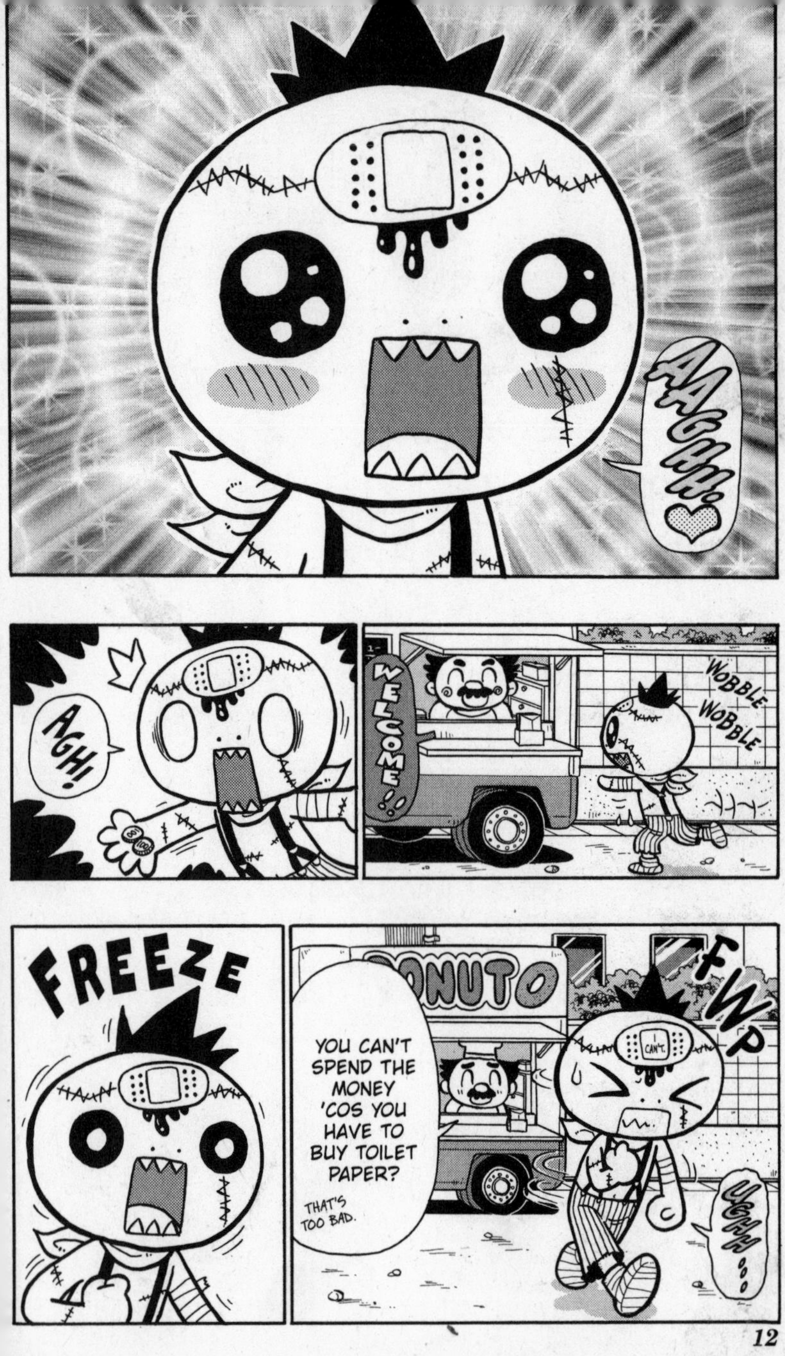
AAGHH♥
WELCOME!!
WOBBLE WOBBLE
AGH!
FWP
YOU CAN'T SPEND THE MONEY 'COS YOU HAVE TO BUY TOILET PAPER?
THAT'S TOO BAD.
I CAN'T.
UGHH...
FREEZE

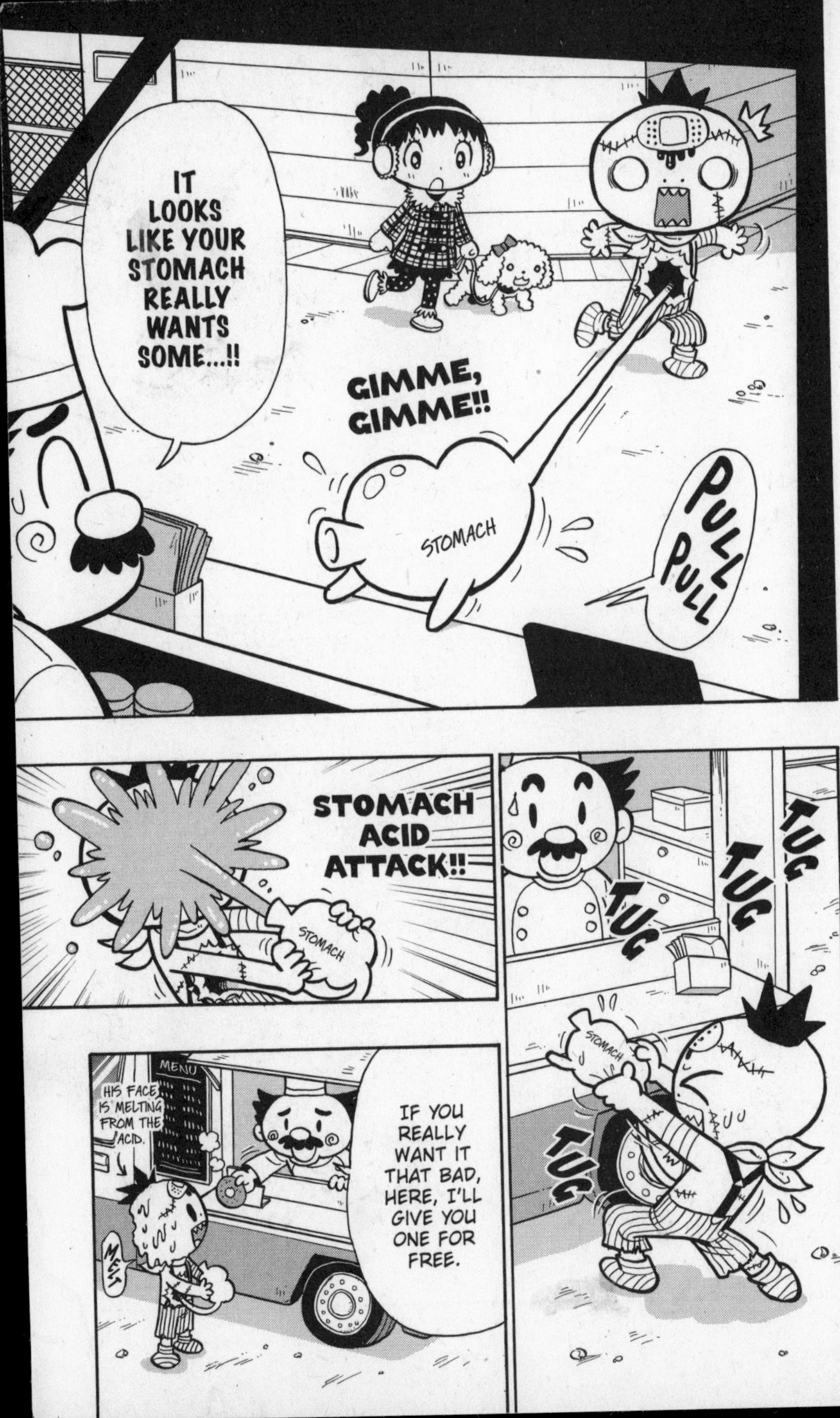
IT LOOKS LIKE YOUR STOMACH REALLY WANTS SOME...!!
GIMME, GIMME!!
STOMACH
PULL PULL
TUG TUG TUG
STOMACH
TUG TUG
STOMACH ACID ATTACK!!
STOMACH
IF YOU REALLY WANT IT THAT BAD, HERE, I'LL GIVE YOU ONE FOR FREE.
MENU
HIS FACE IS MELTING FROM THE ACID.
MELT

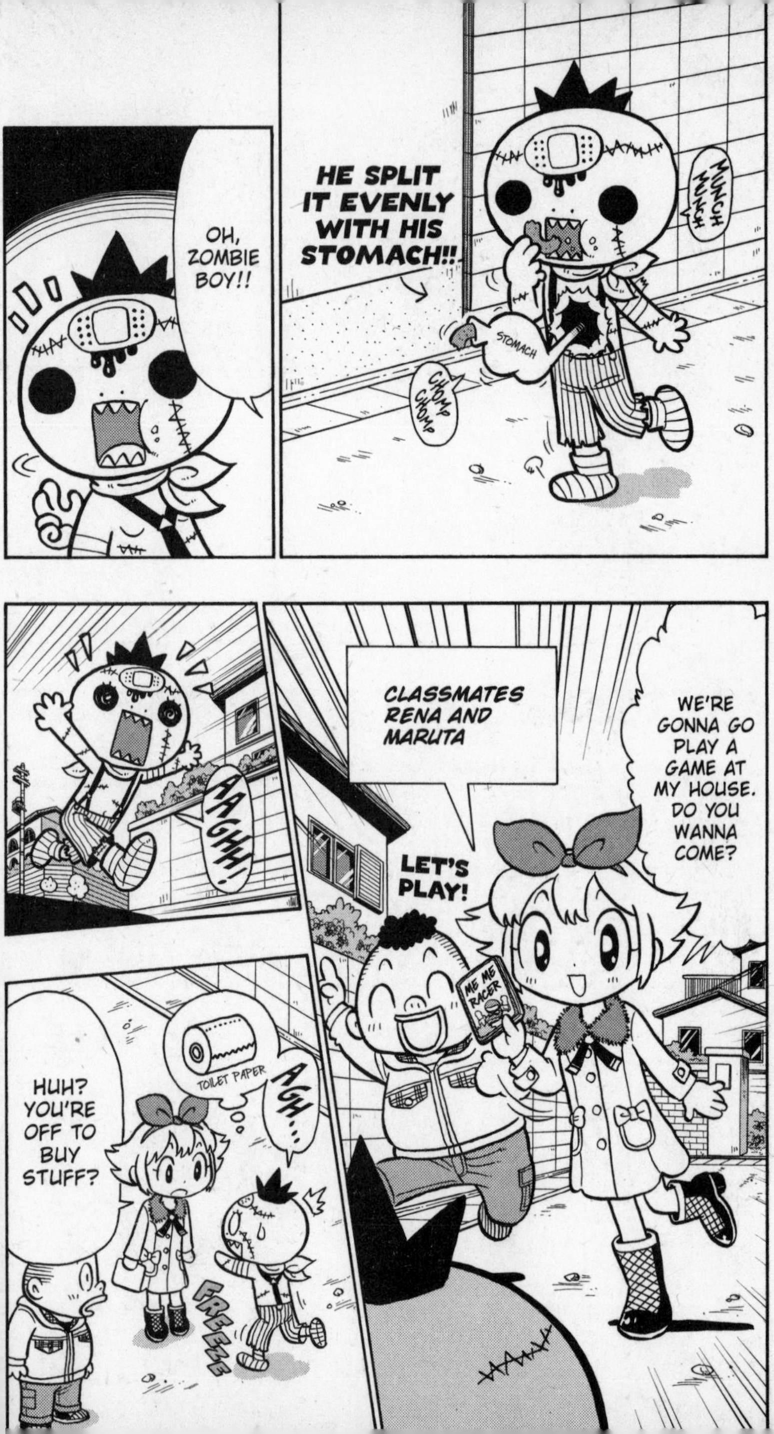
HE SPLIT IT EVENLY WITH HIS STOMACH!!
MUNCH MUNCH
STOMACH
CHOMP CHOMP
OH, ZOMBIE BOY!!
CLASSMATES RENA AND MARUTA
WE'RE GONNA GO PLAY A GAME AT MY HOUSE. DO YOU WANNA COME?
LET'S PLAY!
ME ME RACER
AAGHH!
TOILET PAPER
AGH...
HUH? YOU'RE OFF TO BUY STUFF?
FREEZE

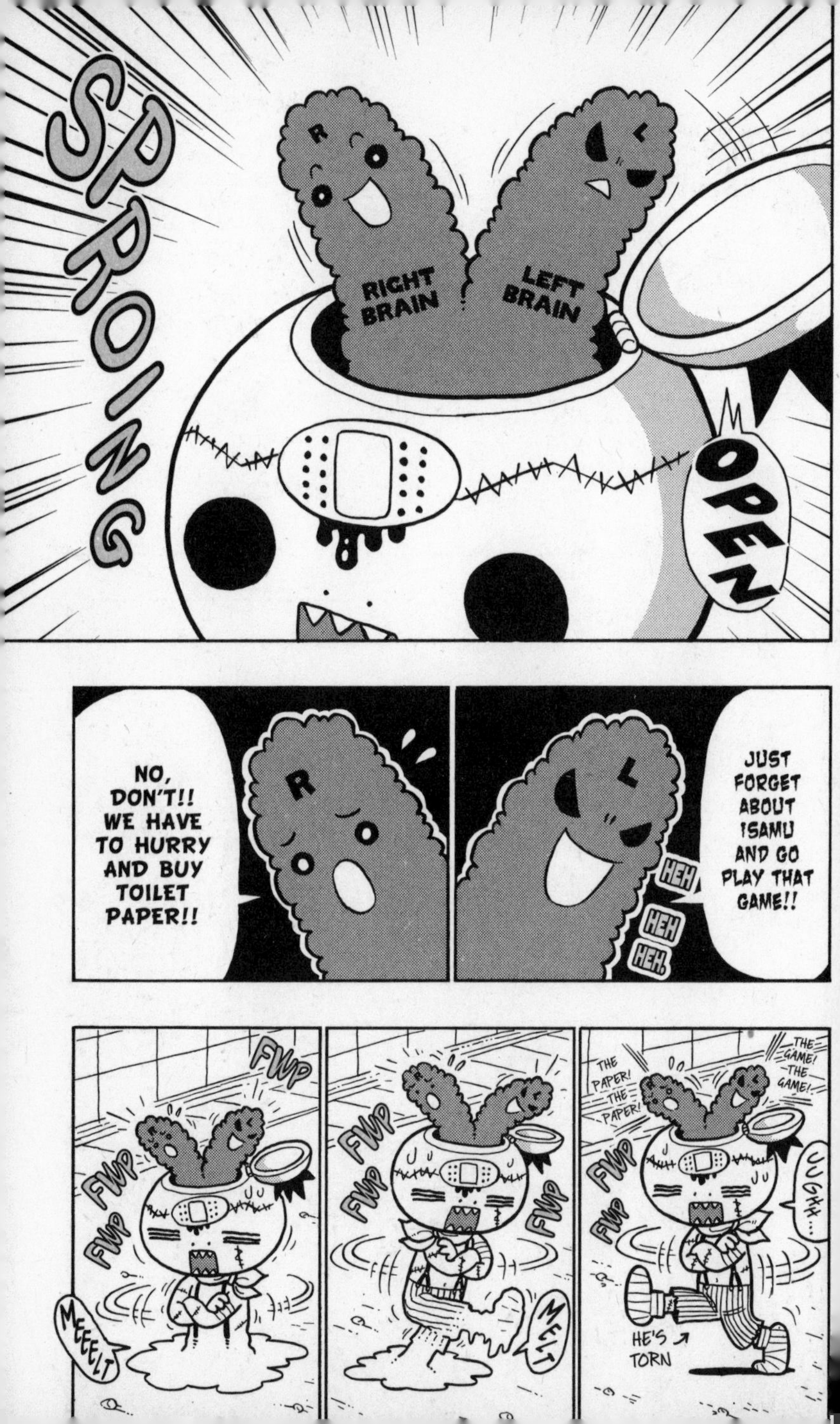
OPEN
LEFT BRAIN
L
RIGHT BRAIN
R
SPROING
JUST FORGET ABOUT ISAMU AND GO PLAY THAT GAME!!
HEH HEH HEH.
L
R
NO, DON'T!! WE HAVE TO HURRY AND BUY TOILET PAPER!!
THE GAME! THE GAME!
THE PAPER! THE PAPER!
UUGHH...
FWP
FWP
HE'S TORN
FWP
FWP
FWP
FWP
MELT
FWP
FWP
FWP
MEEELT

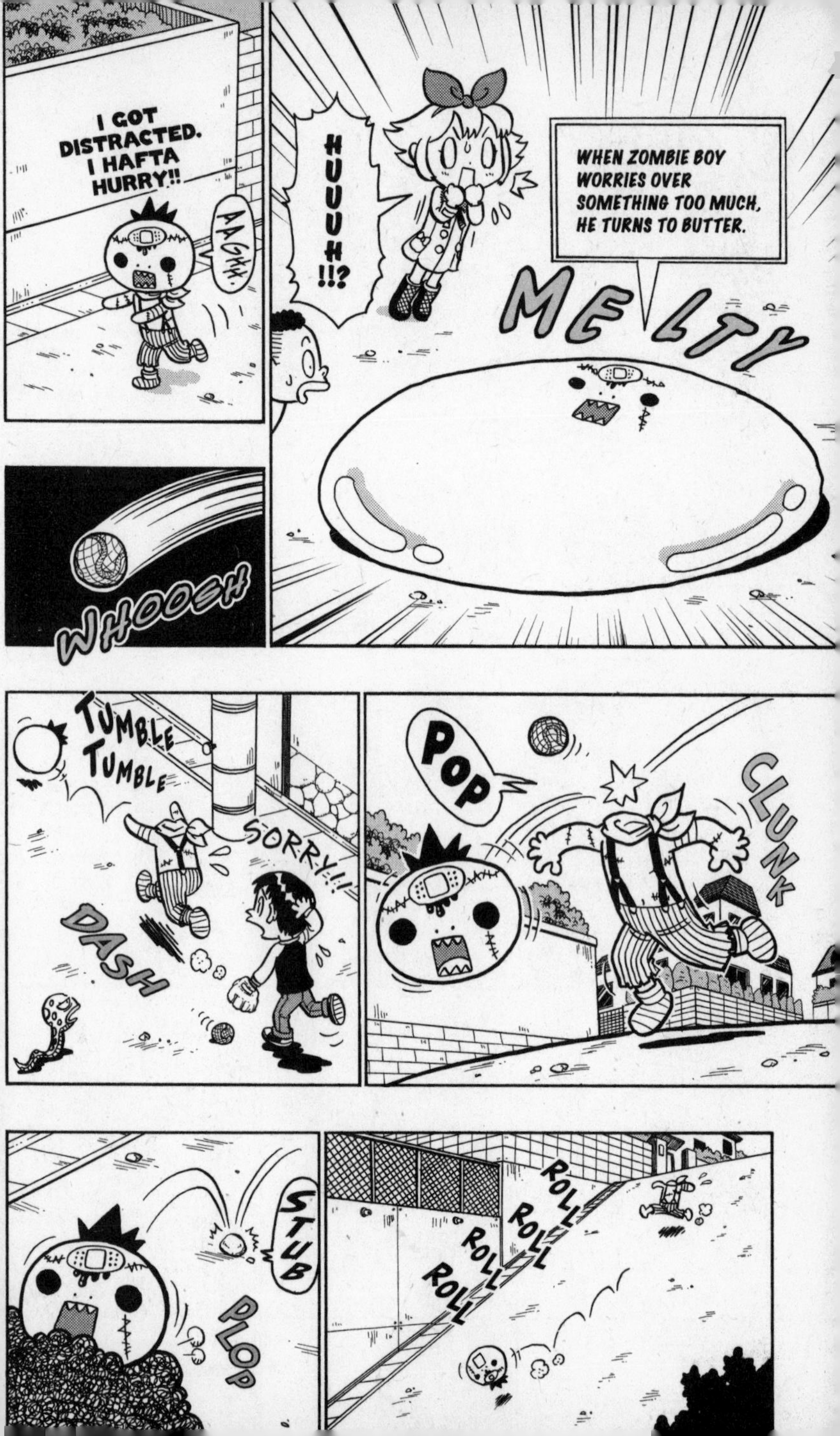
WHEN ZOMBIE BOY WORRIES OVER SOMETHING TOO MUCH, HE TURNS TO BUTTER.
HUUUUH!!?
MELTY
I GOT DISTRACTED. I HAFTA HURRY!!
AAGHK.
WHOOSH
POP
CLUNK
TUMBLE TUMBLE
SORRY!!
DASH
ROLL ROLL ROLL ROLL
STUB
PLOP

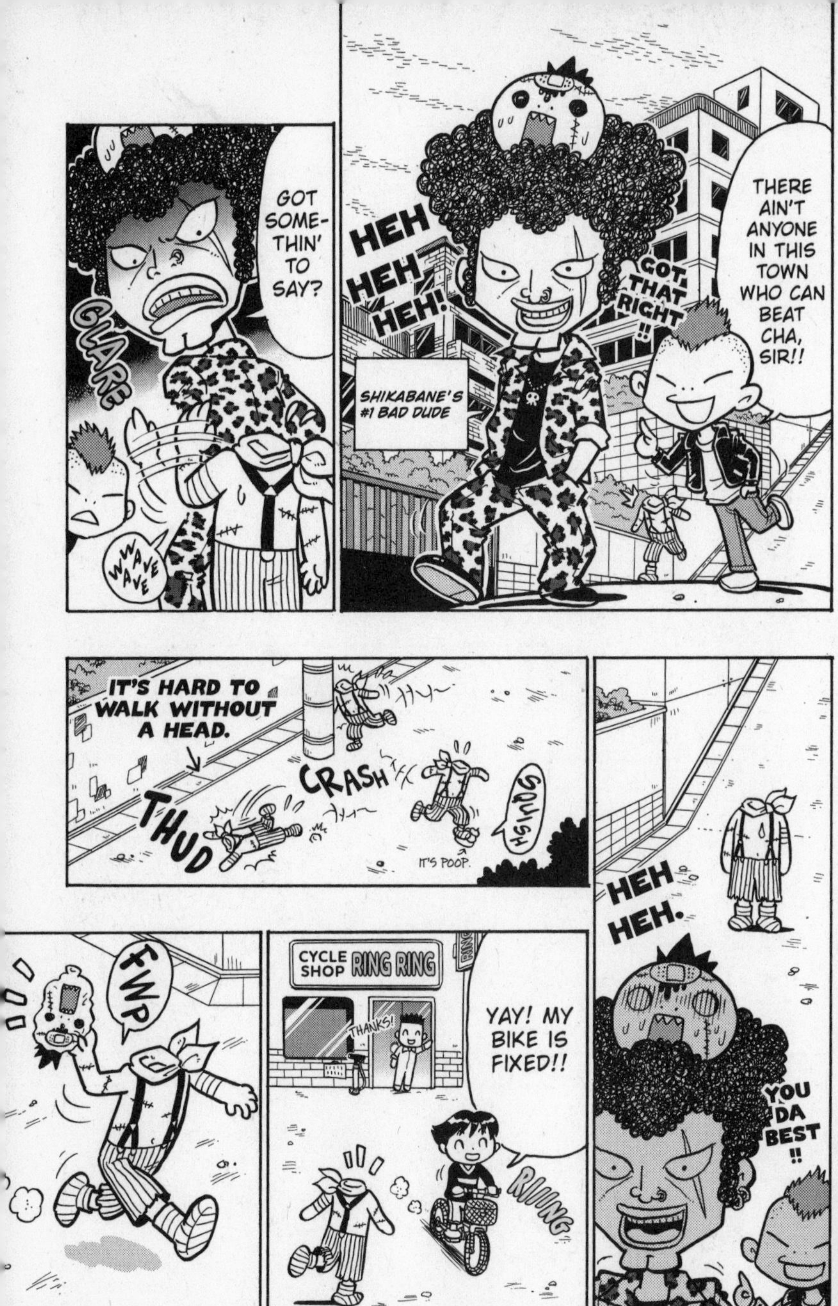
THERE AIN'T ANYONE IN THIS TOWN WHO CAN BEAT CHA, SIR!!
GOT THAT RIGHT!!
HEH HEH HEH!
SHIKABANE'S #1 BAD DUDE
GOT SOME-THIN' TO SAY?
GLARE
WAVE WAVE
HEH HEH.
YOU DA BEST!!
SQUISH
CRASH
IT'S HARD TO WALK WITHOUT A HEAD.
IT'S POOP.
THUD
CYCLE SHOP RING RING
YAY! MY BIKE IS FIXED!!
THANKS!
RIIING
FWP

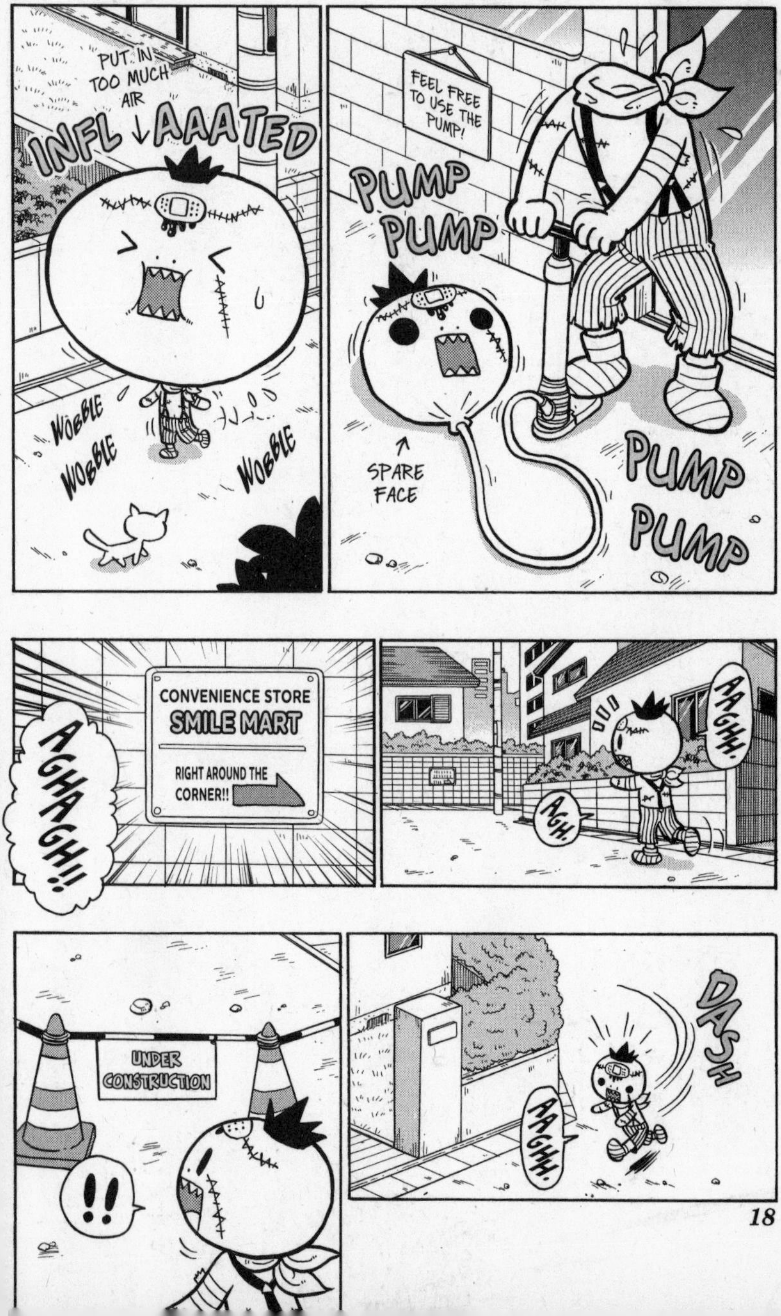
FEEL FREE TO USE THE PUMP!
PUMP PUMP
SPARE FACE
PUMP PUMP
PUT IN TOO MUCH AIR
INFL↓AAATED
WOBBLE WOBBLE
WOBBLE
AAGHH.
AGH.
CONVENIENCE STORE
SMILE MART
RIGHT AROUND THE CORNER!!
AGHAGH!!
DASH
AAGHH.
UNDER CONSTRUCTION
!!

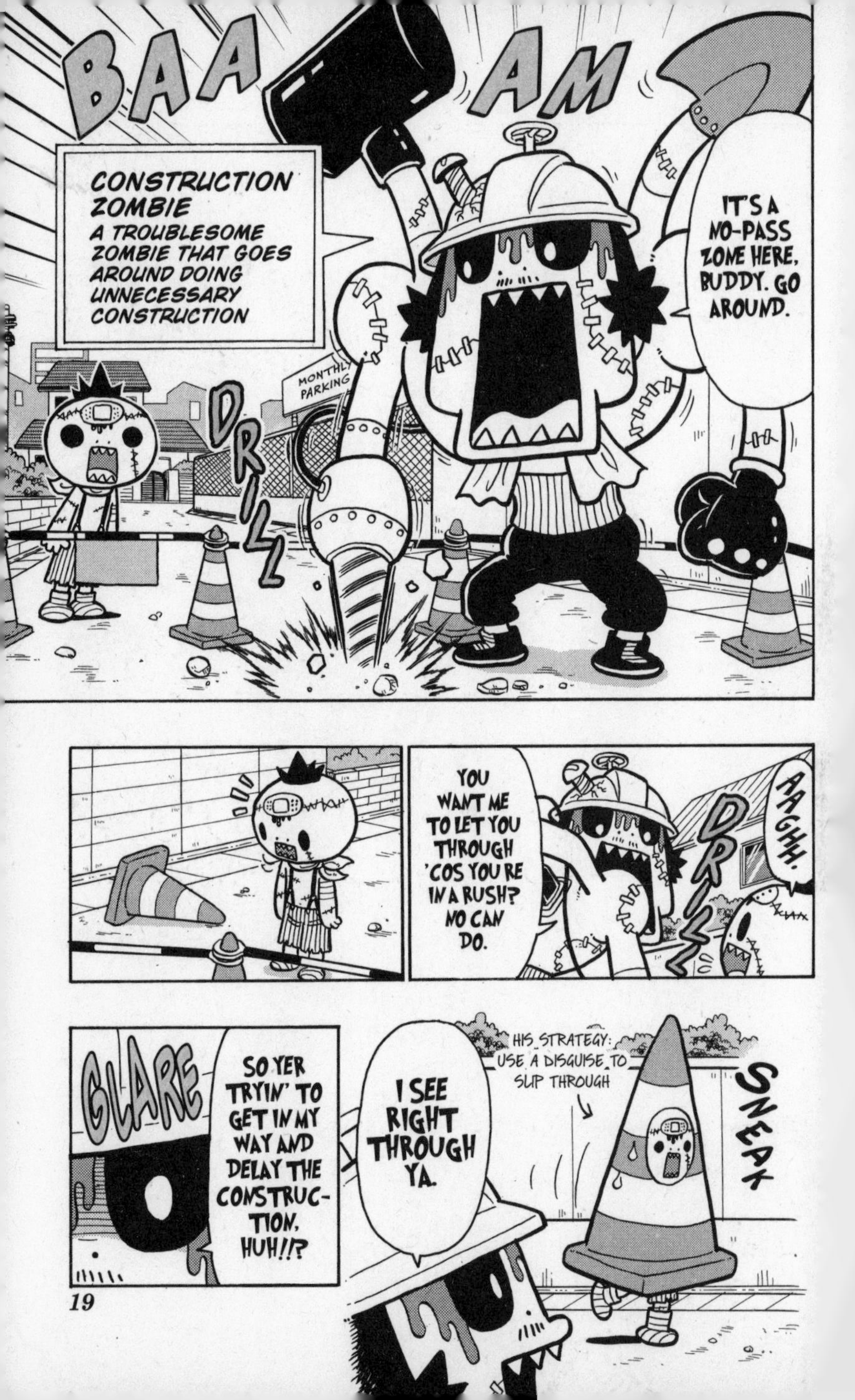
BAAAM
IT'S A NO-PASS ZONE HERE, BUDDY. GO AROUND.
CONSTRUCTION ZOMBIE
A TROUBLESOME ZOMBIE THAT GOES AROUND DOING UNNECESSARY CONSTRUCTION
MONTHLY PARKING
DRILL
AAGHH.
DRILL
YOU WANT ME TO LET YOU THROUGH 'COS YOU'RE IN A RUSH? NO CAN DO.
SNEAK
HIS STRATEGY: USE A DISGUISE TO SLIP THROUGH
I SEE RIGHT THROUGH YA.
SO YER TRYIN' TO GET IN MY WAY AND DELAY THE CONSTRUCTION, HUH!!?
GLARE

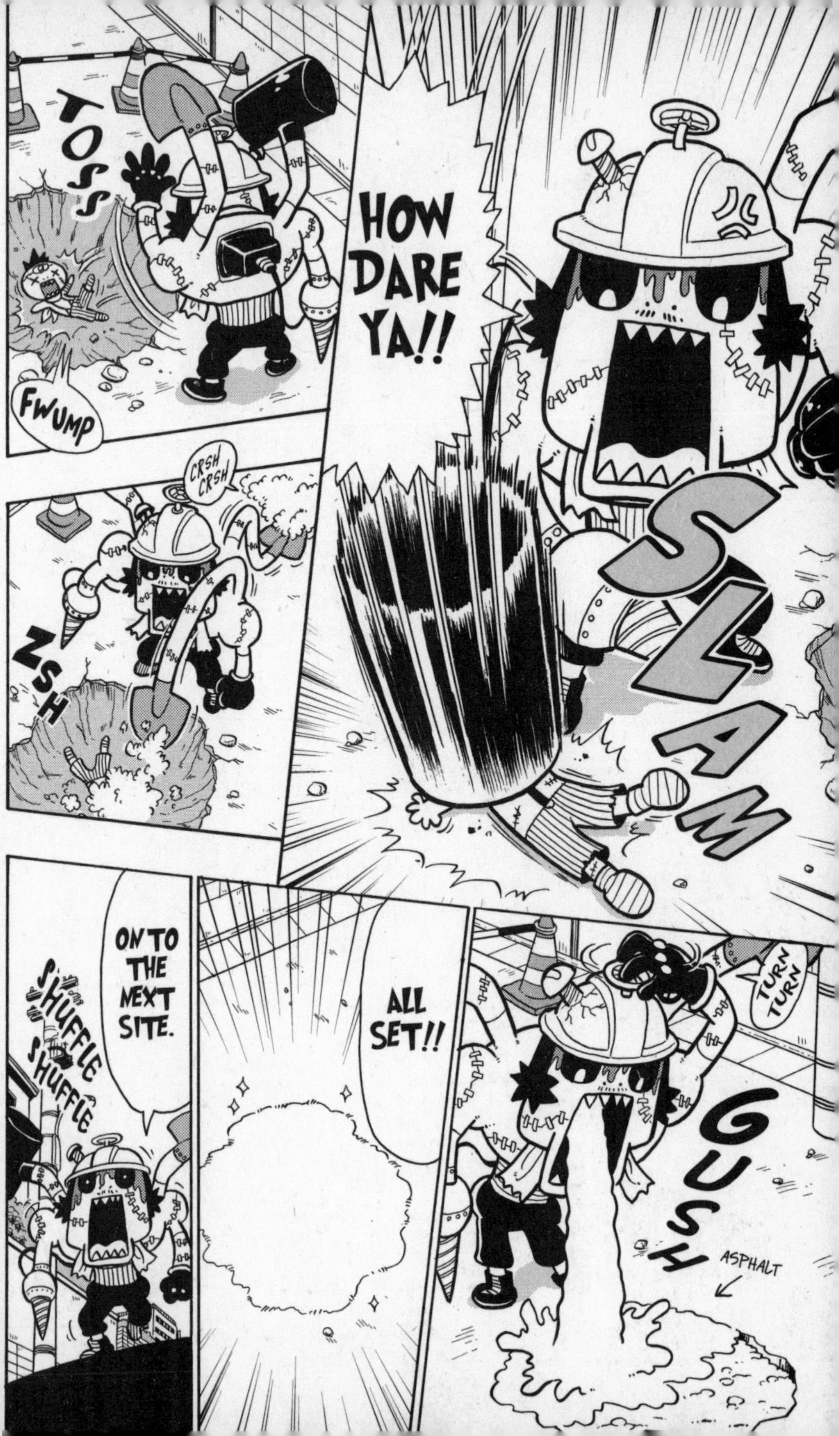
HOW DARE YA!!
SLAM
TOSS
FWUMP
CRSH CRSH
ZSH
TURN TURN
GUSH
ASPHALT
ALL SET!!
ON TO THE NEXT SITE.
SHUFFLE SHUFFLE

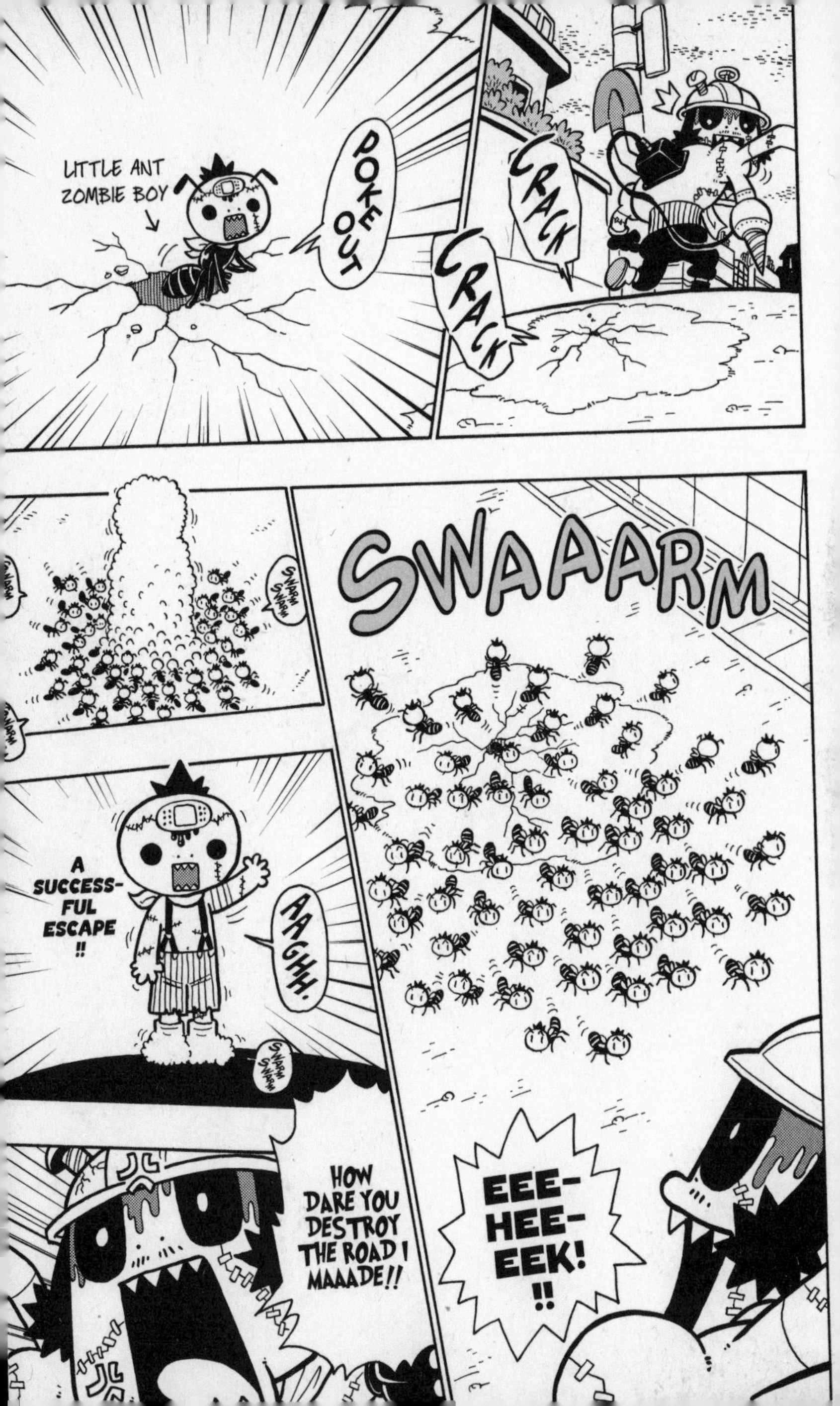
CRACK
CRACK
POKE OUT
LITTLE ANT ZOMBIE BOY
SWAAARM
EEE-HEEE-EEK!!!
SWARM SWARM
AAGHH.
A SUCCESSFUL ESCAPE!!
SWARM SWARM
HOW DARE YOU DESTROY THE ROAD I MAAADE!!

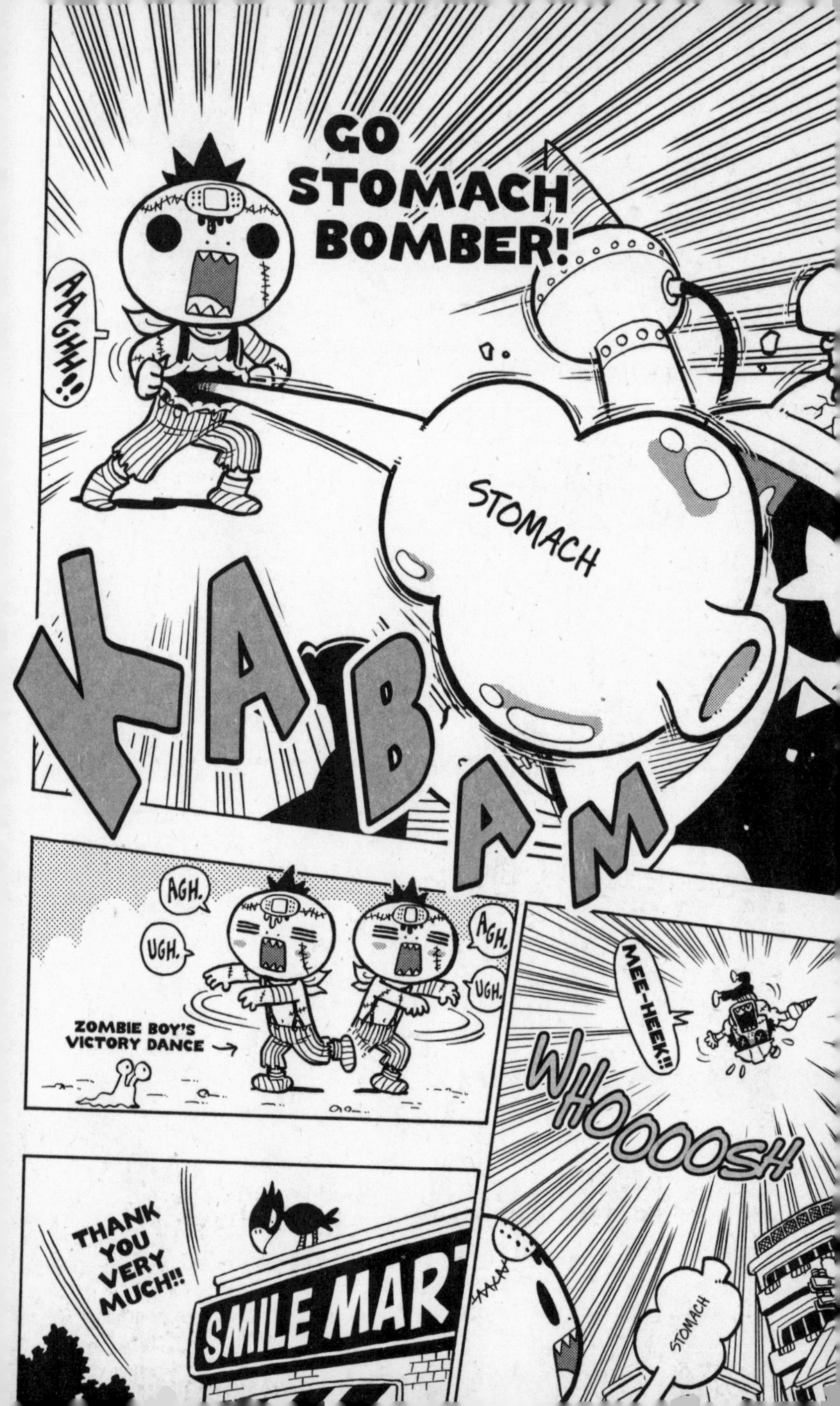
GO STOMACH BOMBER!
AAGHH!!
STOMACH
KABAM
MEE-HEEK!!
WHOOOOSH
STOMACH
AGH.
UGH.
AGH.
UGH.
ZOMBIE BOY'S VICTORY DANCE
THANK YOU VERY MUCH!!
SMILE MAR

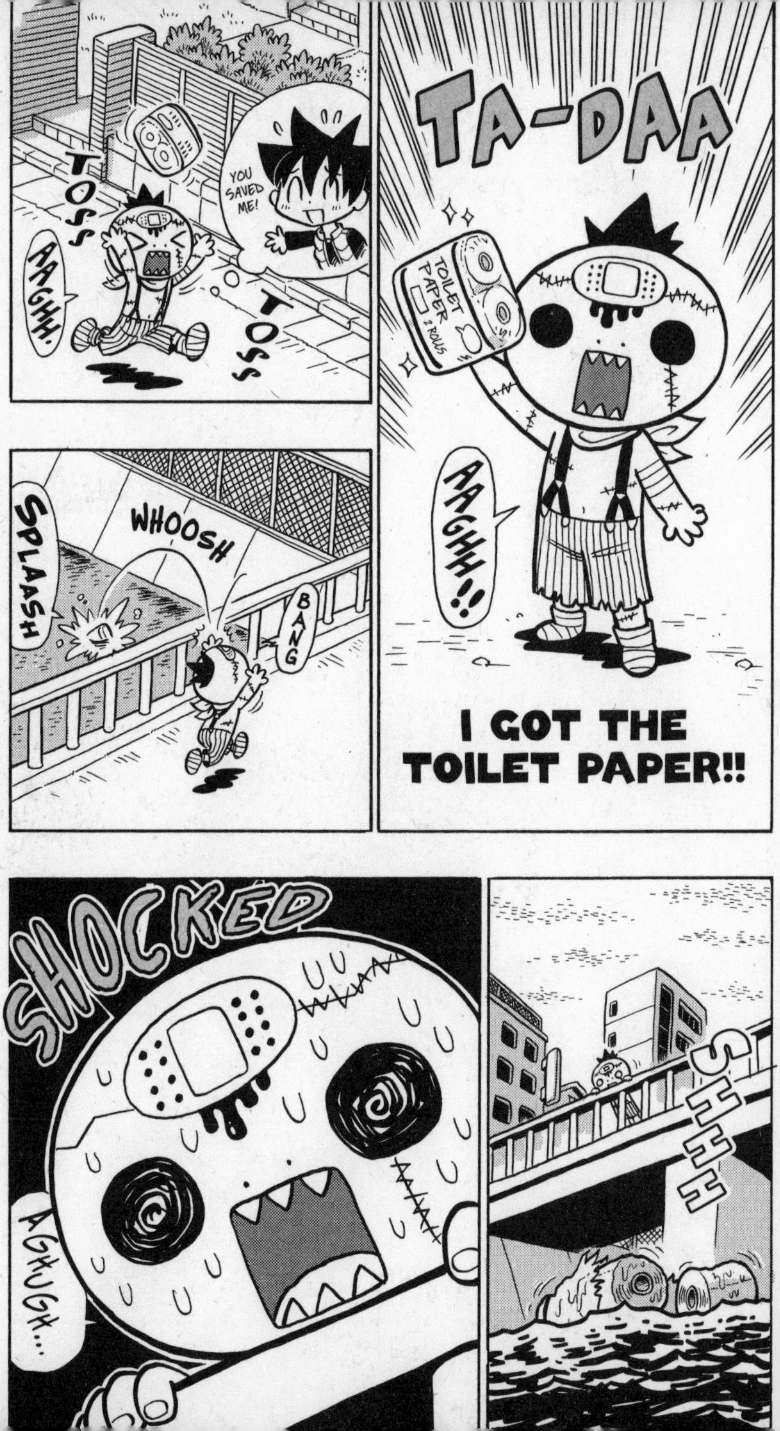

TA-DAA
TOILET PAPER 2 ROLLS
AAGHH!!
I GOT THE TOILET PAPER!!
TOSS
TOSS
YOU SAVED ME!
AAGHH.
WHOOSH
BANG
SPLASH
SHHH
SHOCKED
AGHUGH...

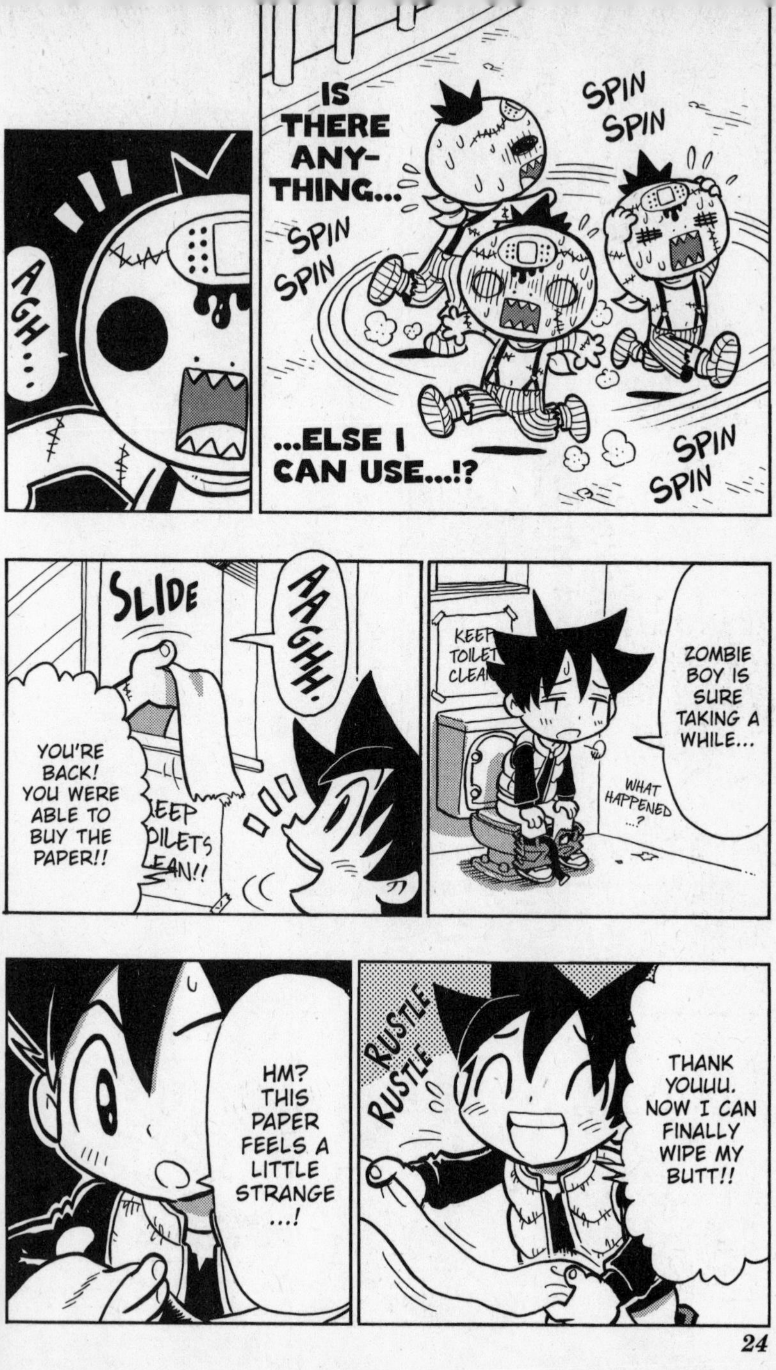

SPIN SPIN
IS THERE ANYTHING...
SPIN SPIN
...ELSE I CAN USE...!?
SPIN SPIN
AGH...
ZOMBIE BOY IS SURE TAKING A WHILE...
WHAT HAPPENED ...?
AAGHH.
SLIDE
YOU'RE BACK! YOU WERE ABLE TO BUY THE PAPER!!
THANK YOUUU. NOW I CAN FINALLY WIPE MY BUTT!!
RUSTLE RUSTLE
HM? THIS PAPER FEELS A LITTLE STRANGE ...!

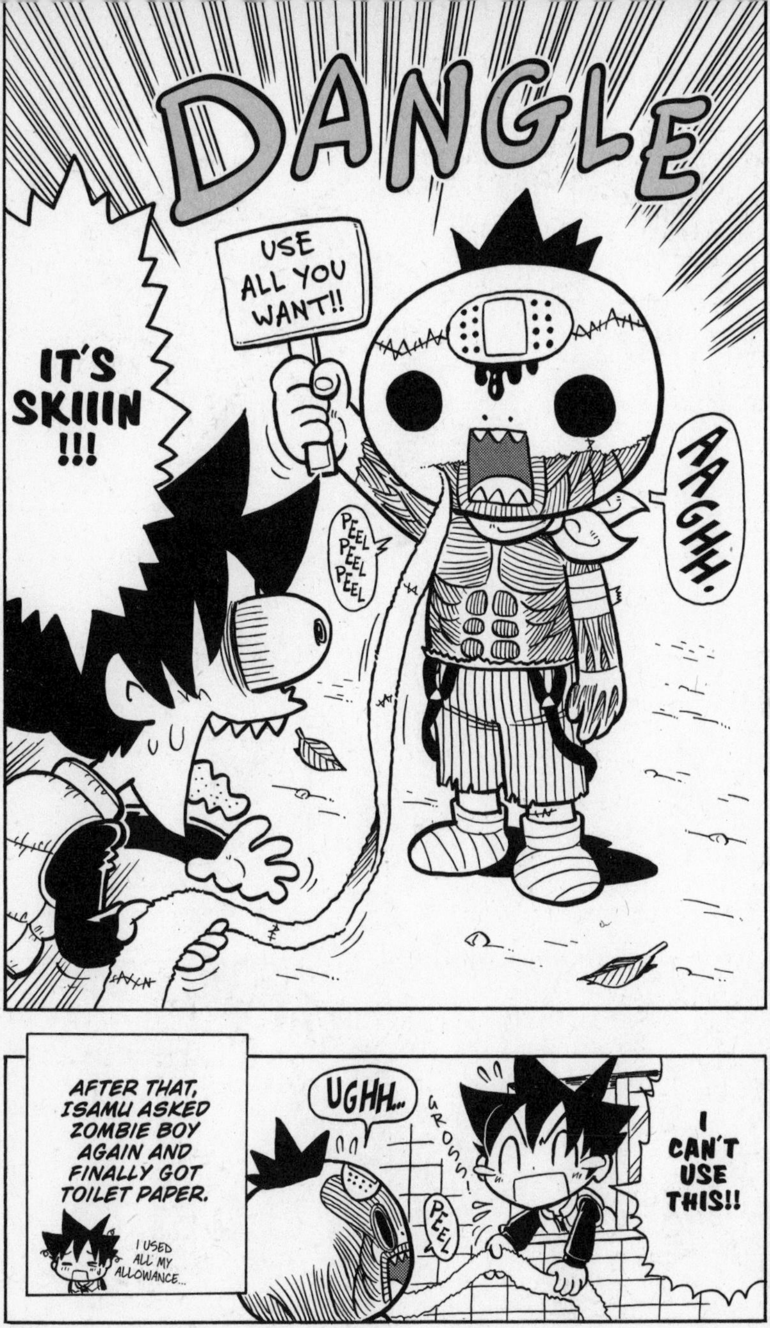
DANGLE
AAGHH.
USE ALL YOU WANT!!
PEEL PEEL PEEL
IT'S SKIIIN!!!
I CAN'T USE THIS!!
GROSS!
PEEL
UGHH...
AFTER THAT, ISAMU ASKED ZOMBIE BOY AGAIN AND FINALLY GOT TOILET PAPER.
I USED ALL MY ALLOWANCE...

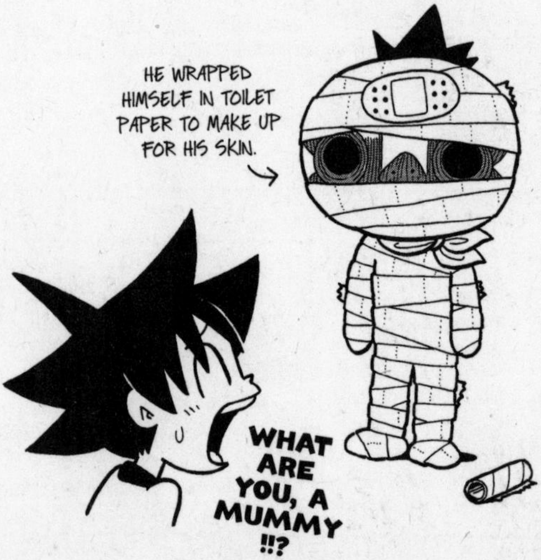
HE WRAPPED HIMSELF IN TOILET PAPER TO MAKE UP FOR HIS SKIN.
WHAT ARE YOU, A MUMMY!!?

FOUR-PANEL GUIDEZ OF NEW ZOMBIE SPECIEZ!

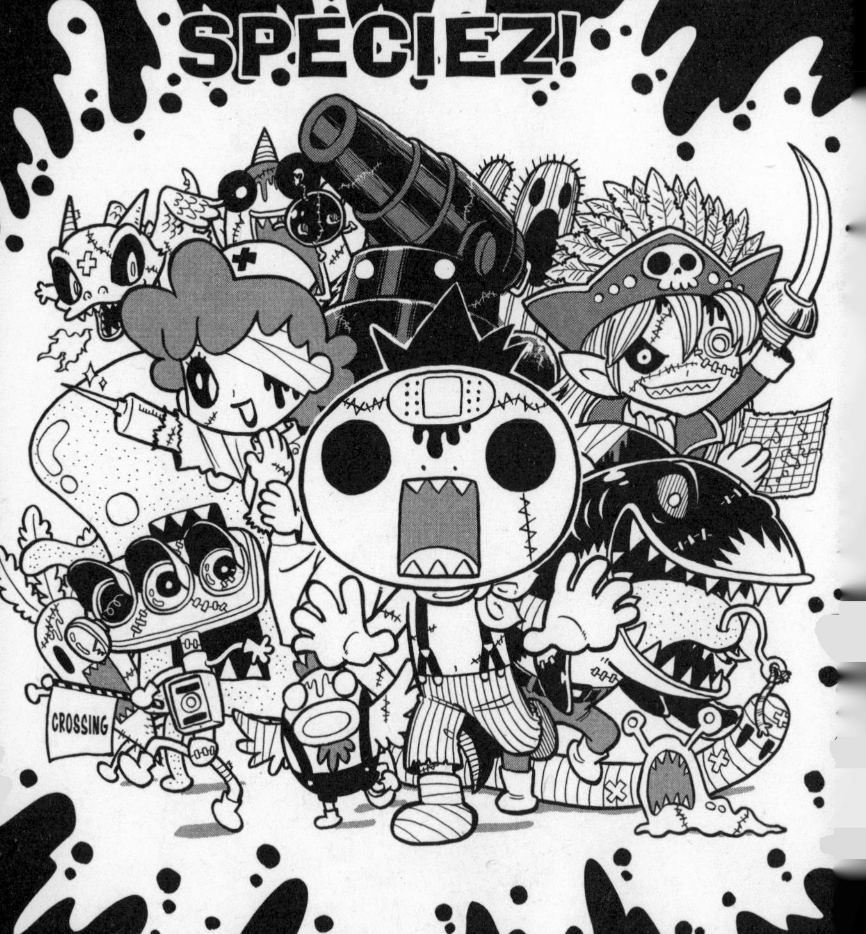
CROSSING

LABEL INDEX

FI = FOUND IN
SC = SPECIAL CHARACTERISTICS
SM = SPECIAL MOVES
FF = FAVORITE FOODS

BASEBALL ZOMBIE

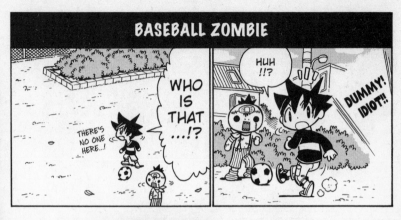

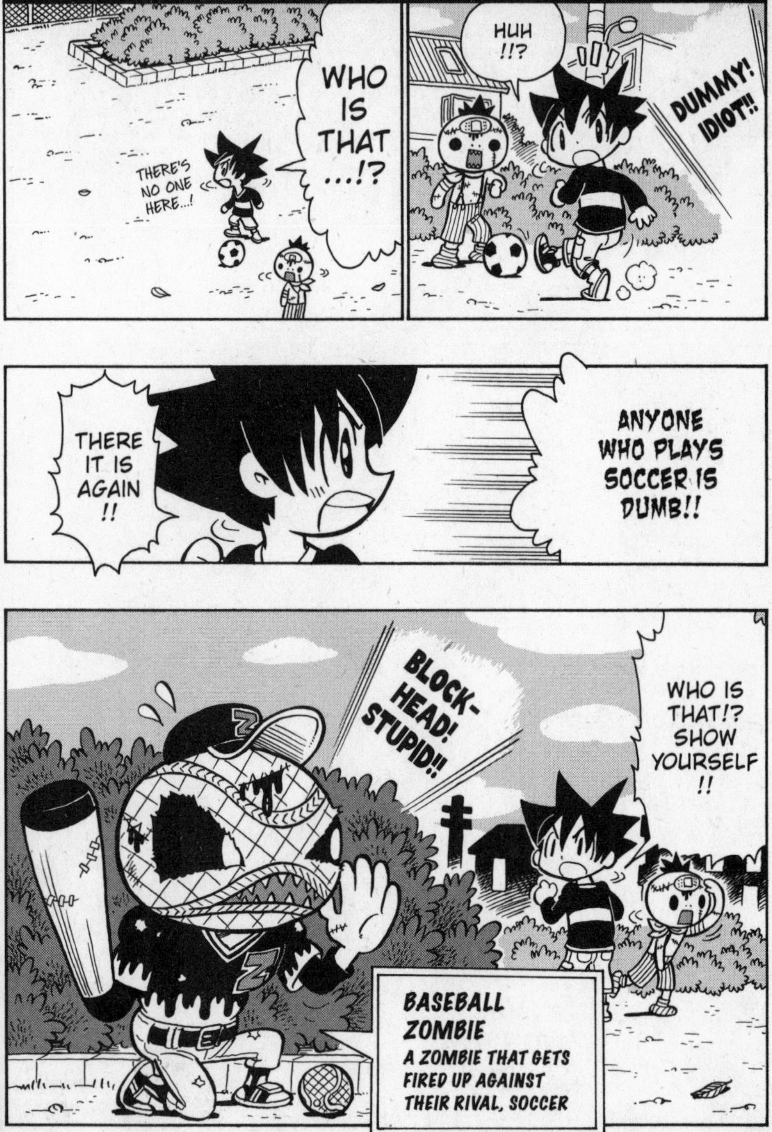
HUH !!?
DUMMY! IDIOT!!
WHO IS THAT ...!?
THERE'S NO ONE HERE...!
ANYONE WHO PLAYS SOCCER IS DUMB!!
THERE IT IS AGAIN !!
WHO IS THAT!? SHOW YOURSELF !!
BLOCK-HEAD! STUPID!!
BASEBALL ZOMBIE
A ZOMBIE THAT GETS FIRED UP AGAINST THEIR RIVAL, SOCCER

SLUG ZOMBIE

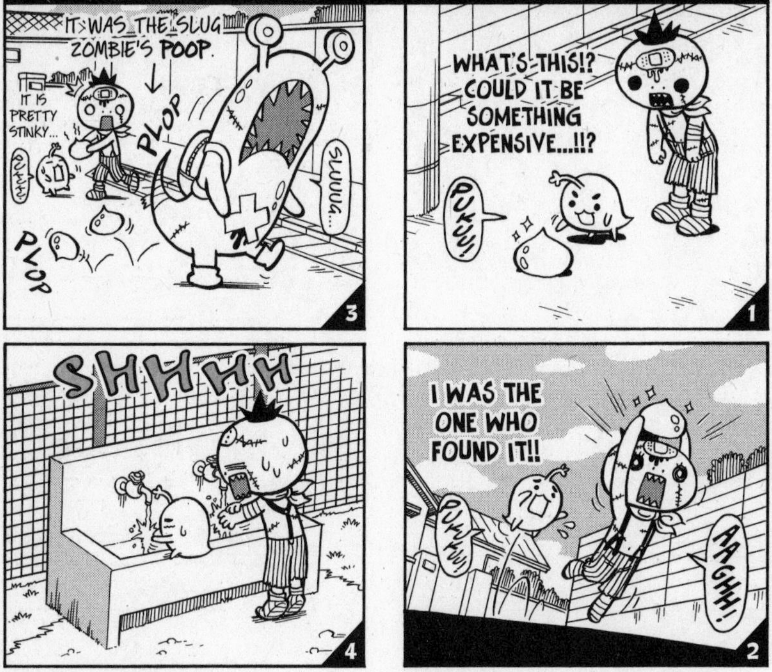
WHAT'S THIS!? COULD IT BE SOMETHING EXPENSIVE...!!?
PUKUU!
I WAS THE ONE WHO FOUND IT!!
PUKUU!
AAGHH!
IT WAS THE SLUG ZOMBIE'S POOP.
IT IS PRETTY STINKY...
PLOP
SLUUUG...
PLOP
SHHHH

SLUG ZOMBIE

FI = GYMNASIUMS AND SPORTS GYMS (PLACES WHERE PEOPLE SWEAT)

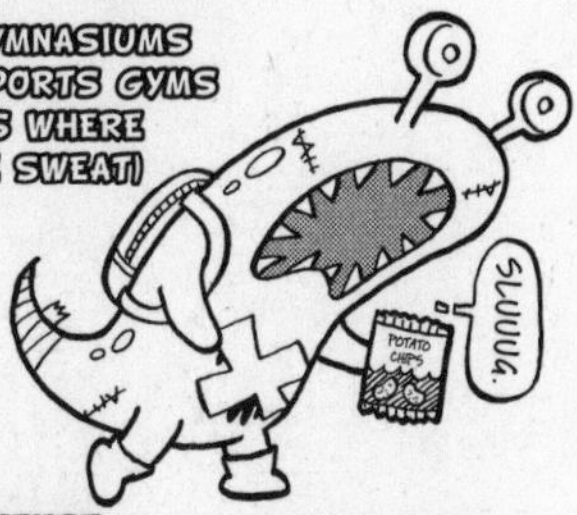
SLUUUG.
POTATO CHIPS

SC = THEY'RE A TROUBLESOME ZOMBIE THAT LOVES SALTY THINGS EVEN THOUGH THEY'RE A SLUG. THEY ALSO OFTEN LICK UP PEOPLE'S SWEAT.

SM = SLIMY SLIME ATTACK

FF = PEOPLE'S SWEAT AND SALT RAMEN

BASEBALL ZOMBIE

FI = BASEBALL FIELDS AND EMPTY LOTS

SC = THEY HATE OTHER SPORTS (ESPECIALLY SOCCER) AND WILL BOTHER ANYONE PLAYING THEM.

SM = INFIELD PUNCH, LEG-LIFT KICK

FF = SOIL FROM THE HIGH SCHOOL NATIONAL BASEBALL CHAMPIONSHIPS FIELD

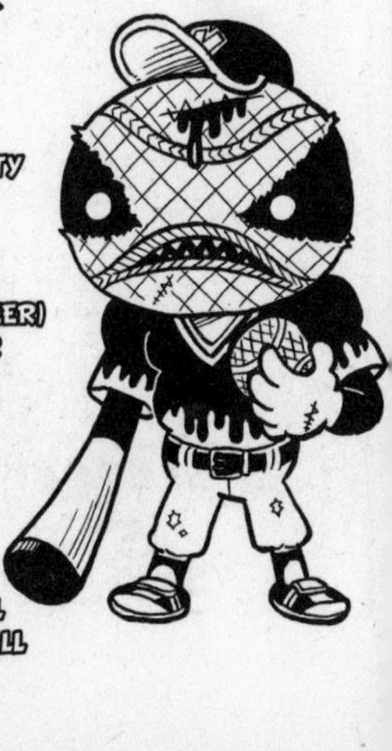

CAMERA ZOMBIE

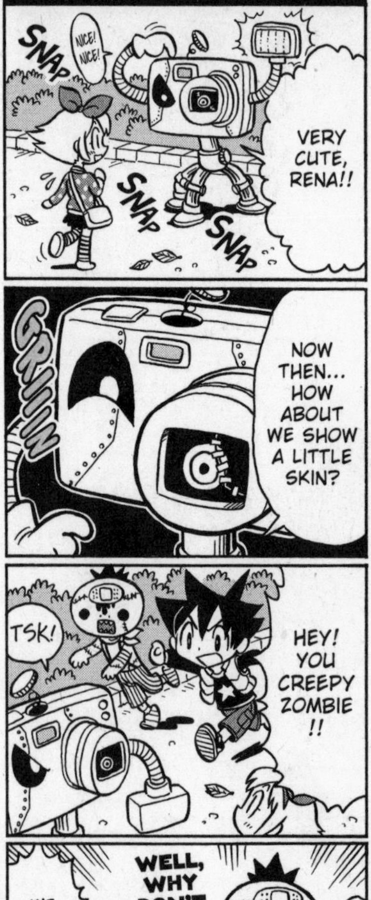
SNAP
NICE! NICE!
VERY CUTE, RENA!!
SNAP
SNAP
NOW THEN... HOW ABOUT WE SHOW A LITTLE SKIN?
GRIIIN
HEY! YOU CREEPY ZOMBIE!!
TSK!
AAGHH.
WELL, WHY DON'T I...?
WE DON'T WANNA SEE THAT!!

BLACK ZOMBIE

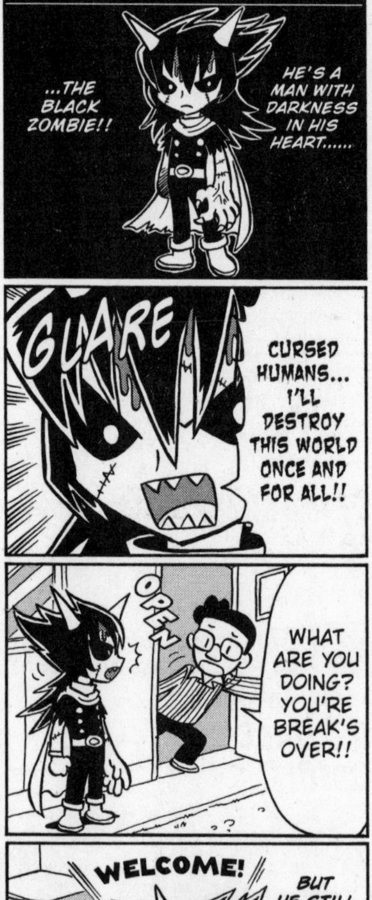
HE'S A MAN WITH DARKNESS IN HIS HEART......
...THE BLACK ZOMBIE!!
CURSED HUMANS... I'LL DESTROY THIS WORLD ONCE AND FOR ALL!!
GLARE
WHAT ARE YOU DOING? YOU'RE BREAK'S OVER!!
OPEN
BUT HE STILL NEEDS TO EARN A LIVING, SO HE WORKS HARD AT HIS PART-TIME JOB.
WELCOME!
COOL!

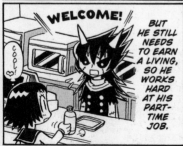

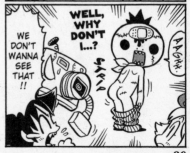

BLACK ZOMBIE

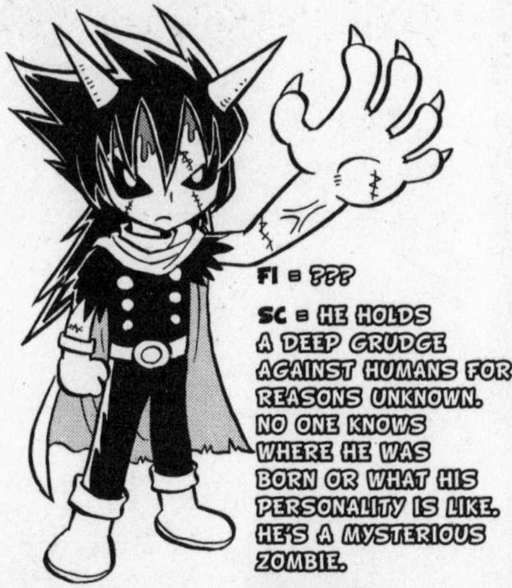

FI = ???

SC = HE HOLDS A DEEP GRUDGE AGAINST HUMANS FOR REASONS UNKNOWN. NO ONE KNOWS WHERE HE WAS BORN OR WHAT HIS PERSONALITY IS LIKE. HE'S A MYSTERIOUS ZOMBIE.

SM = ???

FF = ???

CAMERA ZOMBIE

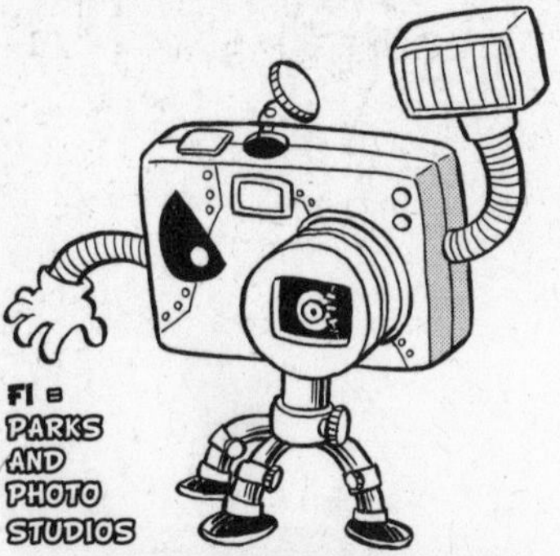

FI = PARKS AND PHOTO STUDIOS

SC = THEY'RE A CREEPY ZOMBIE THAT LOVES CUTE GIRLS BUT IS ACTUALLY VERY TALENTED. IT ALSO SEEMS THAT THEY MIGHT GET THEIR WORK PUBLISHED SOON.

SM = FLASH SHOWER

FF = NAUGHTY PICTURES

BUS ZOMBIE

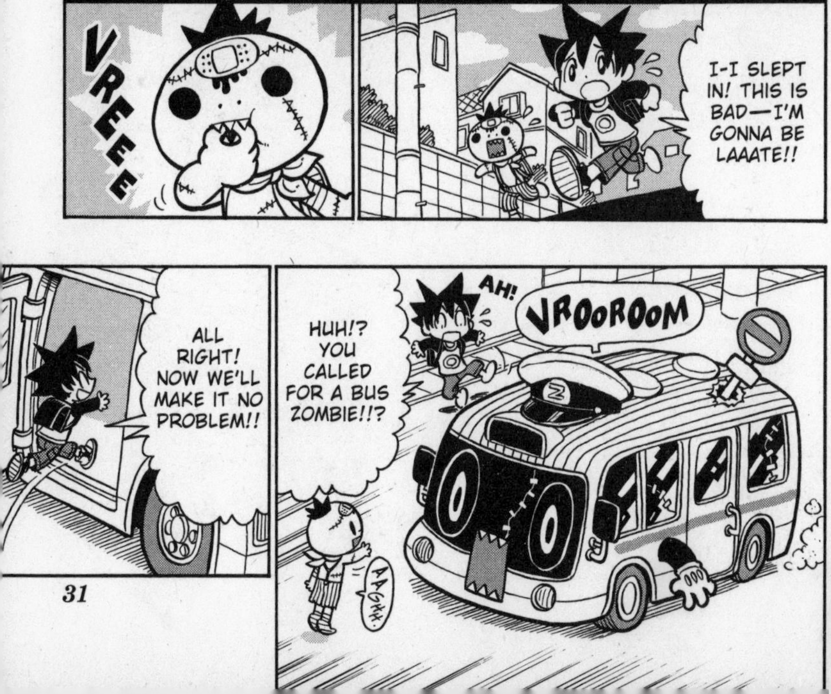
I-I SLEPT IN! THIS IS BAD—I'M GONNA BE LAAATE!!
VREEE
VROOROOM
AH!
HUH!? YOU CALLED FOR A BUS ZOMBIE!!?
AAGHH.
ALL RIGHT! NOW WE'LL MAKE IT NO PROBLEM!!

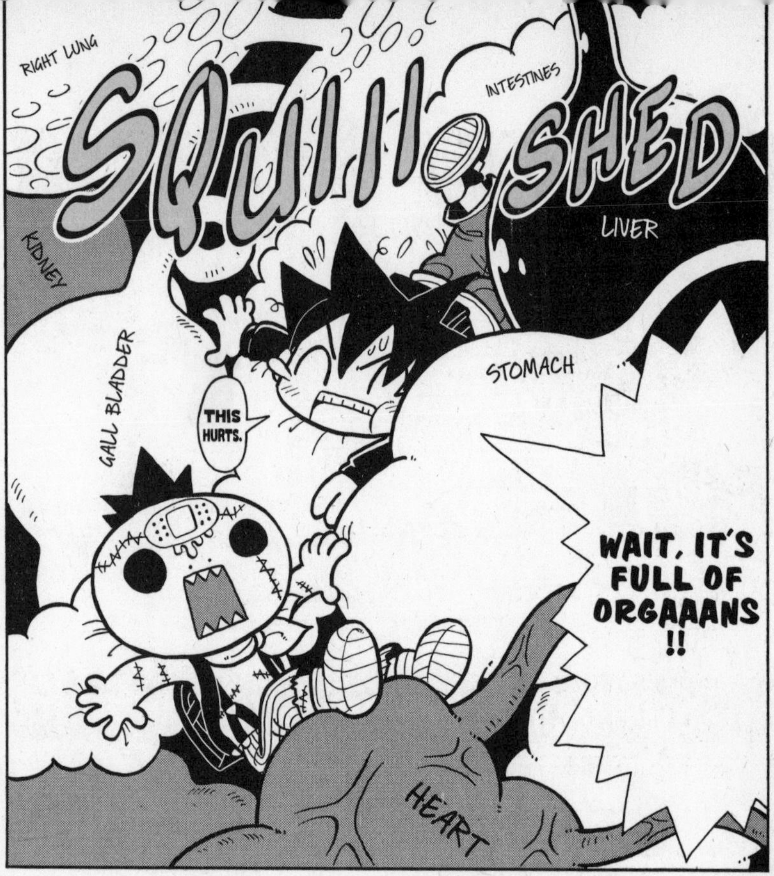
SQUIIISHED
INTESTINES
RIGHT LUNG
LIVER
KIDNEY
STOMACH
THIS HURTS.
GALL BLADDER
WAIT, IT'S FULL OF ORGAAANS !!
HEART

BUS ZOMBIE

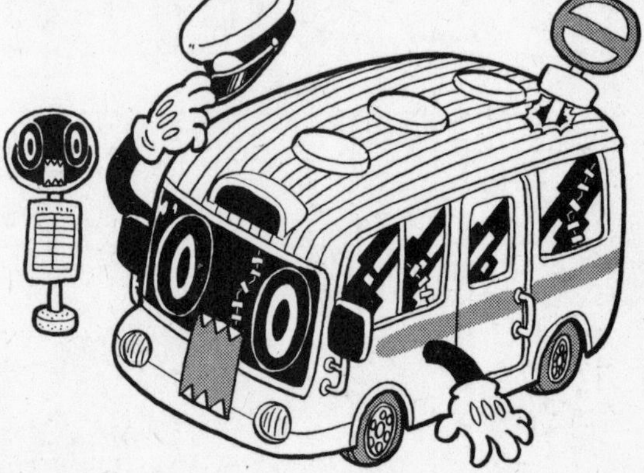

FI = THE STREETS

SC = JUST AS THEIR NAME DESCRIBES, THEY'RE A BUS ZOMBIE. THEY'LL PICK YOU UP IF YOU WAIT AT THEIR SPECIAL BUS STOPS. IF YOU'RE INTERESTED, BE SURE TO LOOK FOR THOSE STOPS.

SM = ONE-MAN CRASH

FF = BUS PASS

PAPER ZOMBIE

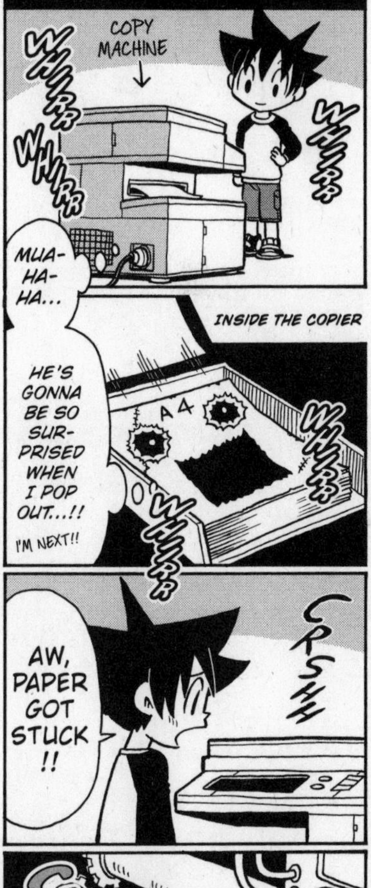
WHIRR
WHIRR
COPY MACHINE
WHIRR
MUA-HA-HA...
INSIDE THE COPIER
WHIRR
HE'S GONNA BE SO SURPRISED WHEN I POP OUT...!!
I'M NEXT!!
WHIRR
CRSHH
AW, PAPER GOT STUCK!!
......
A4
CRUMPLED

PEAR ZOMBIE

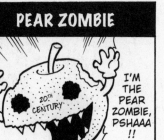

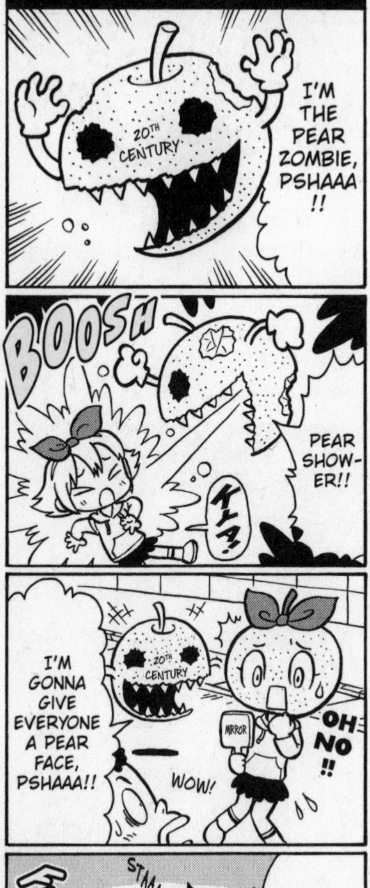
I'M THE PEAR ZOMBIE, PSHAAA!!
20TH CENTURY
PEAR SHOWER!!
BOOSH
OH NO!!
MIRROR
20TH CENTURY
I'M GONNA GIVE EVERYONE A PEAR FACE, PSHAAA!!
WOW!
YOU'RE... LIKE THE EXACT COPY OF A FAMOUS MASCOT...
STAAARE
AAGHH

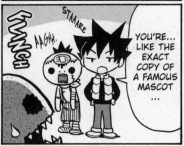

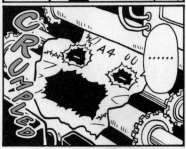

PEAR ZOMBIE

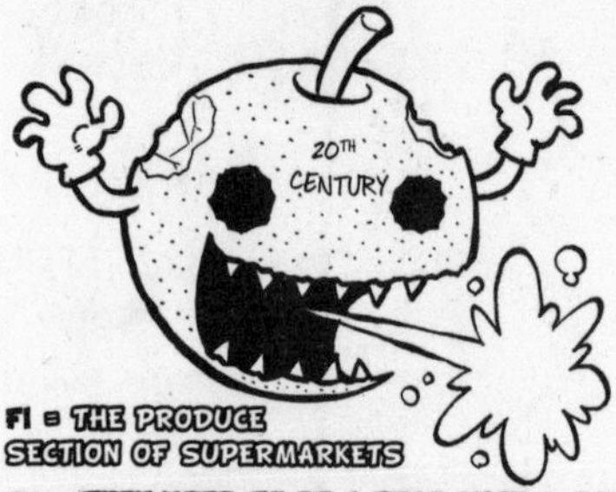
20TH CENTURY

FI = THE PRODUCE SECTION OF SUPERMARKETS

SC = THEY USED TO BE A PEAR WITH A SCRATCH ON IT THAT WASN'T HARVESTED BEFORE TURNING INTO A ZOMBIE. THE REASON THEY'RE A TWENTIETH CENTURY PEAR IS BECAUSE THAT'S THE KIND THAT'S FAMOUS WHERE THE AUTHOR IS FROM—TOTTORI.

SM = PEAR STONES

FF = PICKLED LEEKS (THIS IS ALSO A FAMOUS PRODUCT OF TOTTORI. IT'S PROBABLY NOT HIS FAVORITE—JUST AN AD.)

PAPER ZOMBIE

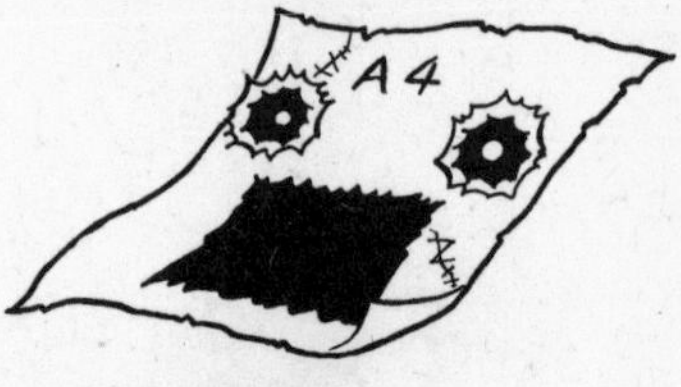
A4

FI = COPY MACHINES

SC = THEY'RE A ZOMBIE THAT WAS ONCE A PAPER CARELESSLY THROWN AWAY. THERE HAVE ALSO BEEN SIGHTINGS OF B4- AND A3-SIZE PAPER ZOMBIES. THEY'VE GOT A FLIMSY PERSONALITY.

SM = FLAP-FLAP CUTTER

FF = ERASER SHAVINGS

HAIRCUT ZOMBIE

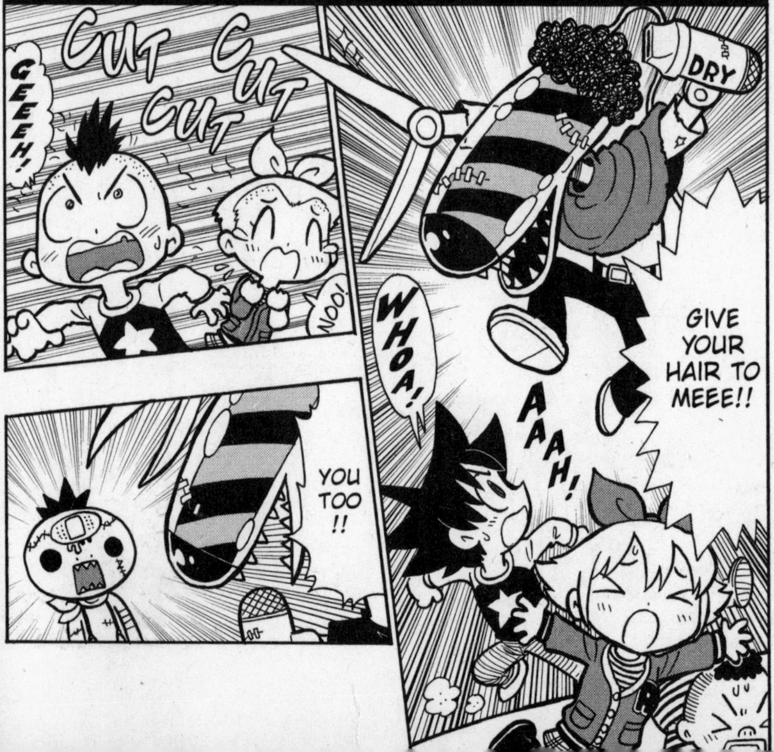
DRY
GIVE YOUR HAIR TO MEEE!!
WHOA!
AAAH!
CUT CUT CUT
GEEEH!
NOO!
YOU TOO!!

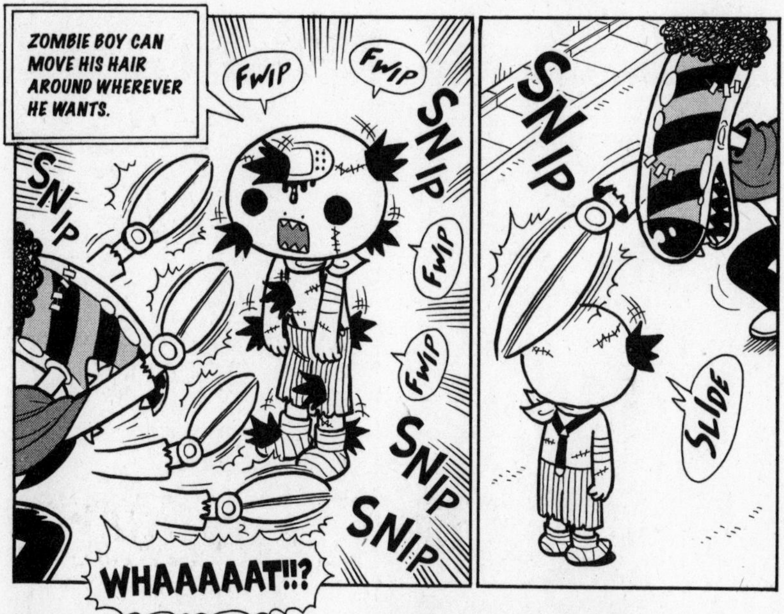
SNIP
SLIDE
ZOMBIE BOY CAN MOVE HIS HAIR AROUND WHEREVER HE WANTS.
FWIP
FWIP
SNIP
SNIP
FWIP
FWIP
SNIP
SNIP
WHAAAAAT!!?

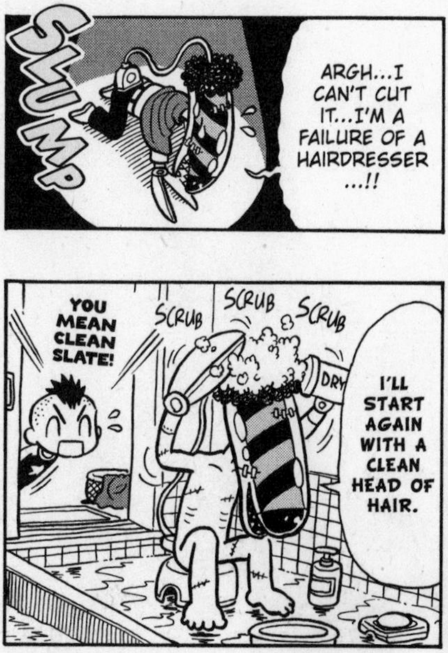
SLUMP
ARGH...I CAN'T CUT IT...I'M A FAILURE OF A HAIRDRESSER ...!!
SCRUB
I'LL START AGAIN WITH A CLEAN HEAD OF HAIR.
SCRUB
SCRUB
YOU MEAN CLEAN SLATE!
DRY

HAIRCUT ZOMBIE

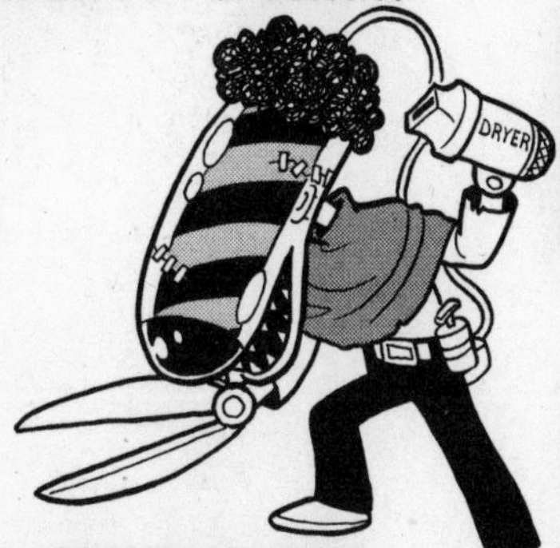
DRYER

FI = SHOPPING DISTRICTS

SC = THEY WERE AN OWNER OF A BARBER SHOP WHO DIED AND BECAME A ZOMBIE WHEN THEY REALIZED THEIR SHOP HAD NO FUTURE. THEY ARE TERRIFIED OF THE ¥1,000 HAIRCUTS THAT ARE GETTING MORE POPULAR DAY BY DAY.

SM = PILEDRYER

FF = SHAMPOO

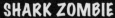

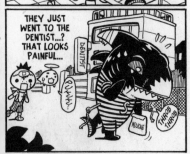

PENCIL ZOMBIE

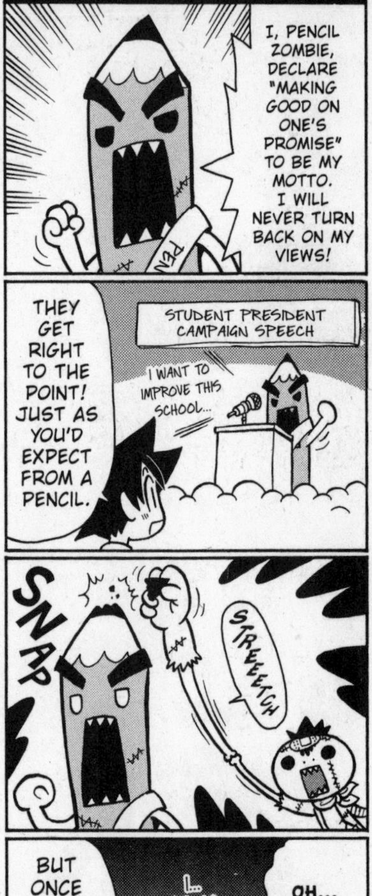
I, PENCIL ZOMBIE, DECLARE "MAKING GOOD ON ONE'S PROMISE" TO BE MY MOTTO. I WILL NEVER TURN BACK ON MY VIEWS!
PEN
STUDENT PRESIDENT CAMPAIGN SPEECH
I WANT TO IMPROVE THIS SCHOOL...
THEY GET RIGHT TO THE POINT! JUST AS YOU'D EXPECT FROM A PENCIL.
STREEEETCH
SNAP
OH... BUT... THERE ARE SOME THINGS I CAN'T DO...
I... I'M NO GOOD...
BUT ONCE THEIR POINT GETS LOST, THEY GET WEAK...
PEN

SHARK ZOMBIE

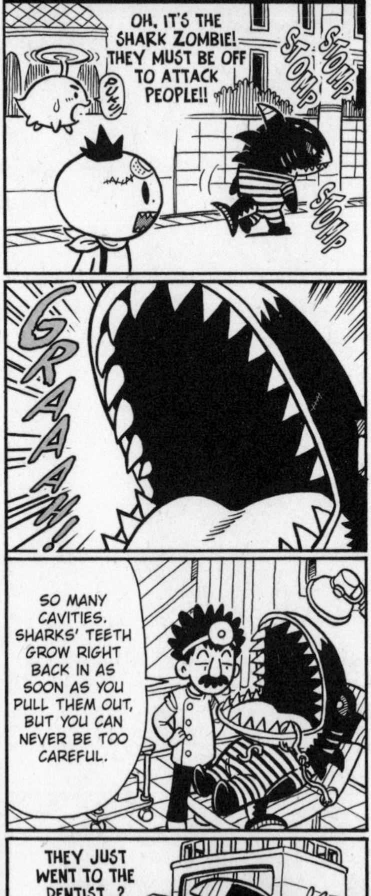
STOMP
STOMP
OH, IT'S THE SHARK ZOMBIE! THEY MUST BE OFF TO ATTACK PEOPLE!!
PUKU!
STOMP
GRAAAAAH!
SO MANY CAVITIES. SHARKS' TEETH GROW RIGHT BACK IN AS SOON AS YOU PULL THEM OUT, BUT YOU CAN NEVER BE TOO CAREFUL.
THROB THROB
MEDICINE
DENTIST
PUKU...
THEY JUST WENT TO THE DENTIST...? THAT LOOKS PAINFUL...

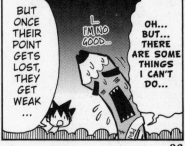

SHARK ZOMBIE

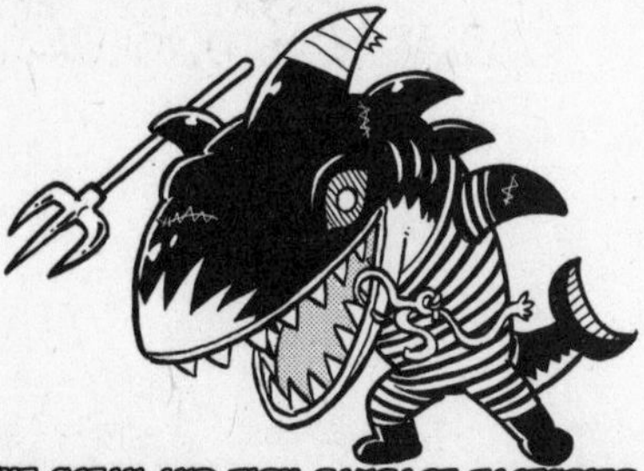

FI = THE OCEAN AND FISH SAUSAGE FACTORIES

SC = THEY ARE FEROCIOUS BUT NOT IN FRONT OF THEIR DENTIST. IT'S A GOOD THING THEIR TEETH JUST GROW BACK IN BECAUSE THEY OFTEN FORGET TO BRUSH THEM AND THEN GET CAVITIES.

SM = SHARK-FILLET SPECIAL

FF = CHOCOLATE

PENCIL ZOMBIE

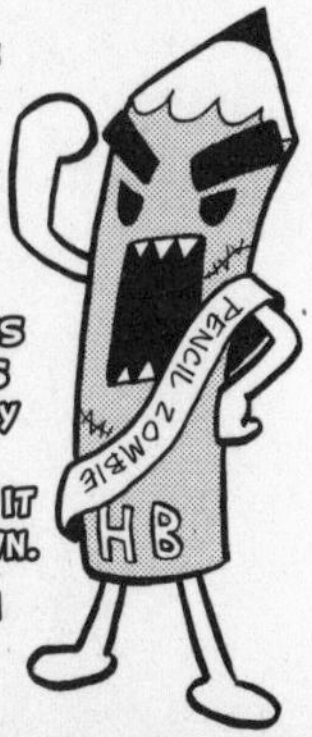
PENCIL ZOMBIE
HB

FI = CLASSROOMS

SC = THEY ARE A PENCIL THAT GREW OLD WITH USE AND TURNED INTO A ZOMBIE. THEY'RE A SERIOUS ZOMBIE WHO PUTS THEIR WHOLE BODY INTO EVERYTHING THEY DO, EVEN IF IT WEARS THEM DOWN.

SM = COAL CRUSH

FF = GRAPHITE

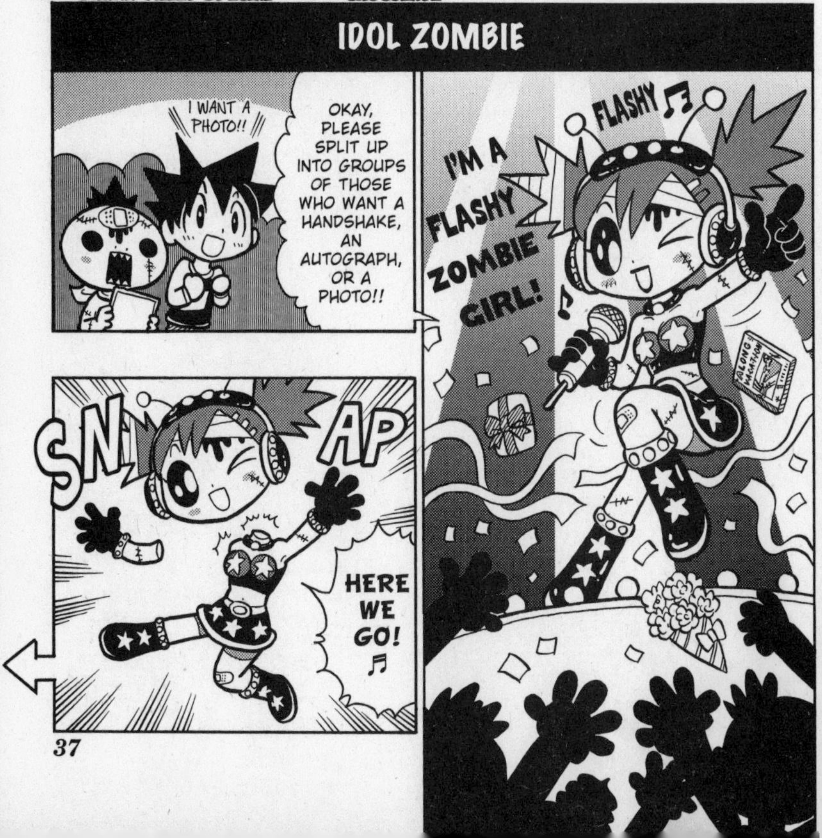
IDOL ZOMBIE
FLASHY ♫
I'M A FLASHY ZOMBIE GIRL!
A LONG VACATION
OKAY, PLEASE SPLIT UP INTO GROUPS OF THOSE WHO WANT A HANDSHAKE, AN AUTOGRAPH, OR A PHOTO!!
I WANT A PHOTO!!
SNAP
HERE WE GO! ♫

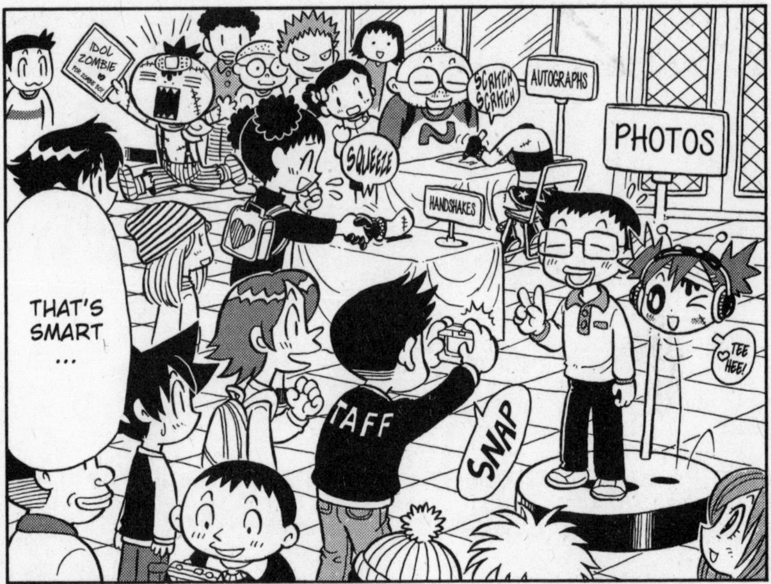
PHOTOS
AUTOGRAPHS
SCRKCH SCRKCH
SQUEEZE
IDOL ZOMBIE
HANDSHAKES
TEE HEE!
SNAP
THAT'S SMART ...

SAMURAI ZOMBIE

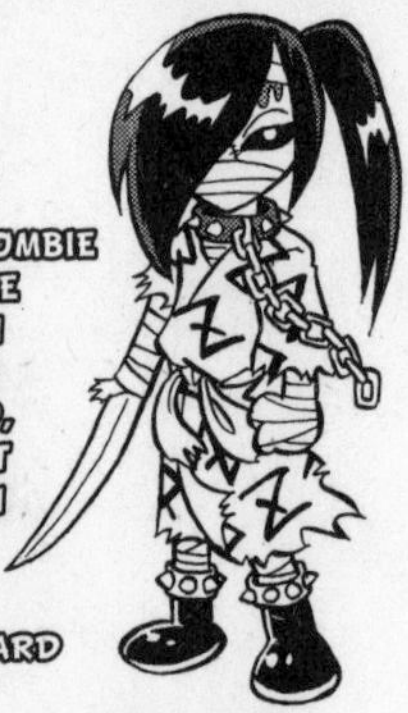

FI = KENDO DOJOS

SC = A SERIOUS ZOMBIE WHO STICKS TO THE SAMURAI CODE. ON TOP OF THAT, HE'S ALWAYS STRESSED, SO HE GETS UPSET STOMACHS. HE CAN GET UPSET AND CRANKY TOO.

SM = BLOOD BLIZZARD STRIKE

FF = RICE BALLS (WITH TUNA FLAKES)

STONE ZOMBIE

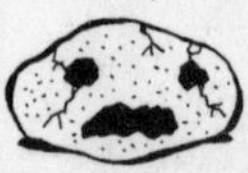

FI = ALONG STREETS

SC = THEY'RE A PEBBLE ZOMBIE THAT ROLLS ALONG THE ROAD. THEY'RE VERY PATIENT AND DON'T MIND BEING ALONE.

SM = TRIPPING PEOPLE

FF = RAINWATER

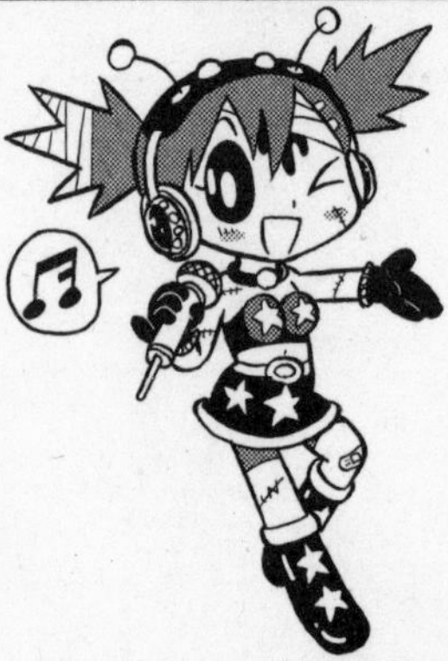

IDOL ZOMBIE

FI = CONCERT HALLS

SC = HER GOAL IS TO BE THE FIRST ZOMBIE IDOL SINGER IN THE WORLD. THANKS TO HER HARD WORK, SHE'S SLOWLY GAINING FANS, AND THE SALES FOR HER NEW SINGLE, "FLASHY☆ZOMBIE GIRL," ARE LOOKING GOOD.

SM = SMILE BEAM

FF = CHEERS FROM HER FANS

SAMURAI ZOMBIE

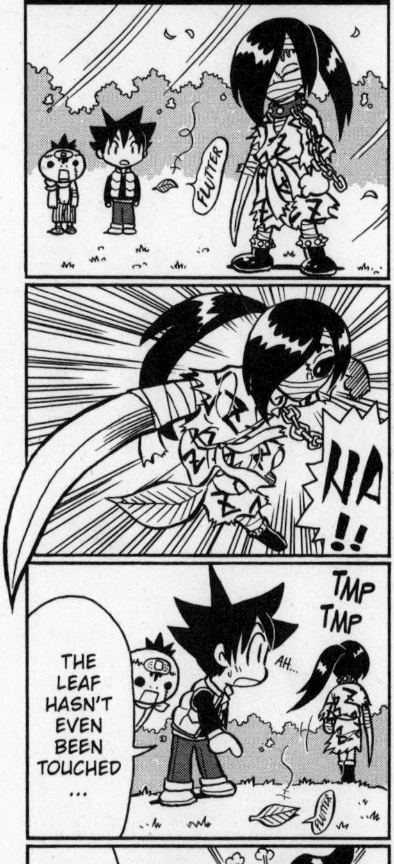
FLUTTER
NP!!
TMP TMP
AH...
THE LEAF HASN'T EVEN BEEN TOUCHED ...
FLUTTER
IT'S NOT MY FAULT!
IT'S ALL THE SWORD'S FAULT, DANG IT!!
BUT SOME-ONE'S GETTING TOUCHY ...!!

STONE ZOMBIE

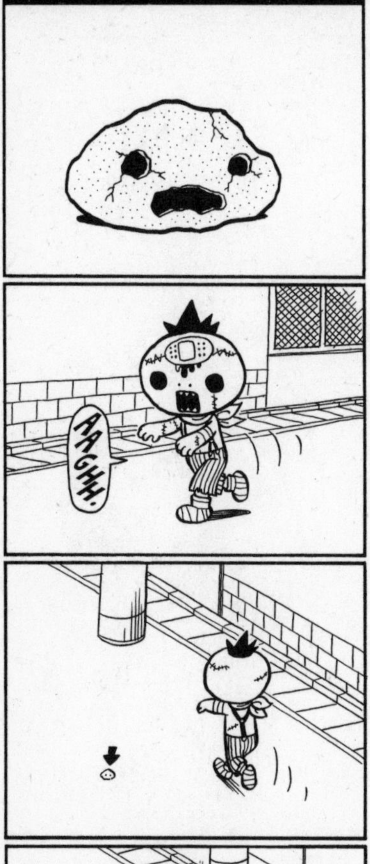
AAGHH.
THEY'RE SO SMALL, ZOMBIE BOY DIDN'T EVEN NOTICE THEM.
...

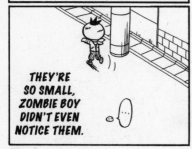

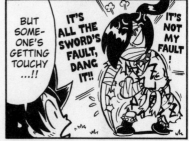

PANDA ZOMBIE

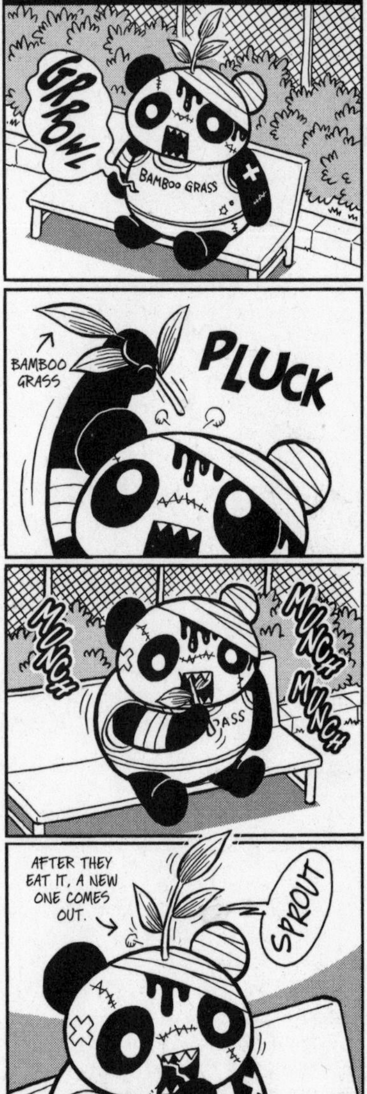
GROWL
BAMBOO GRASS
BAMBOO GRASS
PLUCK
MUNCH
MUNCH
MUNCH
ASS
SPROUT
AFTER THEY EAT IT, A NEW ONE COMES OUT.

ANGEL ZOMBIE

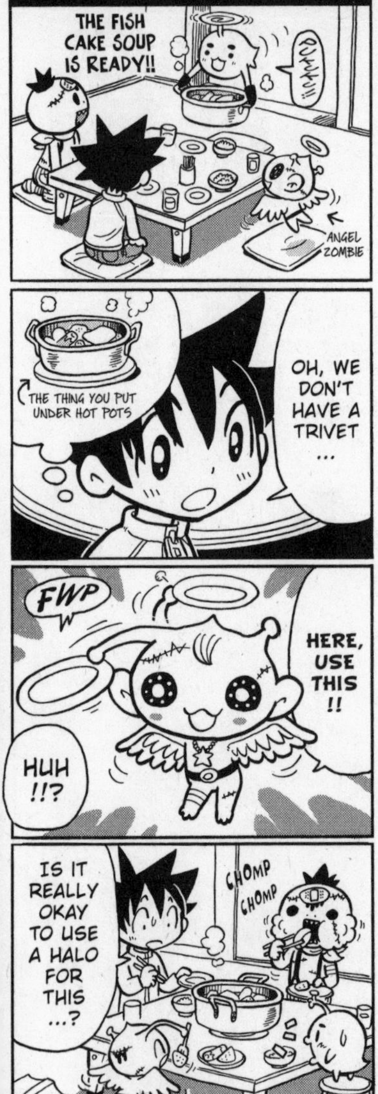
PUKYUU!!
THE FISH CAKE SOUP IS READY!!
ANGEL ZOMBIE
OH, WE DON'T HAVE A TRIVET ...
THE THING YOU PUT UNDER HOT POTS
HERE, USE THIS !!
FWP
HUH !!?
CHOMP CHOMP
IS IT REALLY OKAY TO USE A HALO FOR THIS ...?

ANGEL ZOMBIE

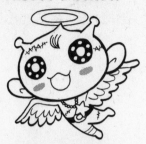

FI = ABOVE THE CLOUDS

SC = NO ONE HAS EVER SEEN THEM GET ANGRY. THEY HAVE AN EXTREMELY GENTLE PERSONALITY BUT IS ACTUALLY ONE OF THE STRONGEST ZOMBIES THERE IS.

SM = HEAVENLY PUNCH, HEAVENLY TAILSPIN

FF = HEAVENLY RICE BOWLS

PANDA ZOMBIE

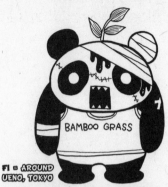

BAMBOO GRASS

FI = AROUND UENO, TOKYO

SC = AS A PANDA, THEY'RE POPULAR DESPITE BEING A ZOMBIE, BUT IT'S GONE TO THEIR HEAD, SO THEIR REPUTATION IS PRETTY BAD IN THE ZOMBIE WORLD.

SM = BLACK-AND-WHITE PRESS

FF = YOU GUESSED IT—BAMBOO GRASS!

TEACHER ZOMBIE

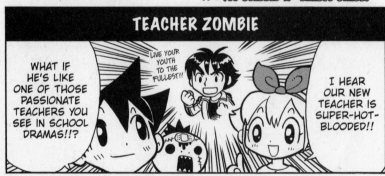

I HEAR OUR NEW TEACHER IS SUPER-HOT-BLOODED!!
LIVE YOUR YOUTH TO THE FULLEST!!
WHAT IF HE'S LIKE ONE OF THOSE PASSIONATE TEACHERS YOU SEE IN SCHOOL DRAMAS!!?
HE'S HERE!!
SLIDE

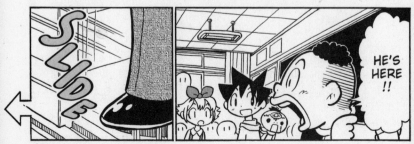

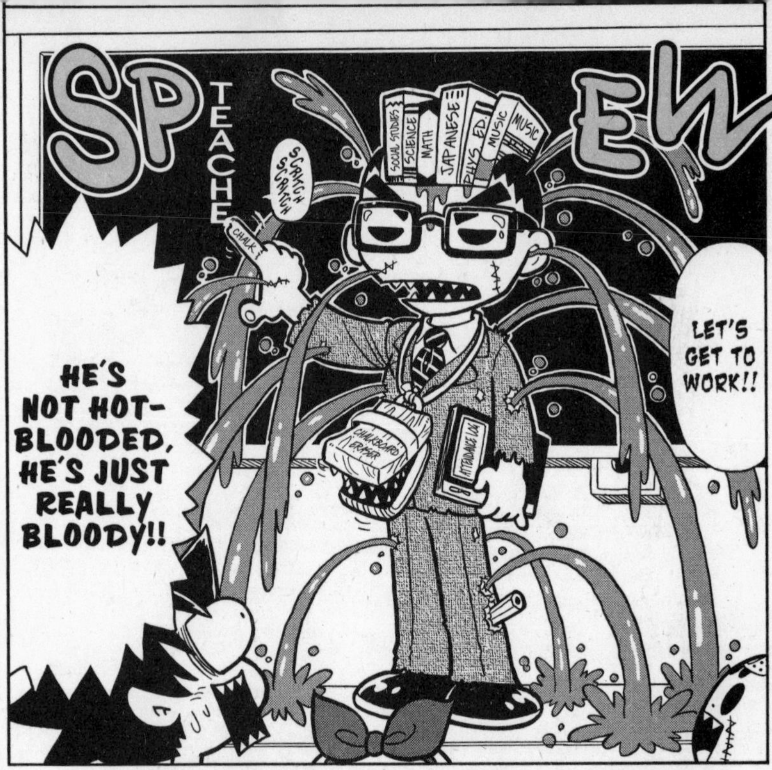
SPEW
LET'S GET TO WORK!!
MUSIC
MUSIC
PHYS. ED.
JAPANESE
MATH
SCIENCE
SOCIAL STUDIES
TEACHE
SCRITCH SCRITCH
CHALK
CHALKBOARD ERASER
ATTENDANCE LOG
HE'S NOT HOT-BLOODED, HE'S JUST REALLY BLOODY!!

KAPPA ZOMBIE

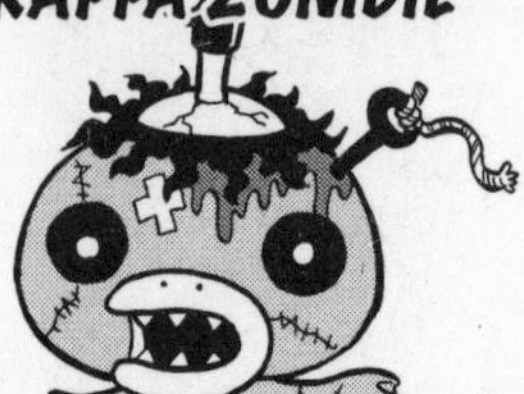

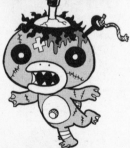

FI = RIVERS AND PONDS

SC = THEY LOVE COMEDY, SO THEY'RE ALWAYS THINKING UP GAG JOKES. THEY ONCE FORMED A COMEDY DUO WITH A KNIFE ZOMBIE CALLED "KOPPER KNIFE."

SM = A-HUNDRED-FURIOUS-GAGS PUNCH

FF = PICKLES

TEACHER ZOMBIE

FI = SCHOOLS

SC = HE'S ALWAYS BLEEDING, SO HE OFTEN GETS ANEMIC AND HAS TO HAVE THE CLASS DO SELF-STUDY. HE WATCHES THE *KINPACHI THE TEACHER II* DVD OVER AND OVER.

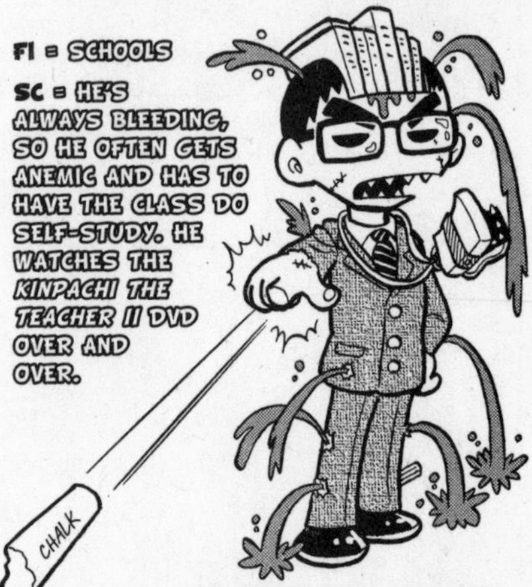
CHALK

SM = SUDDEN-STRIKE CRUSHER

FF = TESTS WITH PERFECT SCORES

KAPPA ZOMBIE

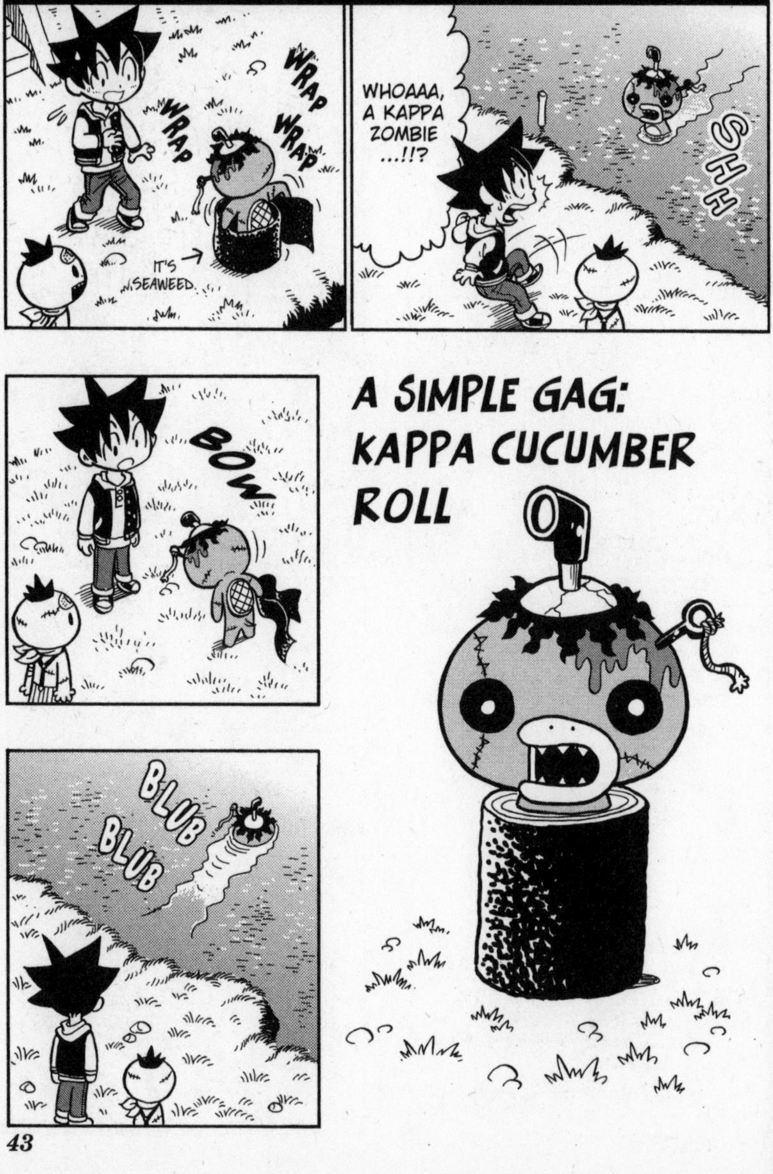
WHOAAA, A KAPPA ZOMBIE ...!!?
SHH
WRAP WRAP WRAP
IT'S SEAWEED
A SIMPLE GAG: KAPPA CUCUMBER ROLL
BOW
B'LUB B'LUB

GENERAL ZOMBIE

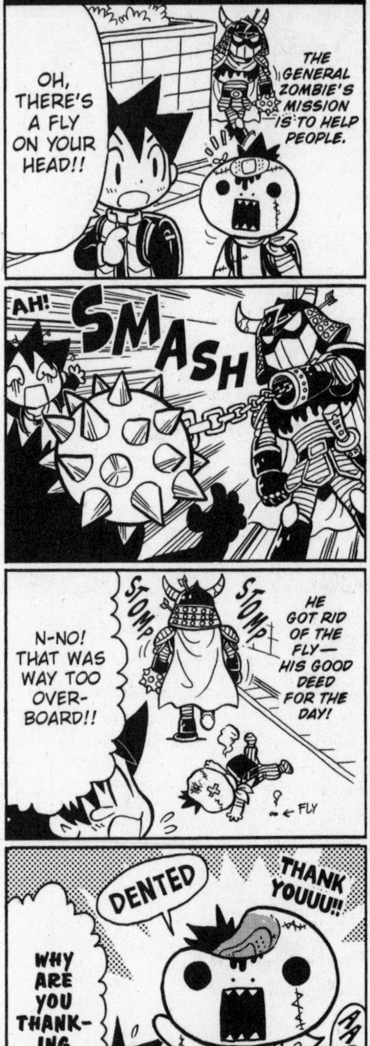
THE GENERAL ZOMBIE'S MISSION IS TO HELP PEOPLE.
OH, THERE'S A FLY ON YOUR HEAD!!
SMASH
AH!
STOMP
HE GOT RID OF THE FLY— HIS GOOD DEED FOR THE DAY!
STOMP
N-NO! THAT WAS WAY TOO OVERBOARD!!
FLY
THANK YOUUU!!
DENTED
WHY ARE YOU THANKING HIM!?
AAGHH!

TELEPHONE ZOMBIE

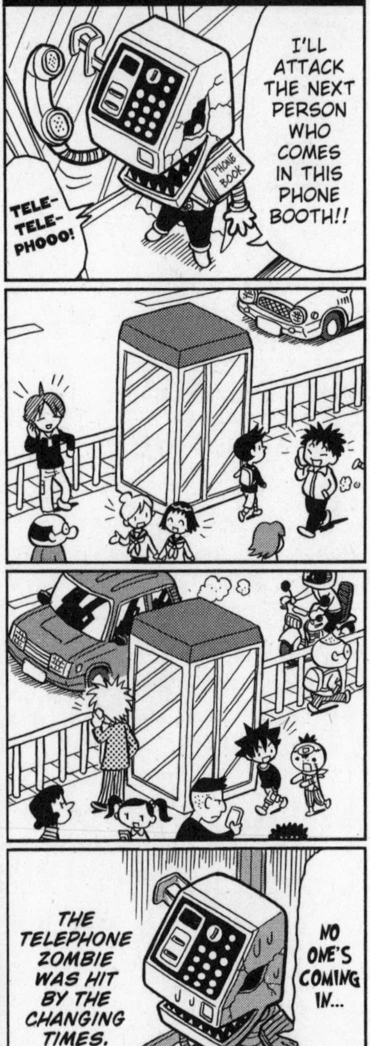
I'LL ATTACK THE NEXT PERSON WHO COMES IN THIS PHONE BOOTH!!
PHONE BOOK
TELE-TELE-PHOOO!
NO ONE'S COMING IN...
THE TELEPHONE ZOMBIE WAS HIT BY THE CHANGING TIMES.

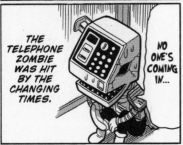

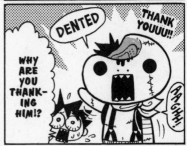

FAIRY ZOMBIE

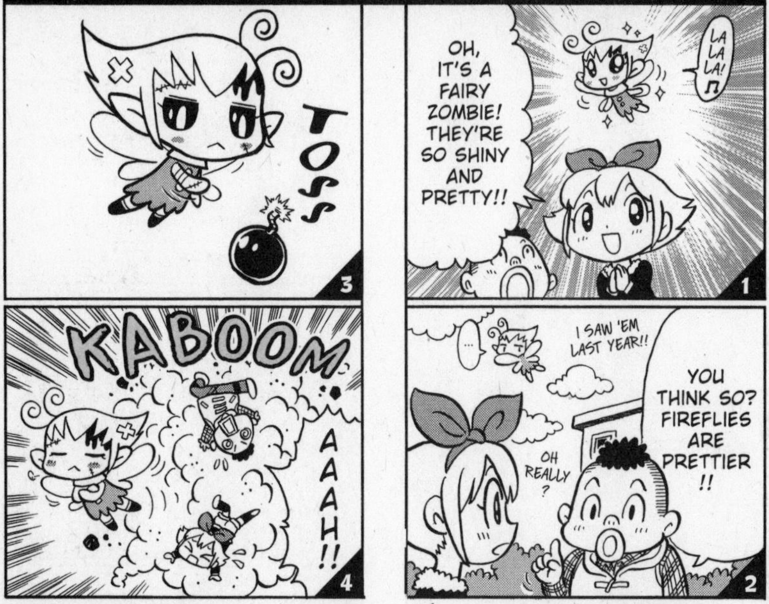
LA LA LA! ♫
OH, IT'S A FAIRY ZOMBIE! THEY'RE SO SHINY AND PRETTY!!
1
I SAW 'EM LAST YEAR!!
YOU THINK SO? FIREFLIES ARE PRETTIER!!
...
OH REALLY?
2
TOSS
3
KABOOM
AAAH!!
4

GENERAL ZOMBIE

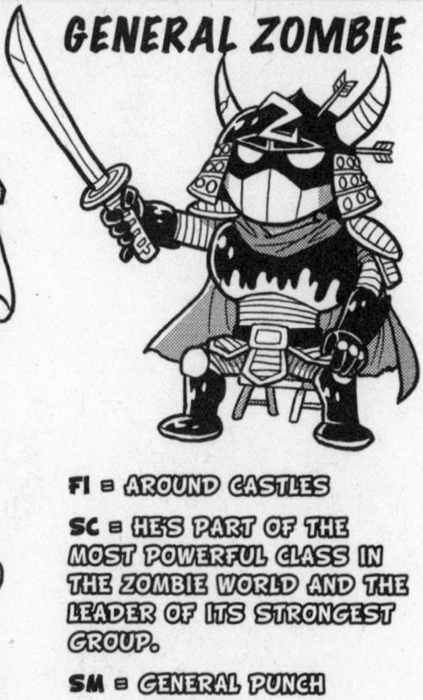

FI = AROUND CASTLES

SC = HE'S PART OF THE MOST POWERFUL CLASS IN THE ZOMBIE WORLD AND THE LEADER OF ITS STRONGEST GROUP.

SM = GENERAL PUNCH

FF = FRIED PORK CUTLET

TELEPHONE ZOMBIE

FI = TELEPHONE BOOTHS

SC = THEY USED TO BE AN UNDERUSED PAY PHONE BEFORE TURNING INTO A ZOMBIE. THEY LOOK SCARY BUT ARE ACTUALLY QUITE SOCIABLE AND A GOOD LISTENER.

SM = TALKING HEADBUTT

FF = PEOPLE'S VOICES

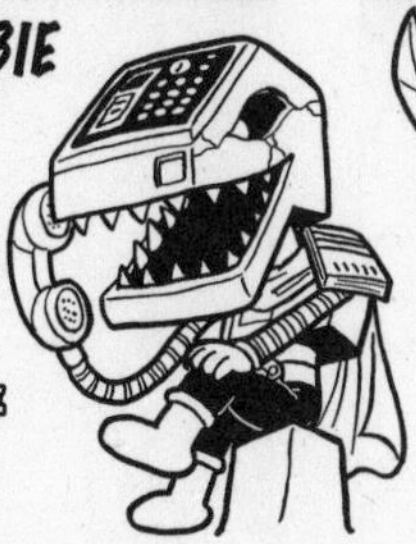

FAIRY ZOMBIE

FI = FORESTS

SC = A ZOMBIFIED FAIRY. THEY'RE SMALL AND CUTE, BUT SUPER-SCARY WHEN ANGRY.

SM = FAIRY BOMB

FF = FLOWER NECTAR

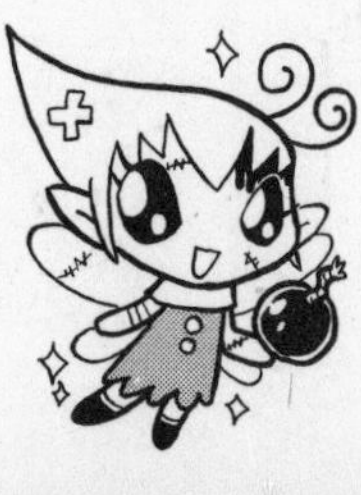

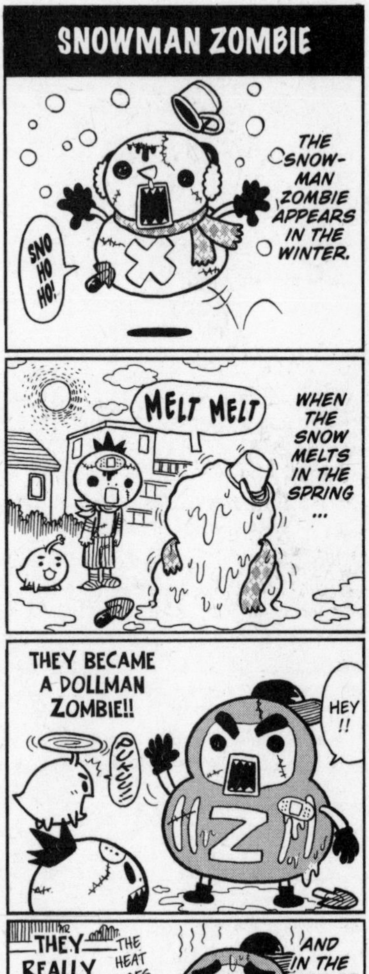
SNOWMAN ZOMBIE
THE SNOW-MAN ZOMBIE APPEARS IN THE WINTER.
SNO HO HO!
WHEN THE SNOW MELTS IN THE SPRING ...
MELT MELT
HEY !!
THEY BECAME A DOLLMAN ZOMBIE!!
PUKU!!
AND IN THE SUMMER ...
SKINNNYYY
THE HEAT DOES THEM IN.
THEY REALLY CAN'T TAKE THE HEAT...
PUKU...

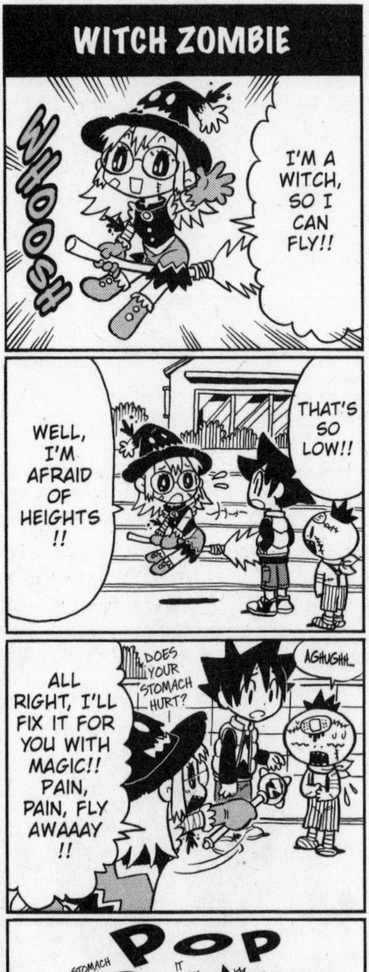
WITCH ZOMBIE
I'M A WITCH, SO I CAN FLY!!
WHOOSH
THAT'S SO LOW!!
WELL, I'M AFRAID OF HEIGHTS !!
AGHUGHH...
DOES YOUR STOMACH HURT?
ALL RIGHT, I'LL FIX IT FOR YOU WITH MAGIC!! PAIN, PAIN, FLY AWAAAY !!
POP
IT REALLY FLEW AWAY !!
STOMACH
ZOMBIE WITCH STILL HAS A LOT TO LEARN.
HUH!?

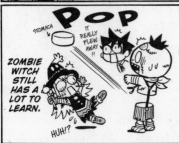

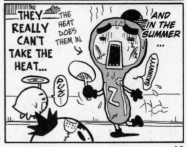

WITCH ZOMBIE

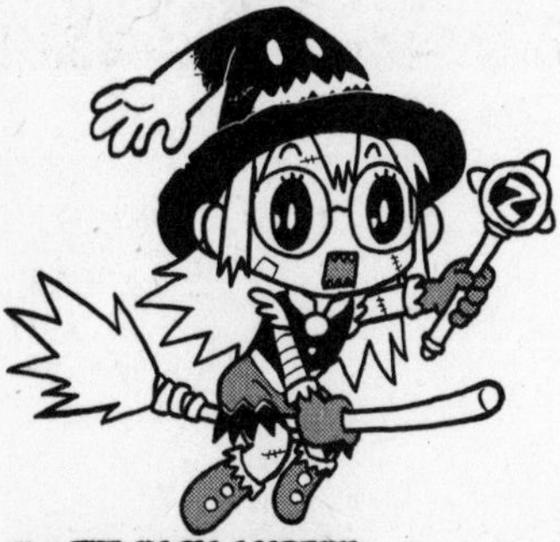

FI = THE MAGIC ACADEMY

SC = SHE'S WORRIED THAT SHE'S NOT GETTING MUCH BETTER AT MAGIC, SO SHE READS MANGA AND WATCHES ANIME ABOUT WITCHES EVERYDAY TO STUDY. HER FAVORITE MANGA IS *QUIET, MS. WITCH!* BY IZUMI TAKEMOTO.

SM = THUNDER WITCH (WORK IN PROGRESS)

FF = MAGIC BREAD

SNOWMAN ZOMBIE

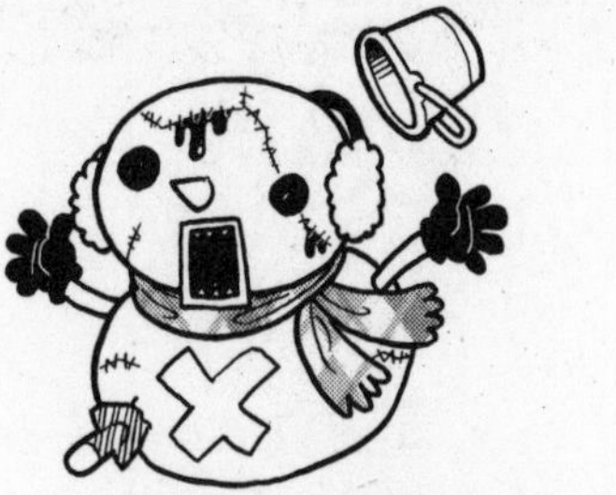

FI = SNOWY STREET CORNERS

SC = THEY ATTACK PEOPLE WHO GET CLOSE TO THEM THINKING THEY'RE A REAL SNOWMAN. THEIR SHAPE CHANGES WITH EACH SEASON. WHAT DO YOU THINK THEY TURN INTO IN THE FALL?

SM = SNOW QUINTET

FF = FROST-COVERED TREES

LUCKY CAT ZOMBIE

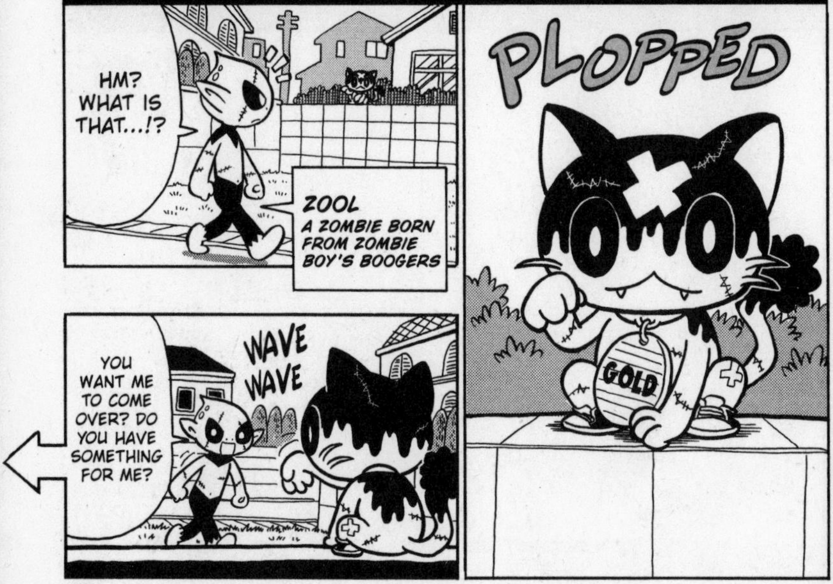
PLOPPED
GOLD
HM? WHAT IS THAT...!?
ZOOL
A ZOMBIE BORN FROM ZOMBIE BOY'S BOOGERS
WAVE WAVE
YOU WANT ME TO COME OVER? DO YOU HAVE SOMETHING FOR ME?

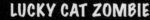

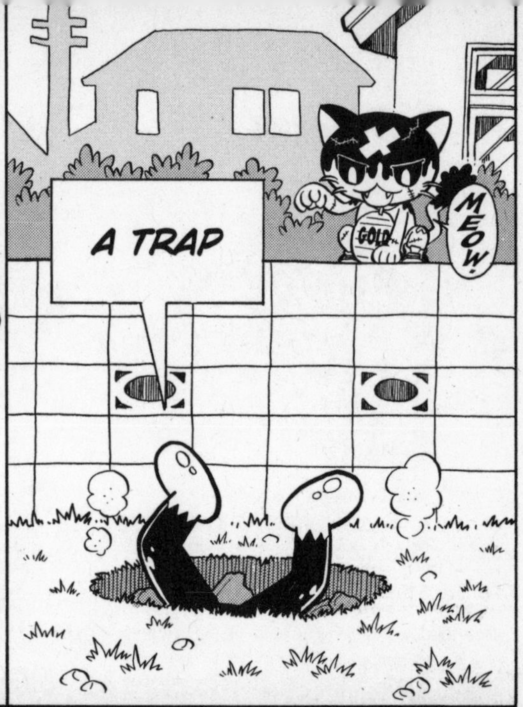
A TRAP
GOLD
MEOW!

LUCKY CAT ZOMBIE

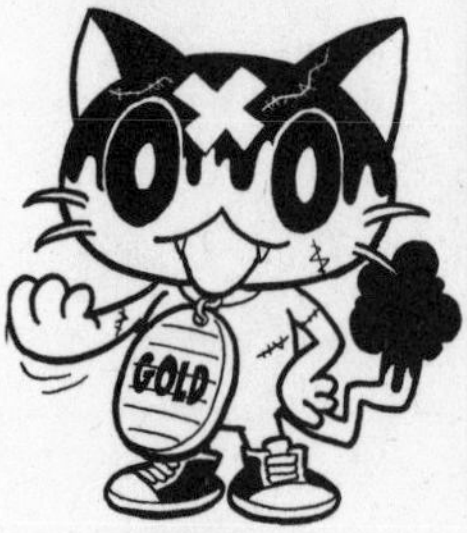
GOLD

FI = ALL AROUND NEIGHBORHOODS

SC = THEY CALL OUT TO PEOPLE PRETENDING TO BE CUTE AND THEN PLAY PRANKS ON THEM. THEY'RE NOT A STRONG FIGHTER, BUT THEY'RE VERY CUNNING.

SM = WELCOME PANIC

FF = SASHIMI SET MEALS

FLOWER ZOMBIE

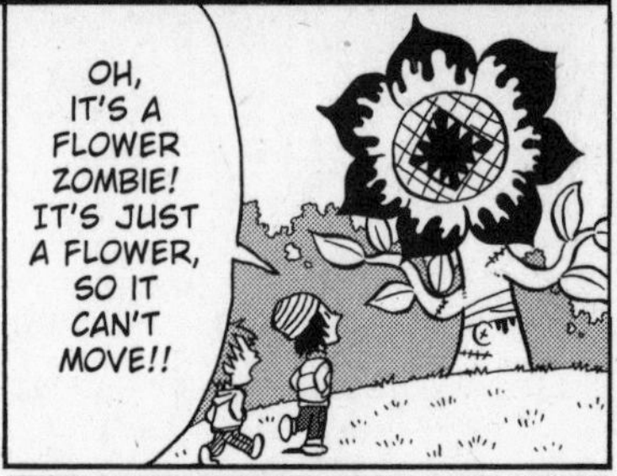
OH, IT'S A FLOWER ZOMBIE! IT'S JUST A FLOWER, SO IT CAN'T MOVE!!

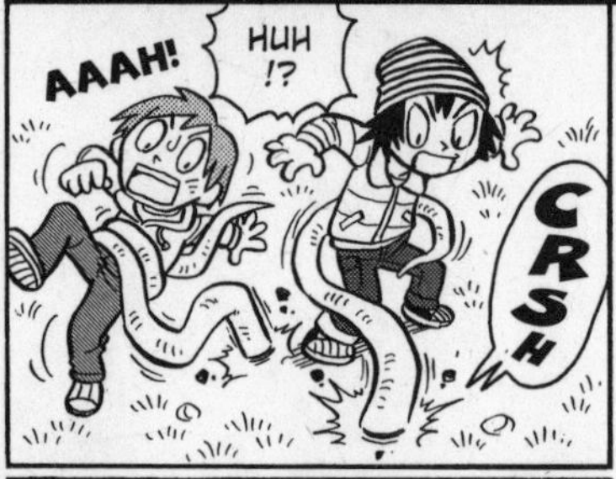
HUH !?
AAAH!
CRSH

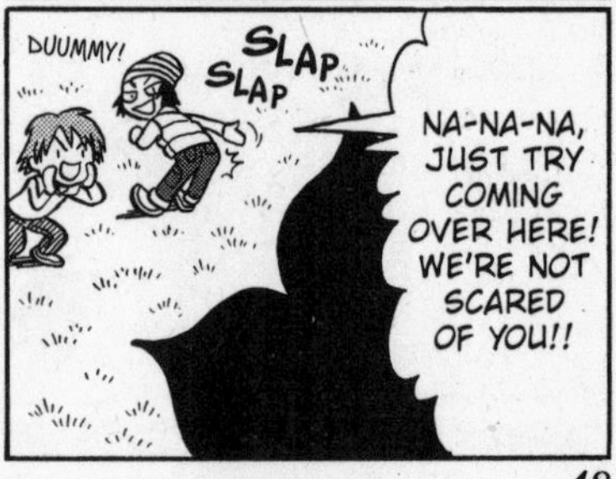
SLAP
SLAP
DUUMMY!
NA-NA-NA, JUST TRY COMING OVER HERE! WE'RE NOT SCARED OF YOU!!

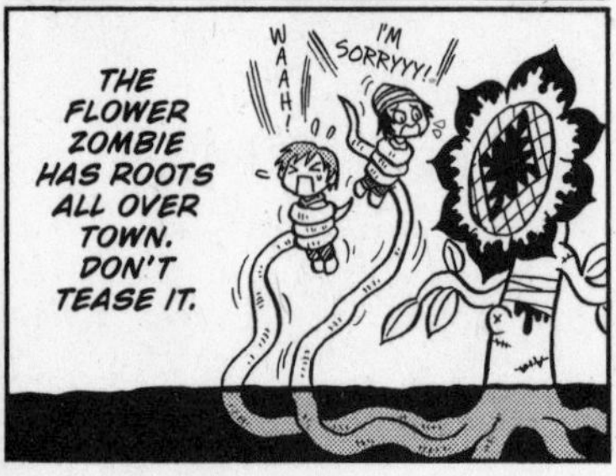
I'M SORRYYY!
WAAH!
THE FLOWER ZOMBIE HAS ROOTS ALL OVER TOWN. DON'T TEASE IT.

SNAKE ZOMBIE

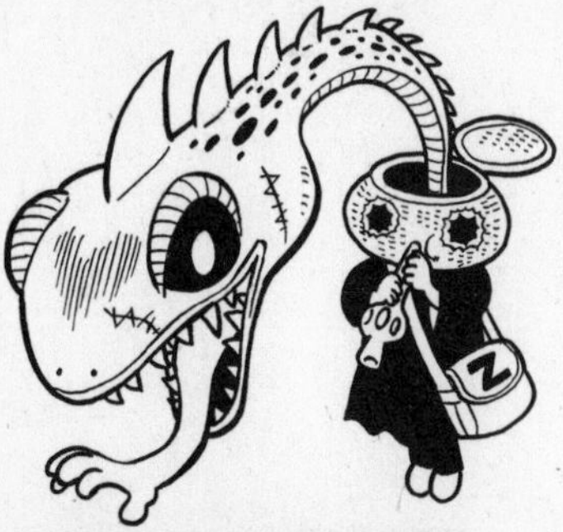

FI = STREET PERFORMANCE GROUNDS

SC = THEY'RE A DANGEROUS ZOMBIE WITH DEADLY POISON. AT FIRST GLANCE, YOU MIGHT THINK "SNAKE CHARMER ZOMBIE" IS A MORE ACCURATE NAME, BUT THE SNAKE HAS BEEN A ZOMBIE LONGER, SO IT COMES FIRST.

SM = SNAKEMAN SHOCK

FF = SNAKE PLANTS

FLOWER ZOMBIE

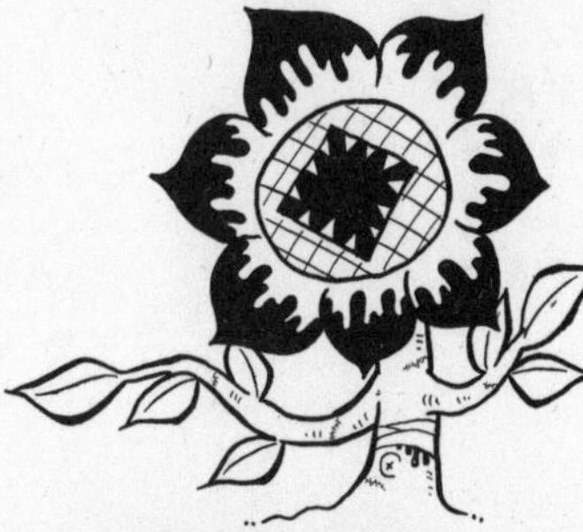

FI = FIELDS OF FLOWERS

SC = WHENEVER IT CAPTURES A PERSON, IT PLANTS NEW SEEDS AND ADDS TO ITS NUMBERS. IT'S QUIET LIKE MOST PLANTS, BUT IT GETS THE JOB DONE WHEN IT NEEDS TO.

SM = PHOTOSYNTHETIC-FLOWER-DESTRUCTION BLIZZARD

FF = HUMAN NUTRIENTS

SNAKE ZOMBIE

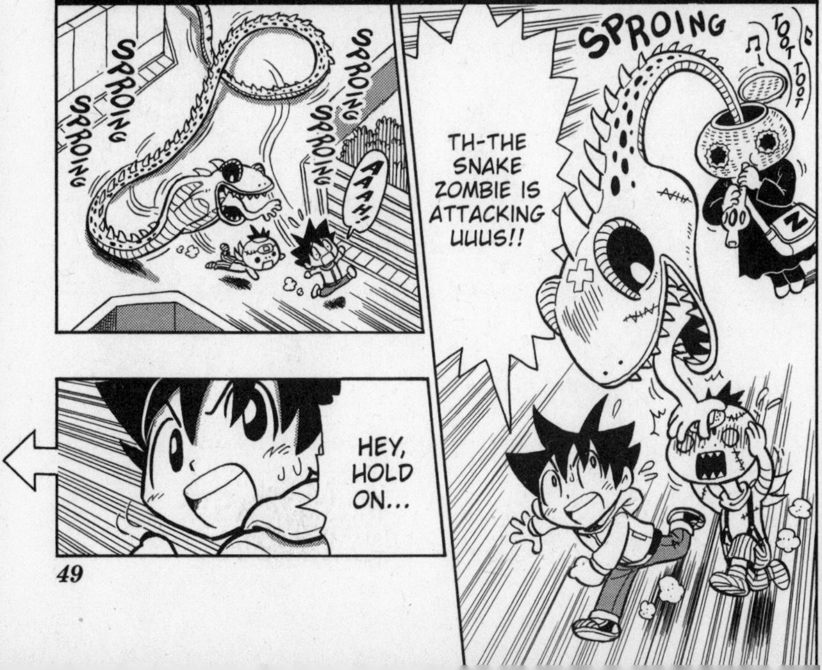
SPROING
TOOT TOOT
TH-THE SNAKE ZOMBIE IS ATTACKING UUUS!!
SPROING
SPROING
SPROING
SPROING
AAAH!
HEY, HOLD ON...

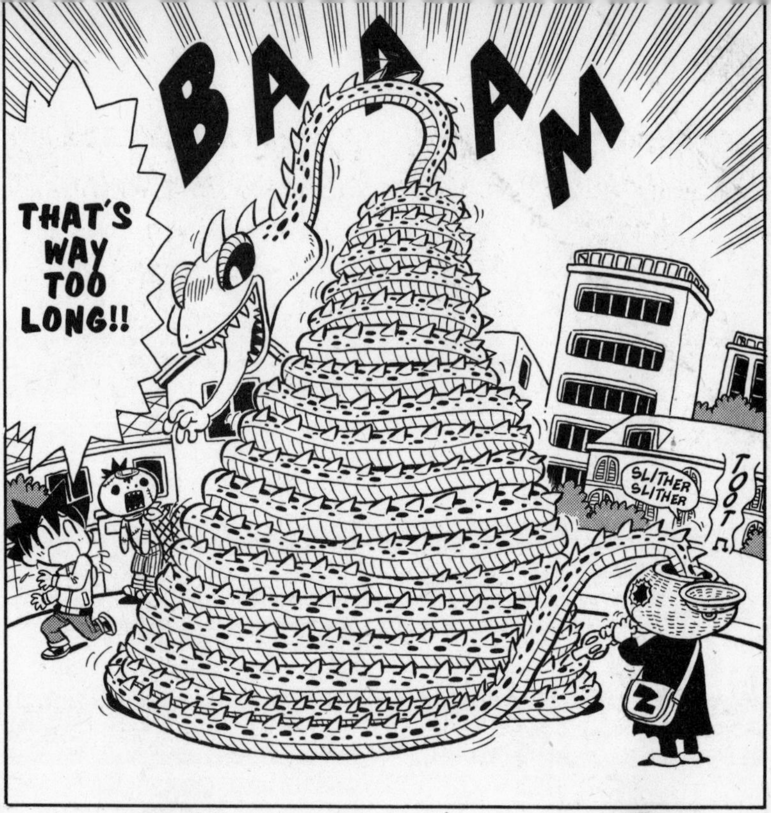
BADAM
THAT'S WAY TOO LONG!!
TOOT ♫
SLITHER SLITHER

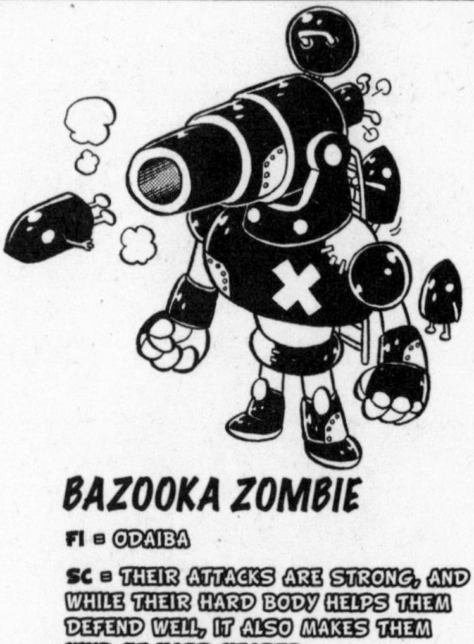

BAZOOKA ZOMBIE

FI = ODAIBA

SC = THEIR ATTACKS ARE STRONG, AND WHILE THEIR HARD BODY HELPS THEM DEFEND WELL, IT ALSO MAKES THEM KIND OF HARD-HEADED.

SM = JUMPING BAZOOKA ATTACK

FF = GUNPOWDER

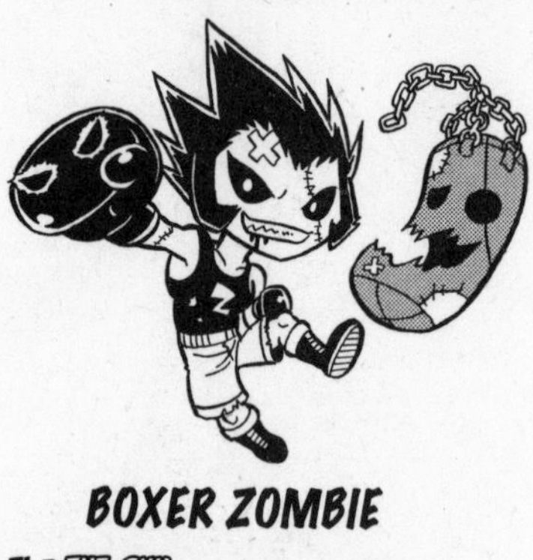

BOXER ZOMBIE

FI = THE GYM

SC = JUST ONE OF HIS PUNCHES CAN DESTROY AN ENTIRE BUILDING. THE SANDBAG ZOMBIE NEXT TO HIM IS HIS TRAINER. THEY OFTEN FIGHT BUT ARE INSEPARABLE FRIENDS.

SM = ATOMIC RAINBOW

FF = SANDBAG ZOMBIE'S HOME-COOKED MEALS

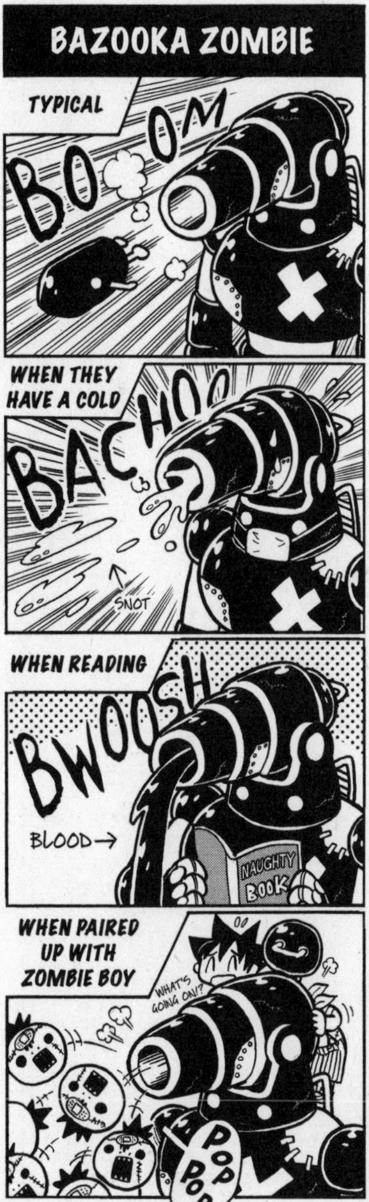
BAZOOKA ZOMBIE
TYPICAL
BOOOM
WHEN THEY HAVE A COLD
BACHOO
SNOT
WHEN READING
BWOOSH
BLOOD→
NAUGHTY BOOK
WHEN PAIRED UP WITH ZOMBIE BOY
WHAT'S GOING ON!?
POP POP POP

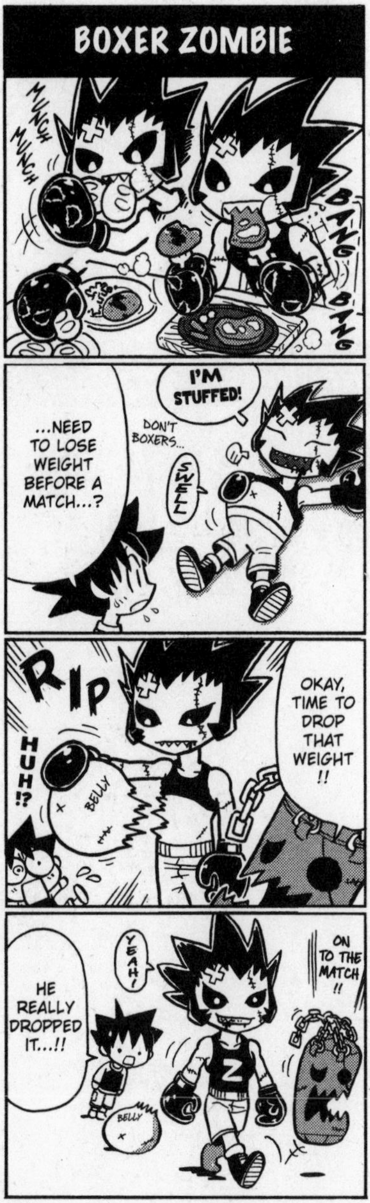
BOXER ZOMBIE
BANG BANG
MUNCH MUNCH
I'M STUFFED!
SWELL
DON'T BOXERS...
...NEED TO LOSE WEIGHT BEFORE A MATCH...?
OKAY, TIME TO DROP THAT WEIGHT!!
RIP
BELLY
HUH!?
ON TO THE MATCH!!
YEAH!
HE REALLY DROPPED IT...!!
BELLY

SPOILED LADY ZOMBIE

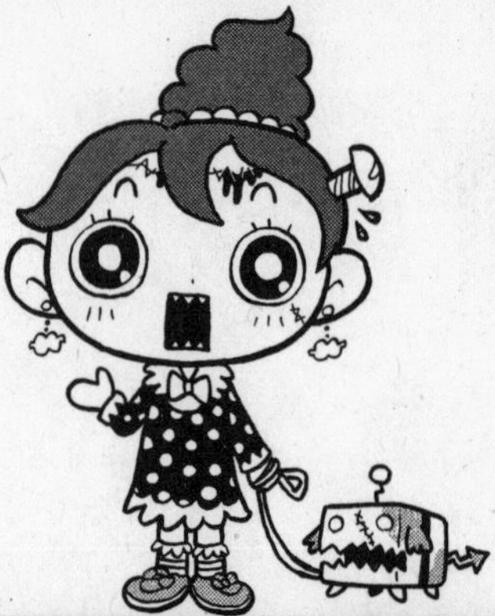

FI = PARTY VENUES

SC = HER FATHER IS THE PRESIDENT OF A LARGE COMPANY THAT HAS ZOMBENIENCE STORES ALL OVER THE COUNTRY. SINCE SHE WAS RAISED AS A SPOILED LADY, SHE'S A BIT SELFISH. SHE SURPRISINGLY LOVES VIDEO GAMES AND OFTEN PLAYS THEM WITH HER MAIDS, BUT GETS VERY CRANKY IF SHE LOSES.

SM = SUPER-EXPENSIVE CHOP

FF = GEMSTONES

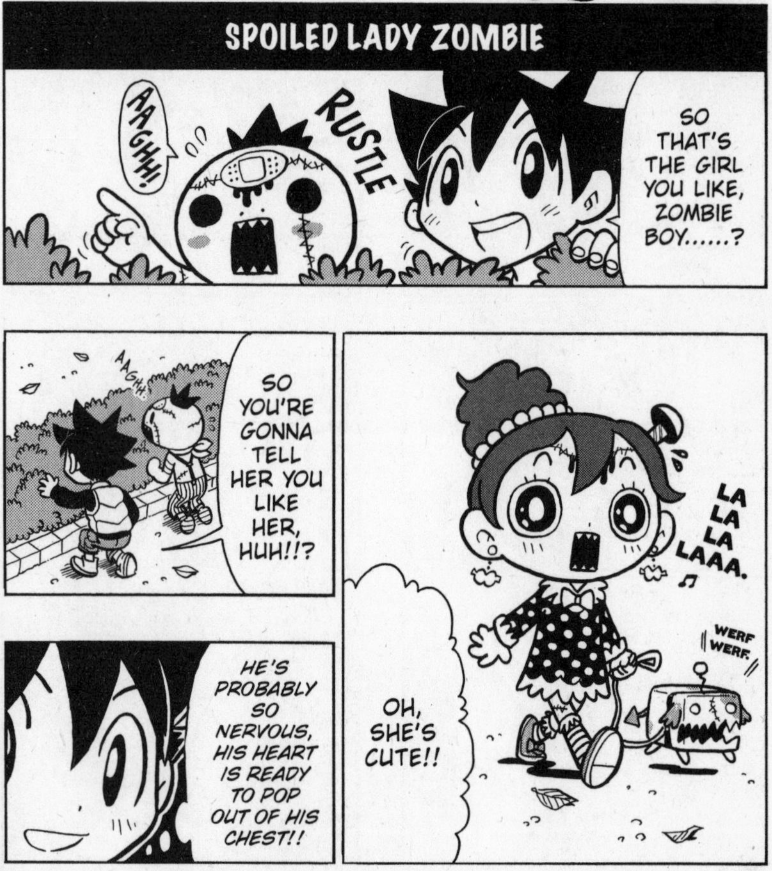
SPOILED LADY ZOMBIE
SO THAT'S THE GIRL YOU LIKE, ZOMBIE BOY......?
RUSTLE
AAGHH!
LA LA LA LAAA.
WERF WERF.
OH, SHE'S CUTE!!
SO YOU'RE GONNA TELL HER YOU LIKE HER, HUH!!?
AAGHH.
HE'S PROBABLY SO NERVOUS, HIS HEART IS READY TO POP OUT OF HIS CHEST!!

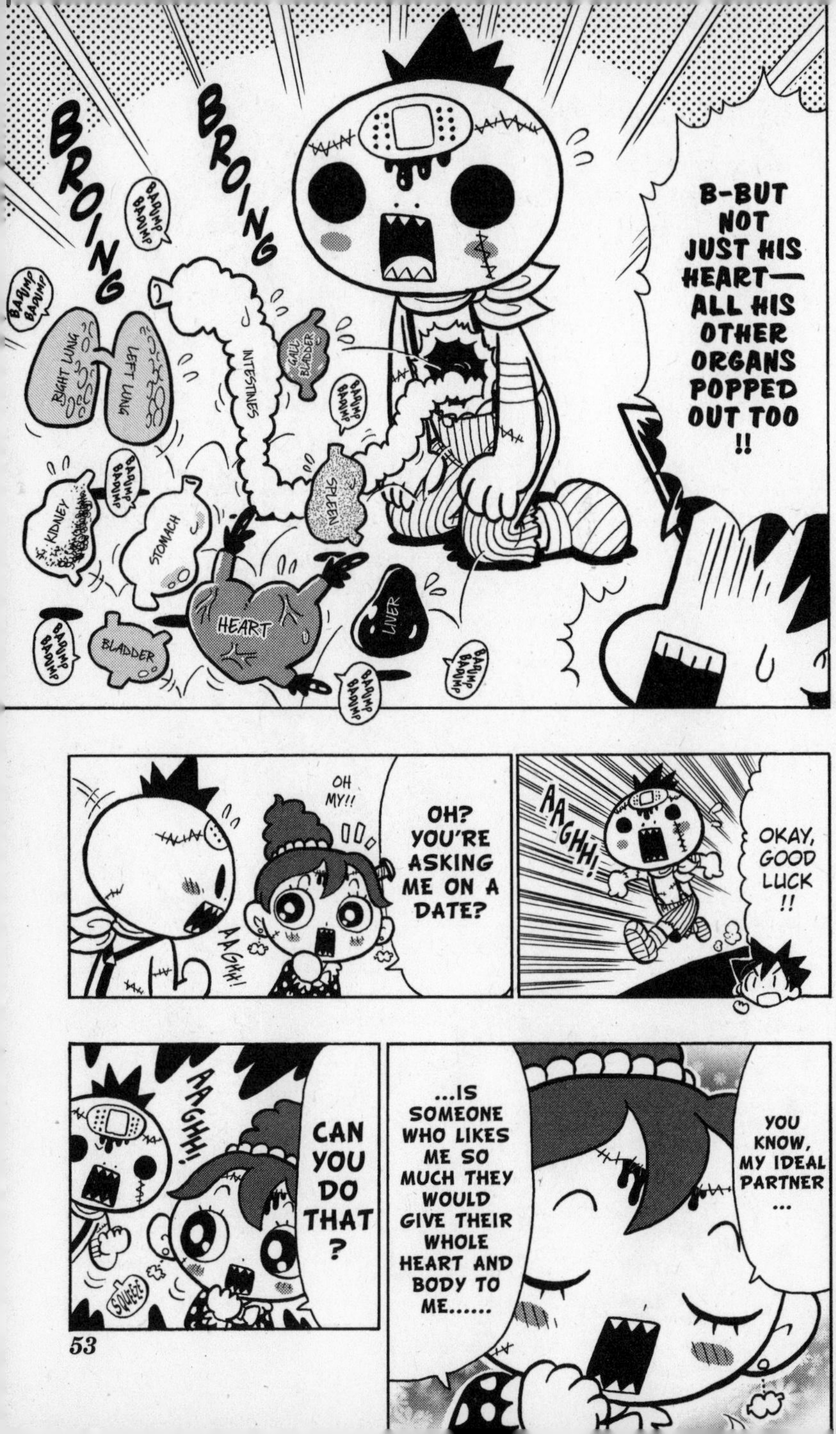

B-BUT NOT JUST HIS HEART— ALL HIS OTHER ORGANS POPPED OUT TOO !!
BROING
BROING
BADUMP BADUMP
BADUMP BADUMP
GALL BLADDER
INTESTINES
RIGHT LUNG
LEFT LUNG
BADUMP BADUMP
BADUMP BADUMP
SPLEEN
KIDNEY
STOMACH
LIVER
HEART
BLADDER
BADUMP BADUMP
BADUMP BADUMP
BADUMP BADUMP
AAGHH!
OKAY, GOOD LUCK !!
OH MY!!
OH? YOU'RE ASKING ME ON A DATE?
AAGHH!
YOU KNOW, MY IDEAL PARTNER ...
...IS SOMEONE WHO LIKES ME SO MUCH THEY WOULD GIVE THEIR WHOLE HEART AND BODY TO ME......
CAN YOU DO THAT ?
AAGHH!
SQUEEZE

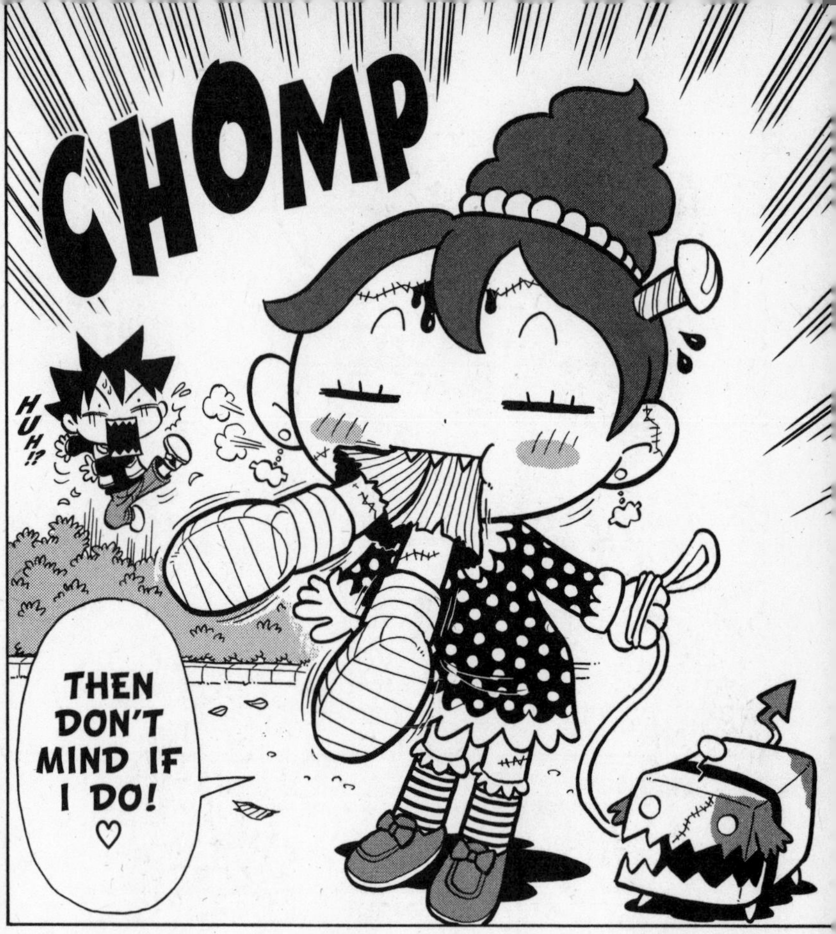
CHOMP
HUH!?
THEN DON'T MIND IF I DO! ♡

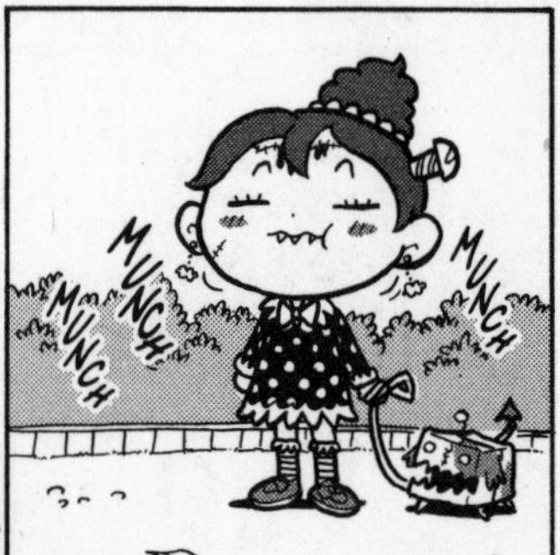
MUNCH
MUNCH
MUNCH

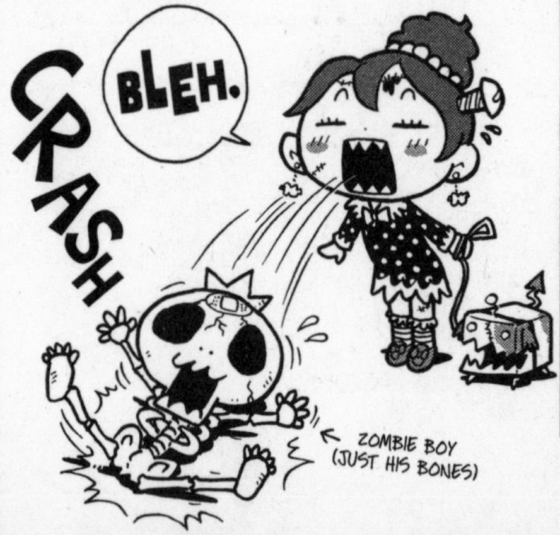
BLEH.
CRASH
ZOMBIE BOY (JUST HIS BONES)

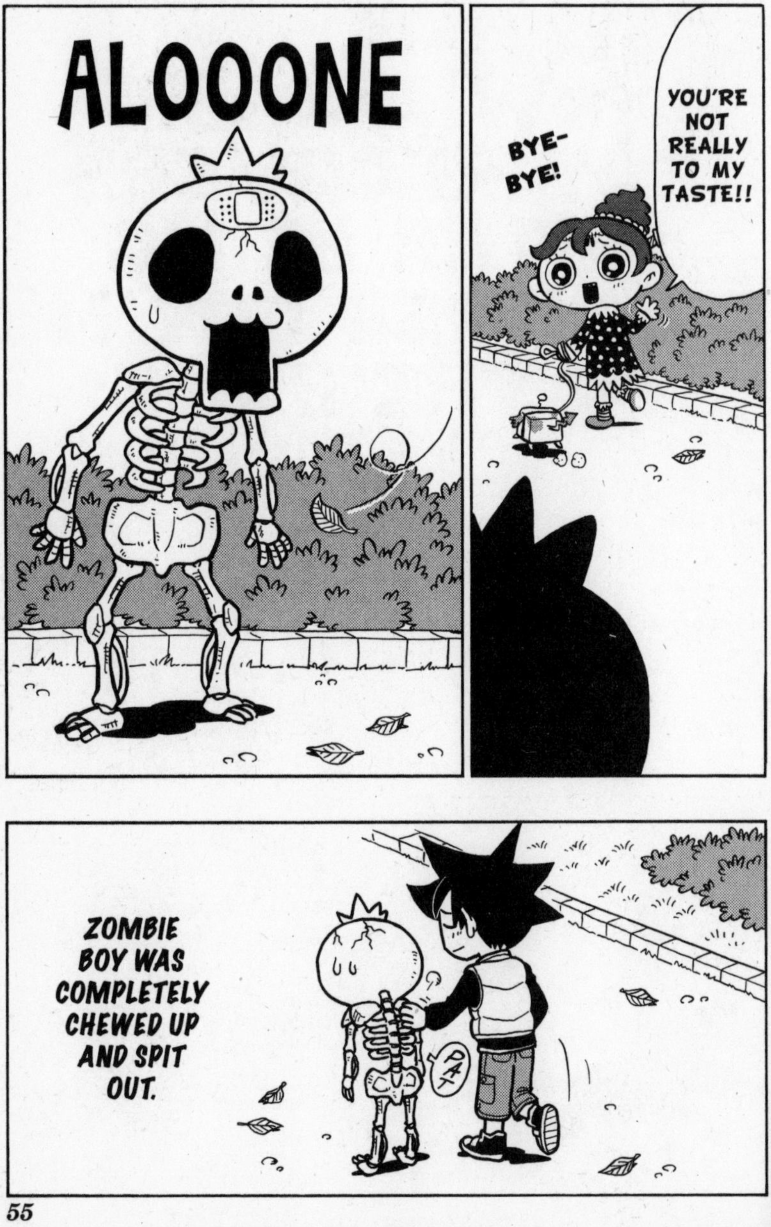
YOU'RE NOT REALLY TO MY TASTE!!
BYE-BYE!
ALOOONE
ZOMBIE BOY WAS COMPLETELY CHEWED UP AND SPIT OUT.
PAT

HOW ZOMBIE BOY RECOVERS AFTER BEING STRIPPED DOWN TO THE BONE:

① DIG A HOLE.

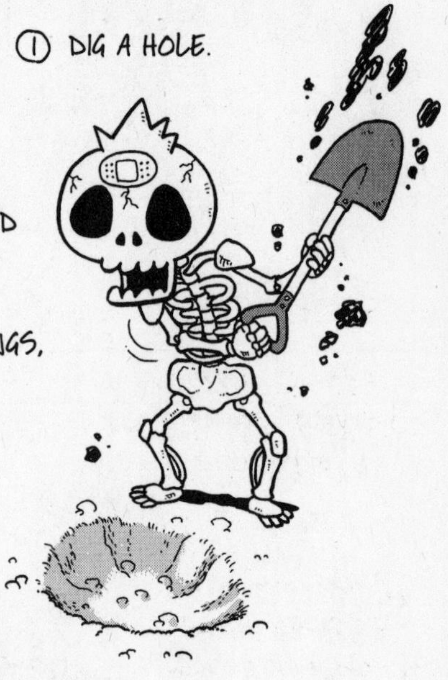

② ADD TWO KILOGRAMS OF MEAT, FIVE HUNDRED GRAMS OF FLOUR, SOY SAUCE, IRON SAND, LEAVES, ERASER SHAVINGS, AND HOT WATER.

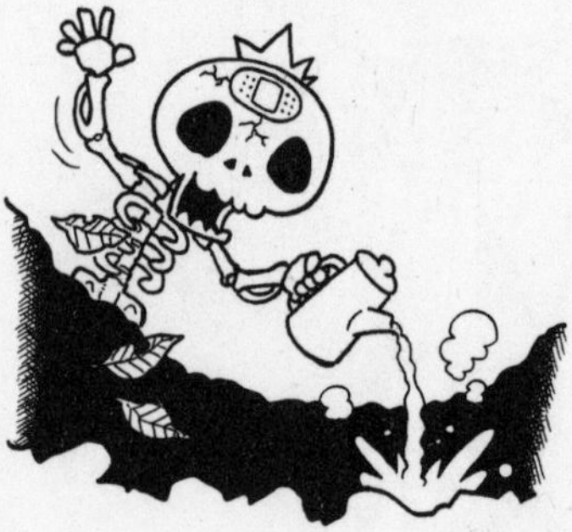

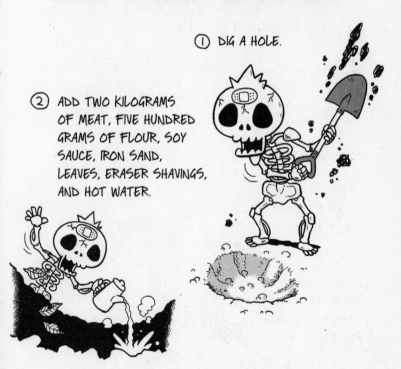

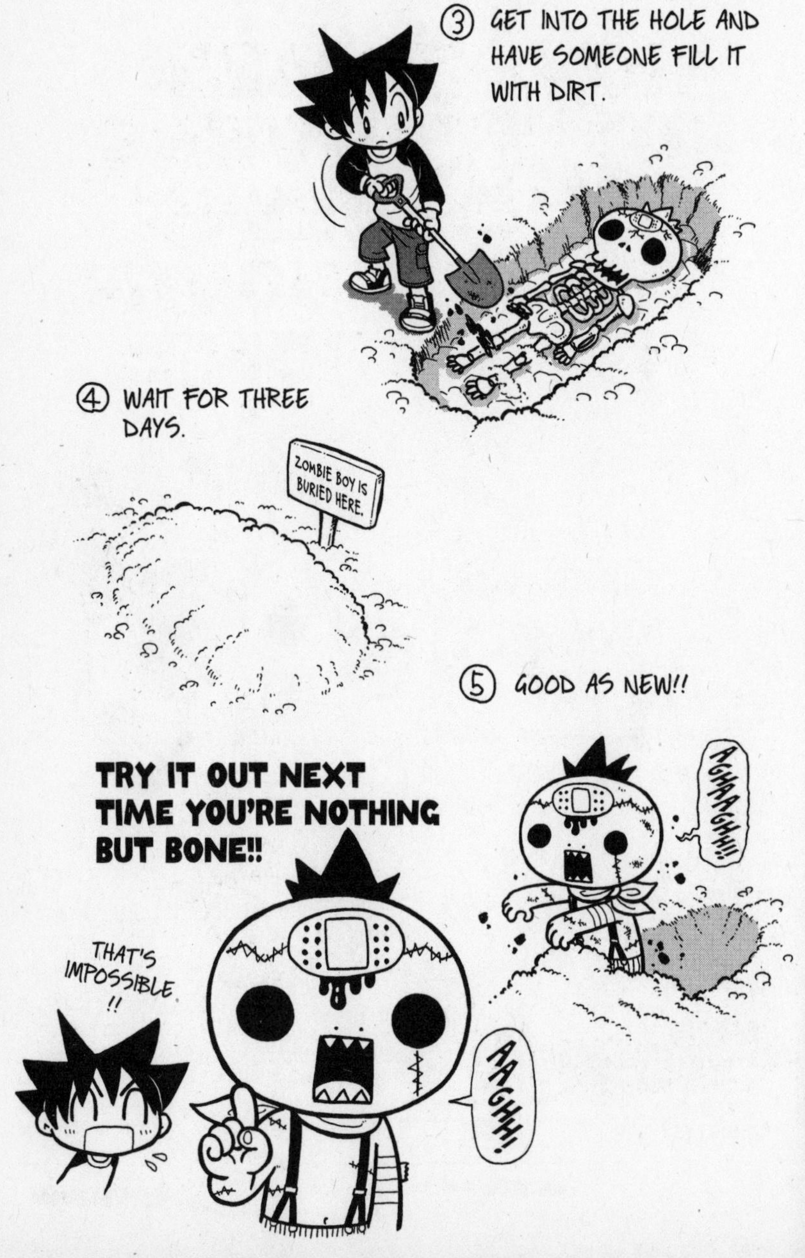
③ GET INTO THE HOLE AND HAVE SOMEONE FILL IT WITH DIRT.
④ WAIT FOR THREE DAYS.
ZOMBIE BOY IS BURIED HERE.
⑤ GOOD AS NEW!!
AGHAAAGHHH!!!
TRY IT OUT NEXT TIME YOU'RE NOTHING BUT BONE!!
AAGHH!
THAT'S IMPOSSIBLE!!

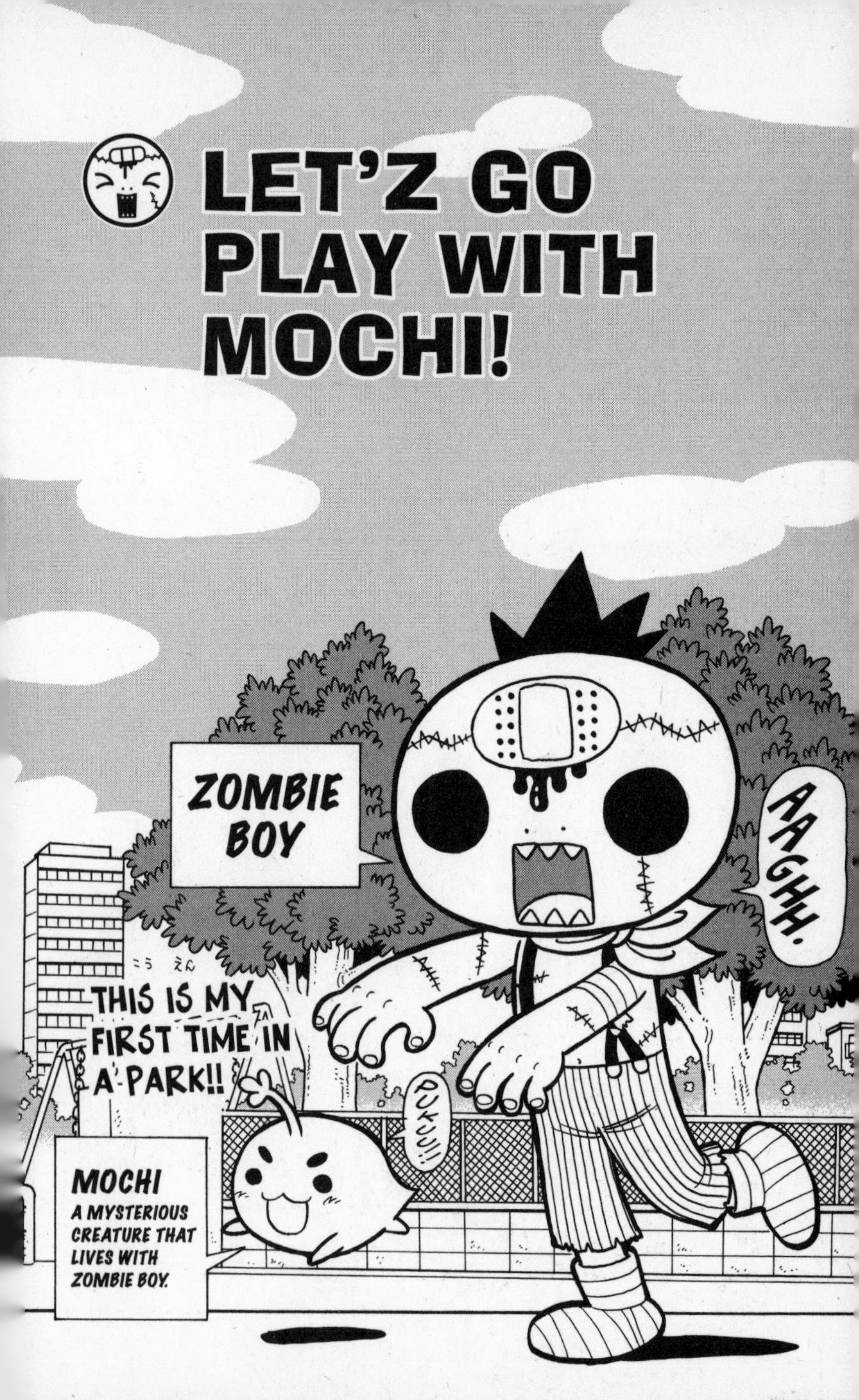
LET'Z GO PLAY WITH MOCHI!
AAGHH.
ZOMBIE BOY
THIS IS MY FIRST TIME IN A PARK!!
PUKU!!
MOCHI
A MYSTERIOUS CREATURE THAT LIVES WITH ZOMBIE BOY.

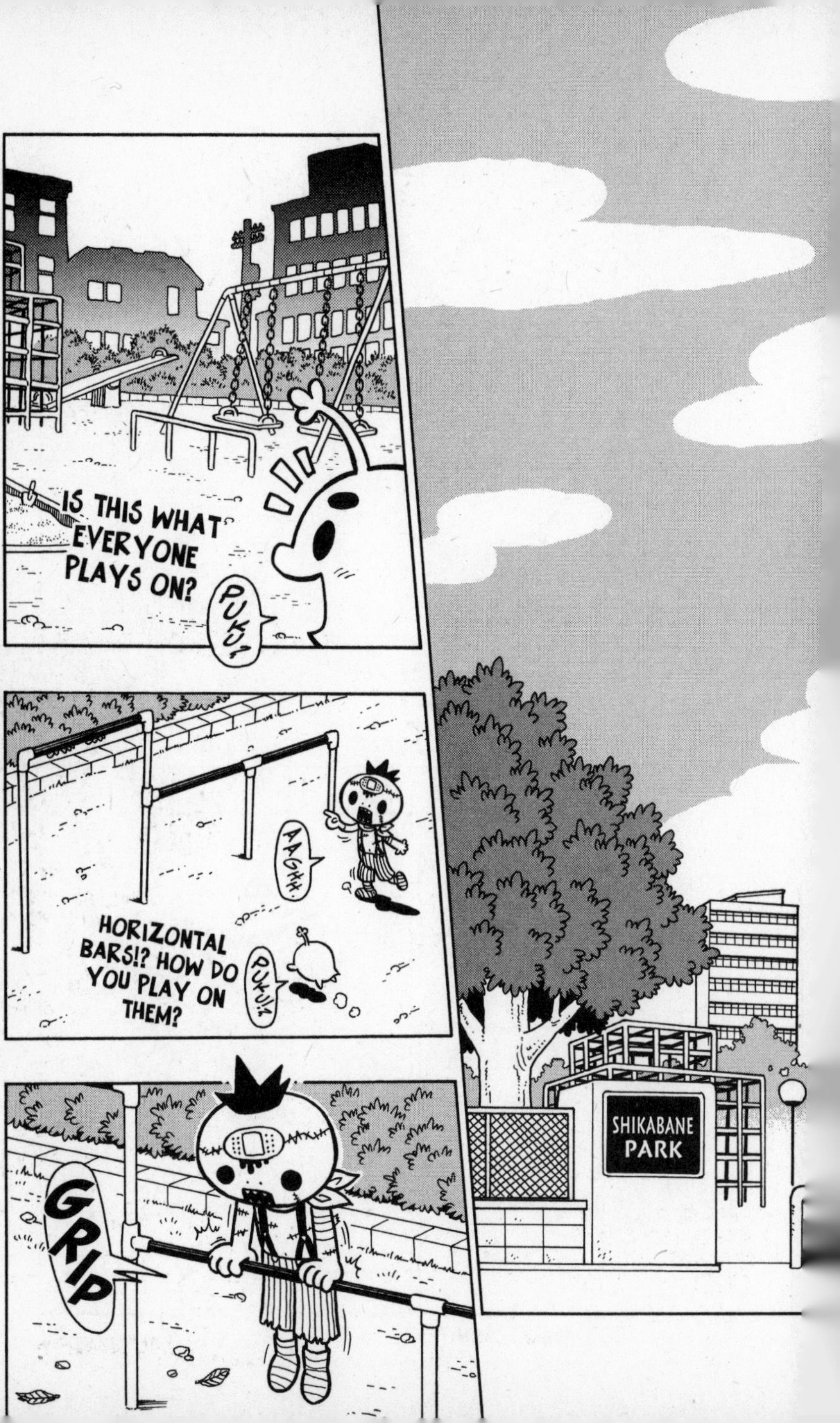
SHIKABANE PARK
IS THIS WHAT EVERYONE PLAYS ON?
PUKU?
AAGHH.
HORIZONTAL BARS!? HOW DO YOU PLAY ON THEM?
PUKU!?
GRIP

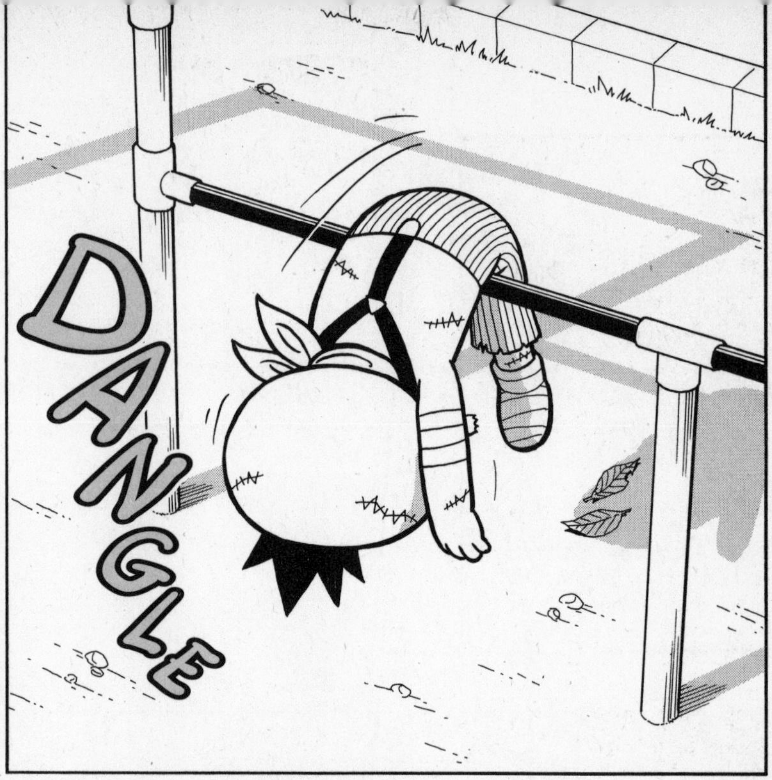
DANGLE
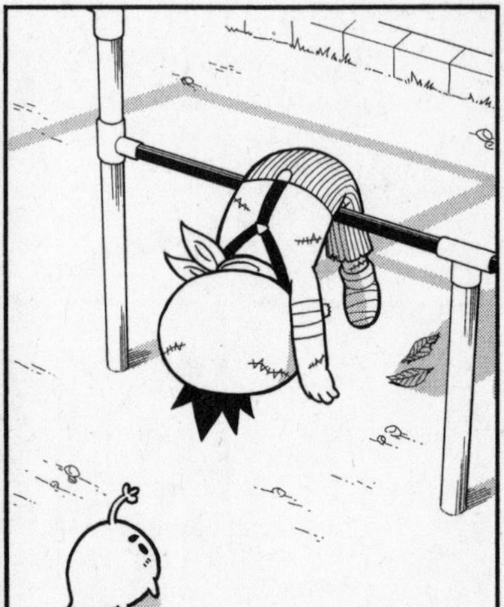
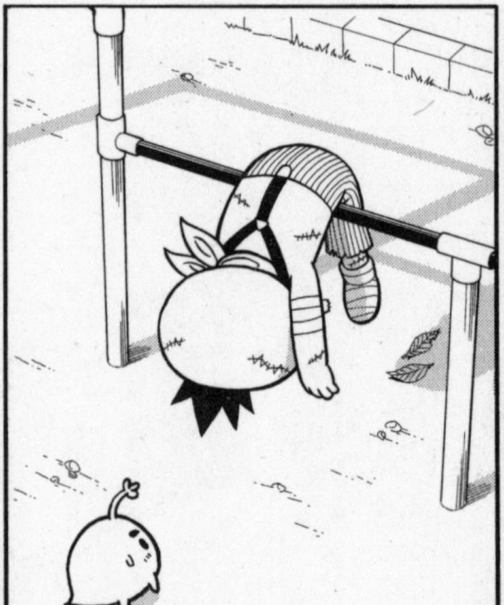

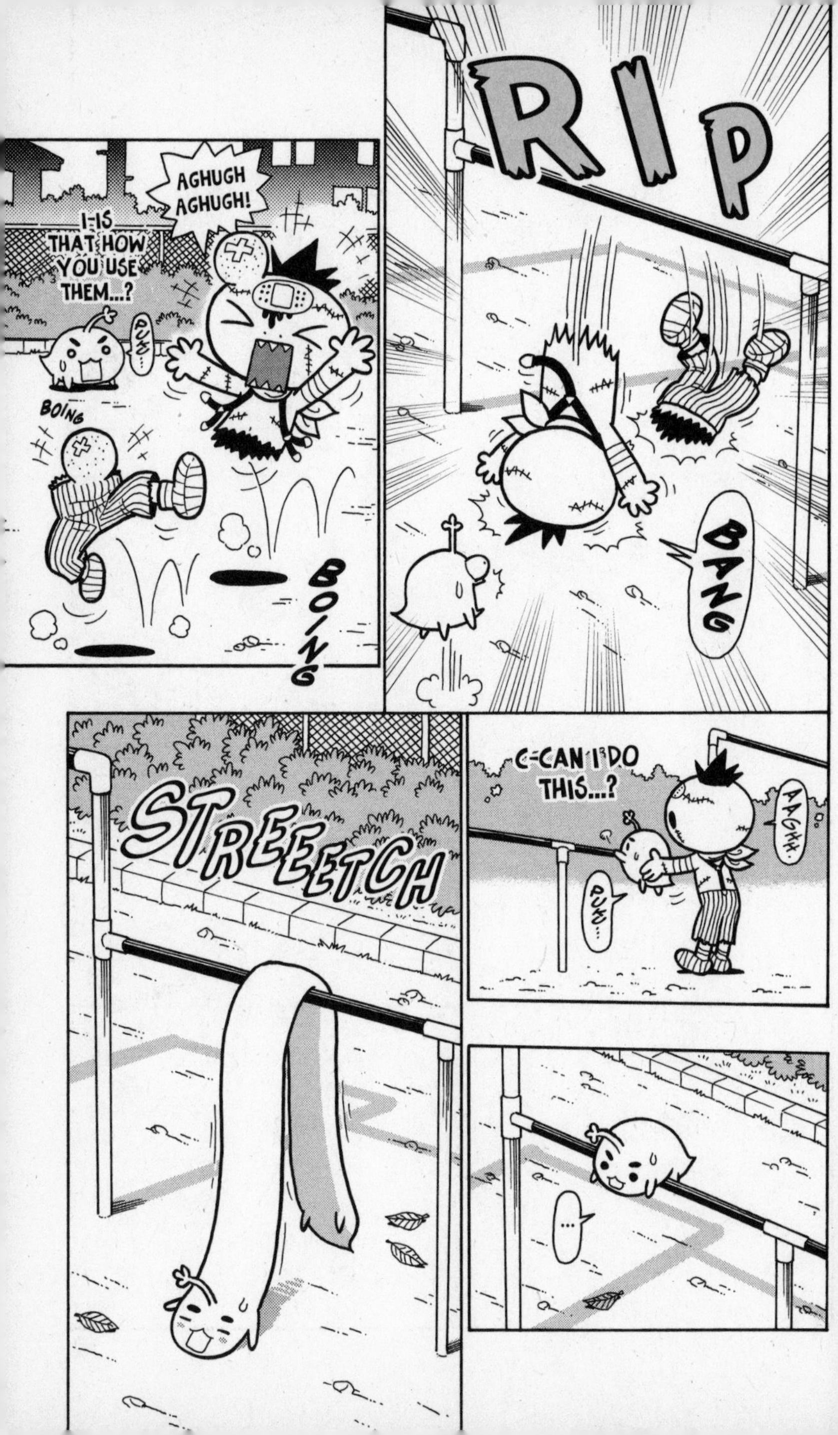
RIP
BANG
AGHUGH AGHUGH!
I-IS THAT HOW YOU USE THEM...?
PUK...
BOING
BOING
C-CAN I DO THIS...?
AAGHH.
PUK...
...
STREEETCH

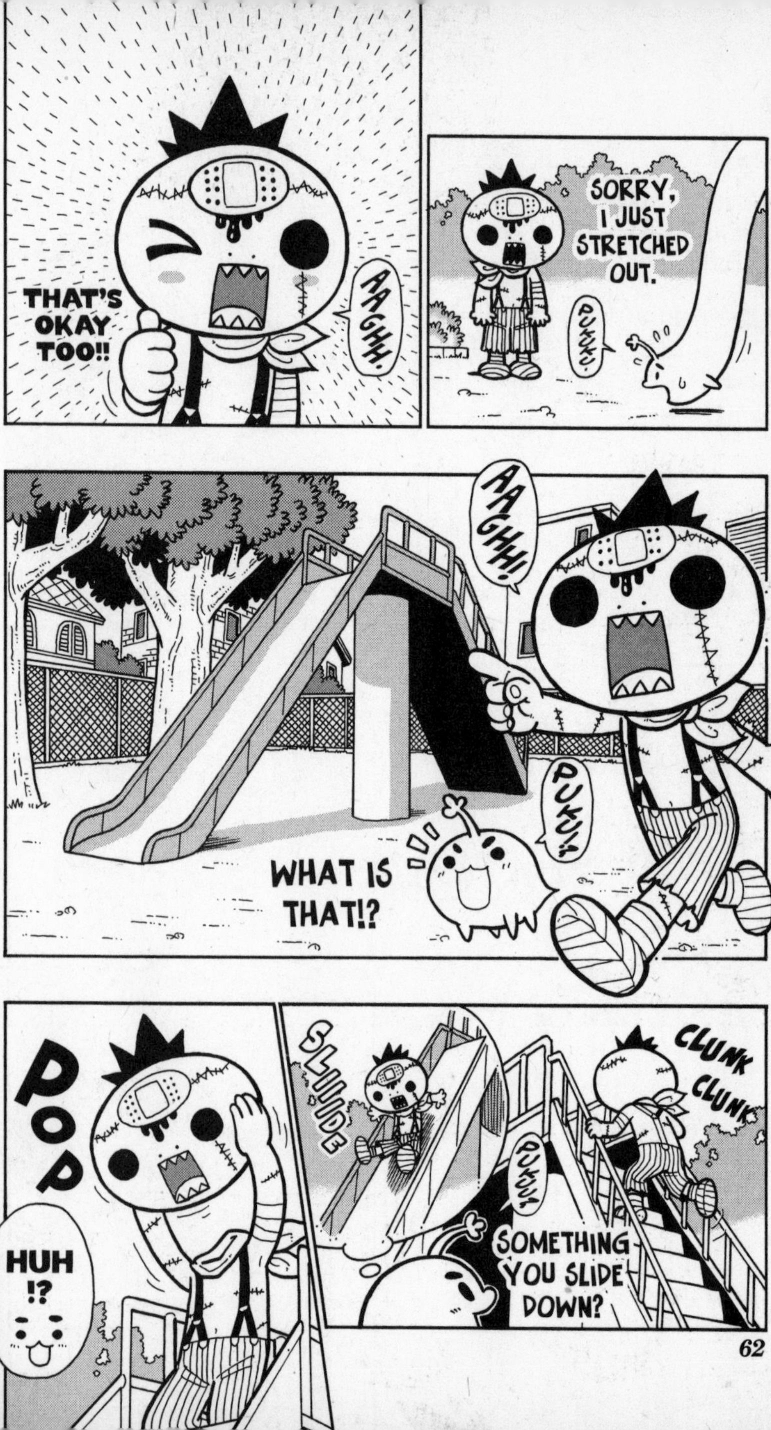

SORRY, I JUST STRETCHED OUT.
PUKUKU.
AAGHH.
THAT'S OKAY TOO!!
AAGHH!
PUKU!?
WHAT IS THAT!?
CLUNK CLUNK
SLIIIDE
PUKU!?
SOMETHING YOU SLIDE DOWN?
POP
HUH!?

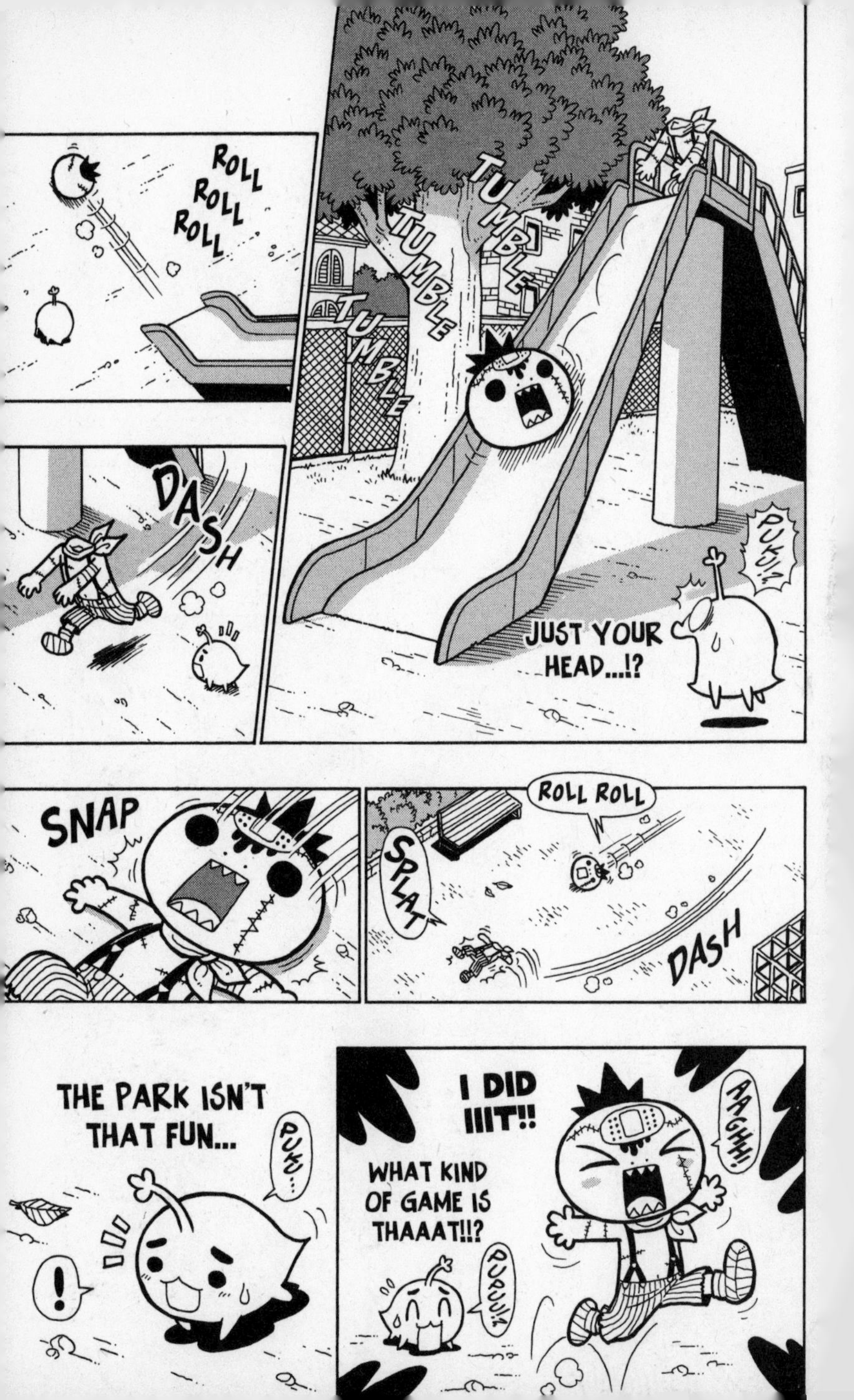
TUMBLE
TUMBLE
TUMBLE
PUKU!?
JUST YOUR HEAD...!?
ROLL ROLL ROLL
DASH
ROLL ROLL
SPLAT
DASH
SNAP
I DID IIIT!!
AAGHH!
WHAT KIND OF GAME IS THAAAT!!?
PUPUU!
THE PARK ISN'T THAT FUN...
PUKU...
!

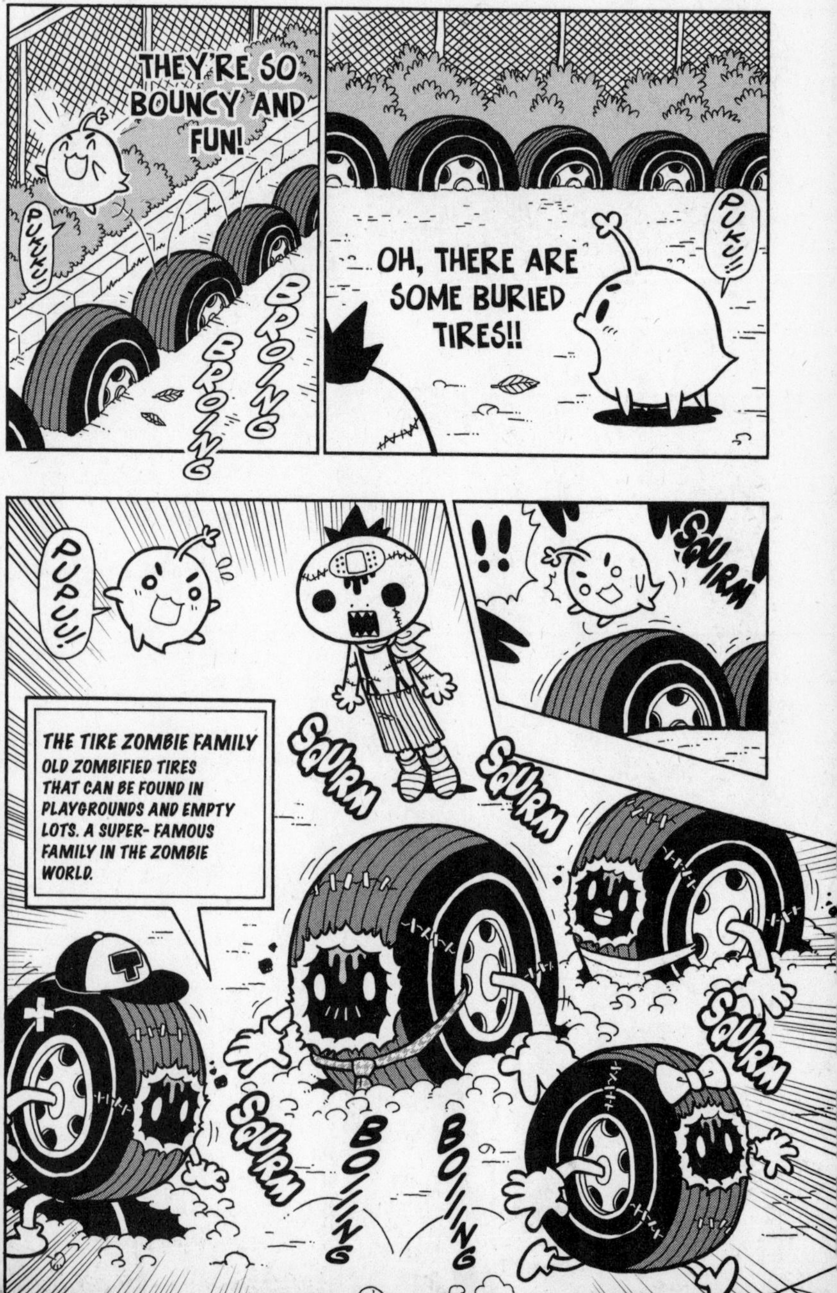
PUKU!!
OH, THERE ARE SOME BURIED TIRES!!
THEY'RE SO BOUNCY AND FUN!
PUKUU!
BROING
BROING
!!
SQUIRM
PUPUU!
SQUIRM
SQUIRM
THE TIRE ZOMBIE FAMILY
OLD ZOMBIFIED TIRES THAT CAN BE FOUND IN PLAYGROUNDS AND EMPTY LOTS. A SUPER-FAMOUS FAMILY IN THE ZOMBIE WORLD.
SQUIRM
SQUIRM
BOING
BOING

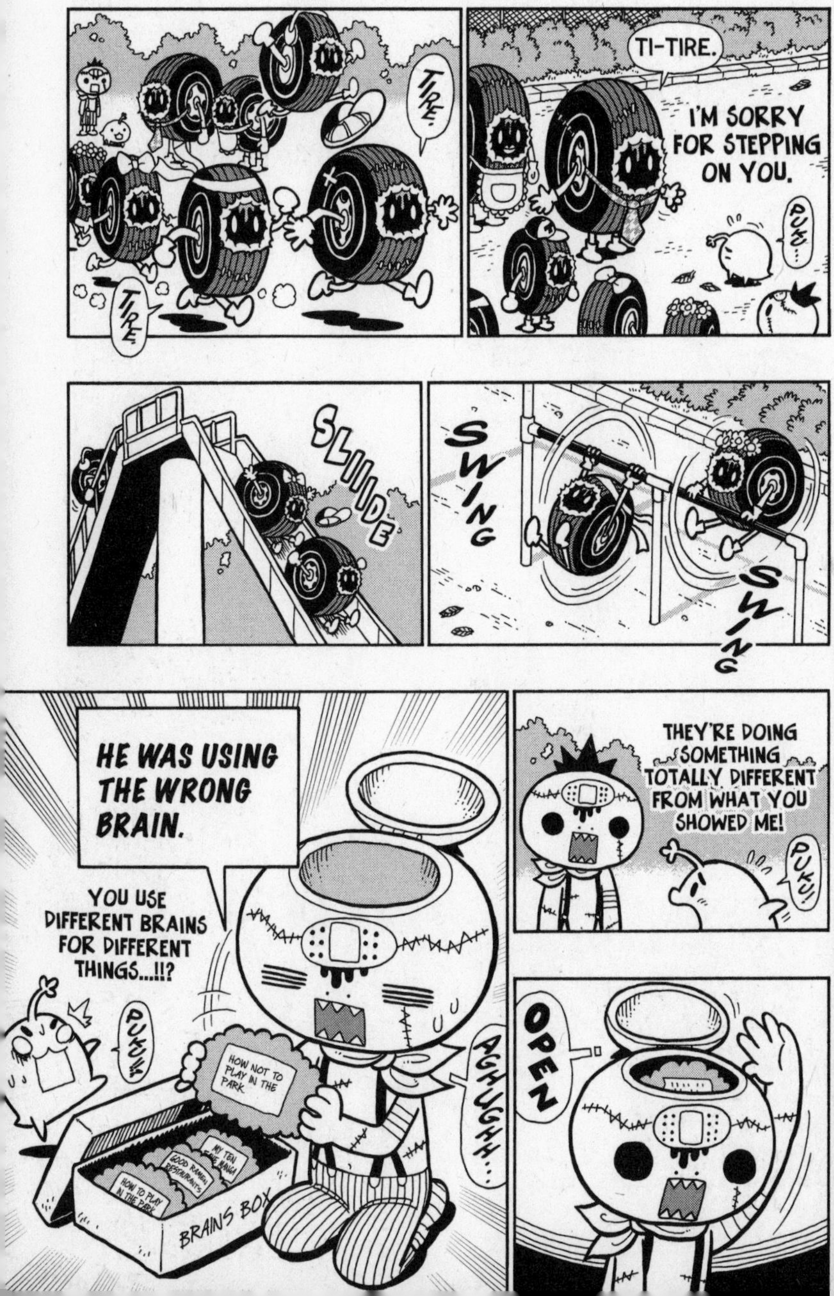
TI-TIRE.
I'M SORRY FOR STEPPING ON YOU.
PUKU...
TIRE.
TIRE.
SWING
SWING
SLIIIDE
THEY'RE DOING SOMETHING TOTALLY DIFFERENT FROM WHAT YOU SHOWED ME!
PUKU!
OPEN
HE WAS USING THE WRONG BRAIN.
YOU USE DIFFERENT BRAINS FOR DIFFERENT THINGS...!!?
PUKU!!
AGHUGHH...
HOW NOT TO PLAY IN THE PARK
GOOD RAMEN RESTAURANTS
HOW TO PLAY IN THE PARK
BRAINS BOX

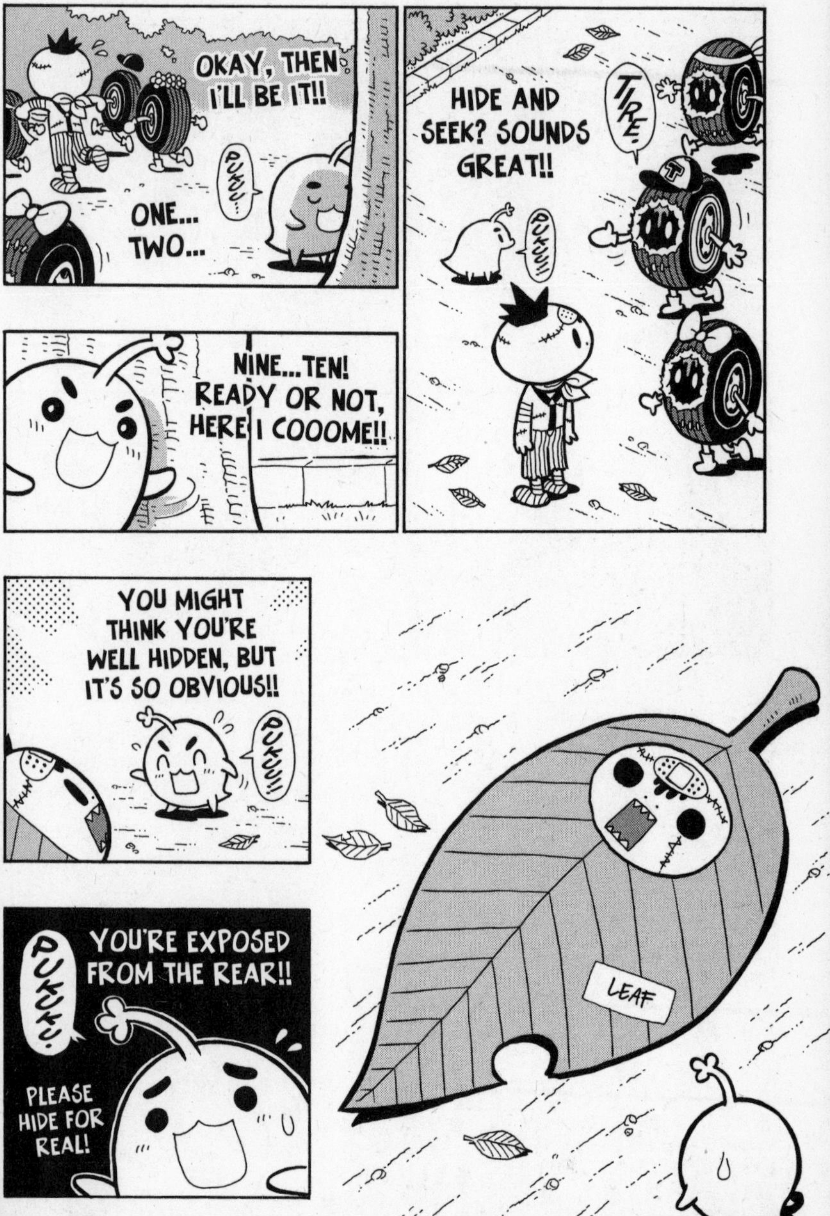
HIDE AND SEEK? SOUNDS GREAT!!
TIRE.
PUKUU!!
OKAY, THEN I'LL BE IT!!
PUKUU...
ONE... TWO...
NINE...TEN! READY OR NOT, HERE I COOOME!!
LEAF
YOU MIGHT THINK YOU'RE WELL HIDDEN, BUT IT'S SO OBVIOUS!!
PUKUU!!
YOU'RE EXPOSED FROM THE REAR!!
PUKUU.
PLEASE HIDE FOR REAL!

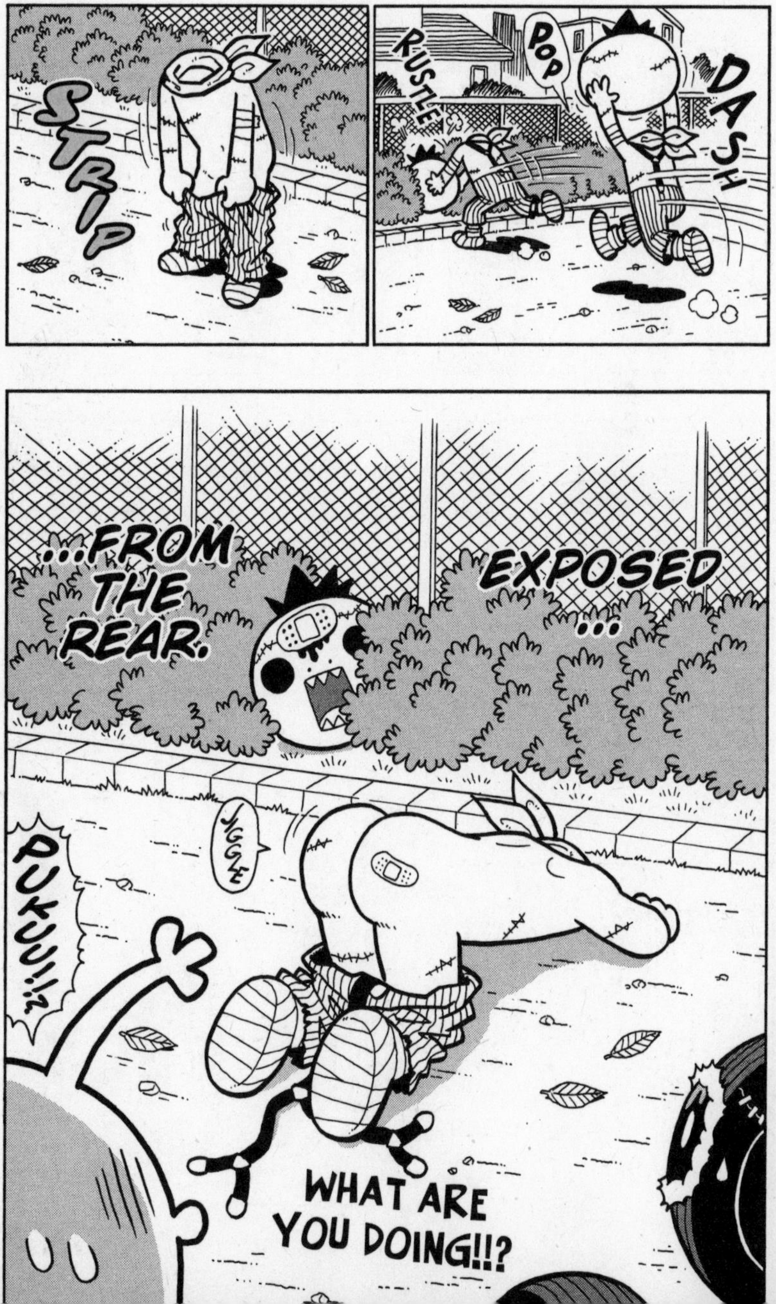
DASH
POP
RUSTLE
STRIP
EXPOSED...
...FROM THE REAR.
JIGGLE
PUKUUU!!?
WHAT ARE YOU DOING!!?

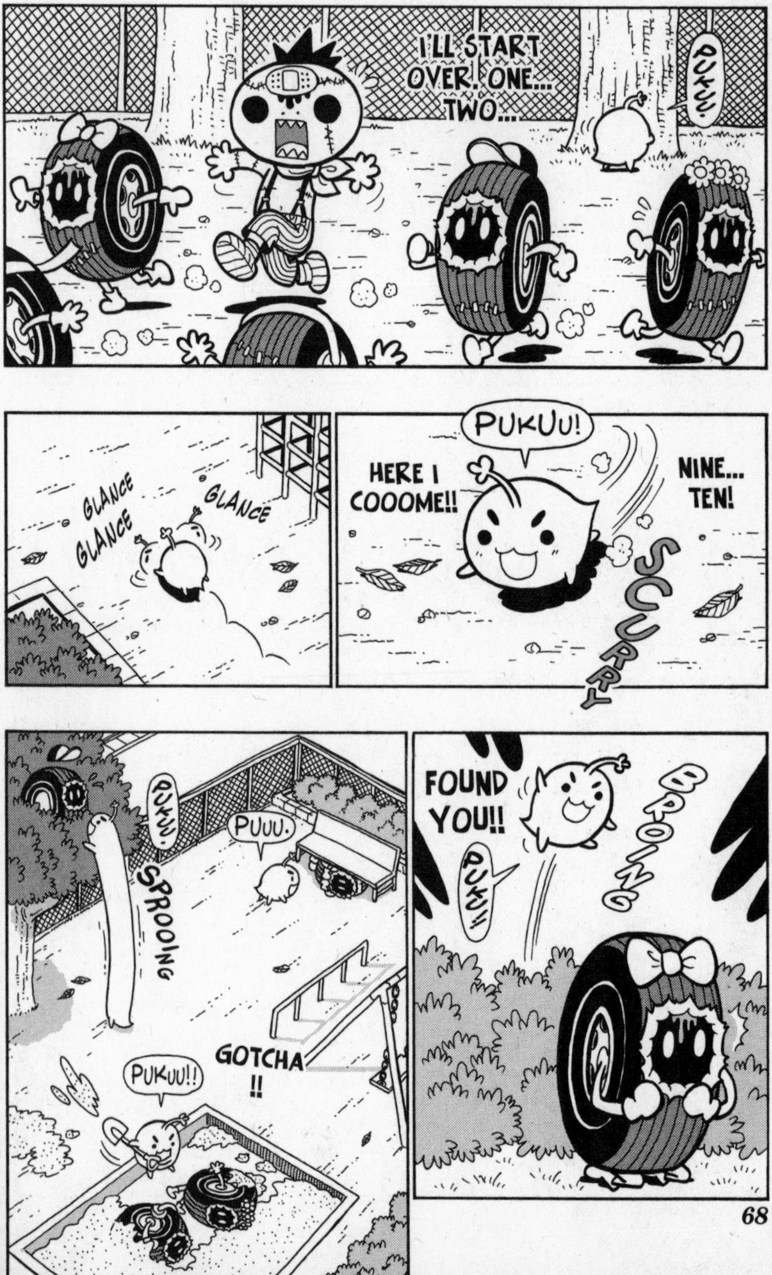

PUKUU.
I'LL START OVER. ONE... TWO...
NINE... TEN!
PUKUU!
HERE I COOOME!!
SCURRY
GLANCE
GLANCE GLANCE
SPROING
FOUND YOU!!
PUKU!!
PUKUU.
PUUU.
SPROOING
GOTCHA!!
PUKUU!!

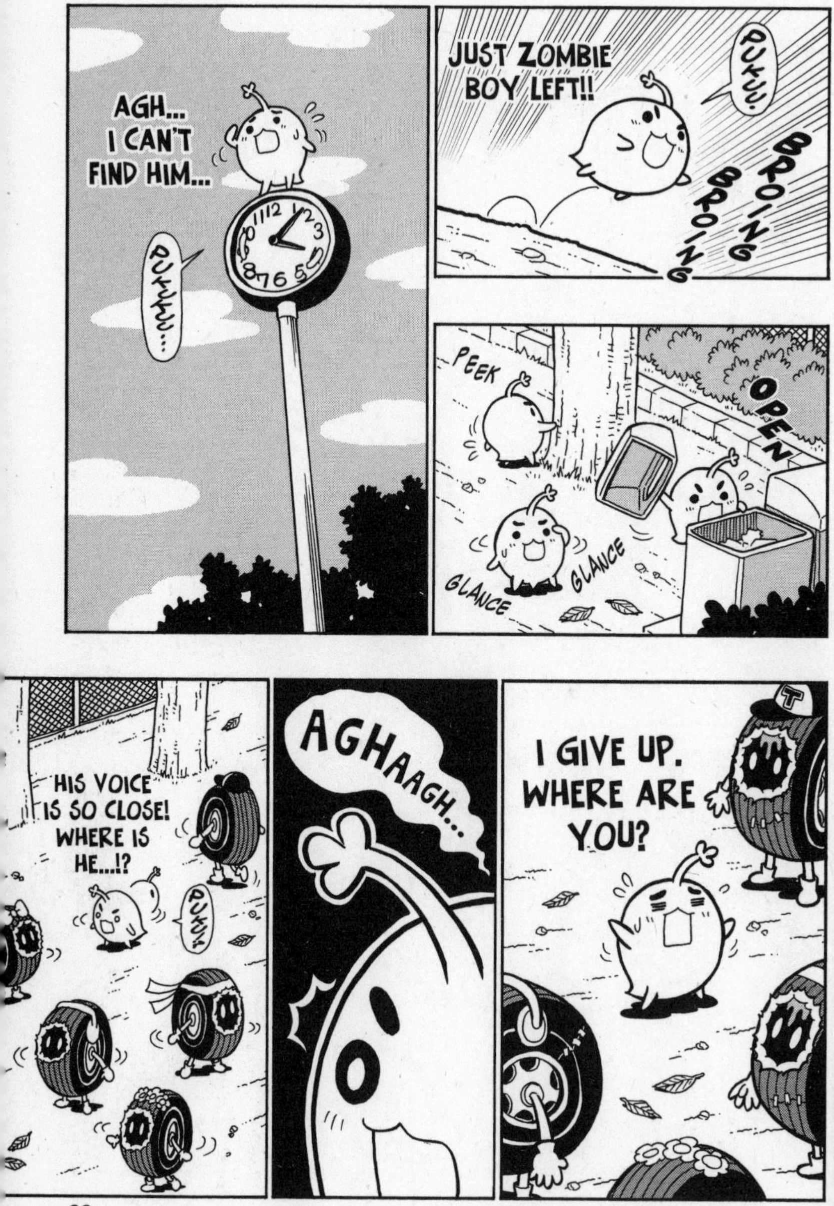
PUKUU.
JUST ZOMBIE BOY LEFT!!
BROING BROING
OPEN
PEEK
GLANCE GLANCE
AGH... I CAN'T FIND HIM...
PUKUUUU...
I GIVE UP. WHERE ARE YOU?
AGHAAGH...
HIS VOICE IS SO CLOSE! WHERE IS HE...!?
PUKU!?

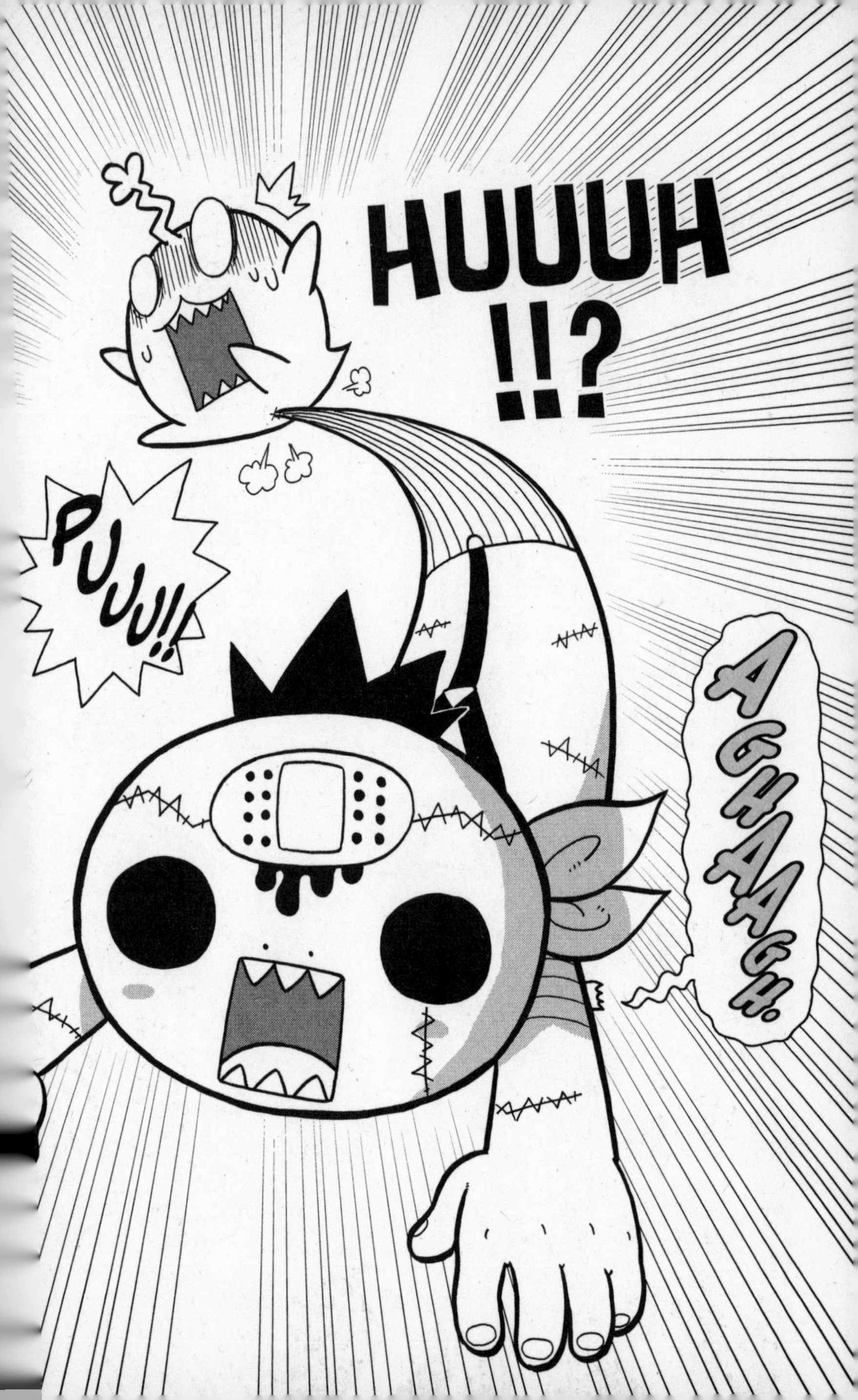
AGHAAAGH.
HUUUH!!?
PUUU!!

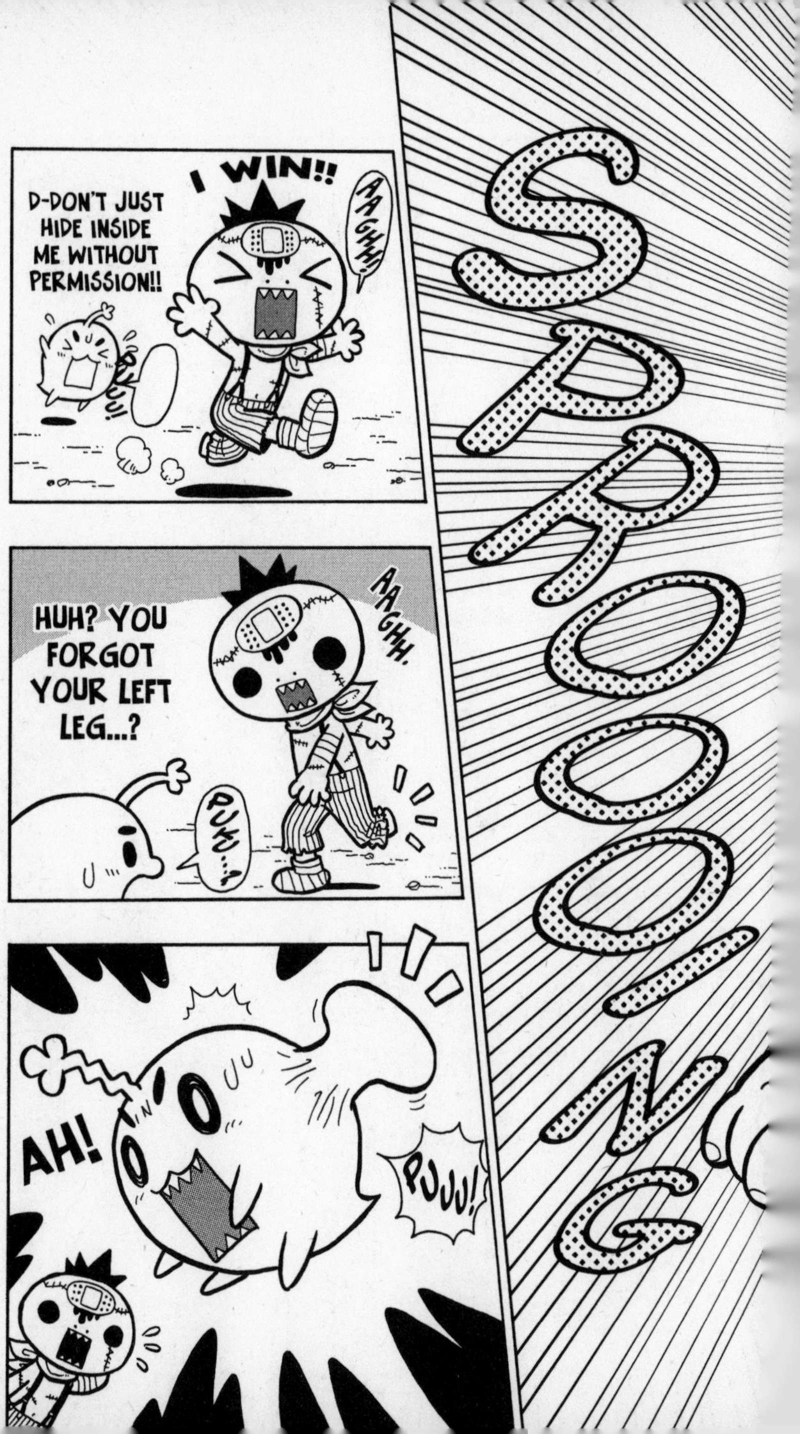
SPROOOING
I WIN!!
AAGHH!
D-DON'T JUST HIDE INSIDE ME WITHOUT PERMISSION!!
PJUJU!
AAGHH.
HUH? YOU FORGOT YOUR LEFT LEG...?
PJUJU...?
PJUJU!
AH!

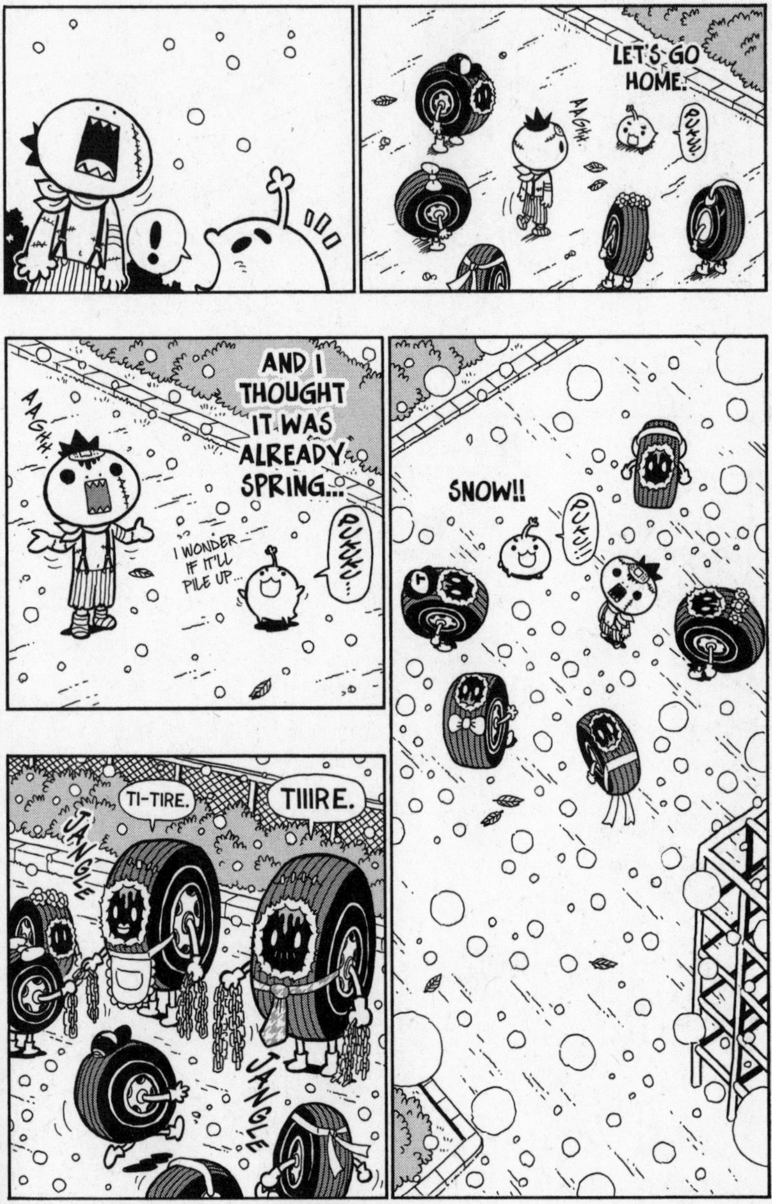
LET'S GO HOME.
PUKU.
AAGHH.
!
SNOW!!
PUKU!!
AND I THOUGHT IT WAS ALREADY SPRING...
PUKUKU...
I WONDER IF IT'LL PILE UP...
AAGHH.
TIIIRE.
TI-TIRE.
JANGLE
JANGLE

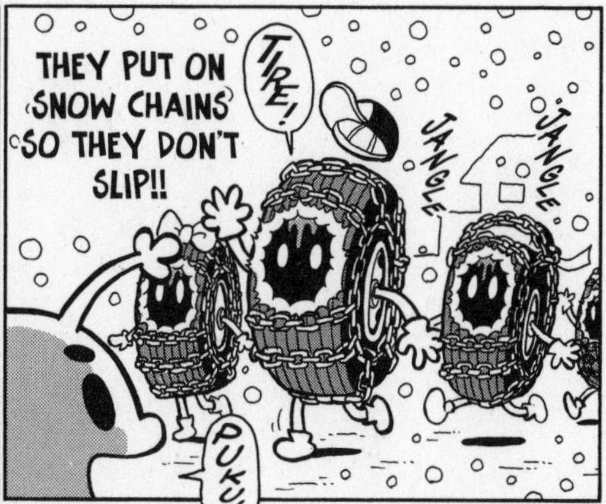
JANGLE
JANGLE
TIRE!
THEY PUT ON SNOW CHAINS SO THEY DON'T SLIP!!
PUKU!

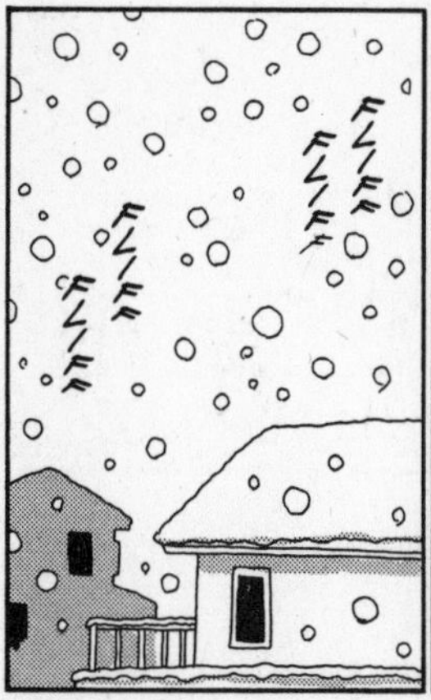
FLIFF FLIFF
FLIFF FLIFF

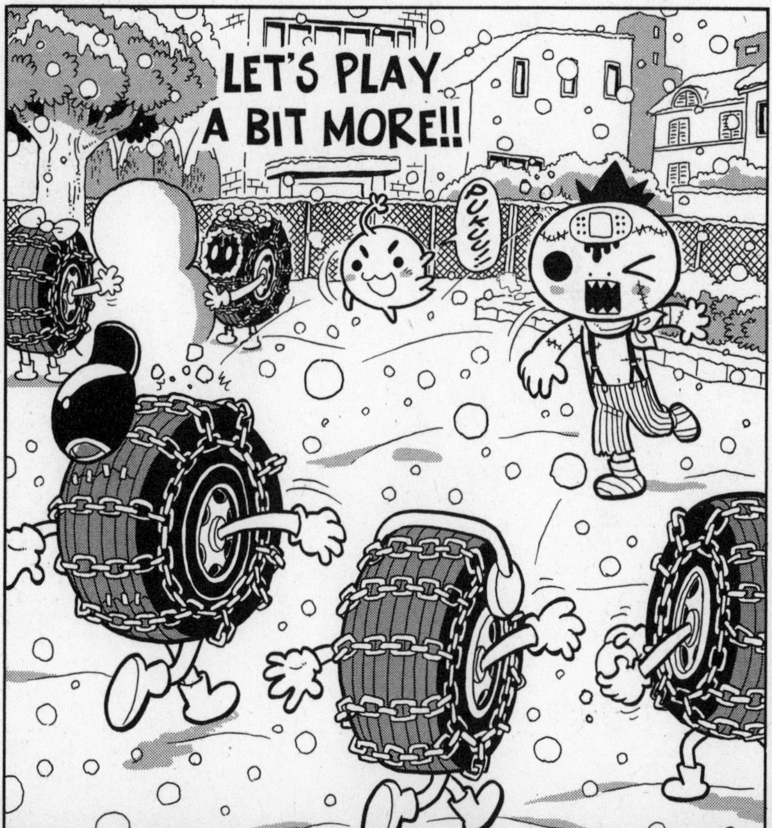
PUKUU!!
LET'S PLAY A BIT MORE!!

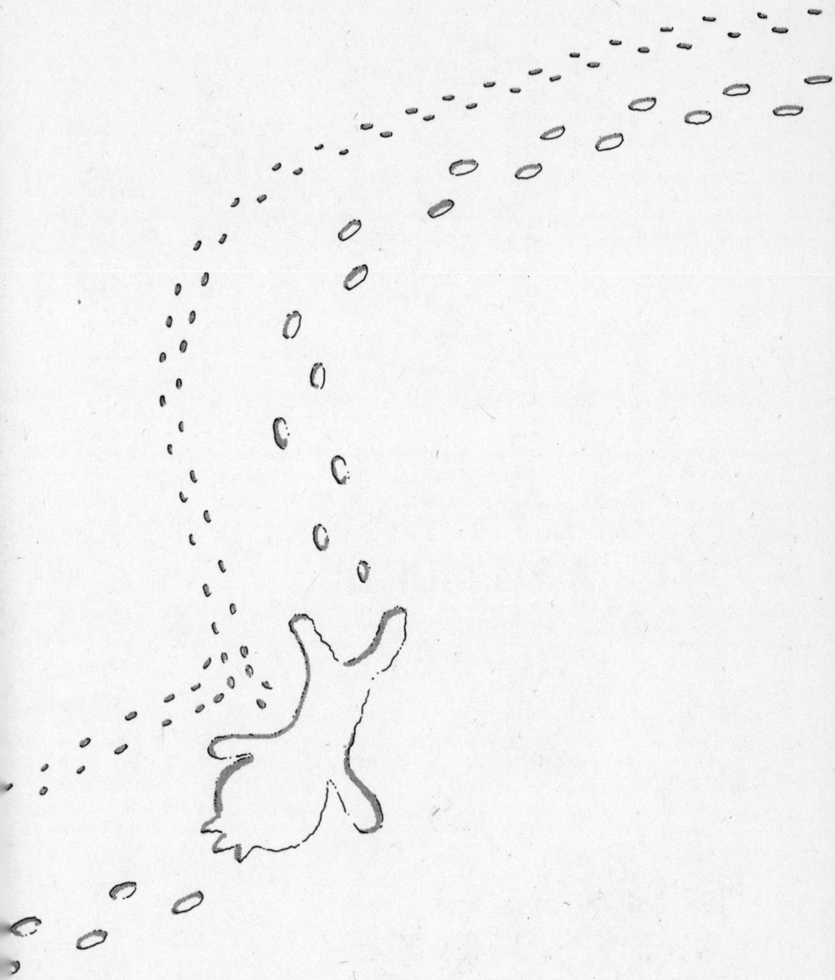

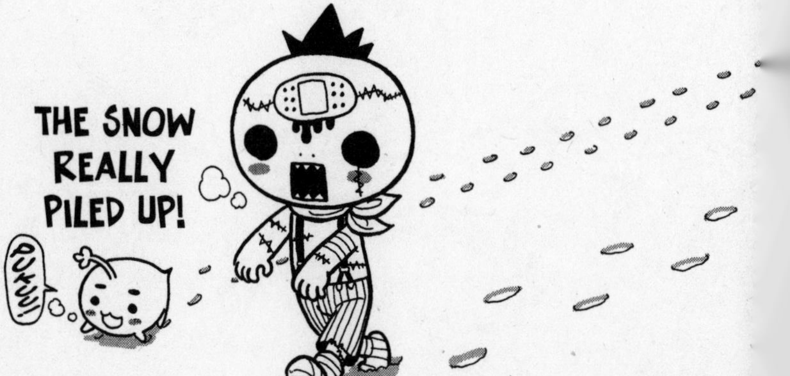
THE SNOW REALLY PILED UP!
PUYU!

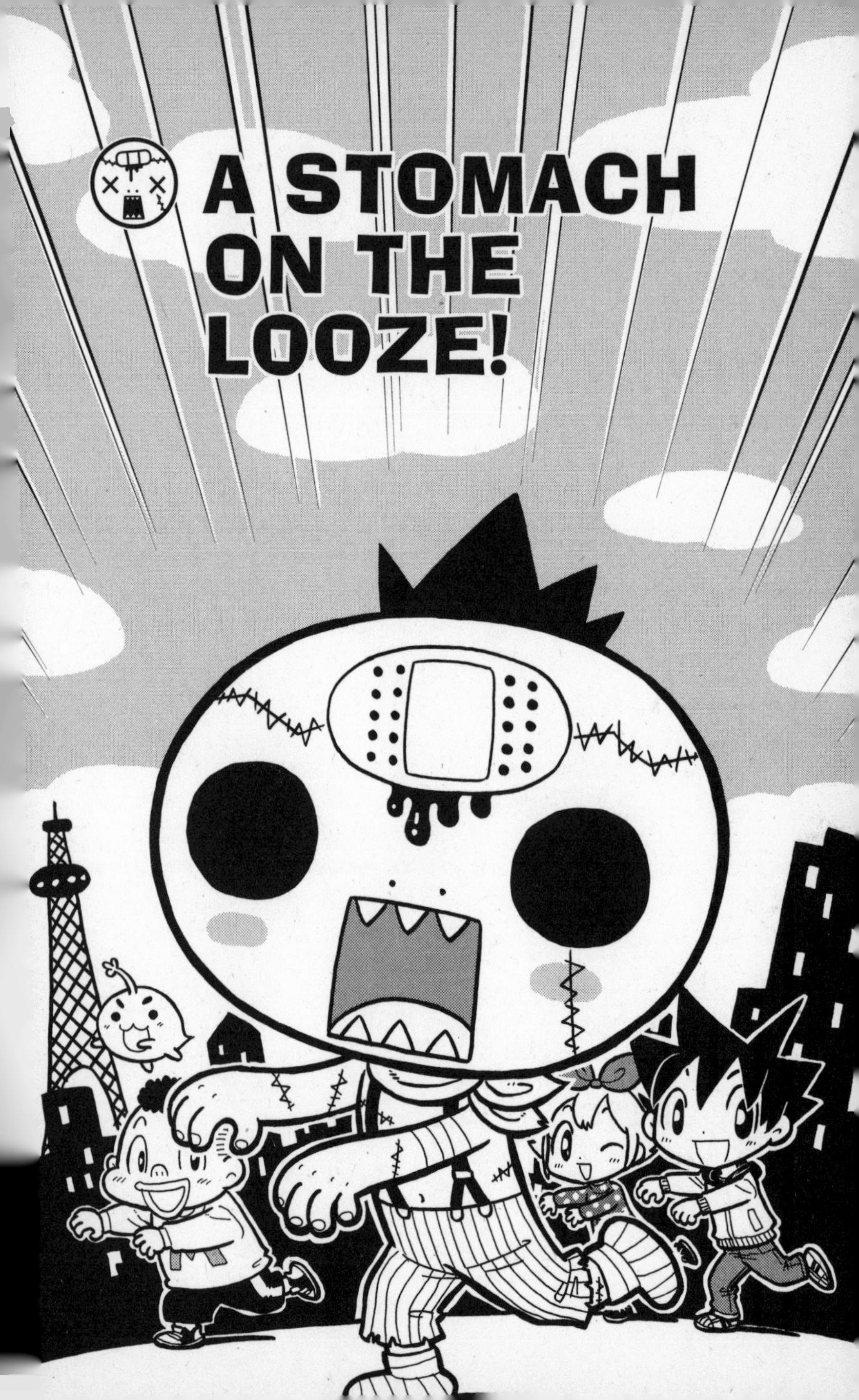
A STOMACH ON THE LOOZE!

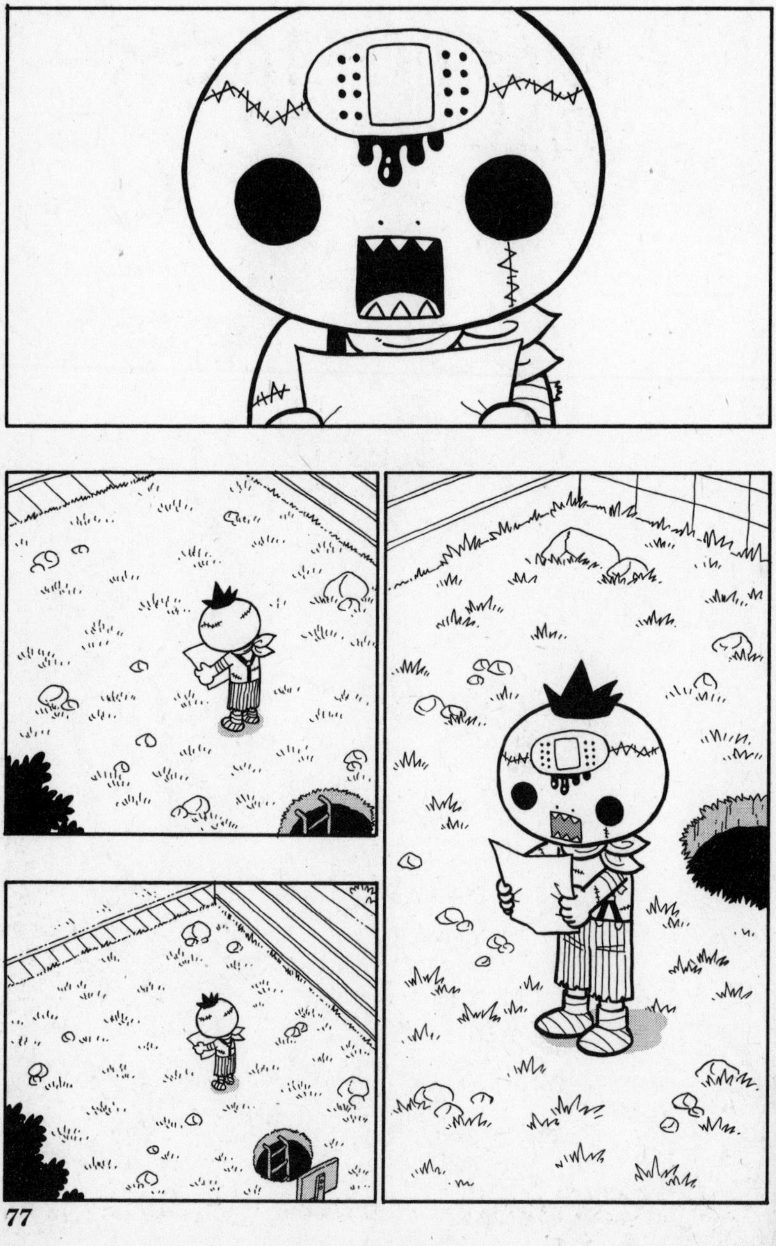

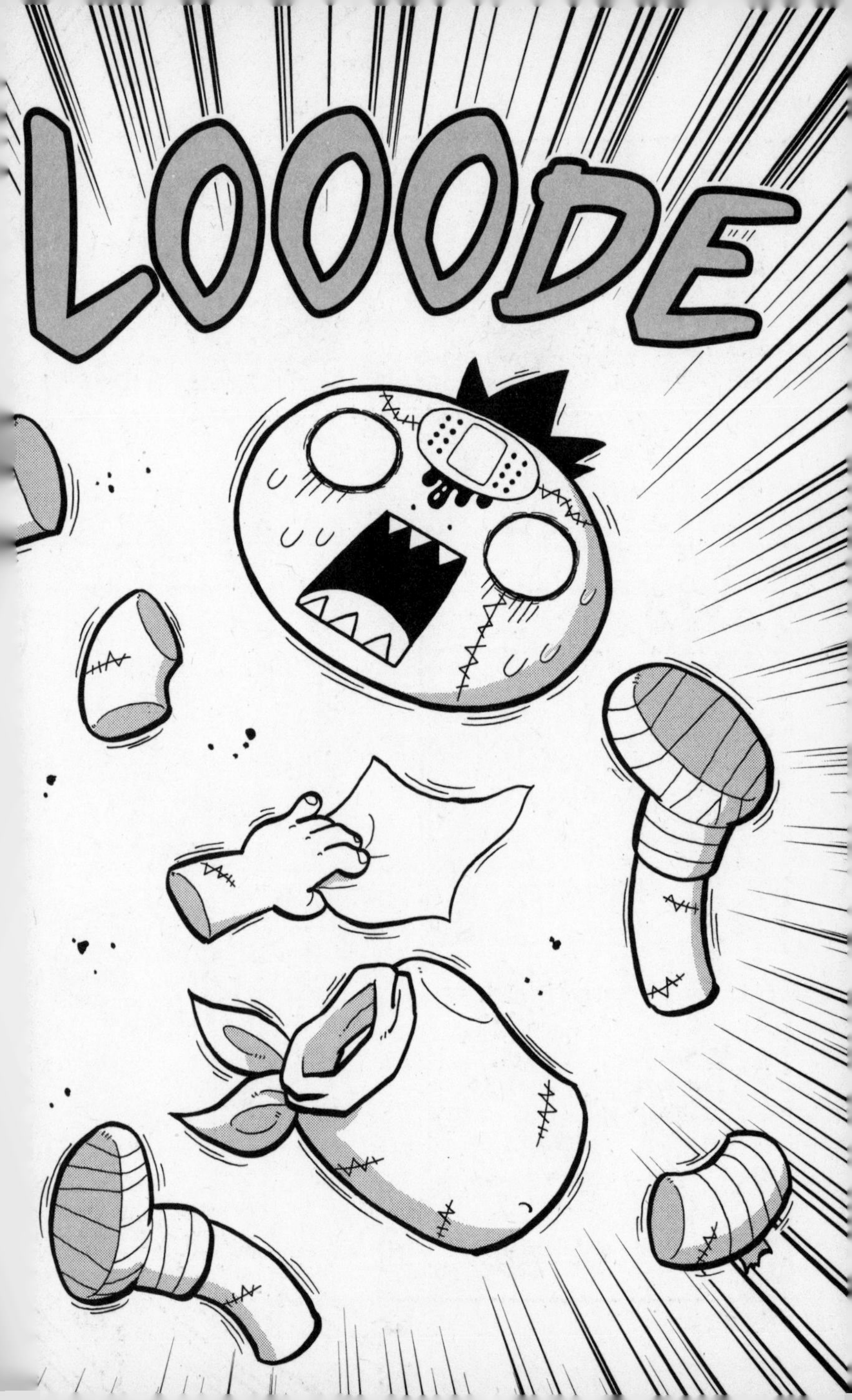
LOOODE

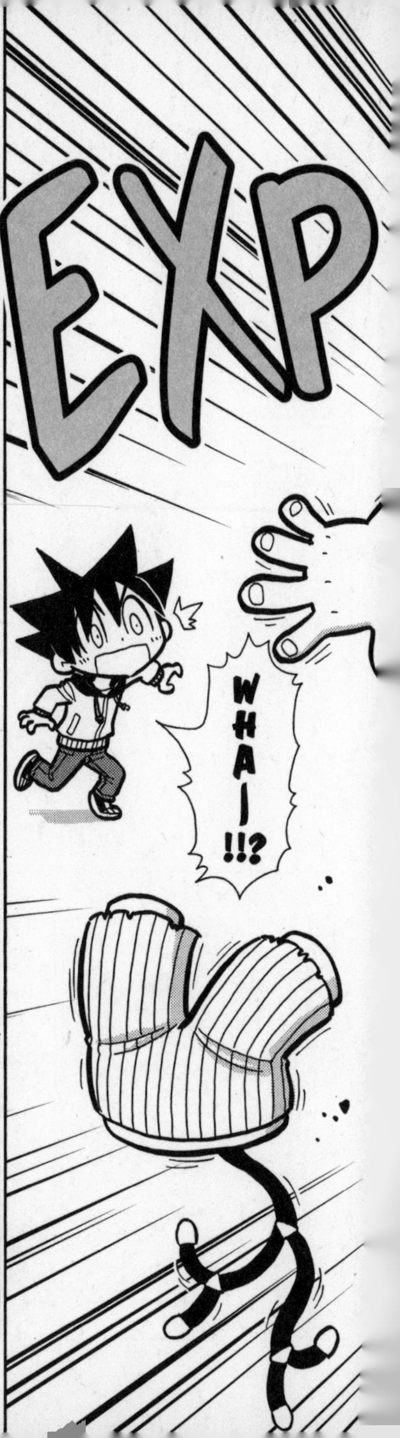
EXP
WHA-!!?

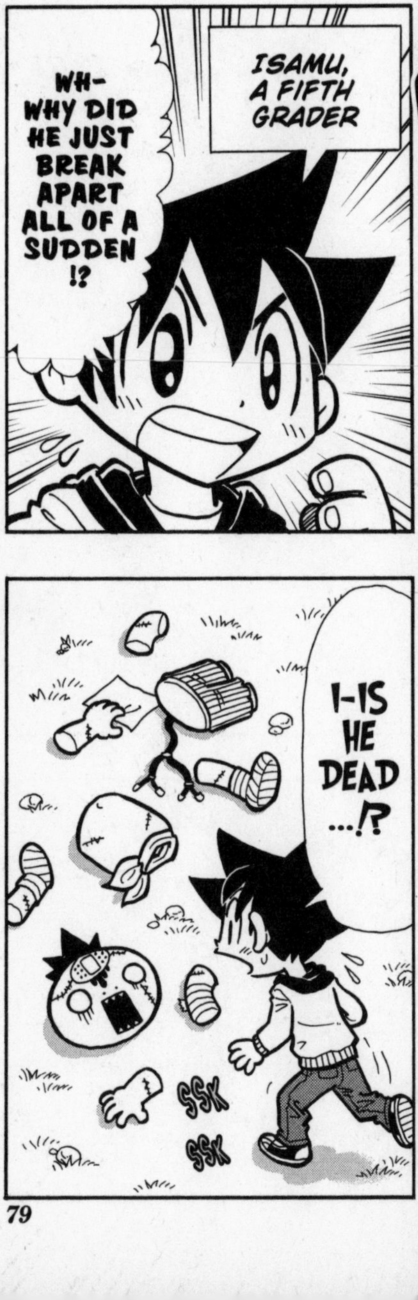
ISAMU, A FIFTH GRADER
WH- WHY DID HE JUST BREAK APART ALL OF A SUDDEN!?
I-IS HE DEAD...!?
SSK
SSK

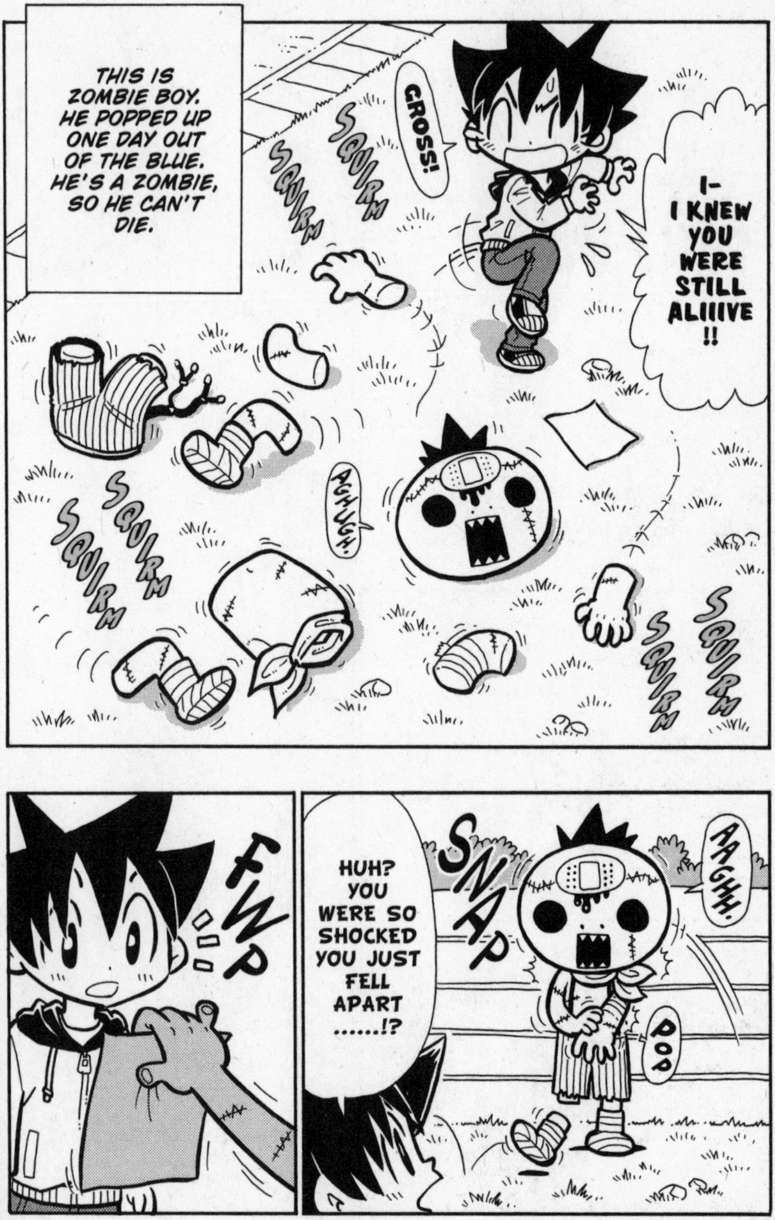
I- I KNEW YOU WERE STILL ALIIIIVE!!
GROSS!
SQUIRM SQUIRM
THIS IS ZOMBIE BOY. HE POPPED UP ONE DAY OUT OF THE BLUE. HE'S A ZOMBIE, SO HE CAN'T DIE.
AGHUGH.
SQUIRM SQUIRM
SQUIRM SQUIRM
AAGHH.
SNAP
POP
HUH? YOU WERE SO SHOCKED YOU JUST FELL APART ......!?
FWP

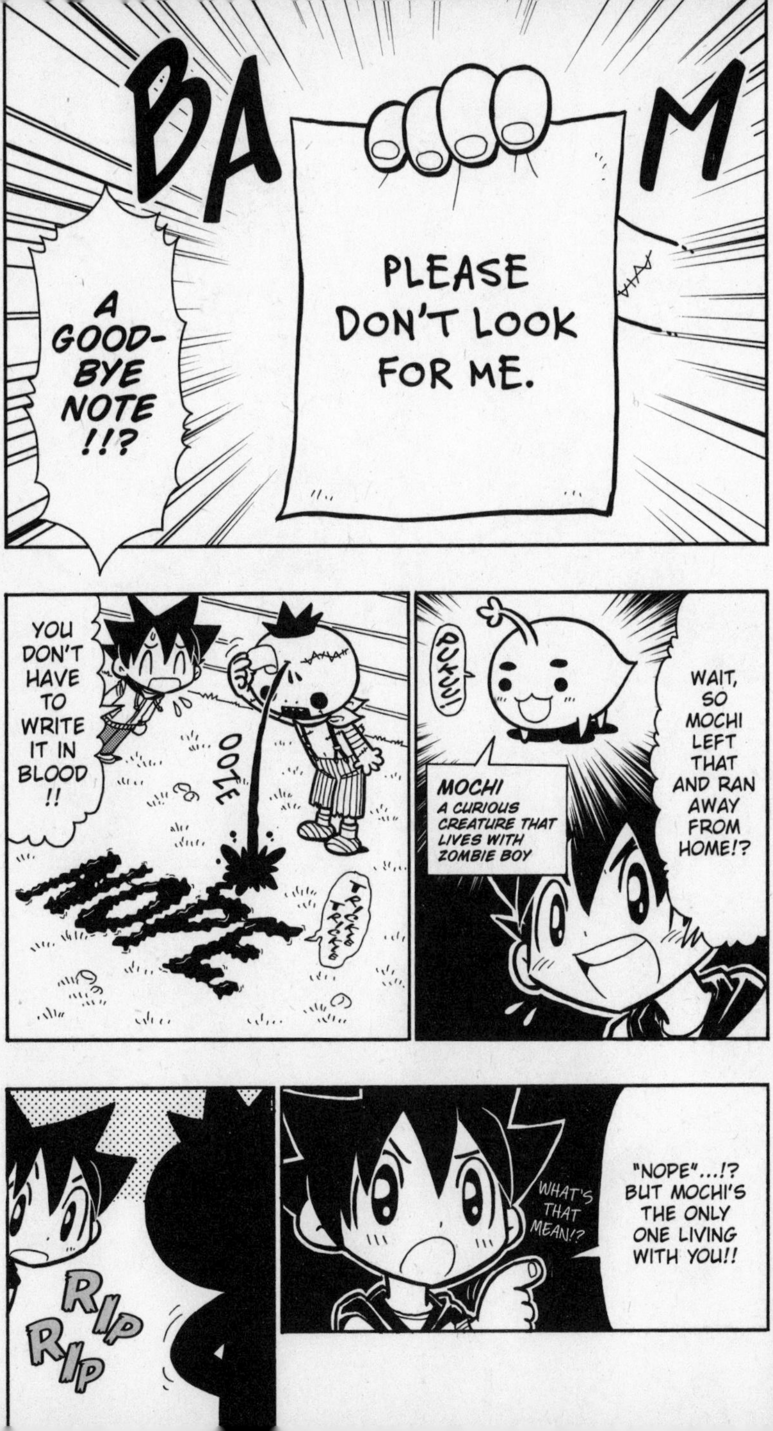
BAM
PLEASE DON'T LOOK FOR ME.
A GOOD-BYE NOTE!!?
WAIT, SO MOCHI LEFT THAT AND RAN AWAY FROM HOME!?
PUKUU!
MOCHI
A CURIOUS CREATURE THAT LIVES WITH ZOMBIE BOY
YOU DON'T HAVE TO WRITE IT IN BLOOD!!
OOZE
TRICKLE TRICKLE
"NOPE"...!? BUT MOCHI'S THE ONLY ONE LIVING WITH YOU!!
WHAT'S THAT MEAN!?
RIP RIP

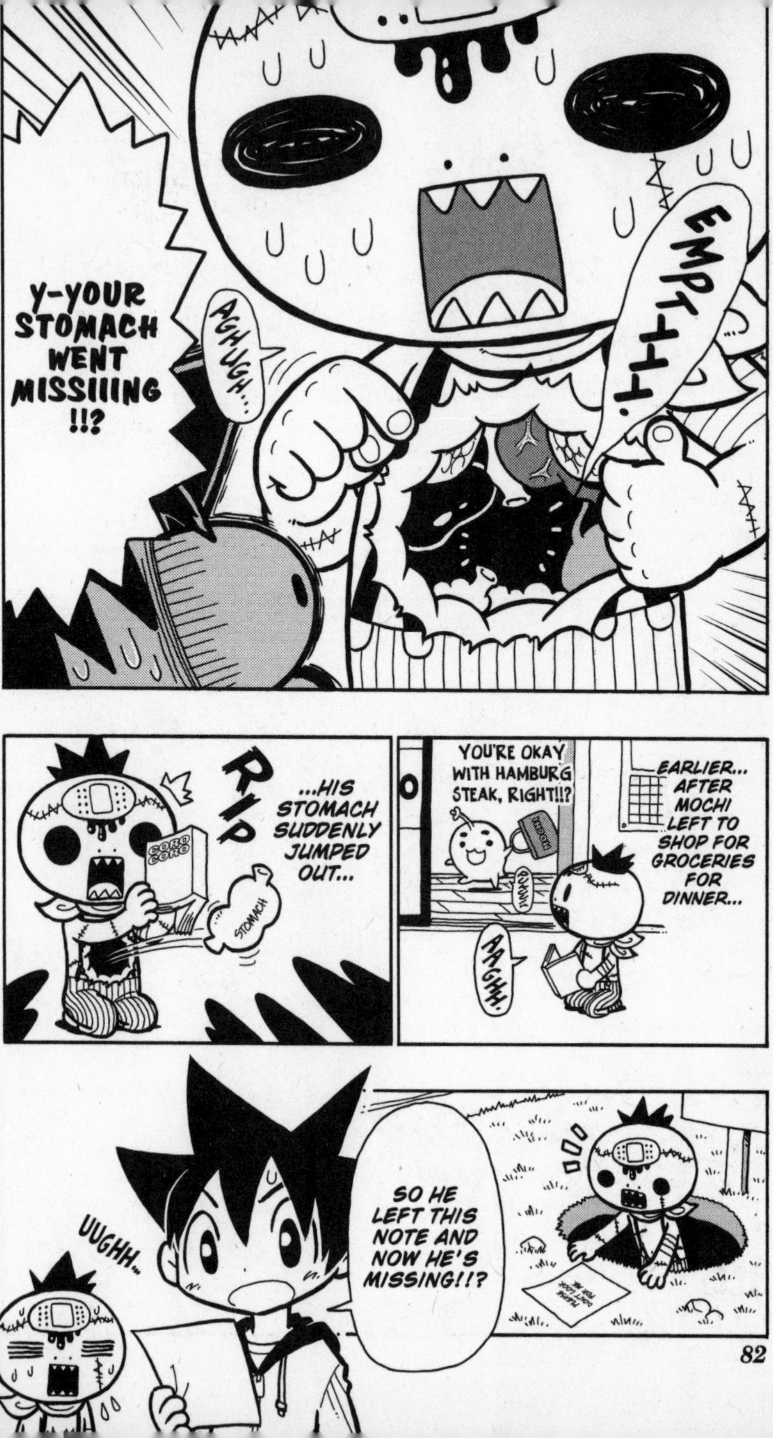
EMPTYYY!
AGHUGH...
Y-YOUR STOMACH WENT MISSIIING!!?
EARLIER... AFTER MOCHI LEFT TO SHOP FOR GROCERIES FOR DINNER...
YOU'RE OKAY WITH HAMBURG STEAK, RIGHT!!?
AAGHH.
RIP
...HIS STOMACH SUDDENLY JUMPED OUT...
CORO CORO
STOMACH
PLEASE DON'T LOOK FOR ME.
SO HE LEFT THIS NOTE AND NOW HE'S MISSING!!?
UUGHH...

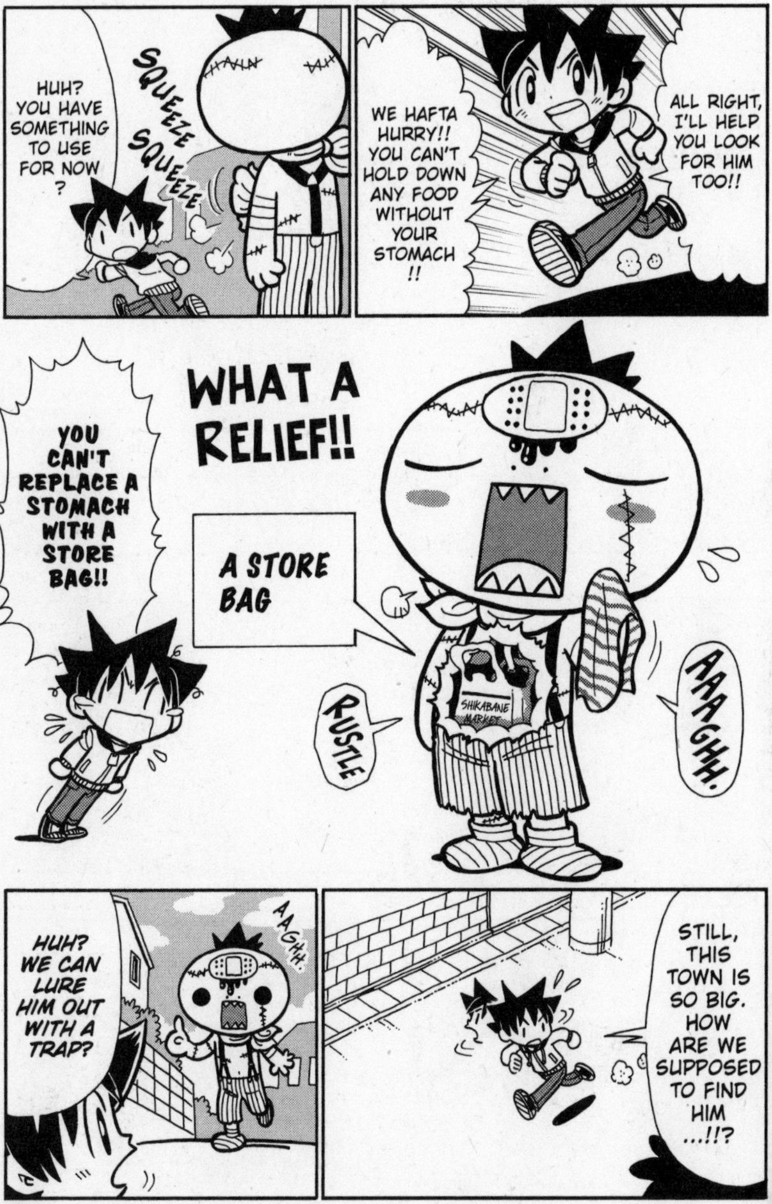
ALL RIGHT, I'LL HELP YOU LOOK FOR HIM TOO!!
WE HAFTA HURRY!! YOU CAN'T HOLD DOWN ANY FOOD WITHOUT YOUR STOMACH !!
SQUEEZE SQUEEZE
HUH? YOU HAVE SOMETHING TO USE FOR NOW ?
AAAGHH.
RUSTLE
SHIKABANE MARKET
A STORE BAG
WHAT A RELIEF!!
YOU CAN'T REPLACE A STOMACH WITH A STORE BAG!!
STILL, THIS TOWN IS SO BIG. HOW ARE WE SUPPOSED TO FIND HIM ...!!?
AAGHH.
HUH? WE CAN LURE HIM OUT WITH A TRAP?

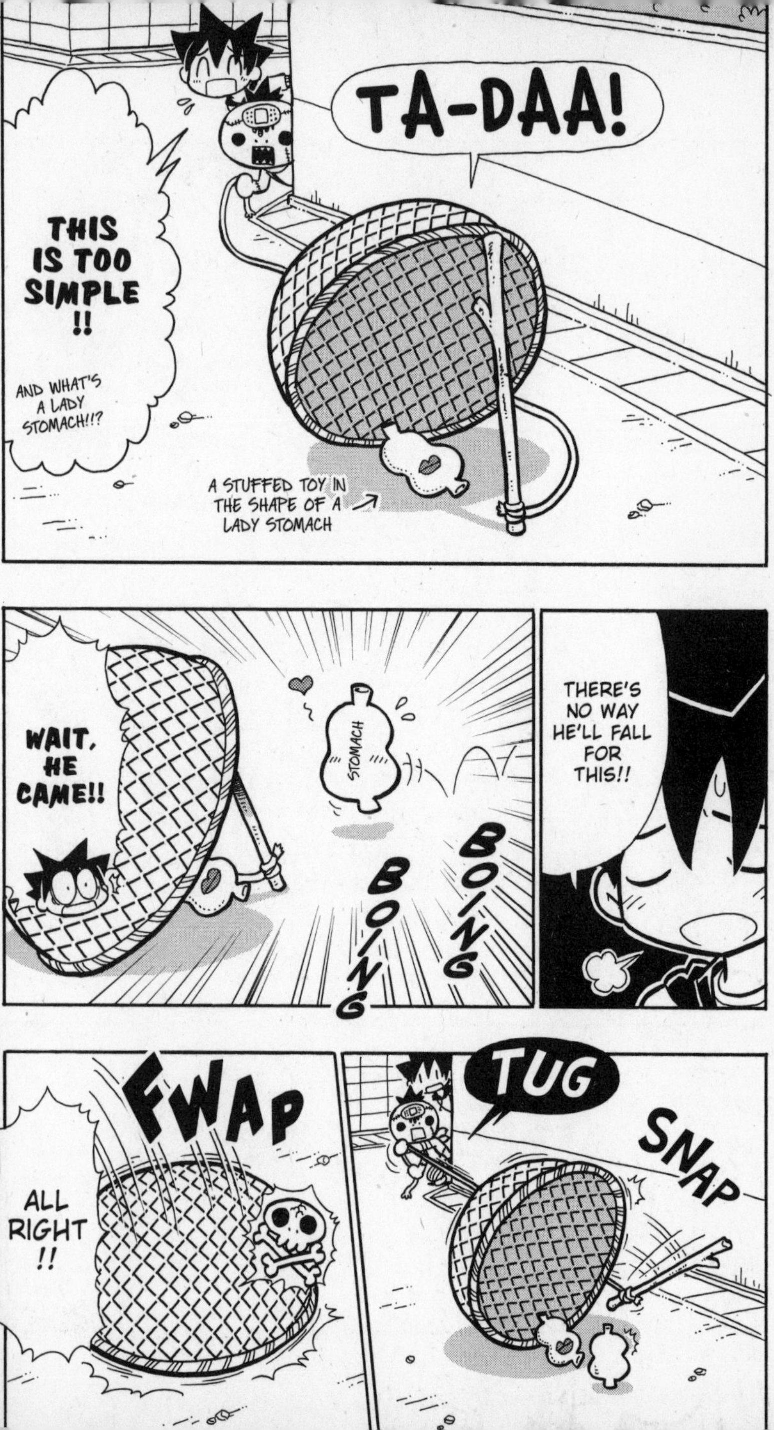
TA-DAA!
THIS IS TOO SIMPLE !!
AND WHAT'S A LADY STOMACH!!?
A STUFFED TOY IN THE SHAPE OF A LADY STOMACH
THERE'S NO WAY HE'LL FALL FOR THIS!!
BOING
BOING
STOMACH
WAIT, HE CAME!!
TUG
SNAP
FWAP
ALL RIGHT !!

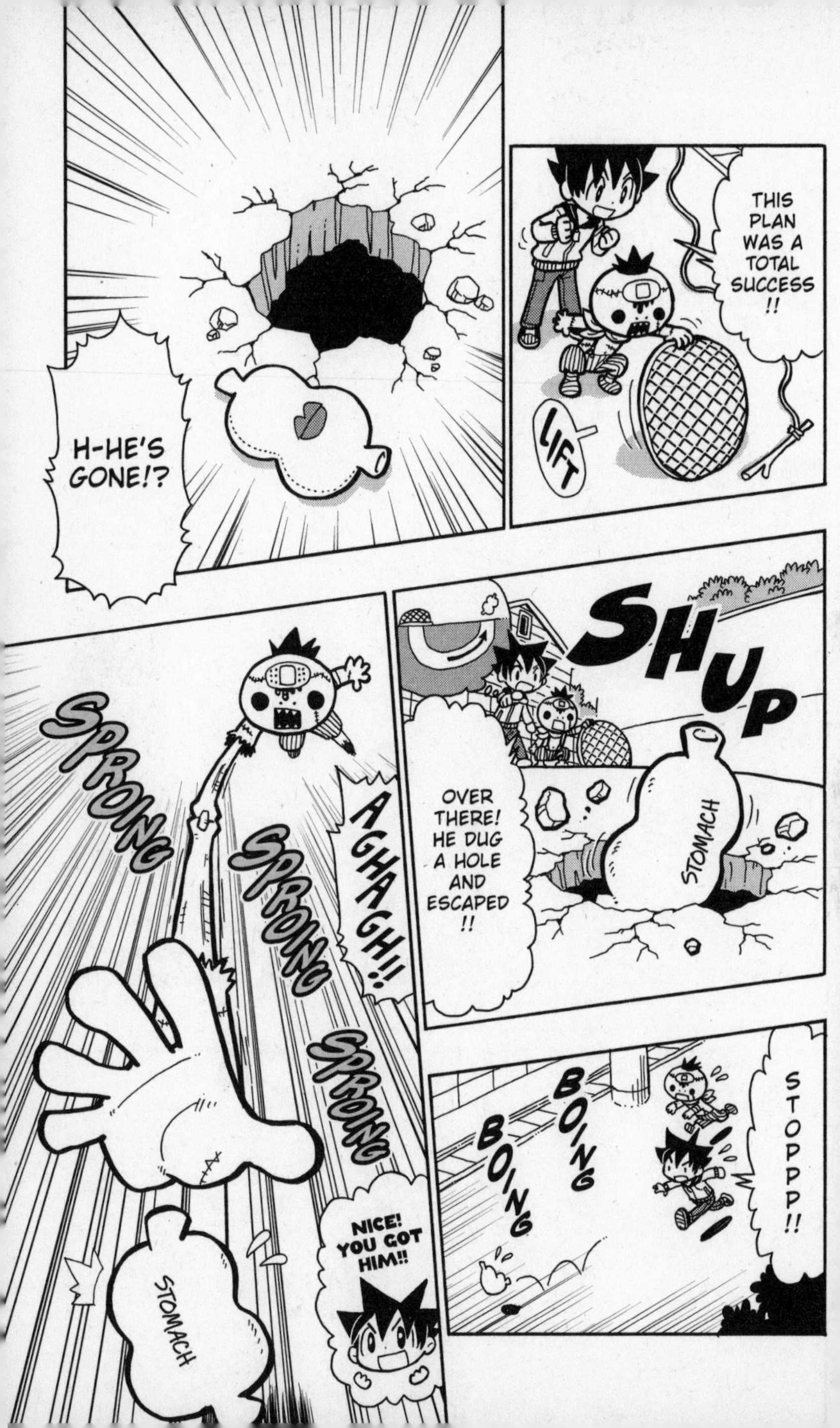
THIS PLAN WAS A TOTAL SUCCESS!!
LIFT
H-HE'S GONE!?
SHUP
OVER THERE! HE DUG A HOLE AND ESCAPED!!
STOMACH
STOPPP!!
BOING
BOING
SPROING
SPROING
SPROING
AGHAGH!!
NICE! YOU GOT HIM!!
STOMACH

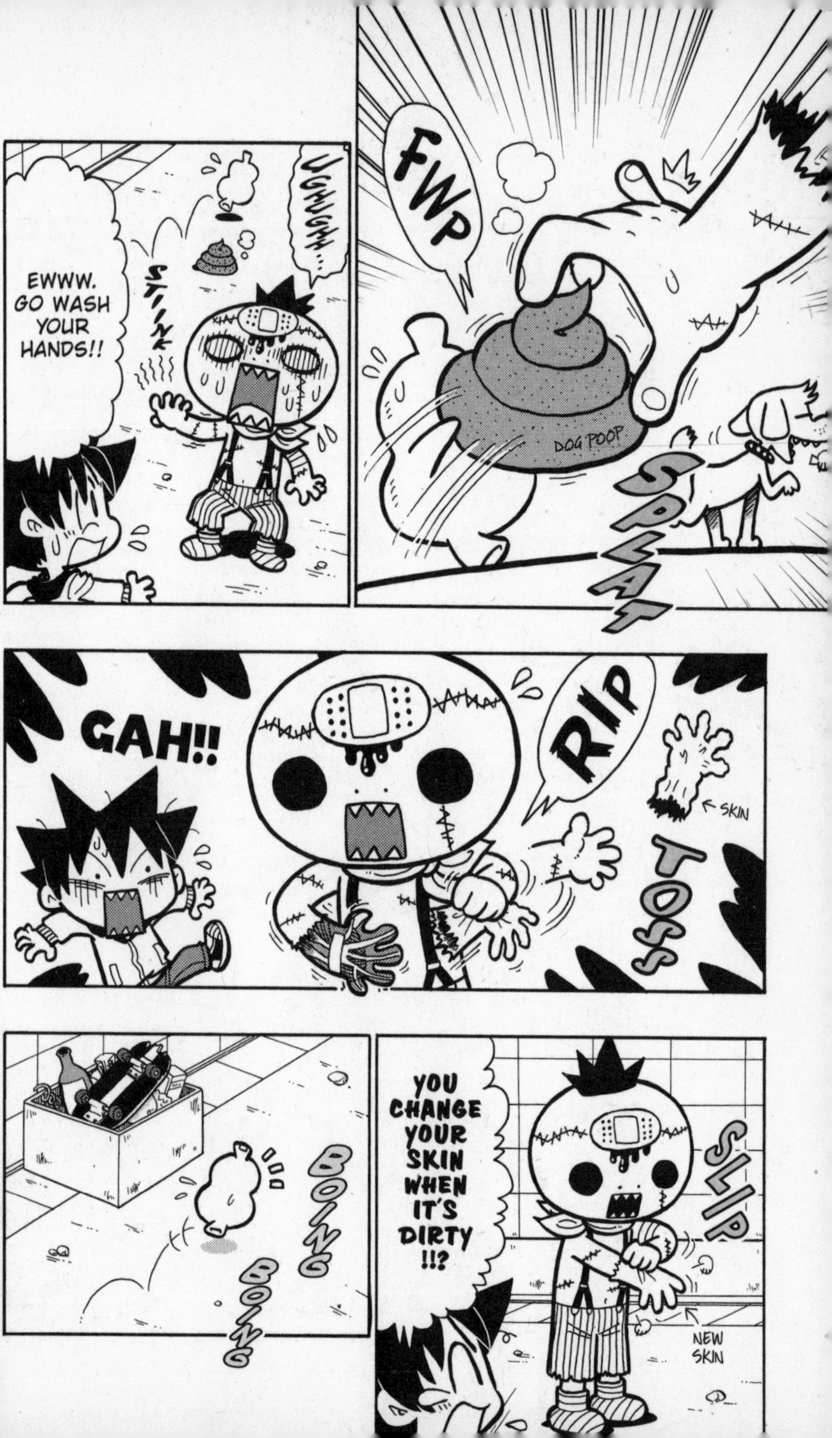
FWP
DOG POOP
SPLAT
UGHUGHH...
STIIINK
EWWW. GO WASH YOUR HANDS!!
RIP
SKIN
TOSS
GAH!!
SLIP
YOU CHANGE YOUR SKIN WHEN IT'S DIRTY !!?
NEW SKIN
BOING
BOING

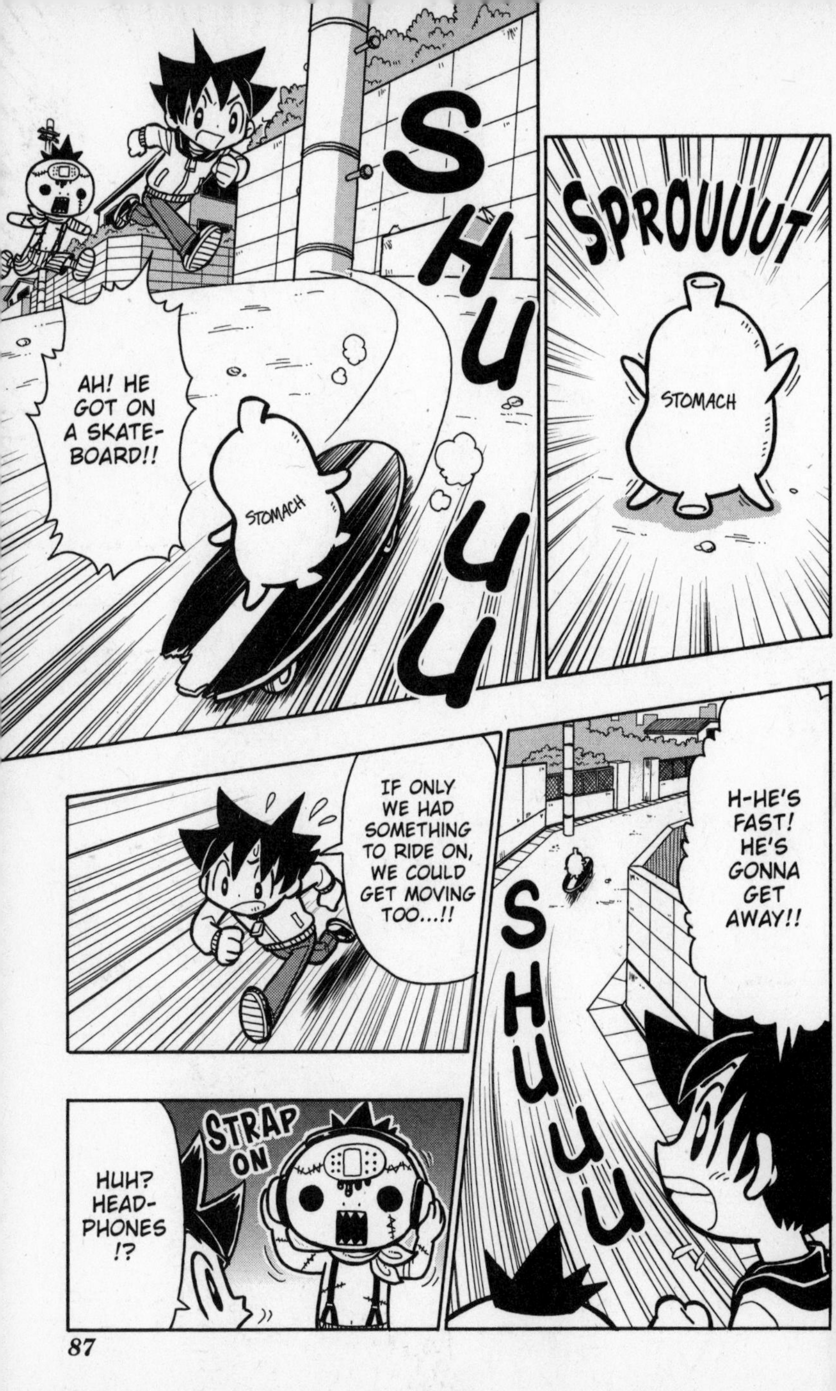

SPROUUUT
STOMACH
SHUUUU
AH! HE GOT ON A SKATE-BOARD!!
STOMACH
H-HE'S FAST! HE'S GONNA GET AWAY!!
SHUUUU
IF ONLY WE HAD SOMETHING TO RIDE ON, WE COULD GET MOVING TOO...!!
STRAP ON
HUH? HEAD-PHONES !?

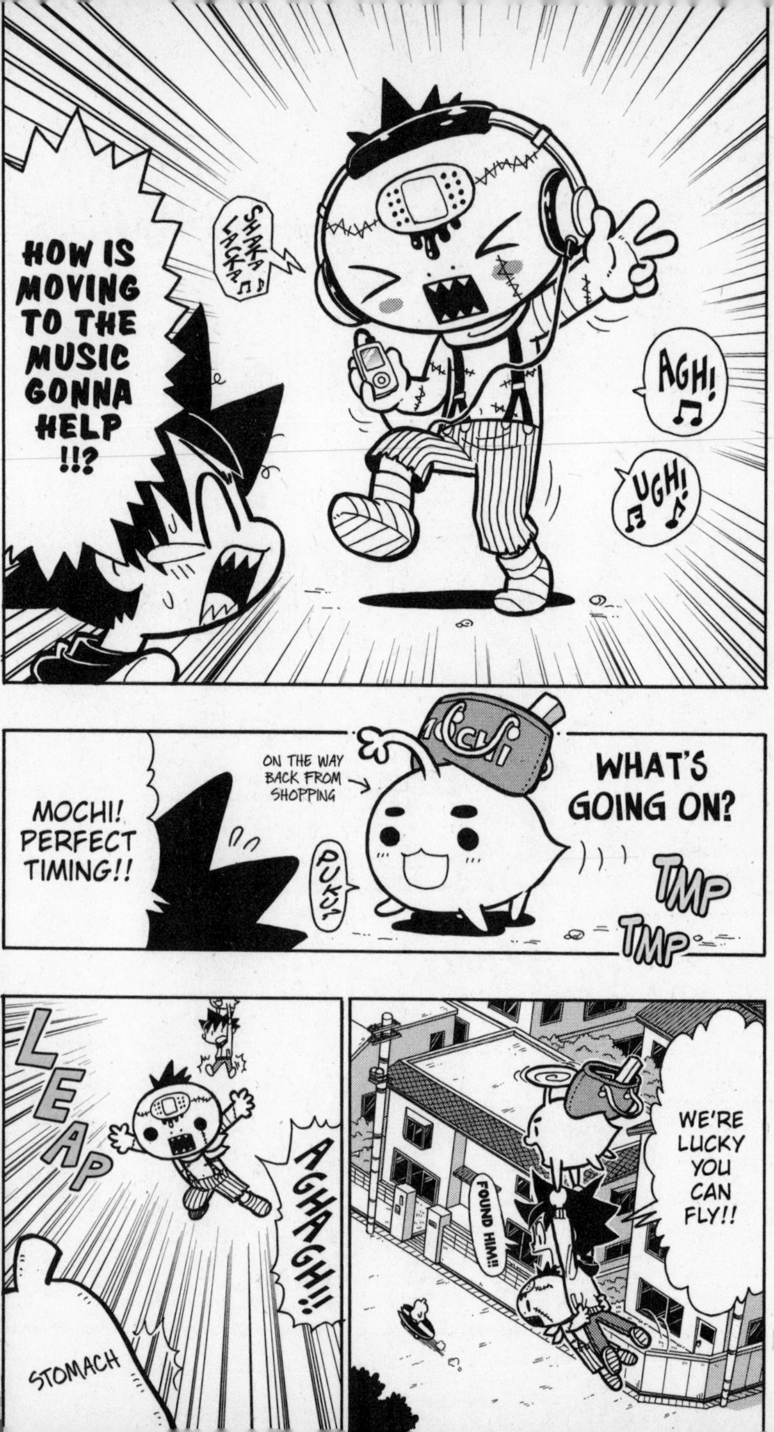
AGH!
UGH!
SHAKA LACKA
HOW IS MOVING TO THE MUSIC GONNA HELP!!?
WHAT'S GOING ON?
TMP
TMP
ON THE WAY BACK FROM SHOPPING
PUKU?
MOCHI! PERFECT TIMING!!
WE'RE LUCKY YOU CAN FLY!!
FOUND HIM!!
AGHAGH!!
LEAP
STOMACH

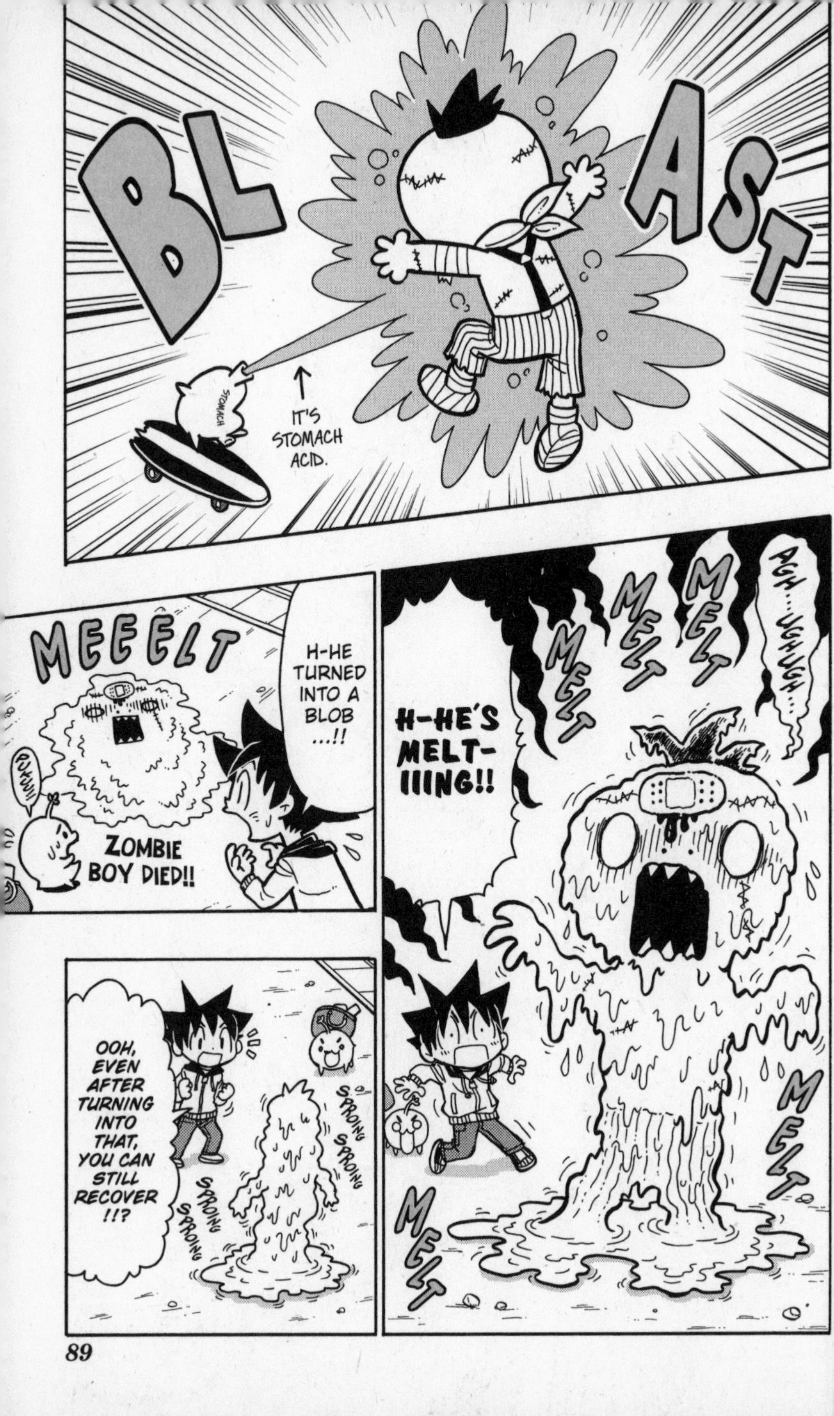
BLAST
STOMACH
IT'S STOMACH ACID.
AGH... UGHUGH...
MELT
MELT
MELT
H-HE'S MELT-IIIING!!
MELT
MELT
MEEELT
H-HE TURNED INTO A BLOB ...!!
ZOMBIE BOY DIED!!
OOH, EVEN AFTER TURNING INTO THAT, YOU CAN STILL RECOVER !!?
SPROING SPROING
SPROING SPROING

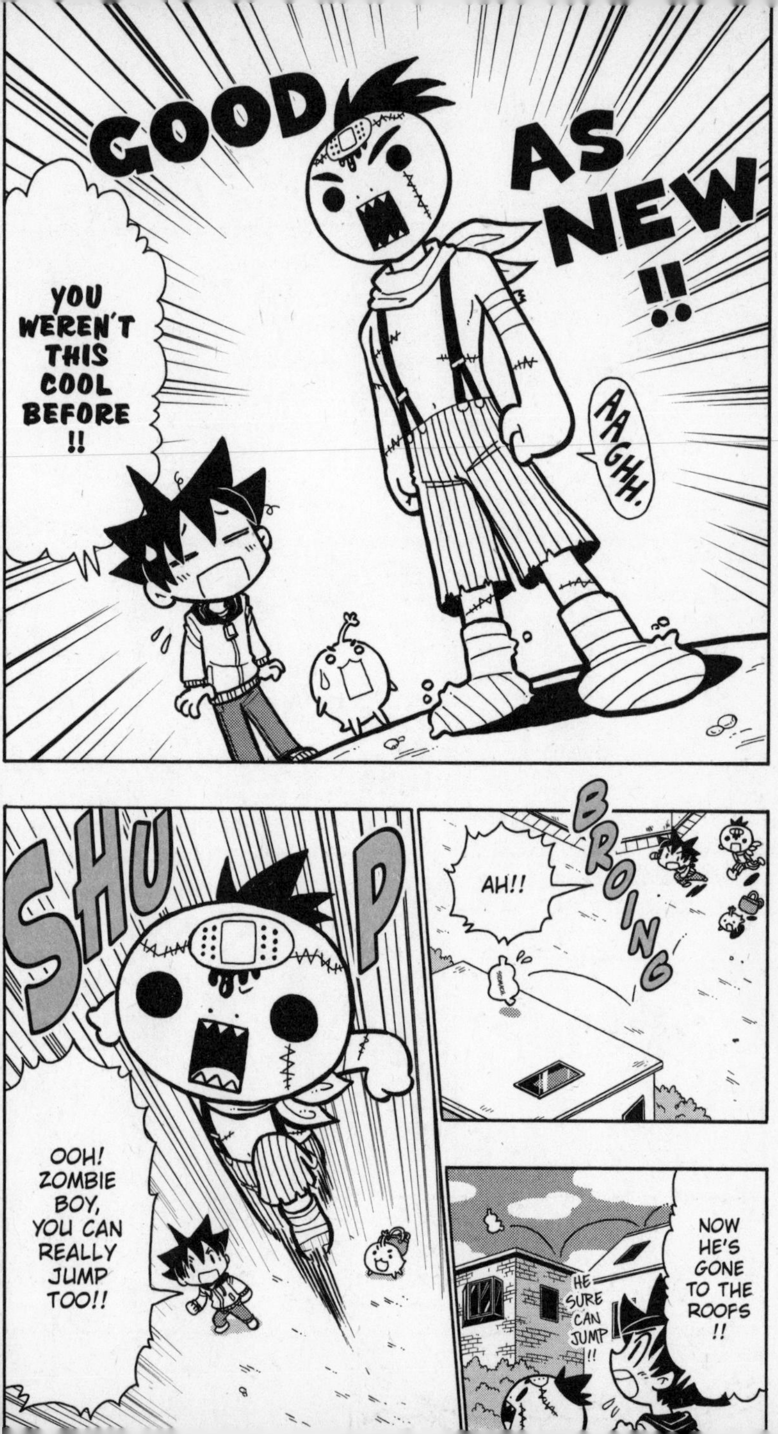
GOOD AS NEW!!
AAGHH.
YOU WEREN'T THIS COOL BEFORE!!
BROING
AH!!
NOW HE'S GONE TO THE ROOFS!!
HE SURE CAN JUMP!!
SHUP
OOH! ZOMBIE BOY, YOU CAN REALLY JUMP TOO!!

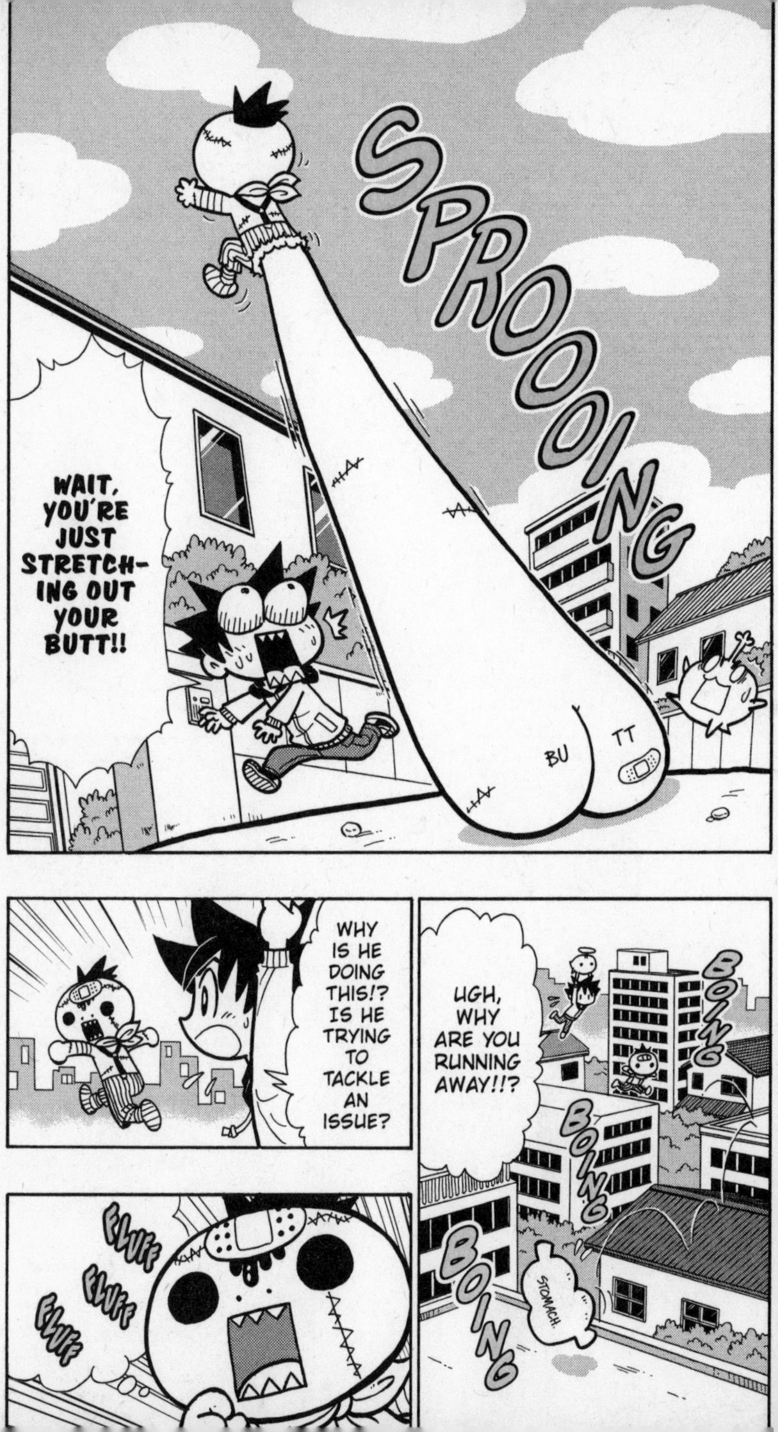
SPROOOING
WAIT, YOU'RE JUST STRETCH-ING OUT YOUR BUTT!!
BU TT
UGH, WHY ARE YOU RUNNING AWAY!!?
BOING
BOING
BOING
STOMACH.
WHY IS HE DOING THIS!? IS HE TRYING TO TACKLE AN ISSUE?
FLUFF
FLUFF
FLUFF

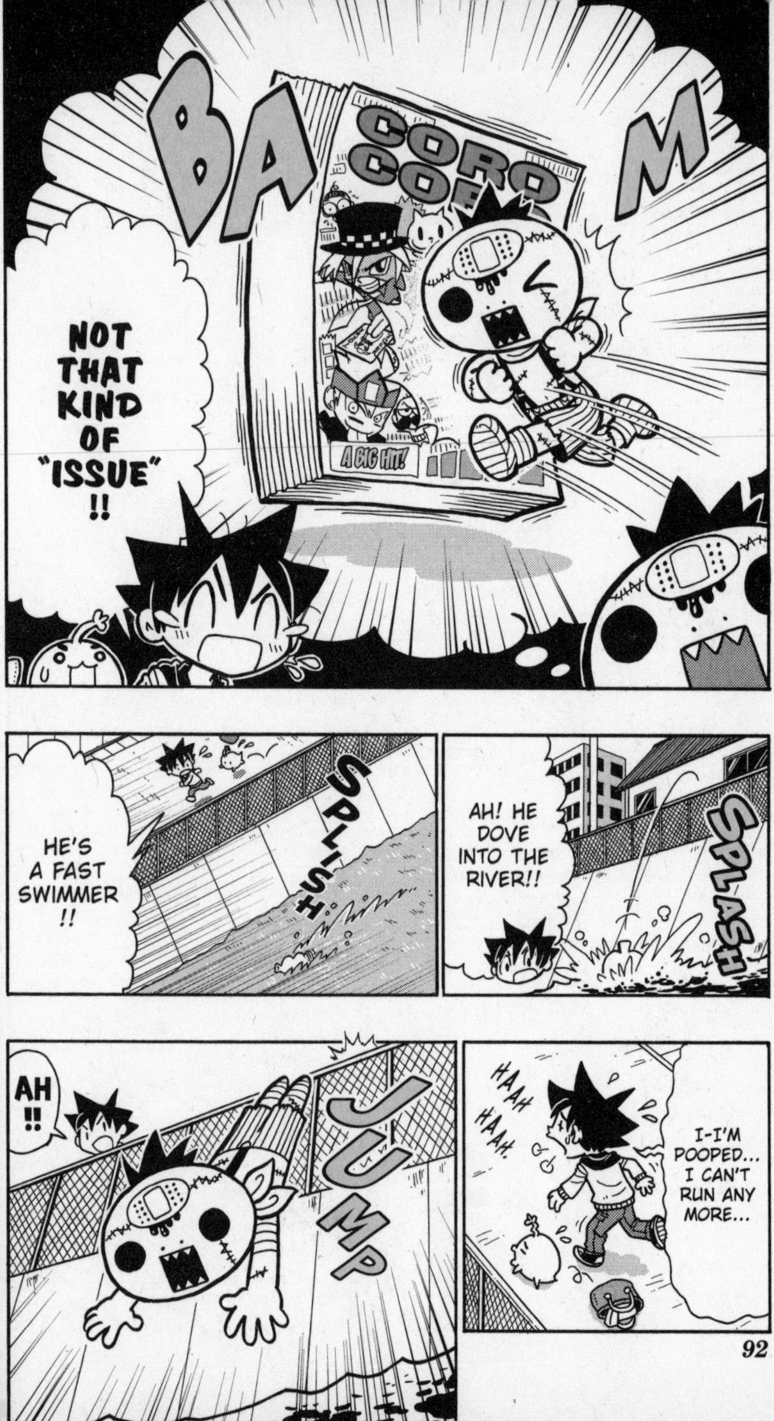
BAM
A BIG HIT!
NOT THAT KIND OF "ISSUE" !!
AH! HE DOVE INTO THE RIVER!!
SPLASH
SPLISH
HE'S A FAST SWIMMER !!
HAAH HAAH
I-I'M POOPED... I CAN'T RUN ANY MORE...
JUMP
AH !!

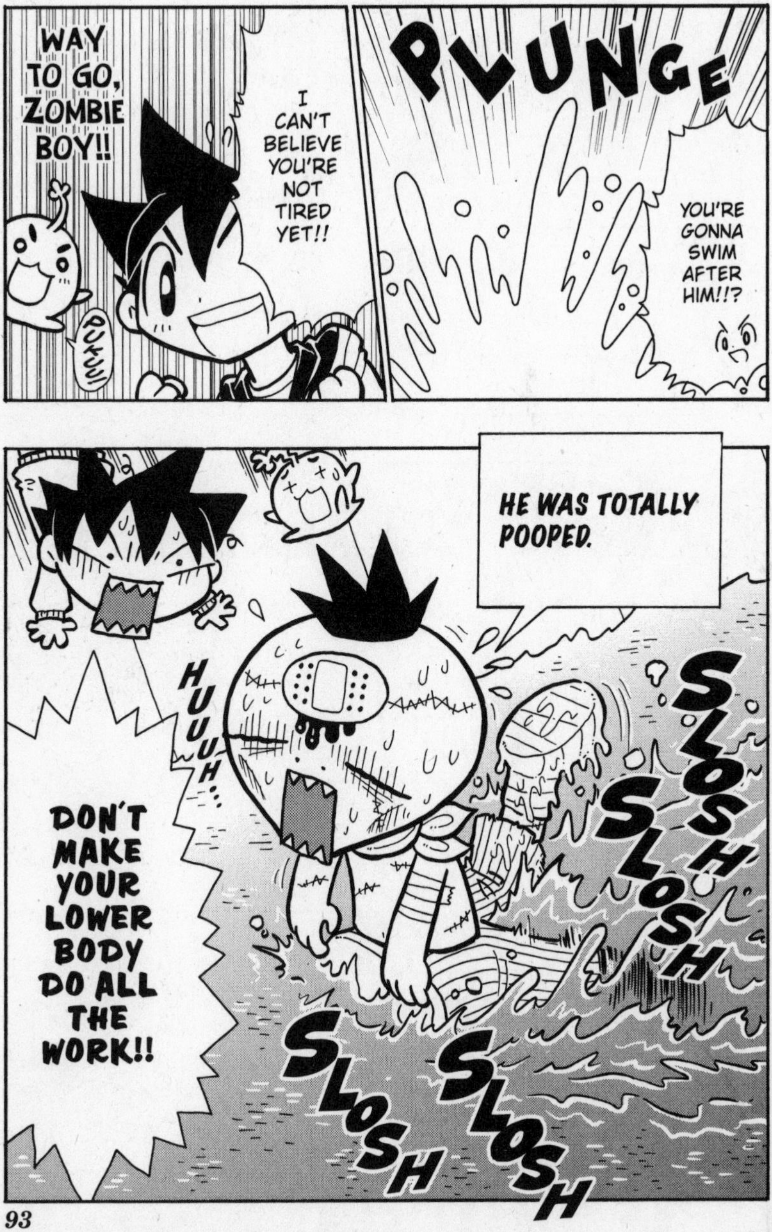

PLUNGE
YOU'RE GONNA SWIM AFTER HIM!!?
I CAN'T BELIEVE YOU'RE NOT TIRED YET!!
WAY TO GO, ZOMBIE BOY!!
PUKU
HE WAS TOTALLY POOPED.
SLOSH SLOSH SLOSH
HUUUH...
DON'T MAKE YOUR LOWER BODY DO ALL THE WORK!!
SLOSH SLOSH

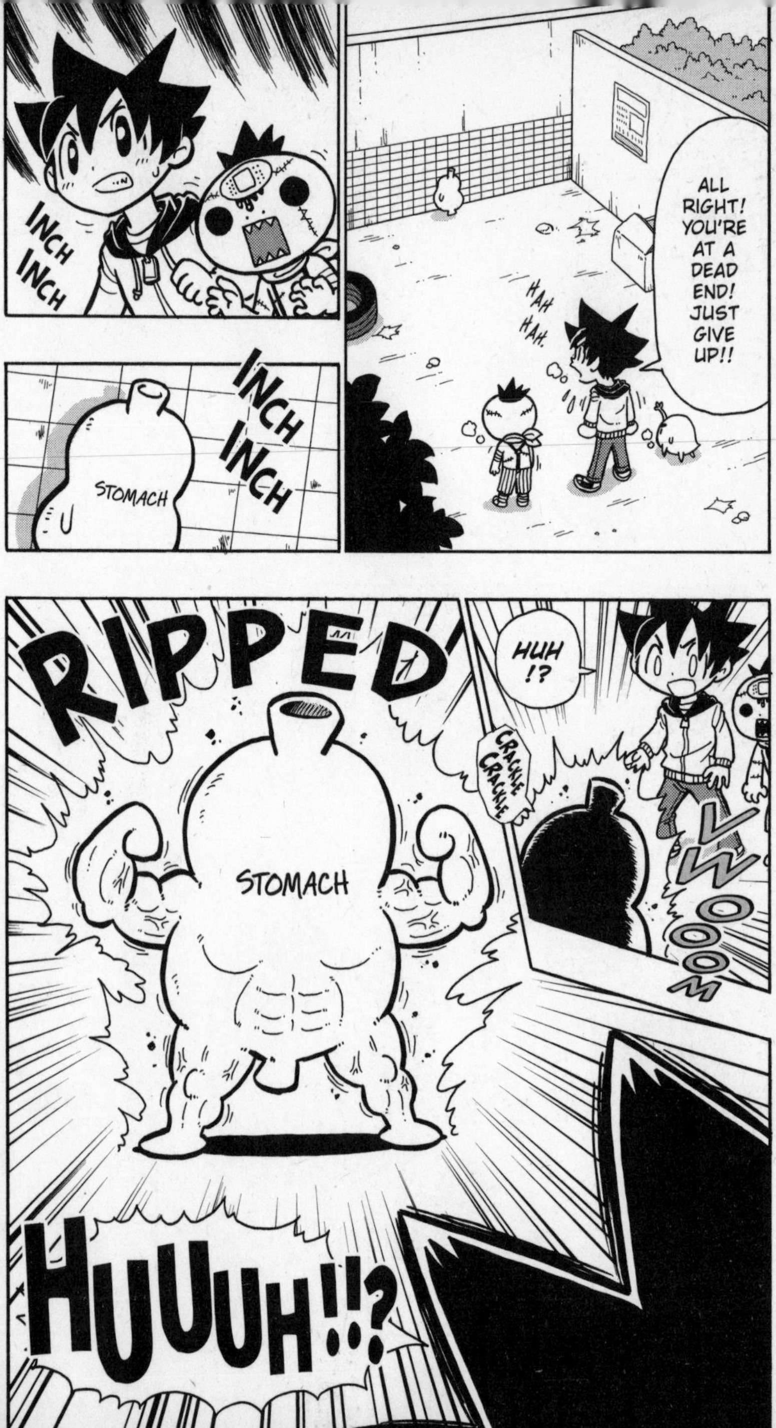

HAH HAH.
ALL RIGHT! YOU'RE AT A DEAD END! JUST GIVE UP!!
INCH INCH
INCH INCH
STOMACH
HUH !?
CRACKLE CRACKLE
VWOOOOM
RIPPED
STOMACH
HUUUH!!?

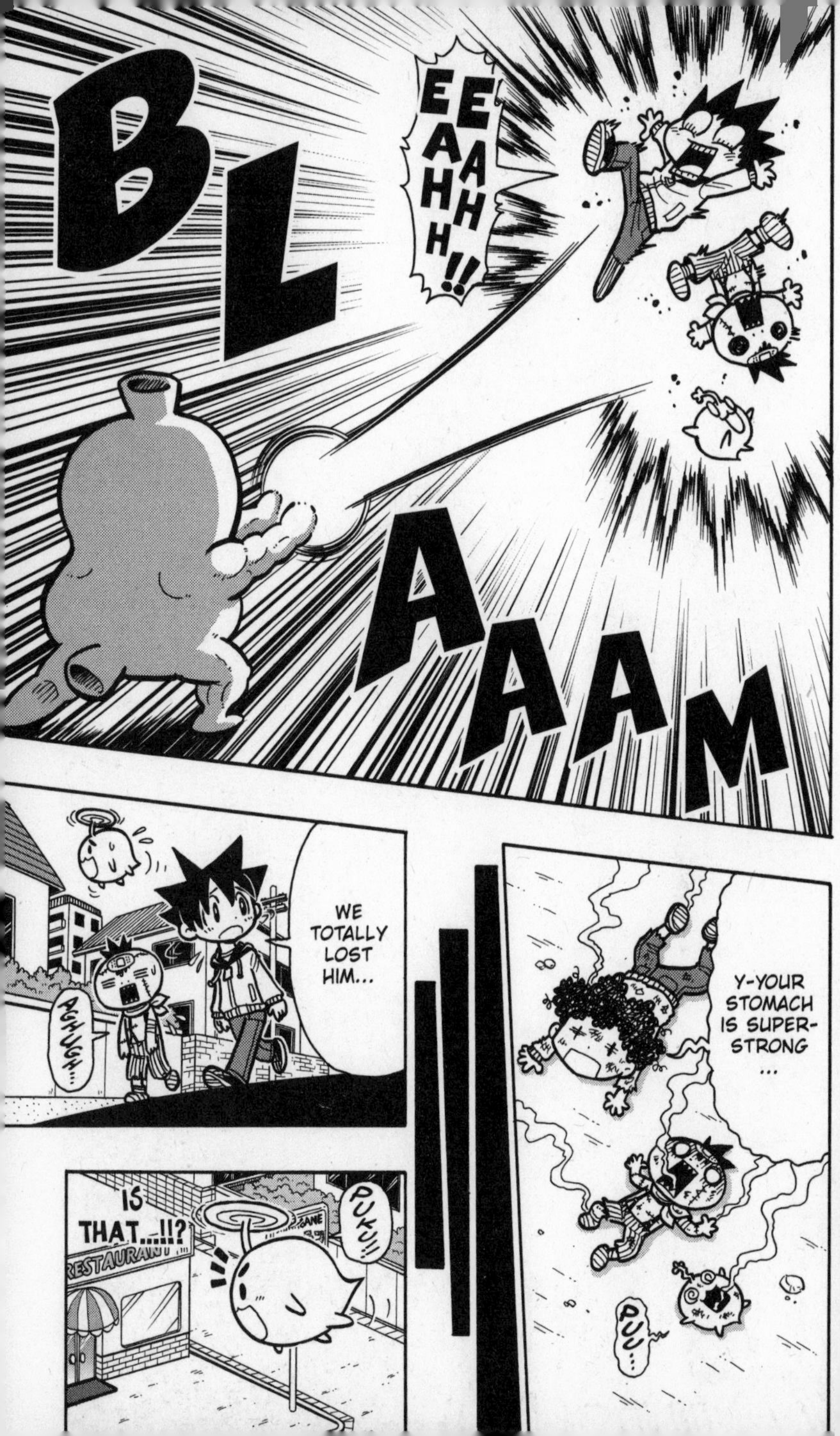
EEAAHHHH!!
BLAAAAM
Y-YOUR STOMACH IS SUPER-STRONG...
PUU...
WE TOTALLY LOST HIM...
ACHUGH...
PUKU!!
IS THAT...!!?
RESTAURANT

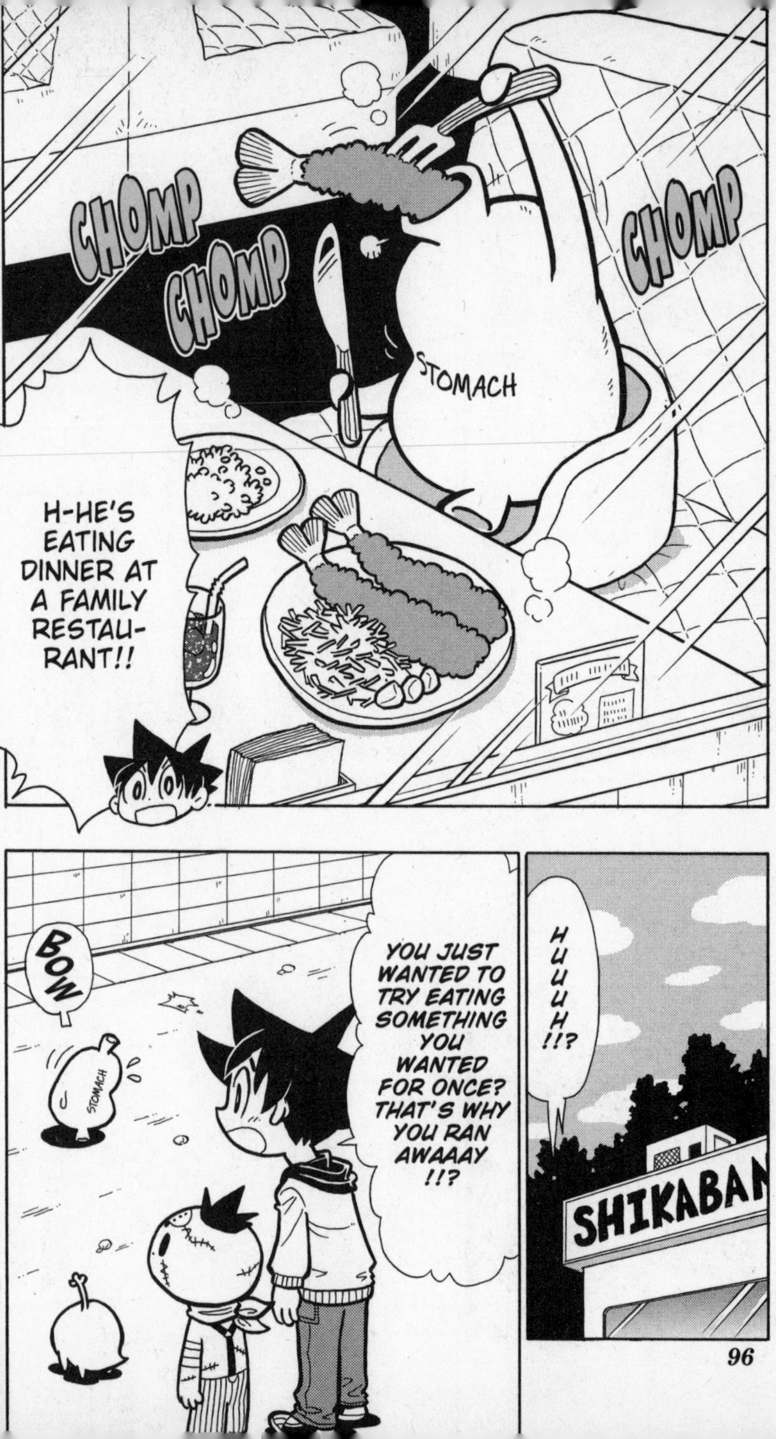
CHOMP
CHOMP
CHOMP
STOMACH
H-HE'S EATING DINNER AT A FAMILY RESTAU-RANT!!
SHIKABAN
HUUUH!!?
YOU JUST WANTED TO TRY EATING SOMETHING YOU WANTED FOR ONCE? THAT'S WHY YOU RAN AWAAAY!!?
BOW
STOMACH

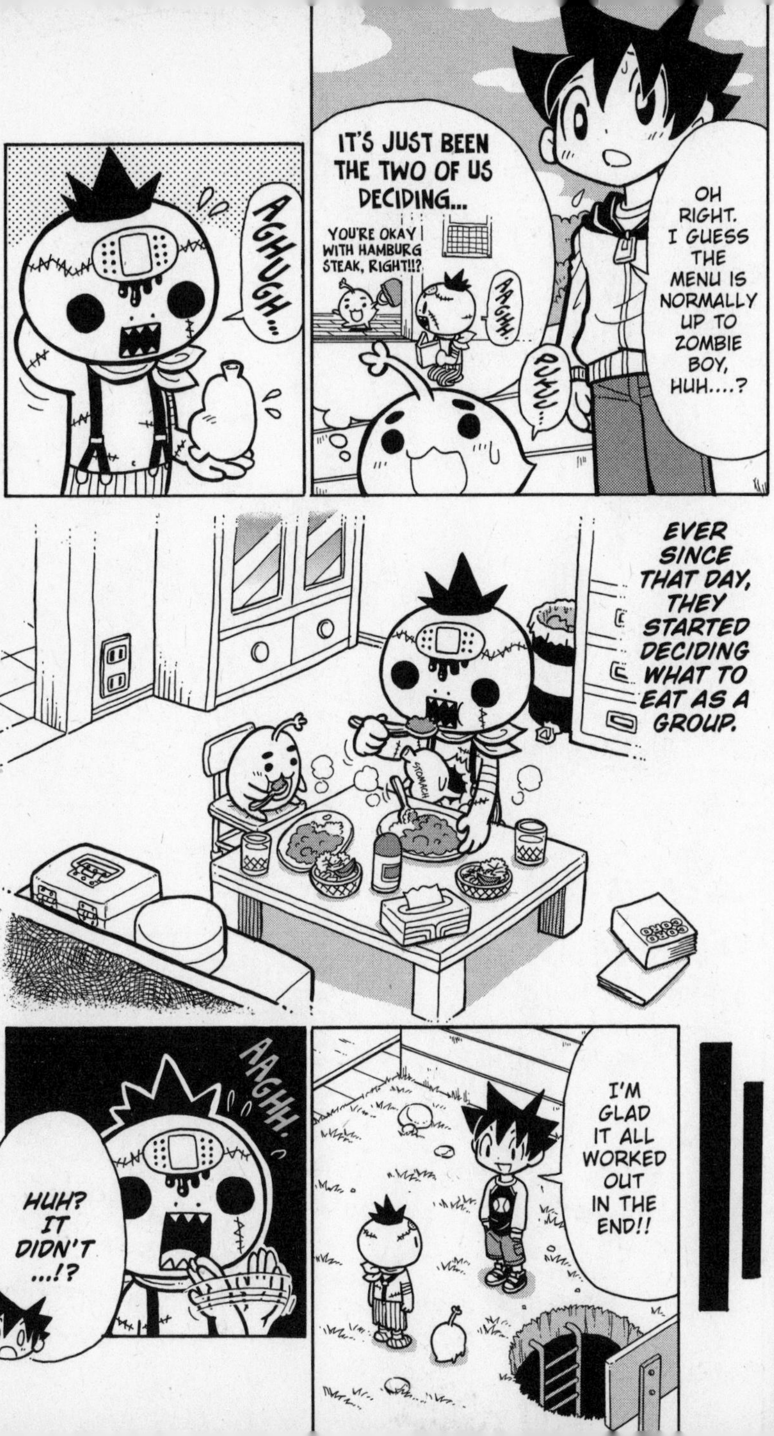
OH RIGHT. I GUESS THE MENU IS NORMALLY UP TO ZOMBIE BOY, HUH....?
IT'S JUST BEEN THE TWO OF US DECIDING...
YOU'RE OKAY WITH HAMBURG STEAK, RIGHT!!?
AAGHH.
PUKUU...
AGHUGH...
EVER SINCE THAT DAY, THEY STARTED DECIDING WHAT TO EAT AS A GROUP.
STOMACH
CORO CORO
I'M GLAD IT ALL WORKED OUT IN THE END!!
AAGHH.
HUH? IT DIDN'T ...!?

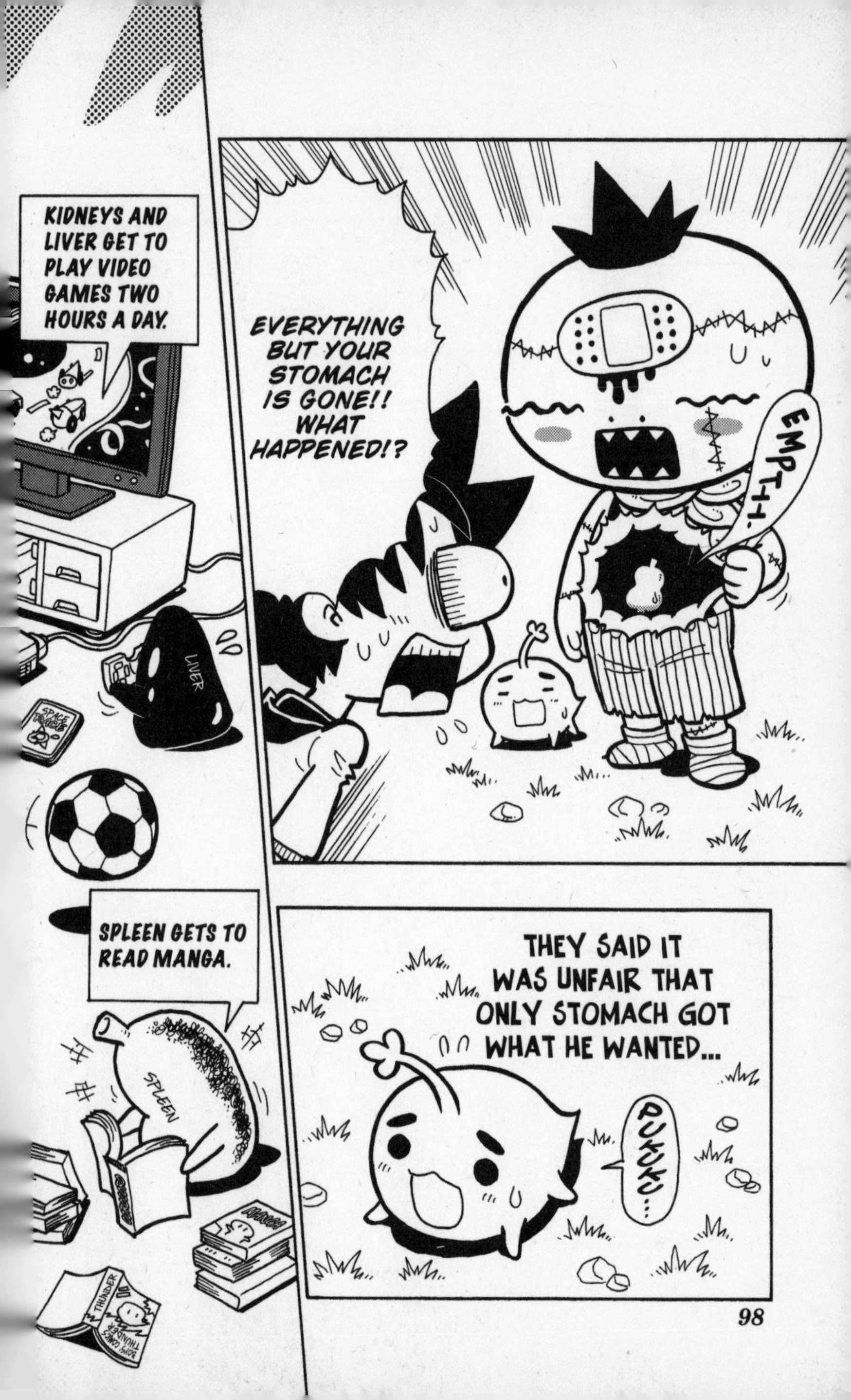

EVERYTHING BUT YOUR STOMACH IS GONE!! WHAT HAPPENED!?
EMPT-Y.
THEY SAID IT WAS UNFAIR THAT ONLY STOMACH GOT WHAT HE WANTED...
PUKUKU...
KIDNEYS AND LIVER GET TO PLAY VIDEO GAMES TWO HOURS A DAY.
LIVER
SPACE RACE
SPLEEN GETS TO READ MANGA.
SPLEEN
THUNDER
BOYS' COMICS THUNDER

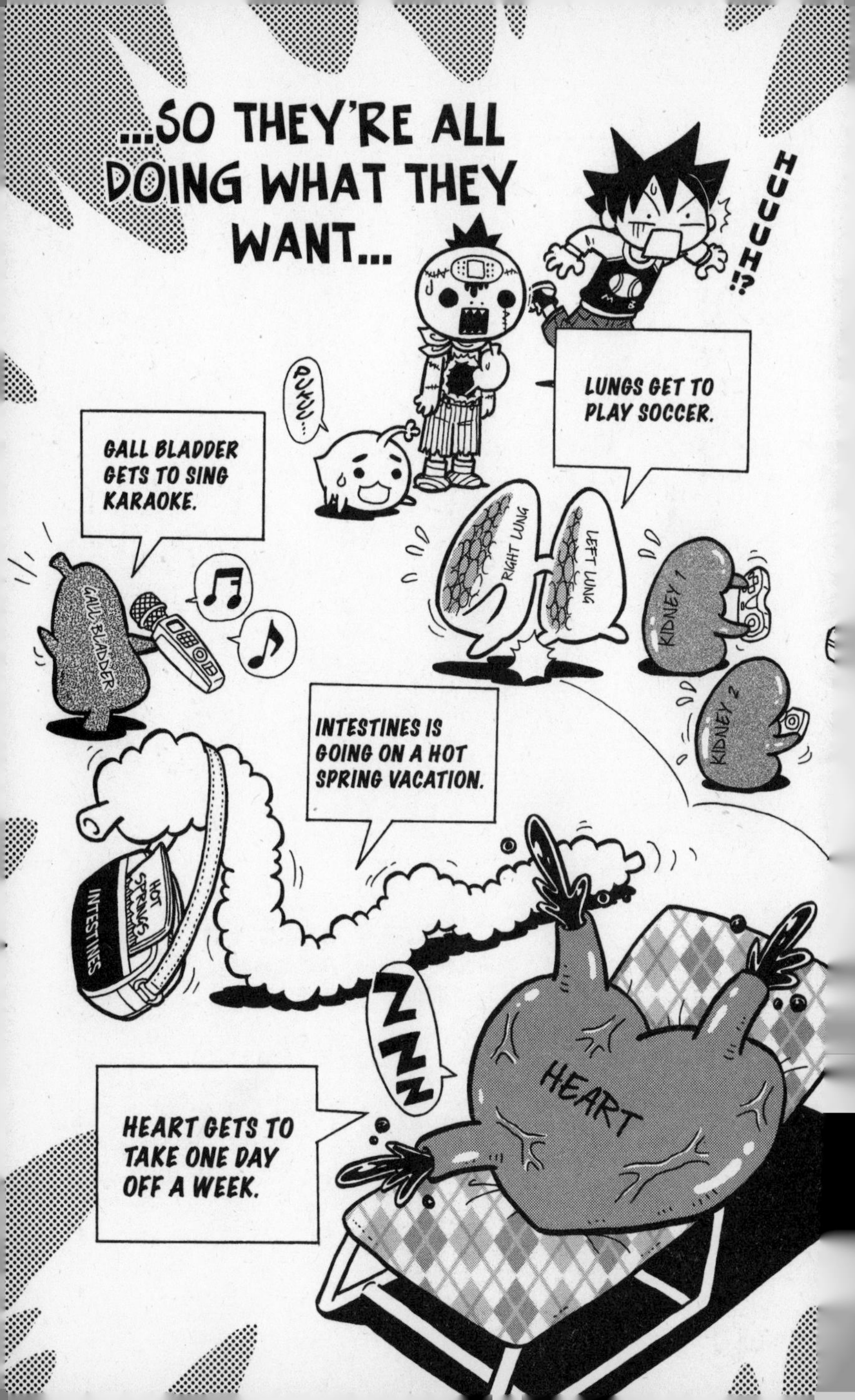
...SO THEY'RE ALL DOING WHAT THEY WANT...
HUUUGH!?
LUNGS GET TO PLAY SOCCER.
PUKUU...
GALL BLADDER GETS TO SING KARAOKE.
RIGHT LUNG
LEFT LUNG
KIDNEY 1
KIDNEY 2
GALL BLADDER
INTESTINES IS GOING ON A HOT SPRING VACATION.
HOT SPRINGS
INTESTINES
NNN
HEART
HEART GETS TO TAKE ONE DAY OFF A WEEK.

BRAIN GETS TO SPEND SOME QUALITY FAMILY TIME.

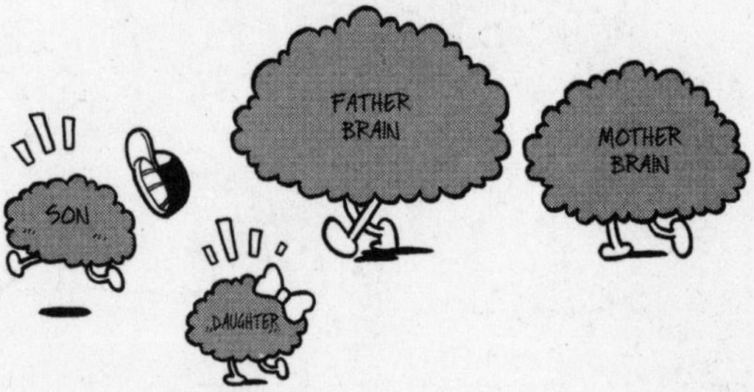
FATHER BRAIN
MOTHER BRAIN
SON
DAUGHTER

ATTACKED BY A GIANT MONZTER!

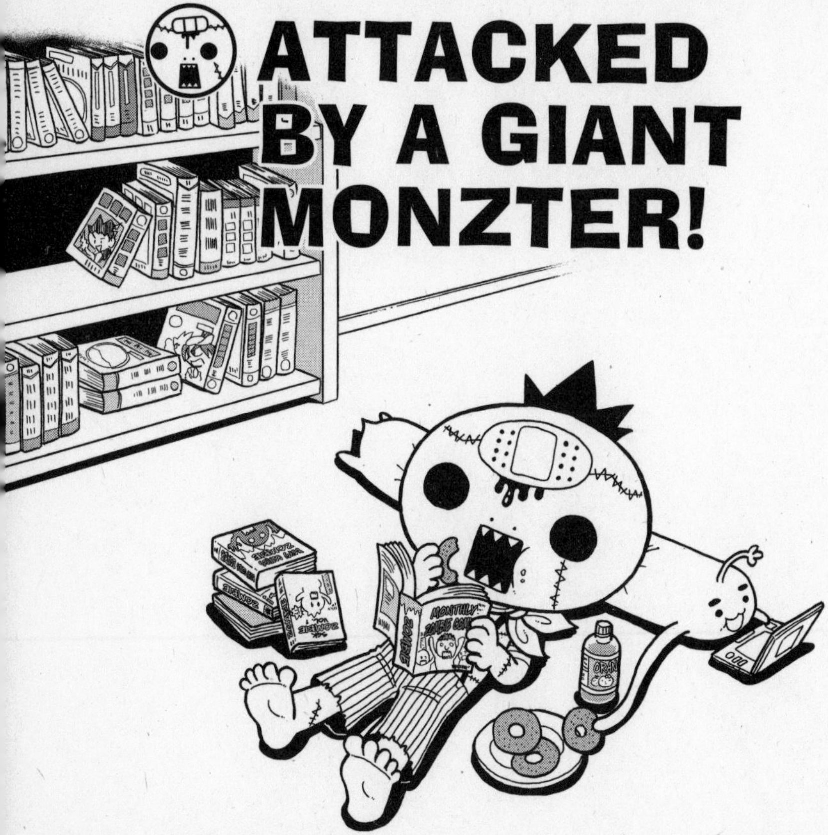

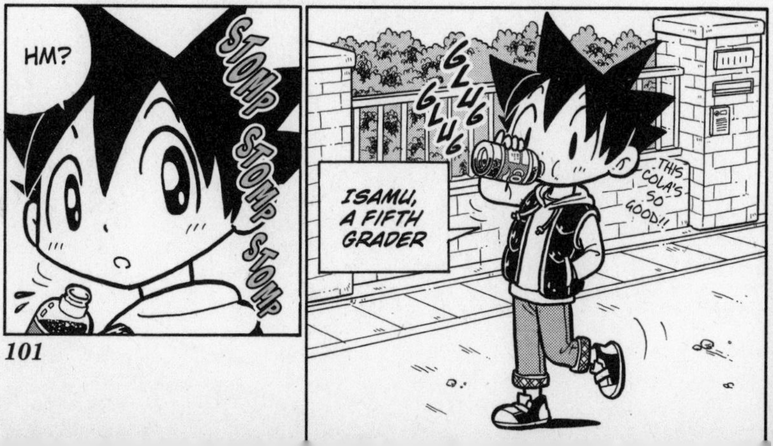

GLUG GLUG
THIS COLA'S SO GOOD!!
ISAMU, A FIFTH GRADER
STOMP STOMP STOMP STOMP
HM?

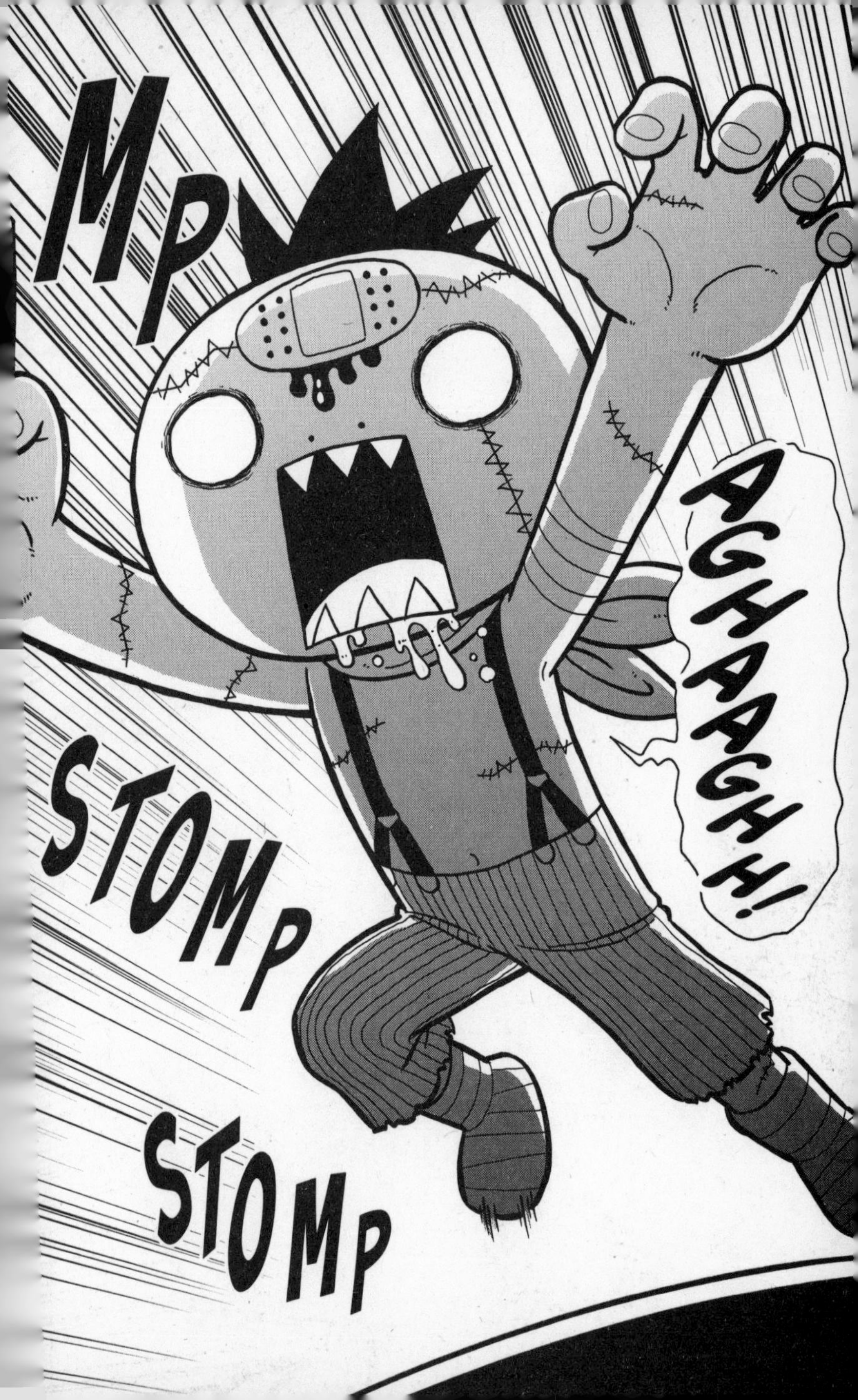
AGHAAAGHH!
MP
STOMP
STOMP

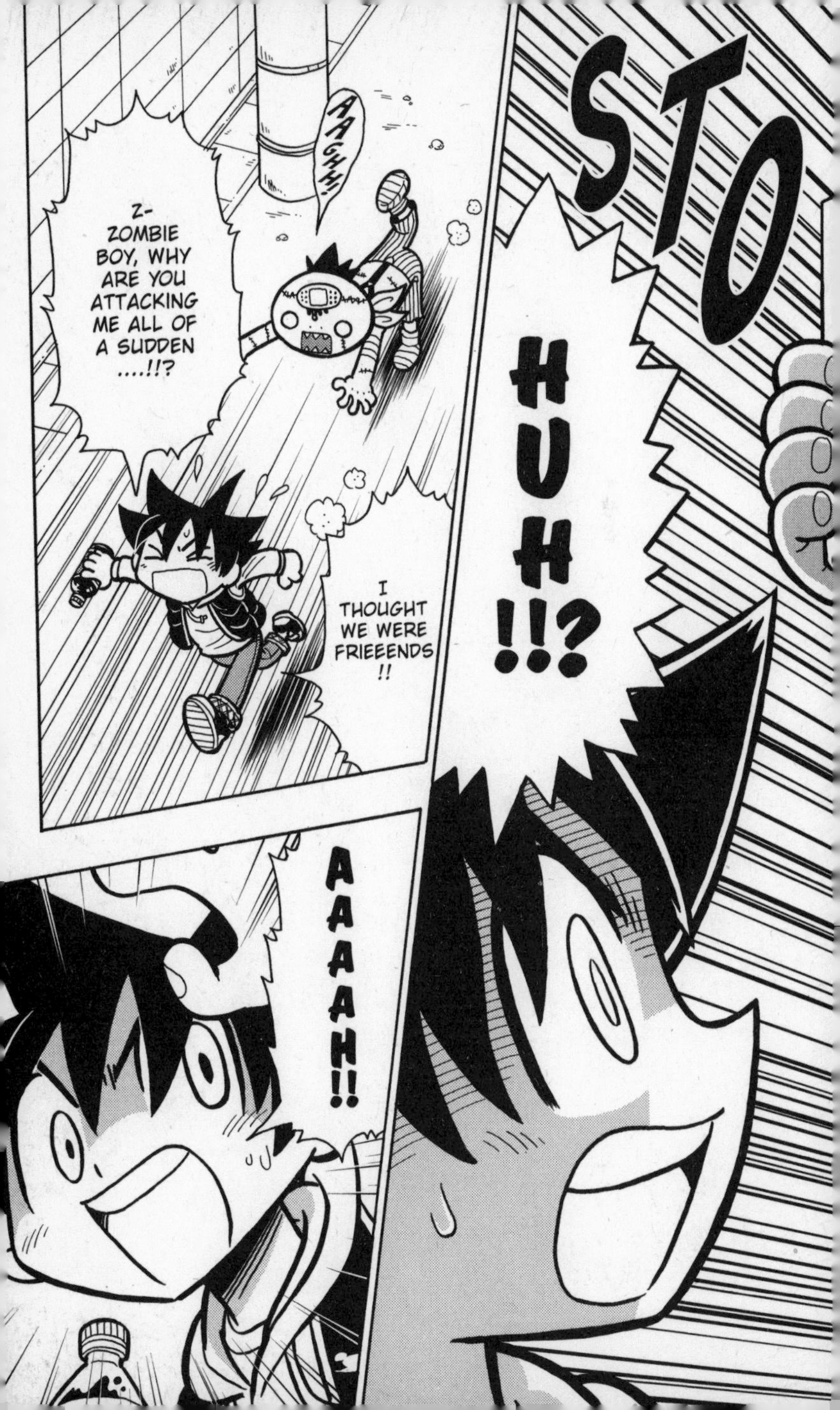
STO
HUH!!?
AAGHH!
Z-ZOMBIE BOY, WHY ARE YOU ATTACKING ME ALL OF A SUDDEN ....!!?
I THOUGHT WE WERE FRIEEENDS!!
AAAAH!!

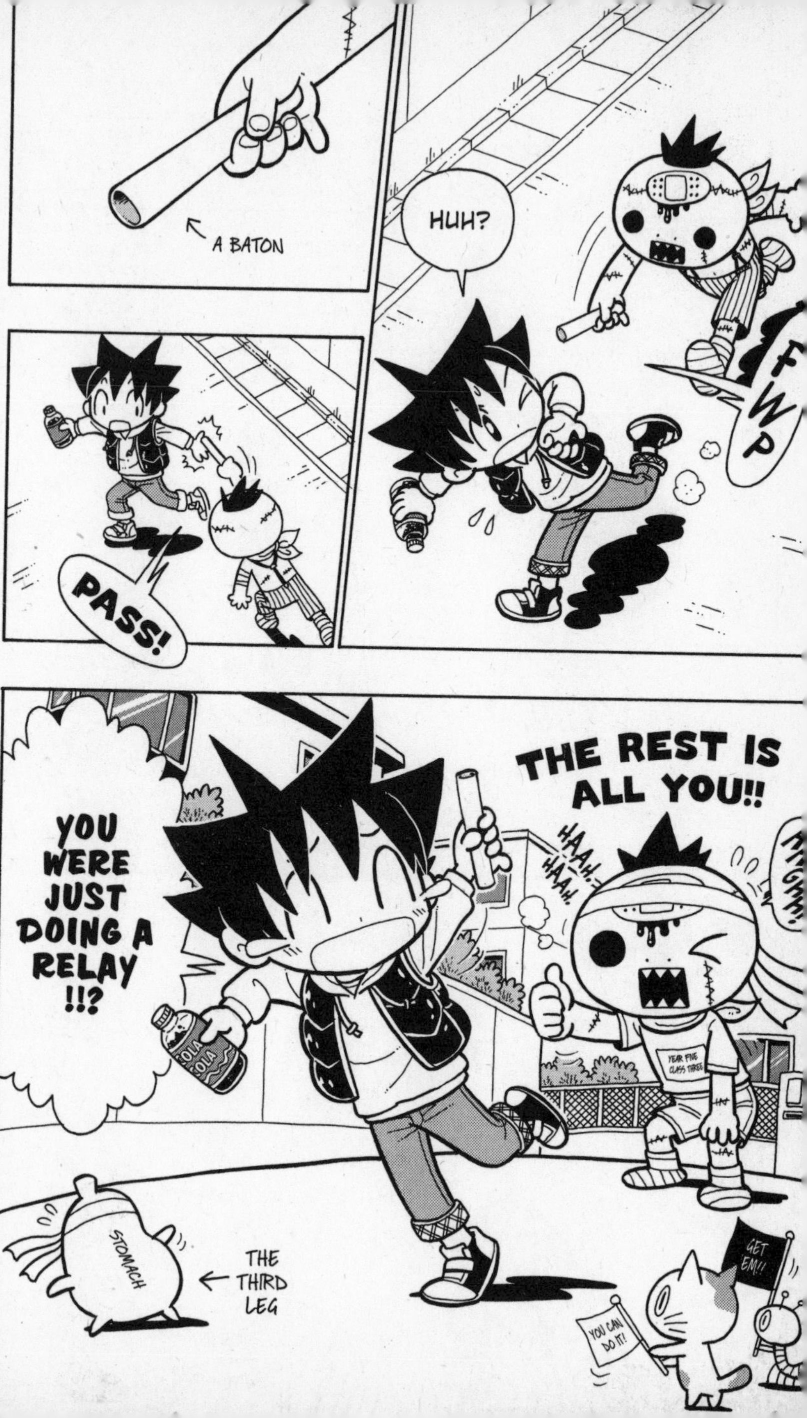
HUH?
FWP
A BATON
PASS!
THE REST IS ALL YOU!!
HAAH... HAAH.
YEAR FIVE CLASS THREE
YOU WERE JUST DOING A RELAY !!?
COLA COLA
GET EM!!
YOU CAN DO IT!
STOMACH
THE THIRD LEG

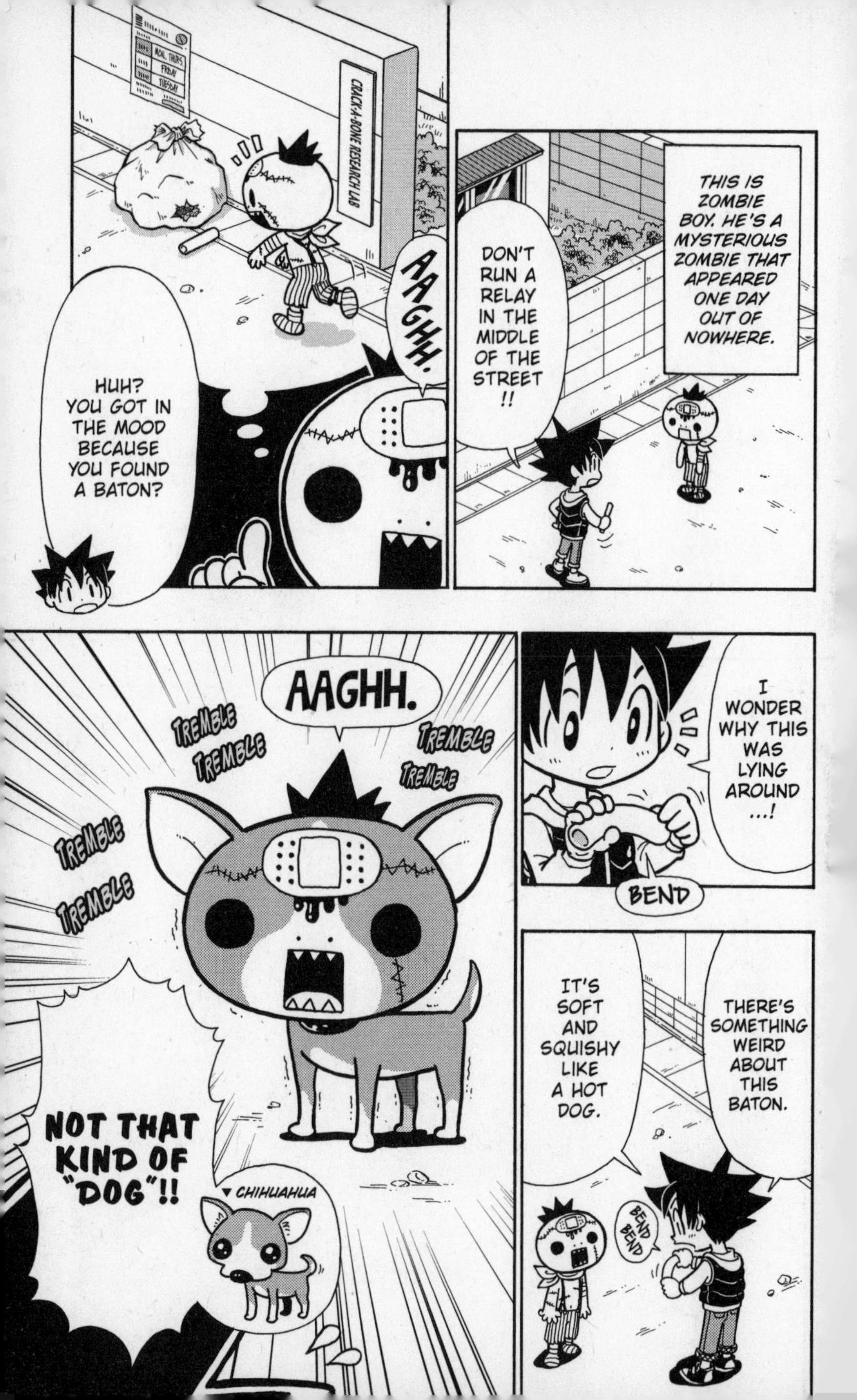
THIS IS ZOMBIE BOY. HE'S A MYSTERIOUS ZOMBIE THAT APPEARED ONE DAY OUT OF NOWHERE.
DON'T RUN A RELAY IN THE MIDDLE OF THE STREET !!
CRACK-A-BONE RESEARCH LAB
MON. THURS.
FRIDAY
TUESDAY
AAGHH.
HUH? YOU GOT IN THE MOOD BECAUSE YOU FOUND A BATON?
I WONDER WHY THIS WAS LYING AROUND ...!
BEND
THERE'S SOMETHING WEIRD ABOUT THIS BATON.
IT'S SOFT AND SQUISHY LIKE A HOT DOG.
BEND BEND
AAGHH.
TREMBLE TREMBLE
TREMBLE TREMBLE
TREMBLE TREMBLE
NOT THAT KIND OF "DOG"!!
▼CHIHUAHUA

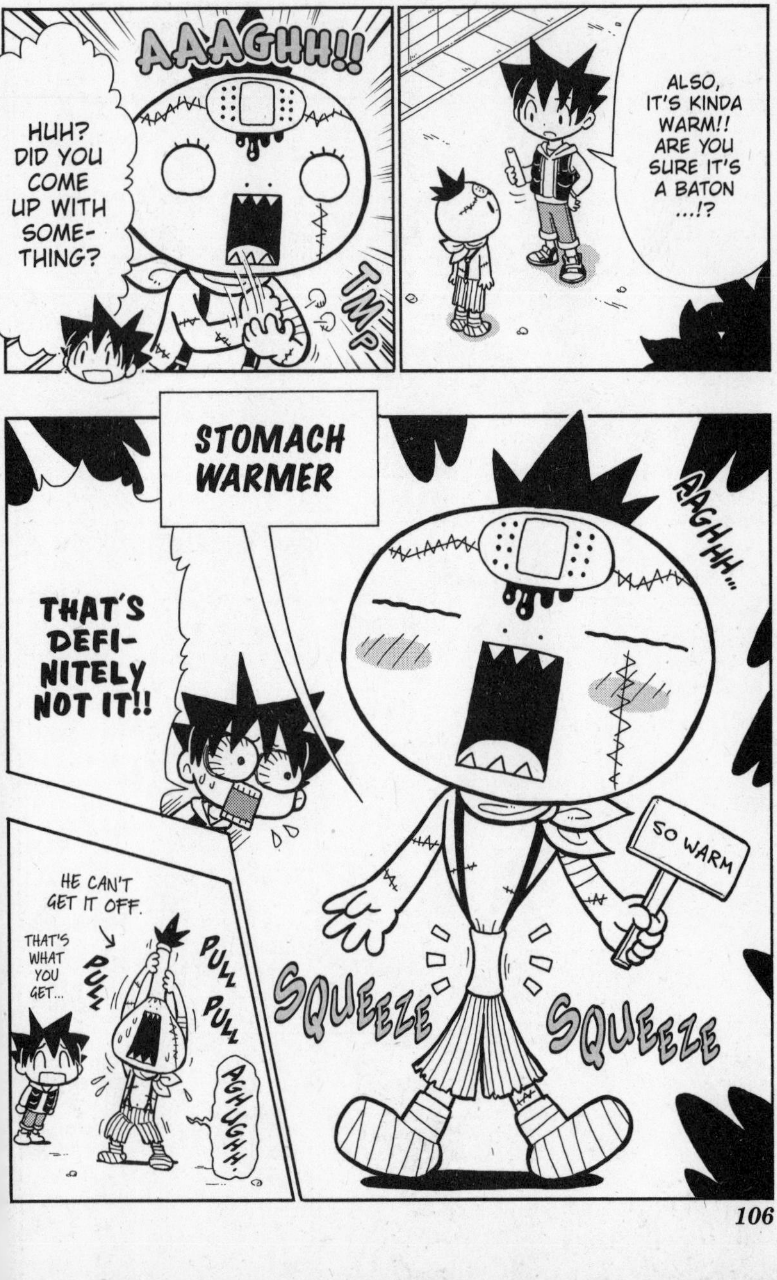
ALSO, IT'S KINDA WARM!! ARE YOU SURE IT'S A BATON ...!?
AAAGHH!!
HUH? DID YOU COME UP WITH SOME-THING?
TMP
STOMACH WARMER
AAGHHH...
THAT'S DEFI-NITELY NOT IT!!
SO WARM
SQUEEZE
SQUEEZE
HE CAN'T GET IT OFF.
PULL
PULL
PULL
AGHUGHH.
THAT'S WHAT YOU GET...

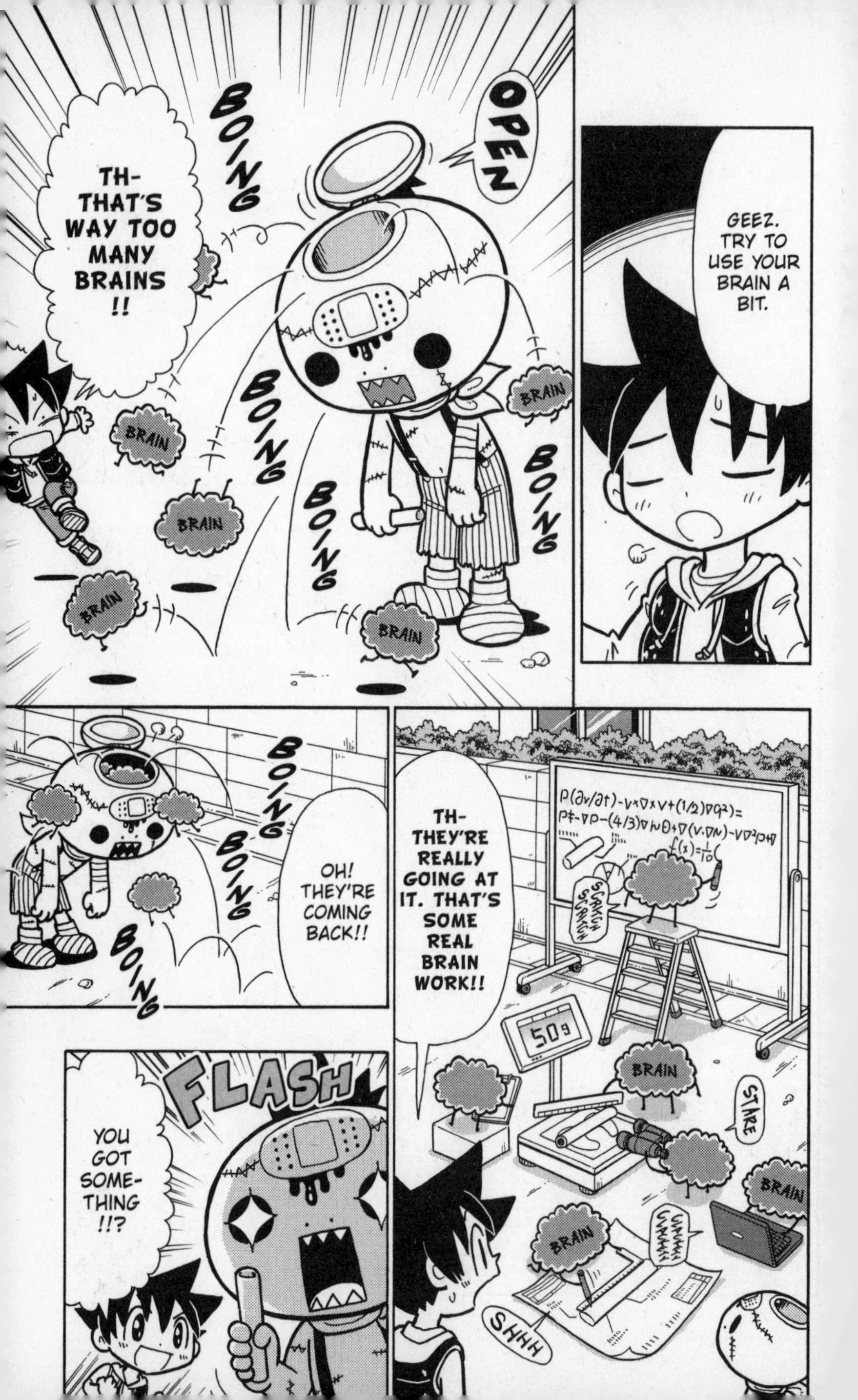
GEEZ. TRY TO USE YOUR BRAIN A BIT.
OPEN
BOING
TH-THAT'S WAY TOO MANY BRAINS!!
BRAIN
BOING
BRAIN
BOING
BRAIN
BRAIN
BOING
BRAIN
TH-THEY'RE REALLY GOING AT IT. THAT'S SOME REAL BRAIN WORK!!
SCRATCH SCRATCH
50g
BRAIN
STARE
BRAIN
BRAIN
SHHH
BOING
BOING
BOING
OH! THEY'RE COMING BACK!!
FLASH
YOU GOT SOMETHING!!?

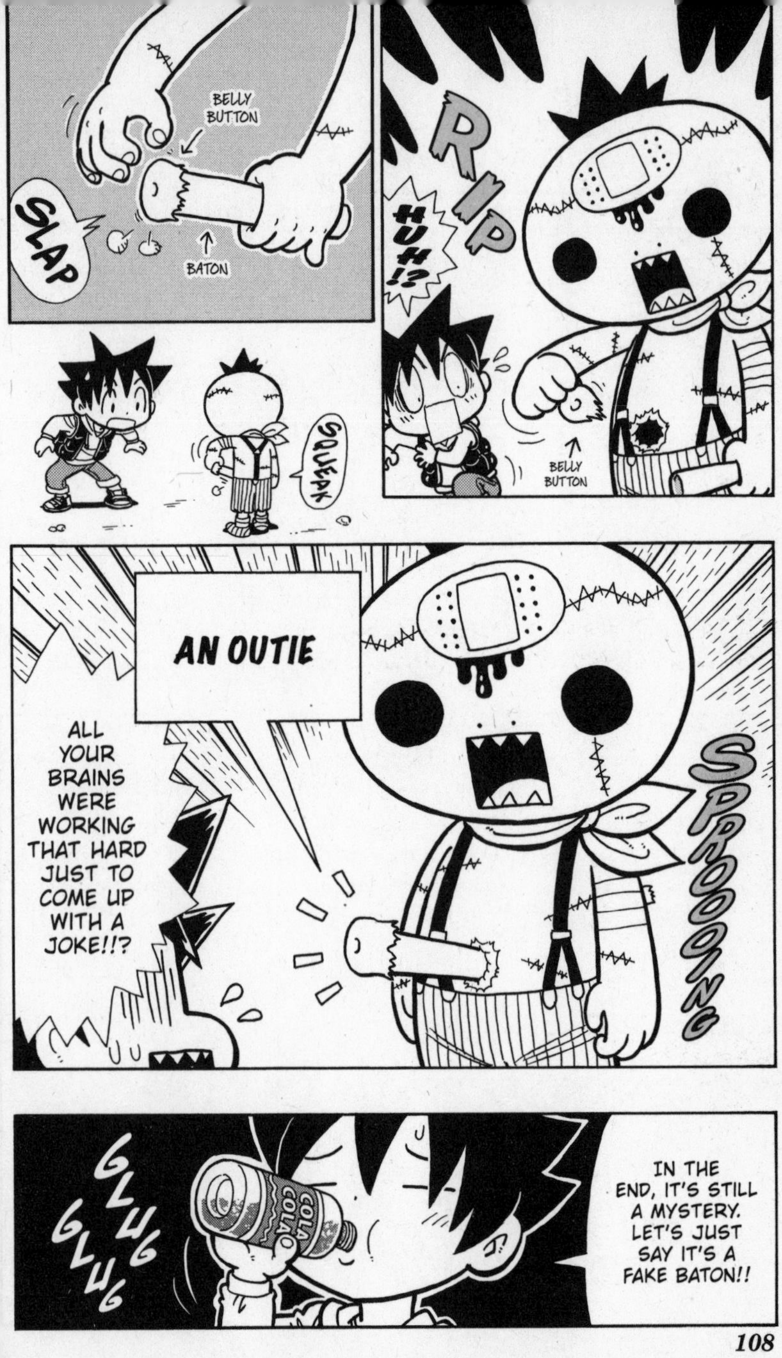
RIP
HUH!?
BELLY BUTTON
BELLY BUTTON
BATON
SLAP
SQUEAK
AN OUTIE
SPROOOING
ALL YOUR BRAINS WERE WORKING THAT HARD JUST TO COME UP WITH A JOKE!!?
IN THE END, IT'S STILL A MYSTERY. LET'S JUST SAY IT'S A FAKE BATON!!
GLUG GLUG
COLA COLA

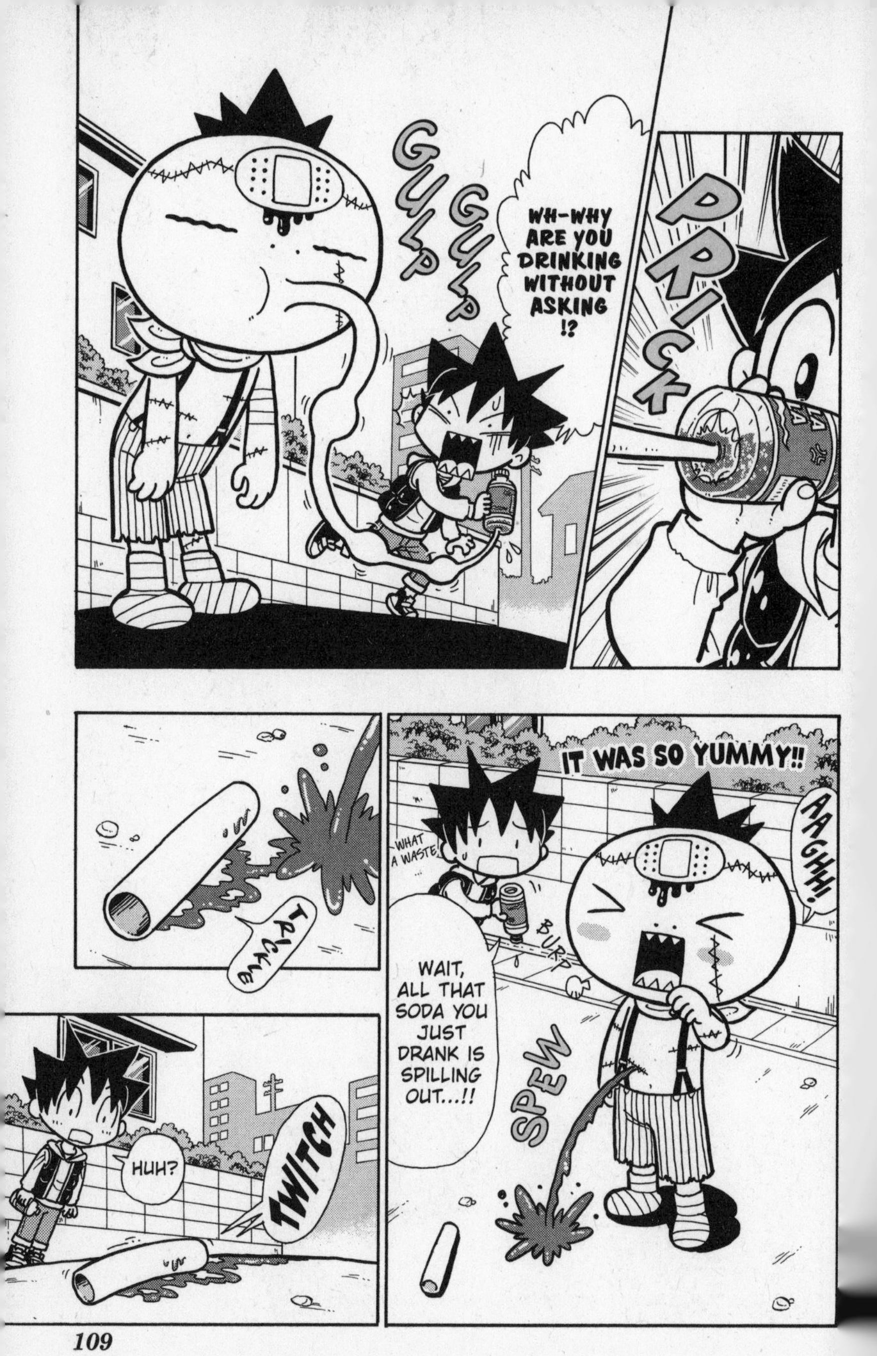
PRICK
WH-WHY ARE YOU DRINKING WITHOUT ASKING !?
GULP
GULP
IT WAS SO YUMMY!!
AAGHH!
WHAT A WASTE...
BURP
WAIT, ALL THAT SODA YOU JUST DRANK IS SPILLING OUT...!!
SPEW
TRICKLE
TWITCH
HUH?

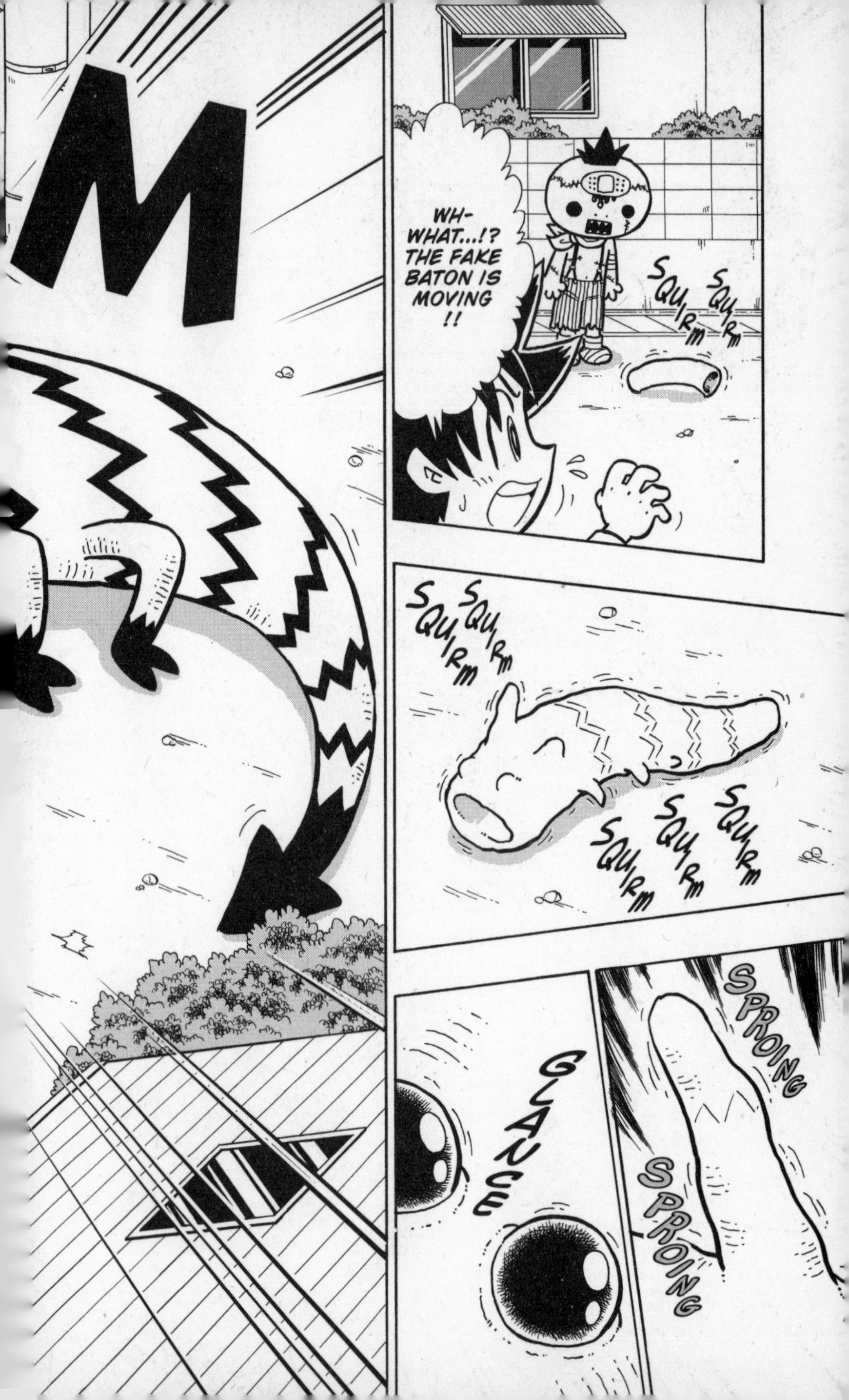

WH-WHAT...!? THE FAKE BATON IS MOVING !!
SQUIRM SQUIRM
SQUIRM SQUIRM
SQUIRM SQUIRM SQUIRM
SPROING
SPROING
GLANCE
M

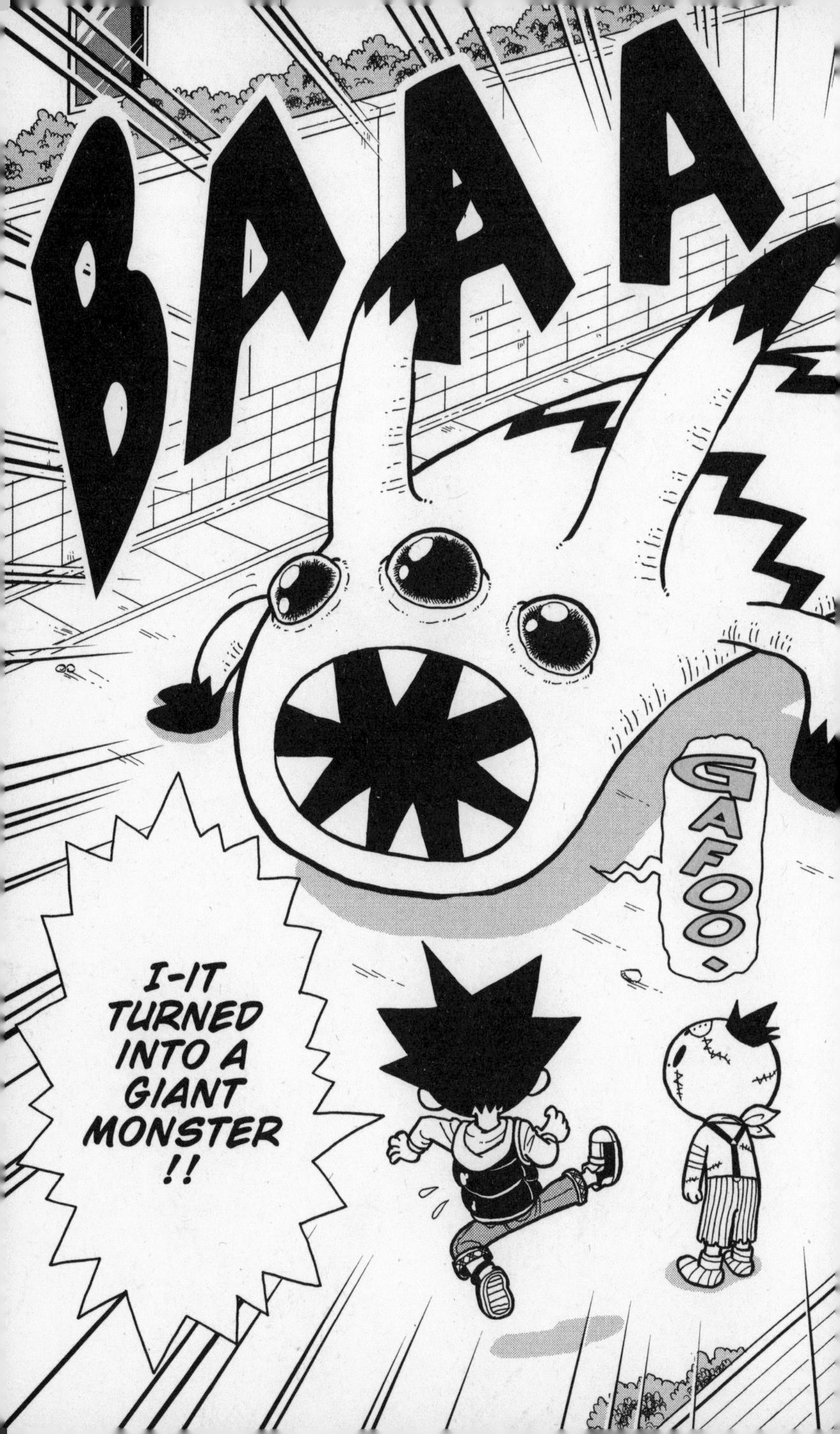
BAAA
GAFOO.
I-IT TURNED INTO A GIANT MONSTER!!

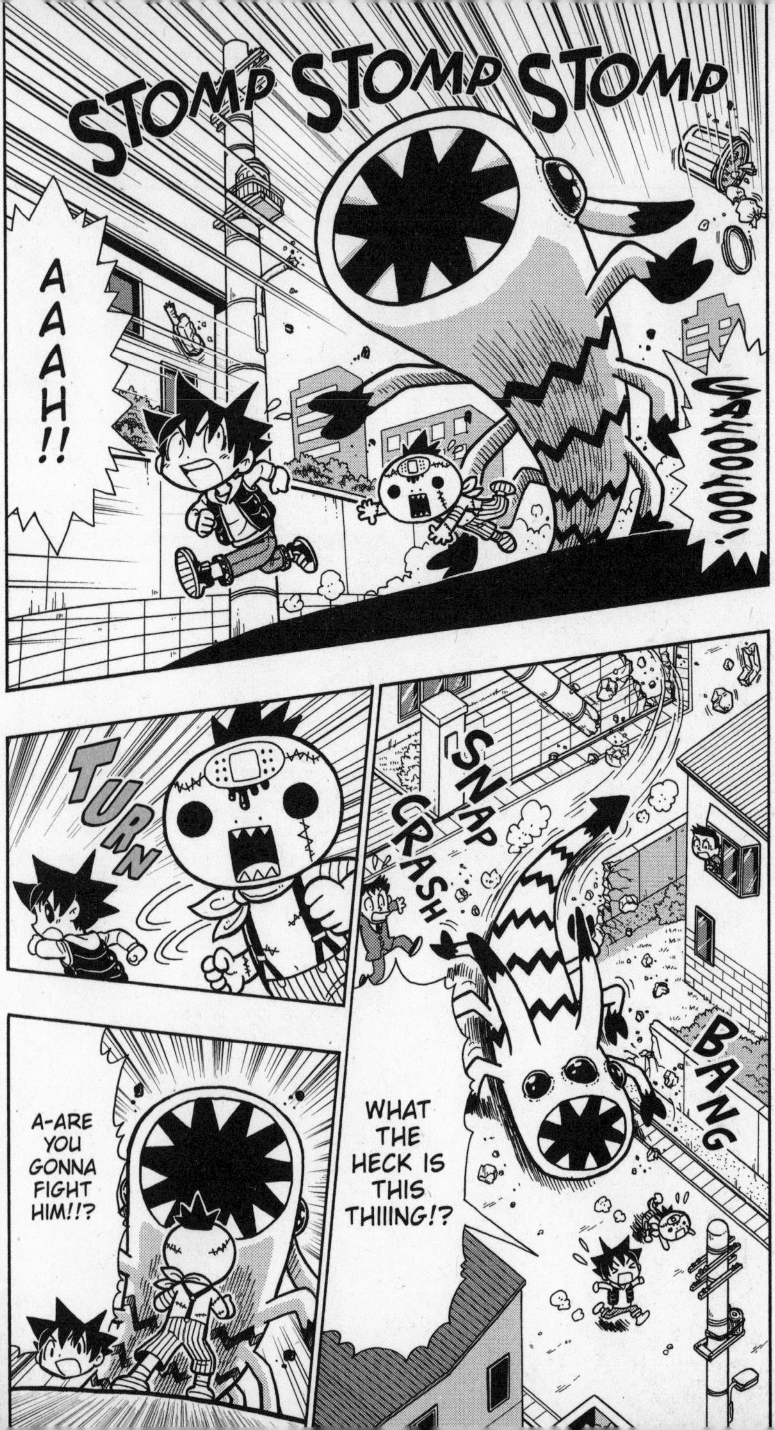
STOMP STOMP STOMP
GAKOOOKOOO!
AAAAH!!
SNAP
CRASH
BANG
WHAT THE HECK IS THIS THIIING!?
TURN
A-ARE YOU GONNA FIGHT HIM!!?

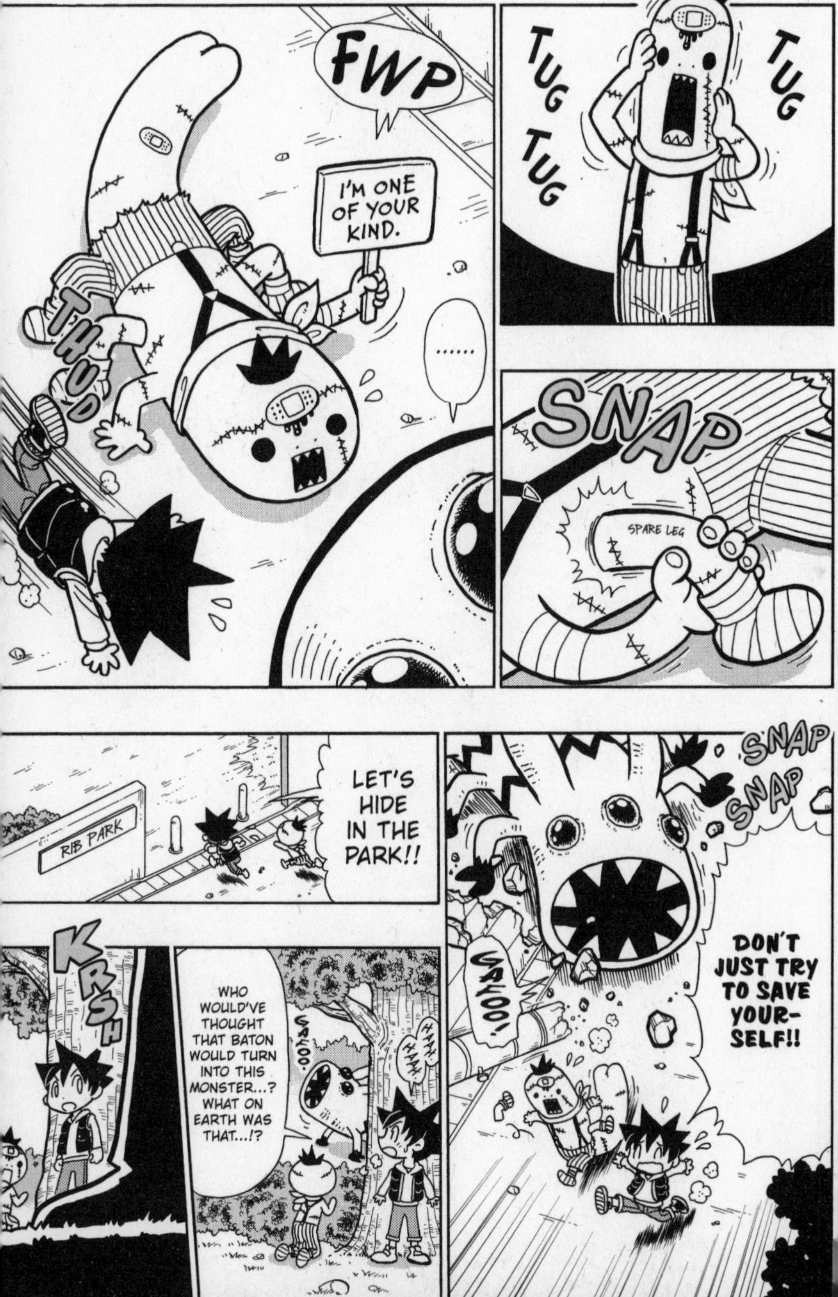
TUG
TUG
TUG
TUG
SNAP
SPARE LEG
FWP
I'M ONE OF YOUR KIND.
....
THUD
SNAP
SNAP
GRROO!
DON'T JUST TRY TO SAVE YOURSELF!!
RIB PARK
LET'S HIDE IN THE PARK!!
WHO WOULD'VE THOUGHT THAT BATON WOULD TURN INTO THIS MONSTER...? WHAT ON EARTH WAS THAT...!?
GRROO.
HAAH HAAH
KRSH

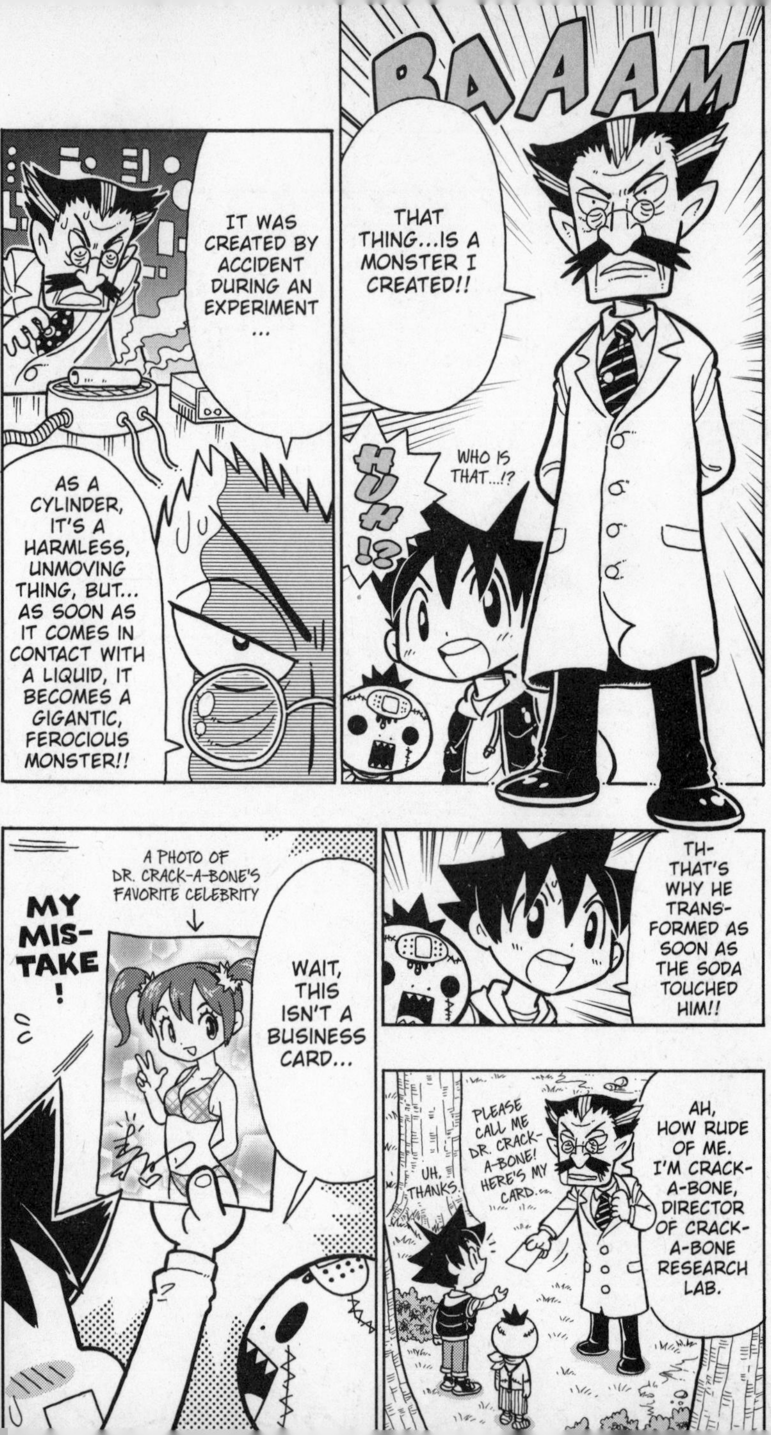
BAAAM
THAT THING...IS A MONSTER I CREATED!!
WHO IS THAT...!?
HUH!?
IT WAS CREATED BY ACCIDENT DURING AN EXPERIMENT ...
AS A CYLINDER, IT'S A HARMLESS, UNMOVING THING, BUT... AS SOON AS IT COMES IN CONTACT WITH A LIQUID, IT BECOMES A GIGANTIC, FEROCIOUS MONSTER!!
TH-THAT'S WHY HE TRANSFORMED AS SOON AS THE SODA TOUCHED HIM!!
AH, HOW RUDE OF ME. I'M CRACK-A-BONE, DIRECTOR OF CRACK-A-BONE RESEARCH LAB.
PLEASE CALL ME DR. CRACK-A-BONE! HERE'S MY CARD.
UH, THANKS.
WAIT, THIS ISN'T A BUSINESS CARD...
A PHOTO OF DR. CRACK-A-BONE'S FAVORITE CELEBRITY
MY MISTAKE!

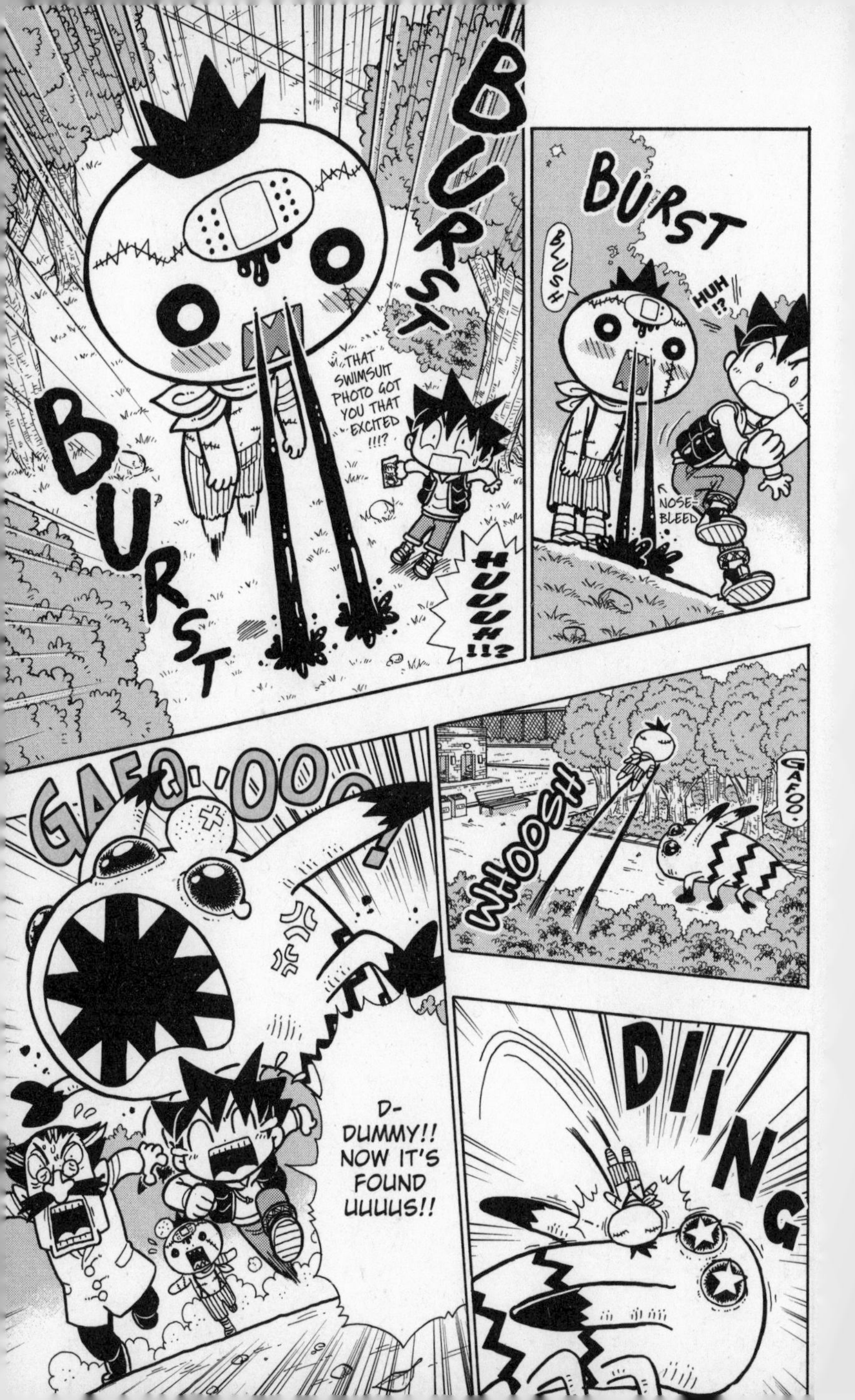
BURST
BLUSH
HUH!?
NOSE-BLEED
BURST
BURST
THAT SWIMSUIT PHOTO GOT YOU THAT EXCITED!!!?
HUUUUH!!?
GAFOO
WHOOSH
GAFOOOO
DIIING
D-DUMMY!! NOW IT'S FOUND UUUUS!!

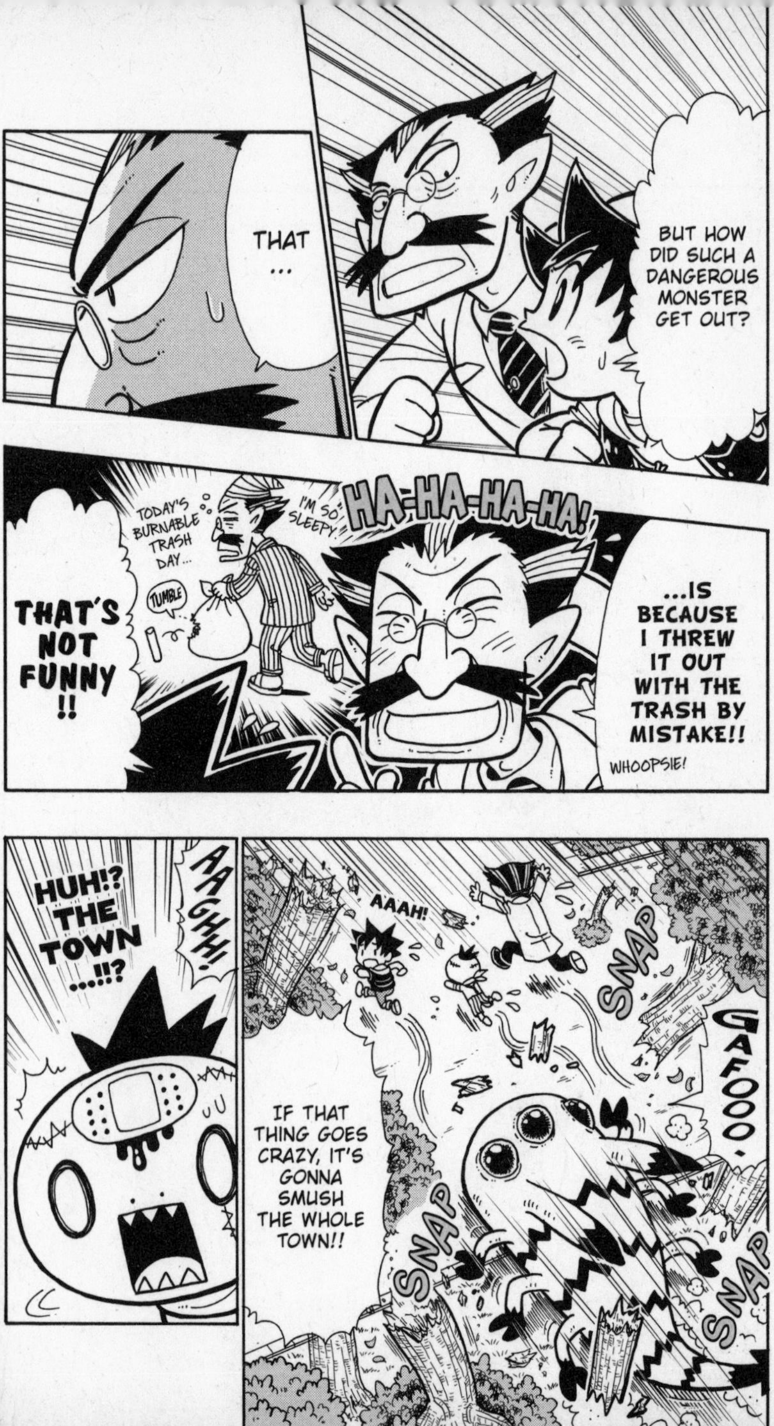
BUT HOW DID SUCH A DANGEROUS MONSTER GET OUT?
THAT ...
...IS BECAUSE I THREW IT OUT WITH THE TRASH BY MISTAKE!!
WHOOPSIE!
HA-HA-HA-HA!
I'M SO SLEEPY
TODAY'S BURNABLE TRASH DAY...
TUMBLE
THAT'S NOT FUNNY!!
GAFOOO.
SNAP
AAAH!
IF THAT THING GOES CRAZY, IT'S GONNA SMUSH THE WHOLE TOWN!!
SNAP
SNAP
AAGHH!
HUH!? THE TOWN ...!!?

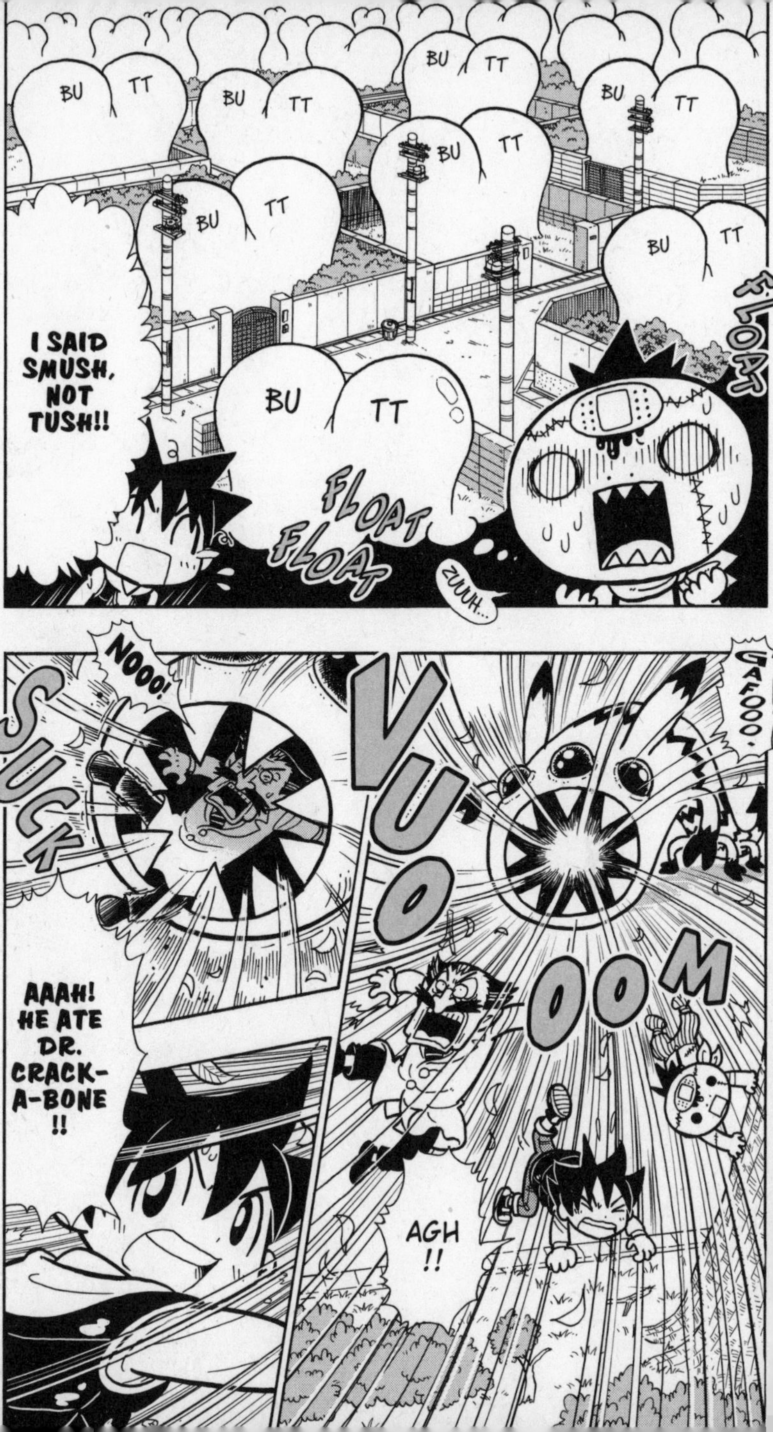
BU TT
BU TT
BU TT
BU TT
BU TT
BU TT
BU TT
BU TT
FLOAT
I SAID SMUSH, NOT TUSH!!
FLOAT FLOAT
ZUUUH...
GAFOOO.
VUOOOM
NOOO!
SUCK
AAAH! HE ATE DR. CRACK-A-BONE!!
AGH!!

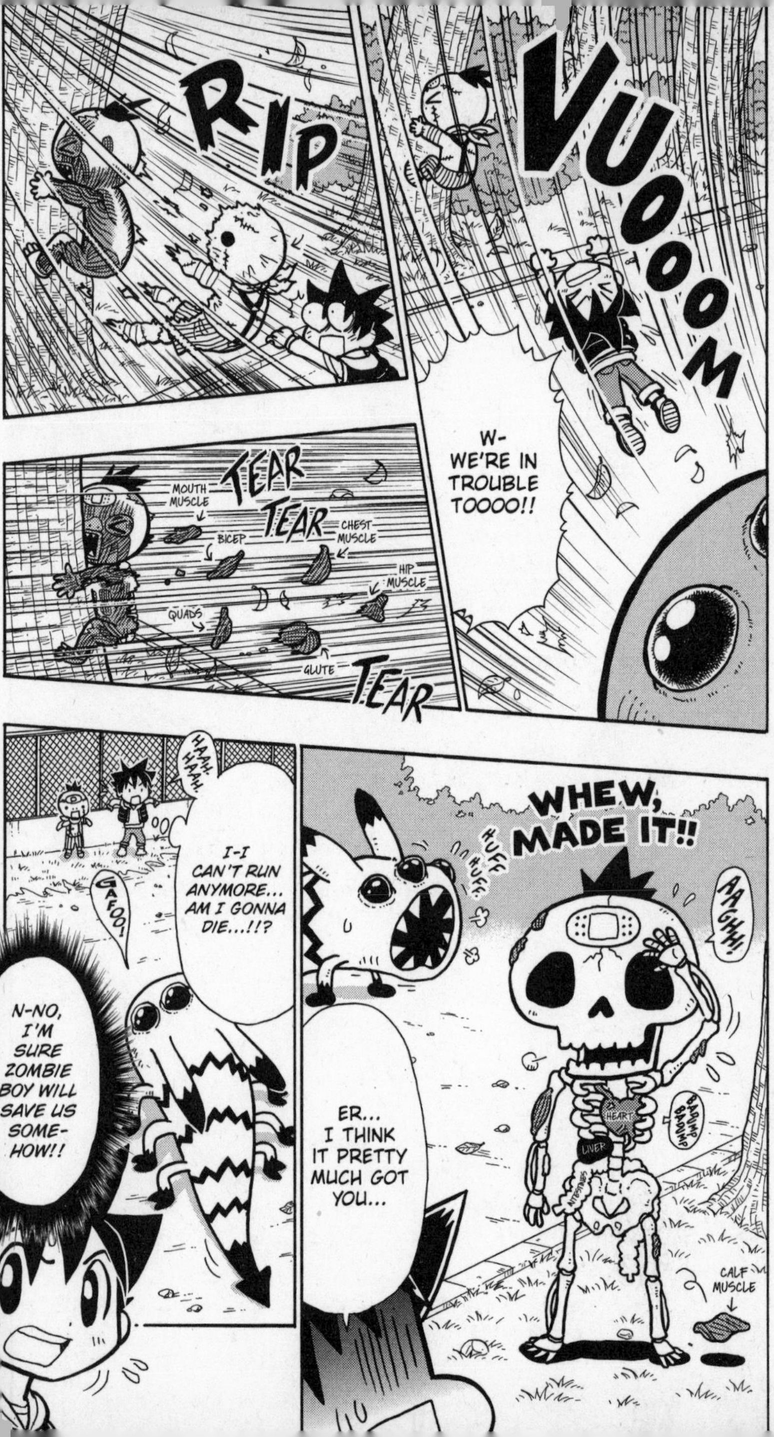
VUOOOOM
W- WE'RE IN TROUBLE TOOOO!!
RIP
TEAR
TEAR
MOUTH MUSCLE
BICEP
CHEST MUSCLE
HIP MUSCLE
QUADS
GLUTE
TEAR
WHEW, MADE IT!!
HUFF HUFF
AAGHH!
HEART
LIVER
BADUMP BADUMP
CALF MUSCLE
ER... I THINK IT PRETTY MUCH GOT YOU...
HAAH HAAH
I-I CAN'T RUN ANYMORE... AM I GONNA DIE...!!?
GAFOO!
N-NO, I'M SURE ZOMBIE BOY WILL SAVE US SOME-HOW!!

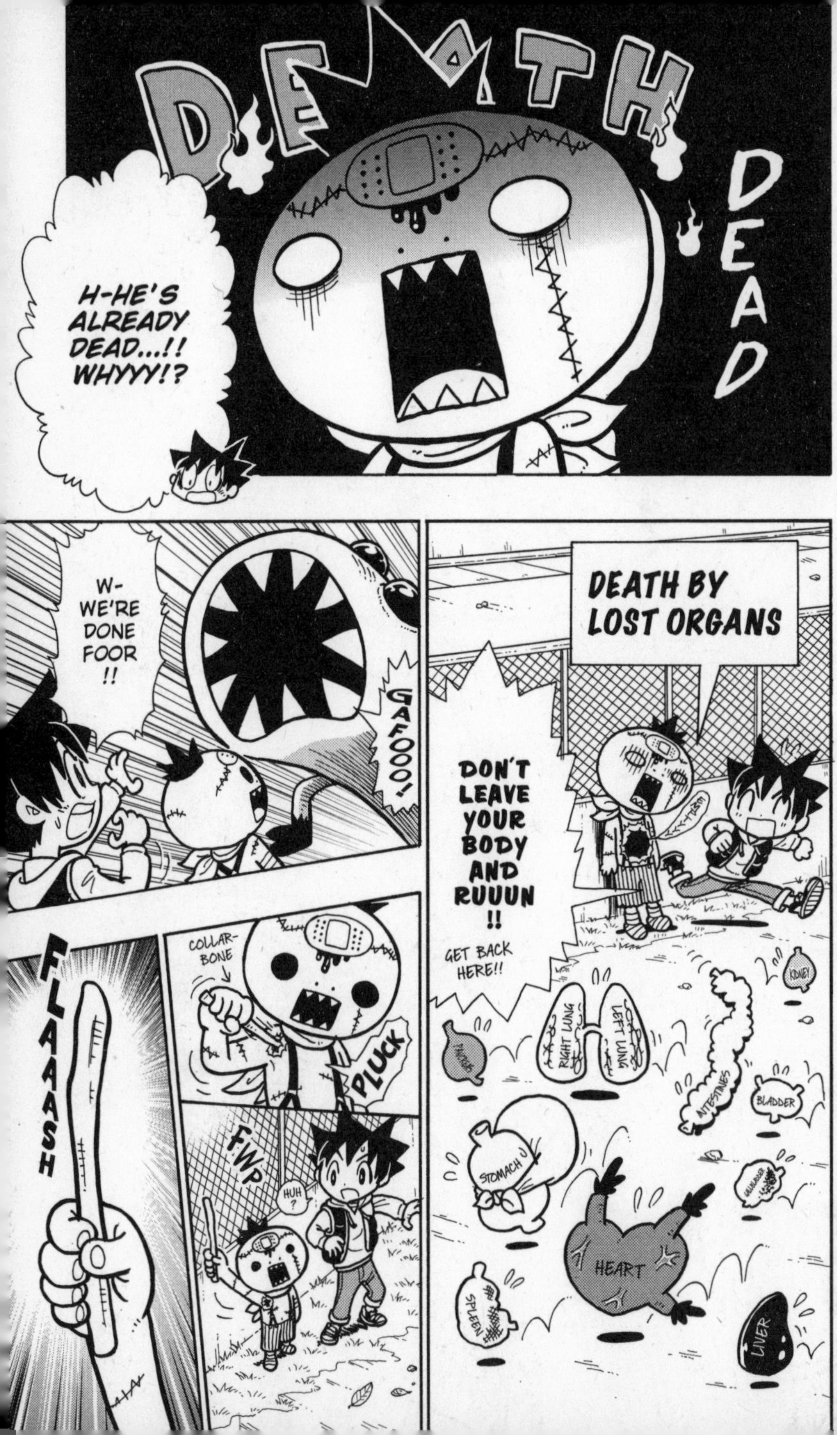
DEATH
DEAD
H-HE'S ALREADY DEAD...!! WHYYY!?
W-WE'RE DONE FOOR !!
GAFOOO!
COLLAR-BONE
PLUCK
FLAAAASH
FWP
HUH ?
DEATH BY LOST ORGANS
DON'T LEAVE YOUR BODY AND RUUUN !!
GET BACK HERE!!
KIDNEY
RIGHT LUNG
LEFT LUNG
INTESTINES
BLADDER
STOMACH
HEART
SPLEEN
LIVER

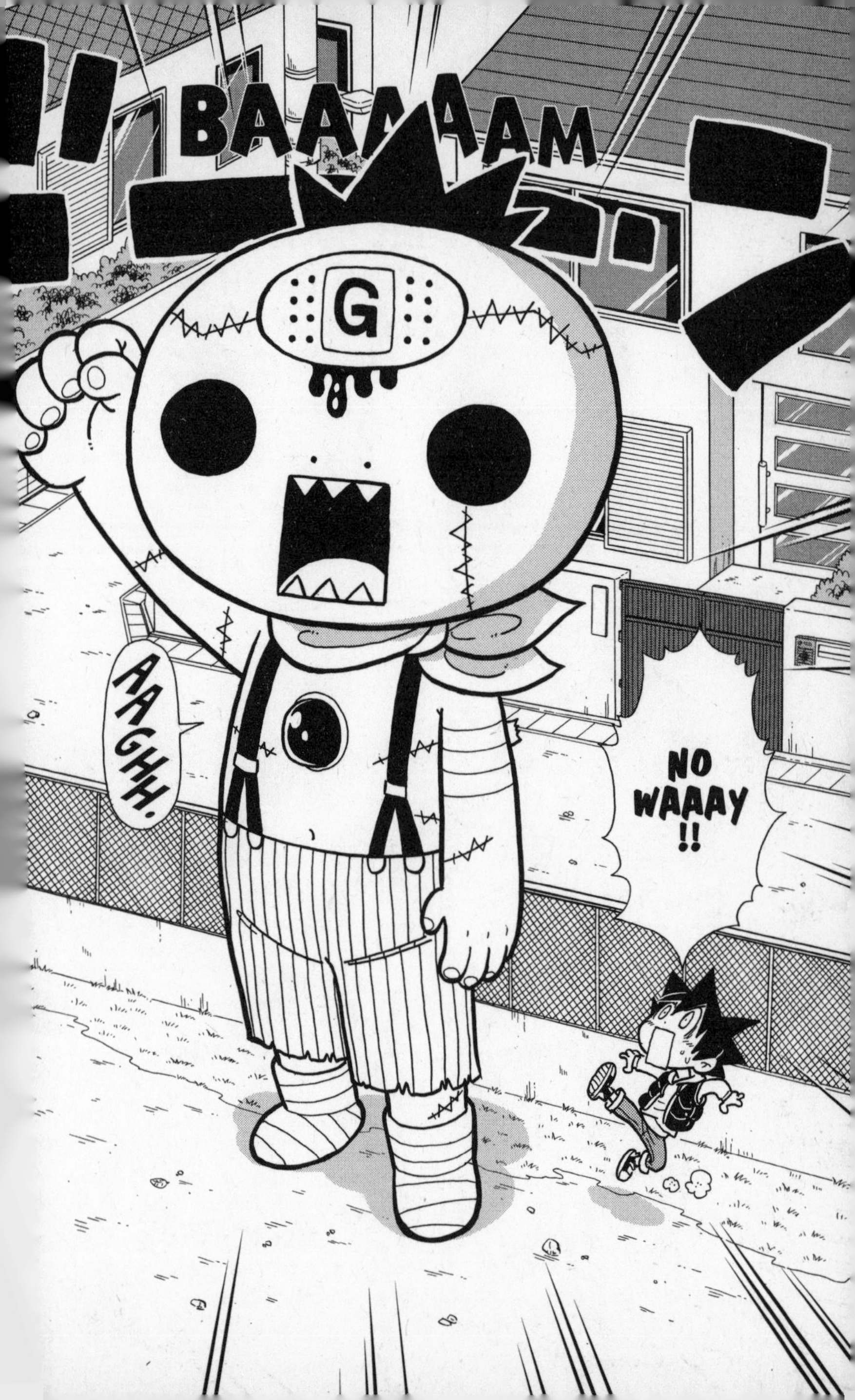
BAAAAAAM
AAGHH.
NO WAAAY!!

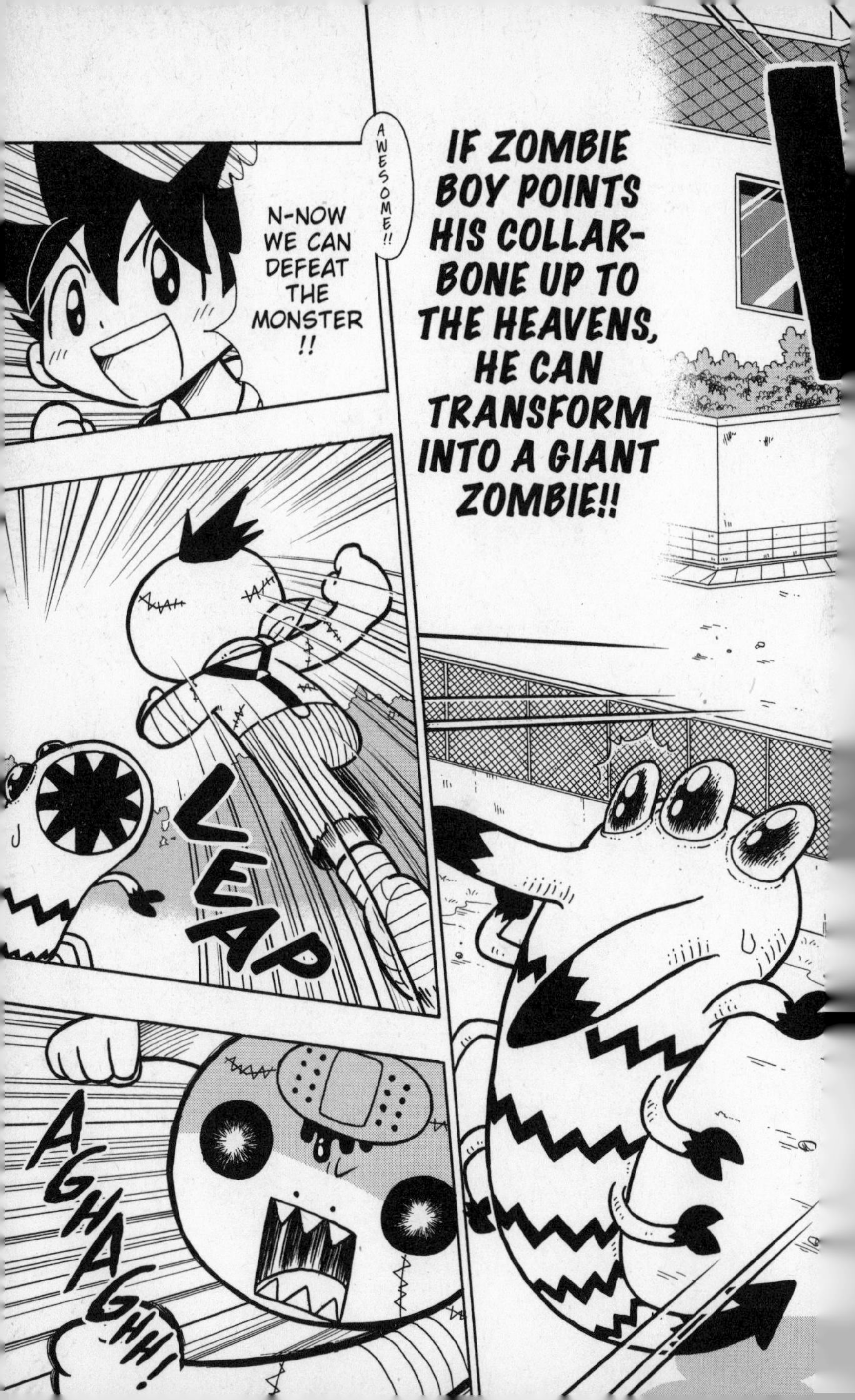
IF ZOMBIE BOY POINTS HIS COLLAR-BONE UP TO THE HEAVENS, HE CAN TRANSFORM INTO A GIANT ZOMBIE!!
AWESOME!!
N-NOW WE CAN DEFEAT THE MONSTER!!
LEAP
AGHAGHH!

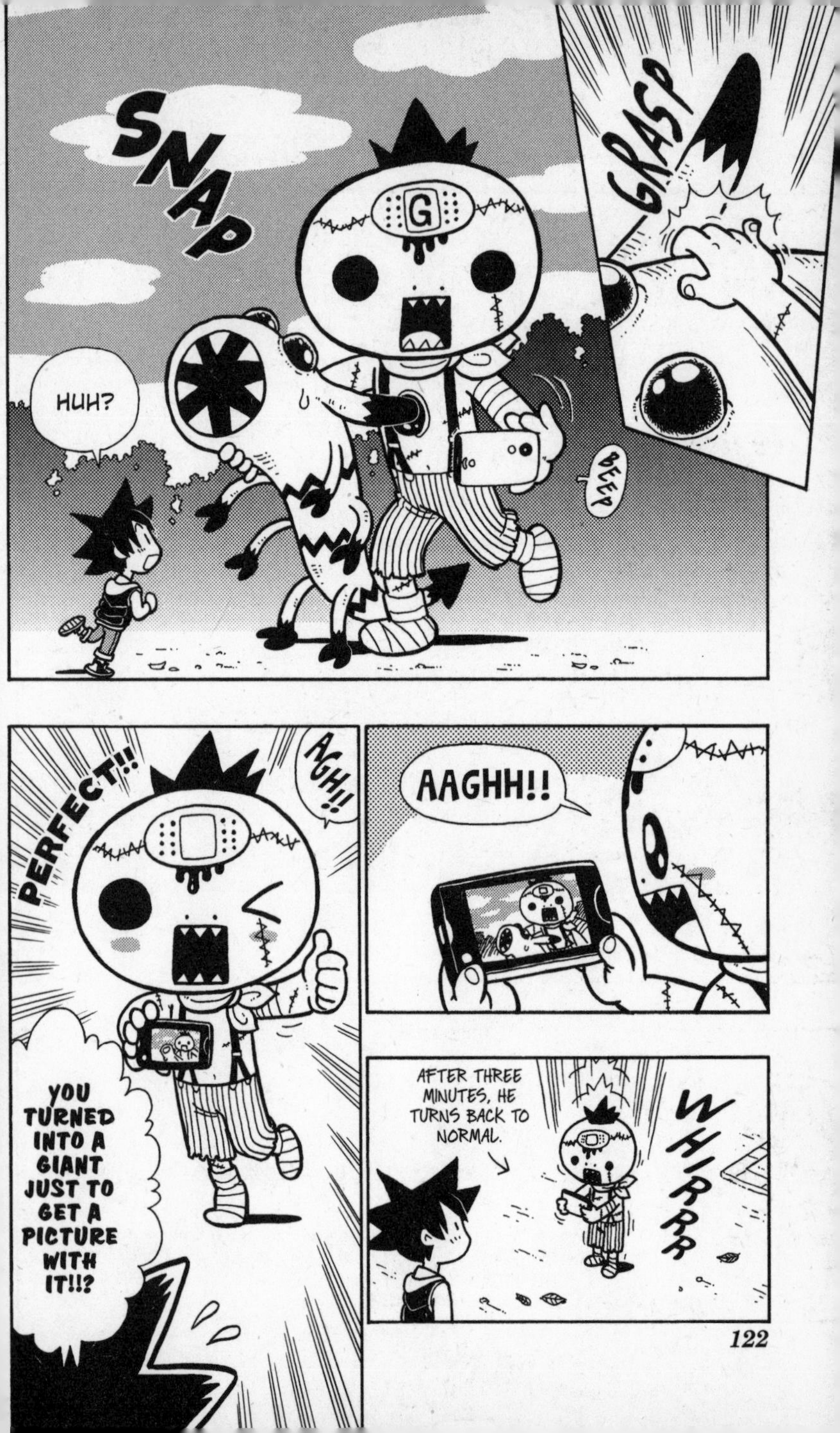
GRASP
SNAP
BEEP
HUH?
AAGHH!!
AFTER THREE MINUTES, HE TURNS BACK TO NORMAL.
WHIRRR
AGH!!
PERFECT!!
YOU TURNED INTO A GIANT JUST TO GET A PICTURE WITH IT!!?

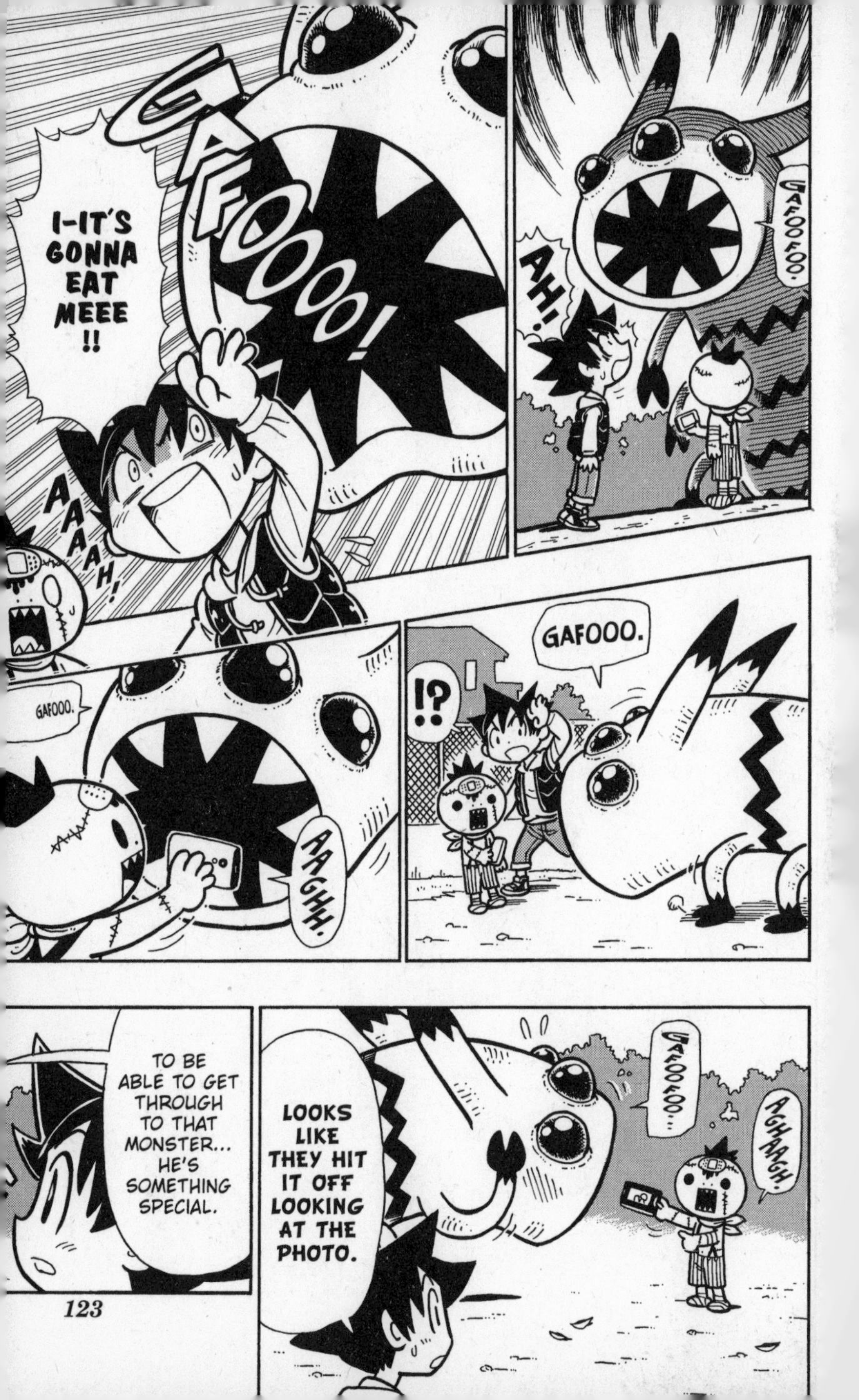
GAFOOFOO.
AH!
GAFOOOO!
I-IT'S GONNA EAT MEEE!!
AAAAH!
GAFOOO.
!?
GAFOOO.
AAGHH.
GAFOOFOO...
AGHAAGH.
LOOKS LIKE THEY HIT IT OFF LOOKING AT THE PHOTO.
TO BE ABLE TO GET THROUGH TO THAT MONSTER... HE'S SOMETHING SPECIAL.

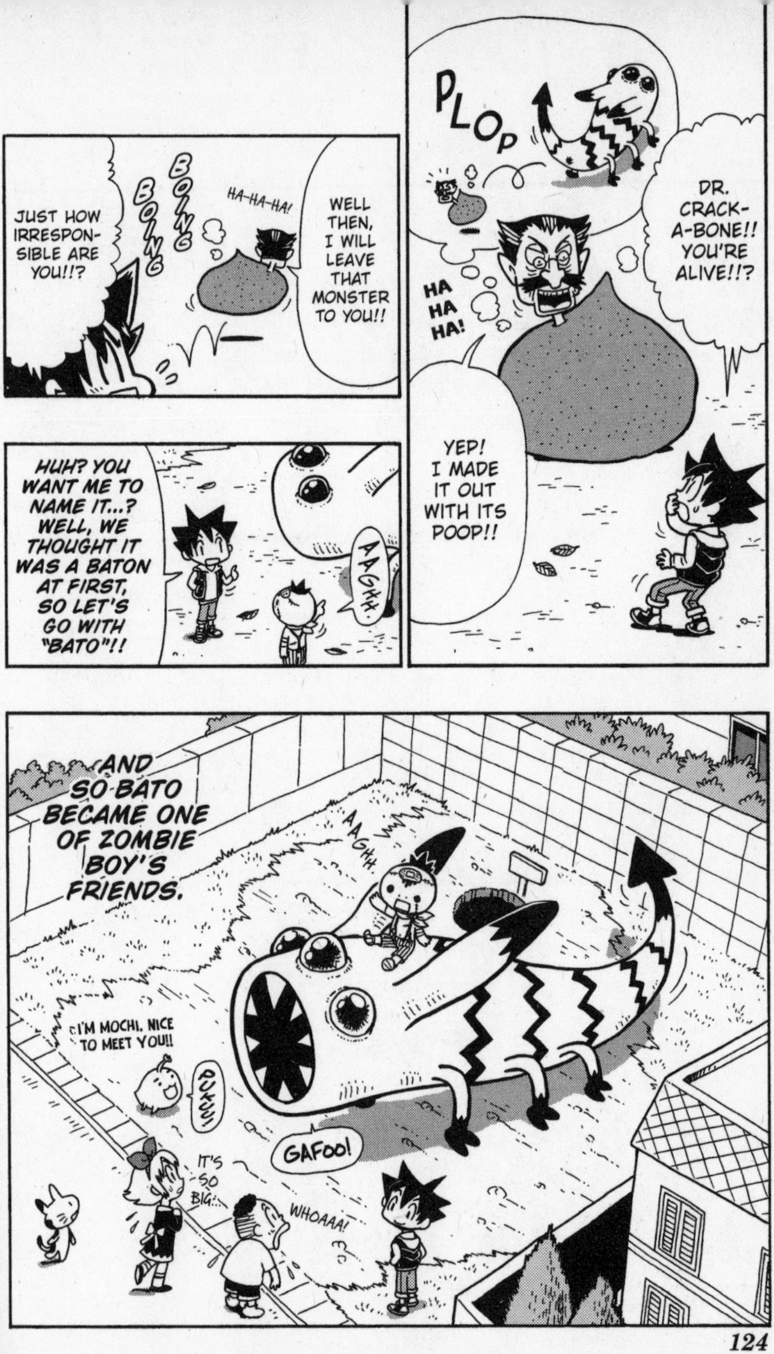
PLOP
DR. CRACK-A-BONE!! YOU'RE ALIVE!!?
HA HA HA!
YEP! I MADE IT OUT WITH ITS POOP!!
WELL THEN, I WILL LEAVE THAT MONSTER TO YOU!!
HA-HA-HA!
BOING BOING
JUST HOW IRRESPON-SIBLE ARE YOU!!?
AAGHH
HUH? YOU WANT ME TO NAME IT...? WELL, WE THOUGHT IT WAS A BATON AT FIRST, SO LET'S GO WITH "BATO"!!
AND SO BATO BECAME ONE OF ZOMBIE BOY'S FRIENDS.
AAGHH
I'M MOCHI. NICE TO MEET YOU!!
PUKUU!
GAFOO!
IT'S SO BIG...
WHOAAA!

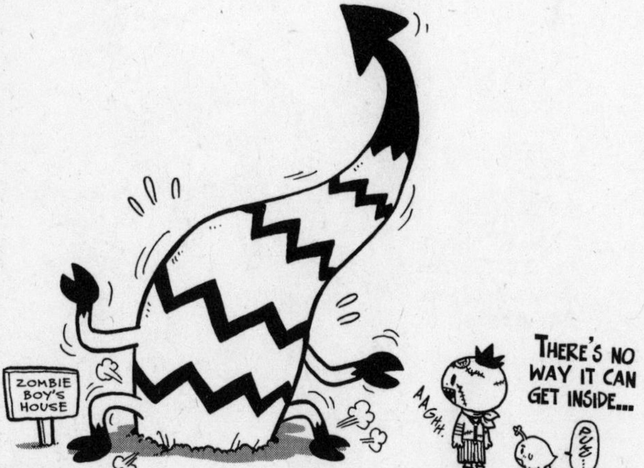
THERE'S NO WAY IT CAN GET INSIDE...
AAGHH.
ZOMBIE BOY'S HOUSE

WHAT'S THE NEXT STORY?

IT HAS SOMETHING TO DO WITH A VENDING MACHINE...

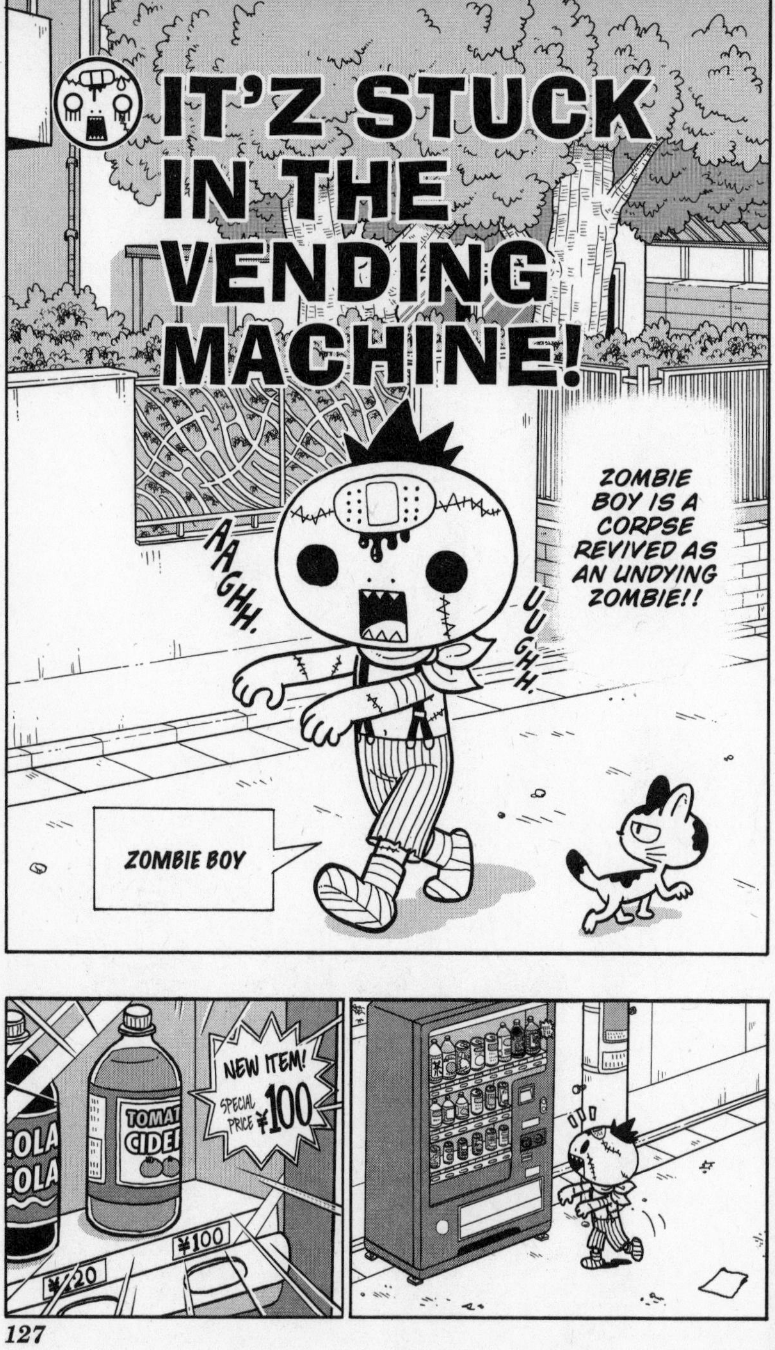
IT'Z STUCK IN THE VENDING MACHINE!
ZOMBIE BOY IS A CORPSE REVIVED AS AN UNDYING ZOMBIE!!
UUGHH.
AAGHH.
ZOMBIE BOY
NEW ITEM! SPECIAL PRICE ¥100
TOMAT CIDE
COLA COLA
¥100

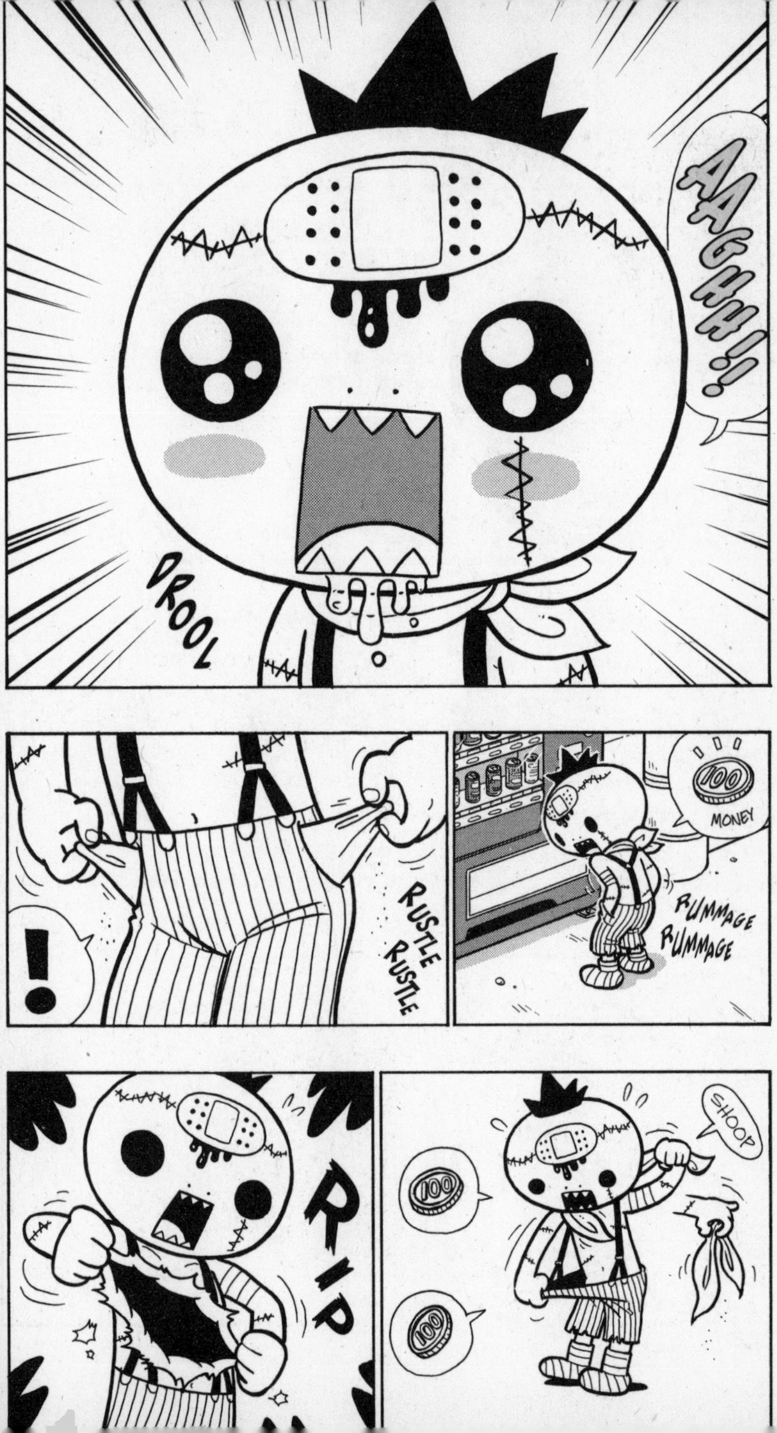
AAGHHH!!!
DROOL
100
MONEY
RUMMAGE
RUMMAGE
RUSTLE
RUSTLE
!
SHOOP
100
100
RIP

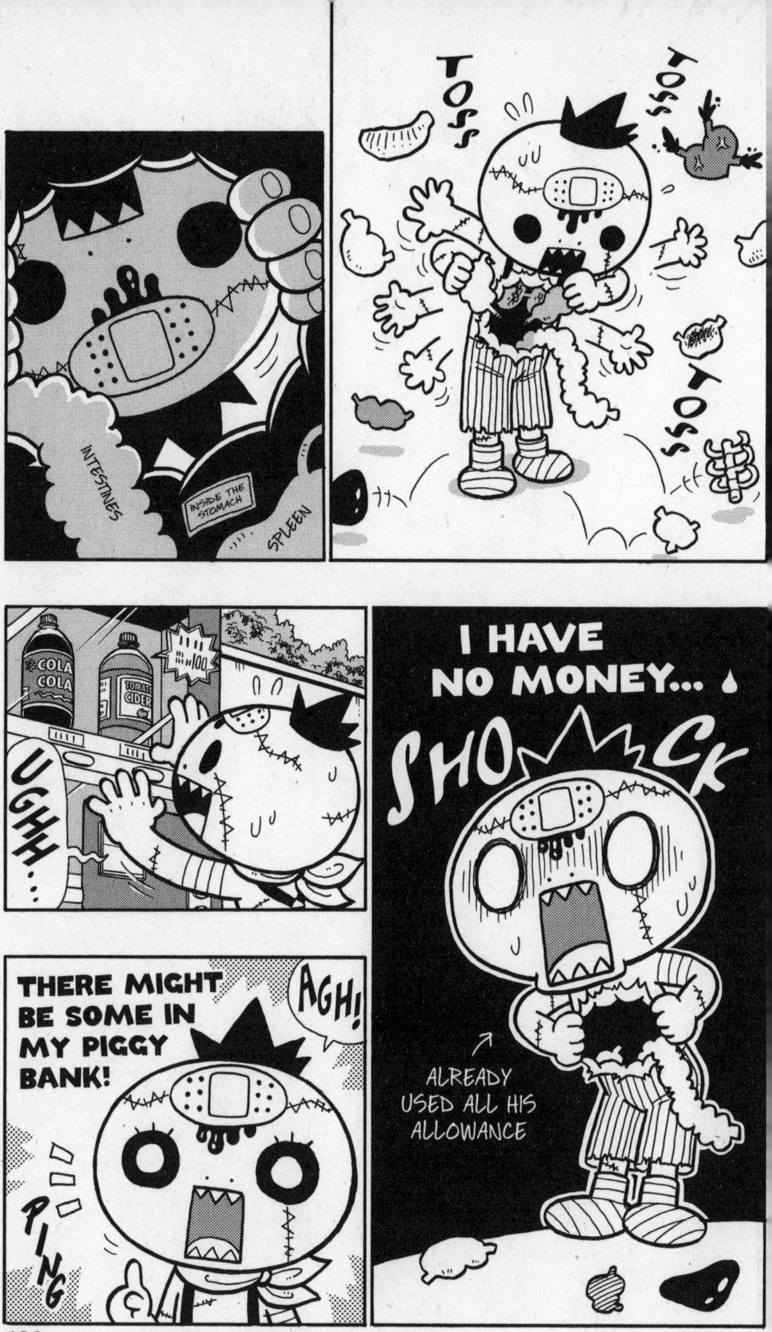
TOSS
TOSS
TOSS
INTESTINES
INSIDE THE STOMACH
SPLEEN
I HAVE NO MONEY...
SHOCK
ALREADY USED ALL HIS ALLOWANCE
COLA COLA
TOMATO CIDER
100
UGHH...
THERE MIGHT BE SOME IN MY PIGGY BANK!
AGH!
PING

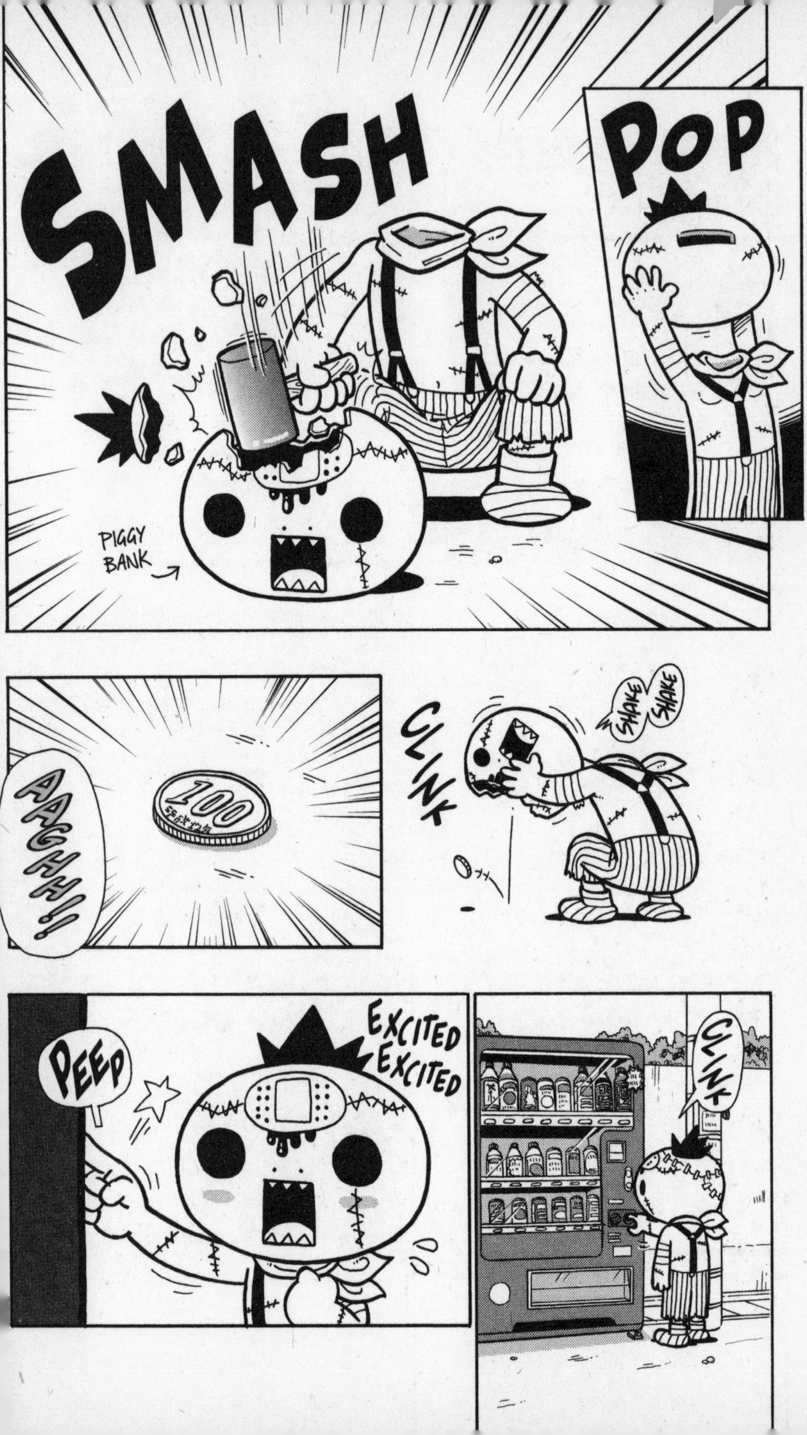
POP
SMASH
PIGGY BANK
SHAKE SHAKE
CLINK
AAGHH!!
100
CLINK
EXCITED EXCITED
PEEP

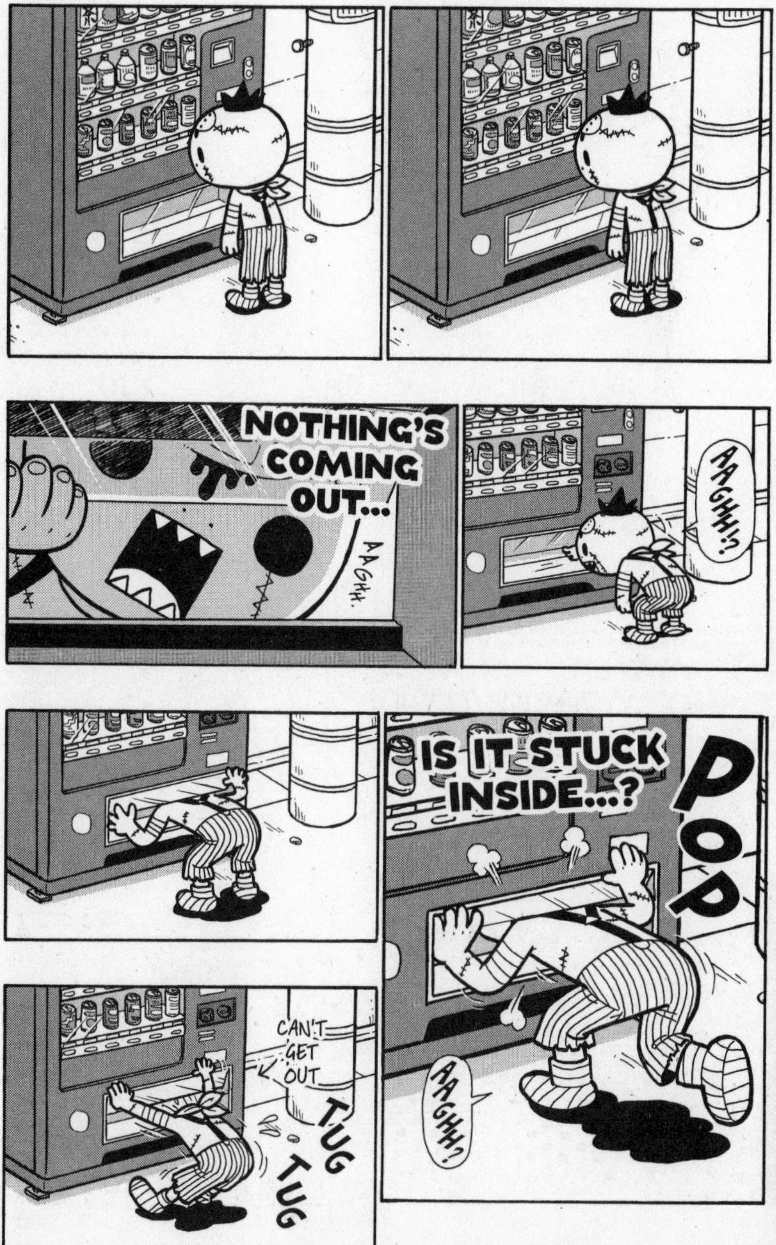
AAGHH!?
NOTHING'S COMING OUT...
AAGHH.
IS IT STUCK INSIDE...?
POP
AAGHH?
CAN'T GET OUT
TUG TUG

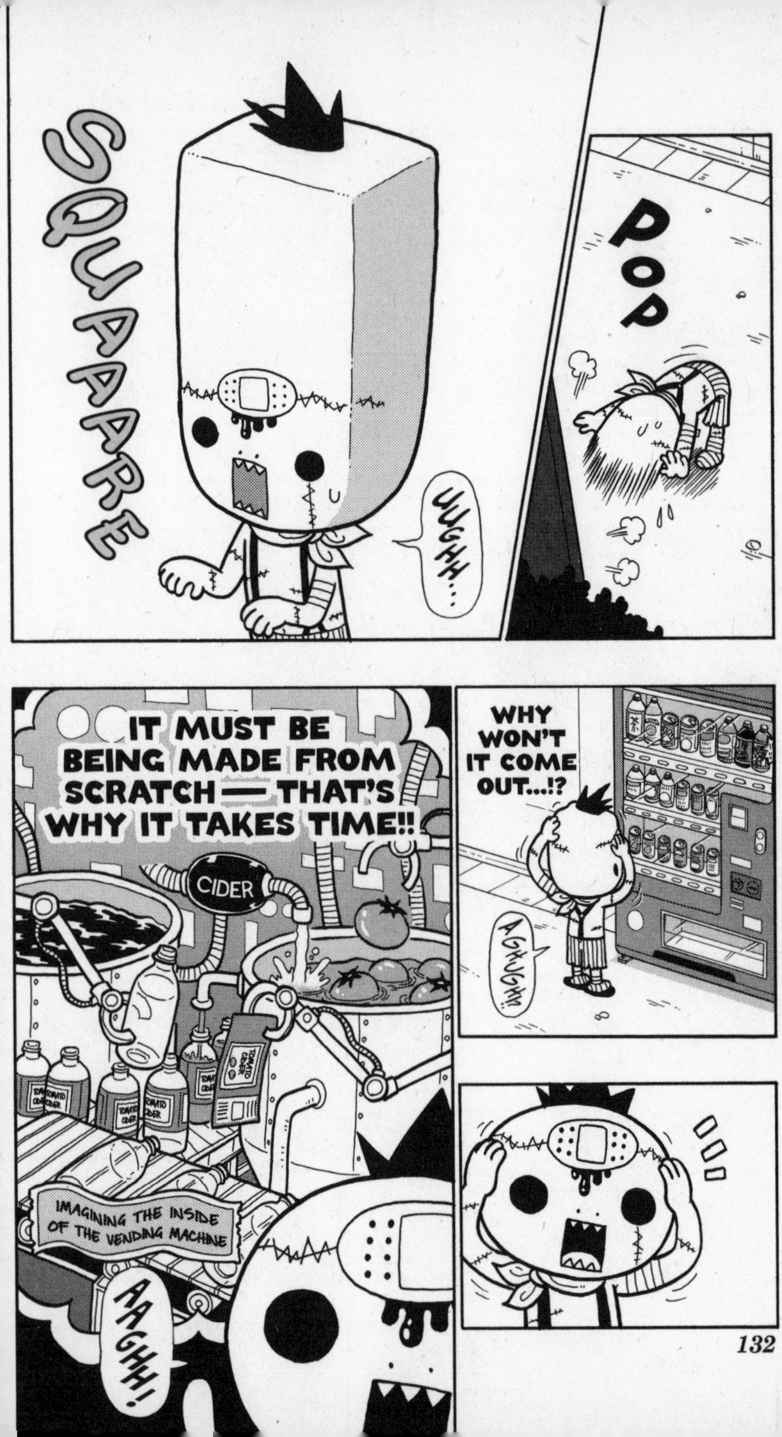
POP
SQUAAARE
UUGHH...
WHY WON'T IT COME OUT...!?
AGHUGHH!!
IT MUST BE BEING MADE FROM SCRATCH — THAT'S WHY IT TAKES TIME!!
CIDER
TOMATO CIDER
IMAGINING THE INSIDE OF THE VENDING MACHINE
AAGHH!

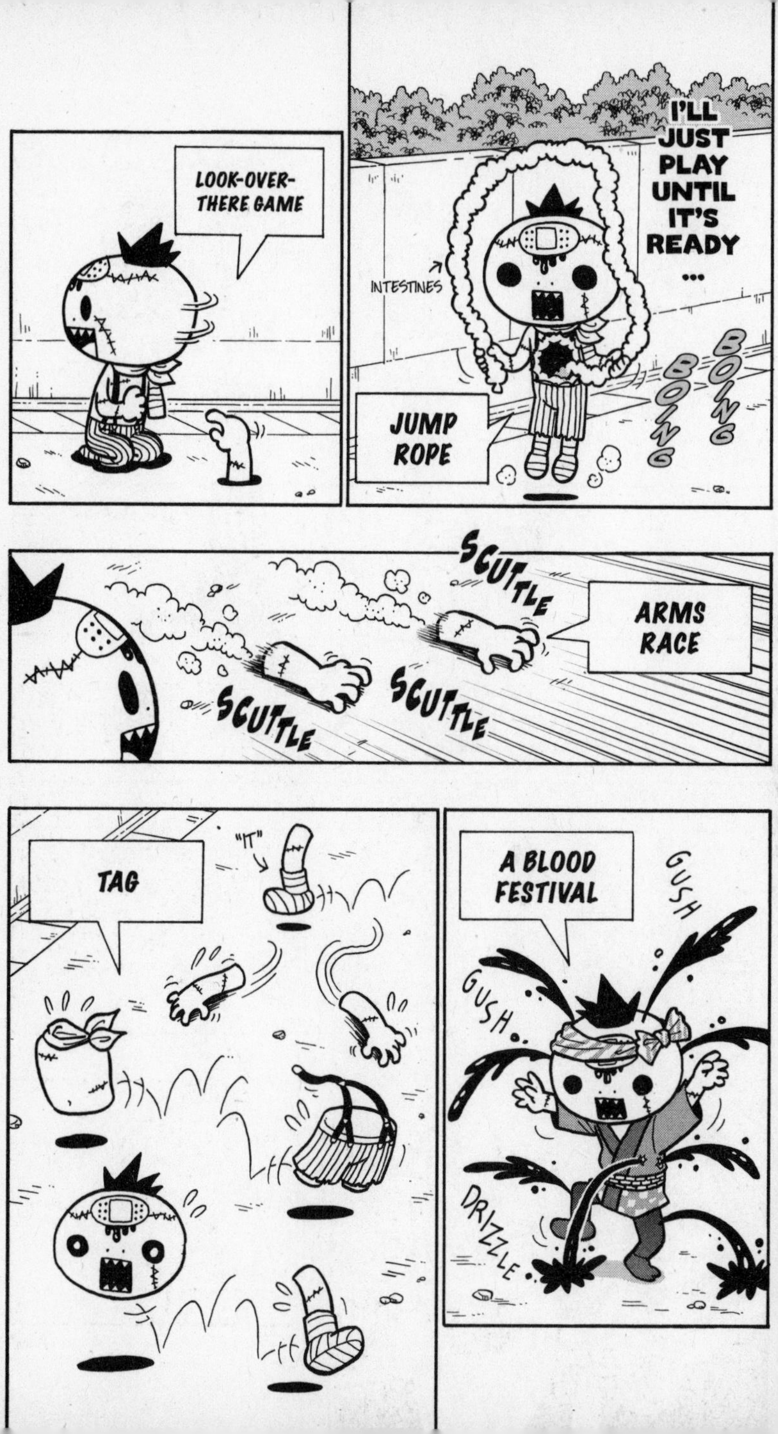
I'LL JUST PLAY UNTIL IT'S READY ...
BOING
BOING
INTESTINES
JUMP ROPE
LOOK-OVER-THERE GAME
SCUTTLE
ARMS RACE
SCUTTLE
SCUTTLE
A BLOOD FESTIVAL
GUSH
GUSH
DRIZZLE
"IT"
TAG

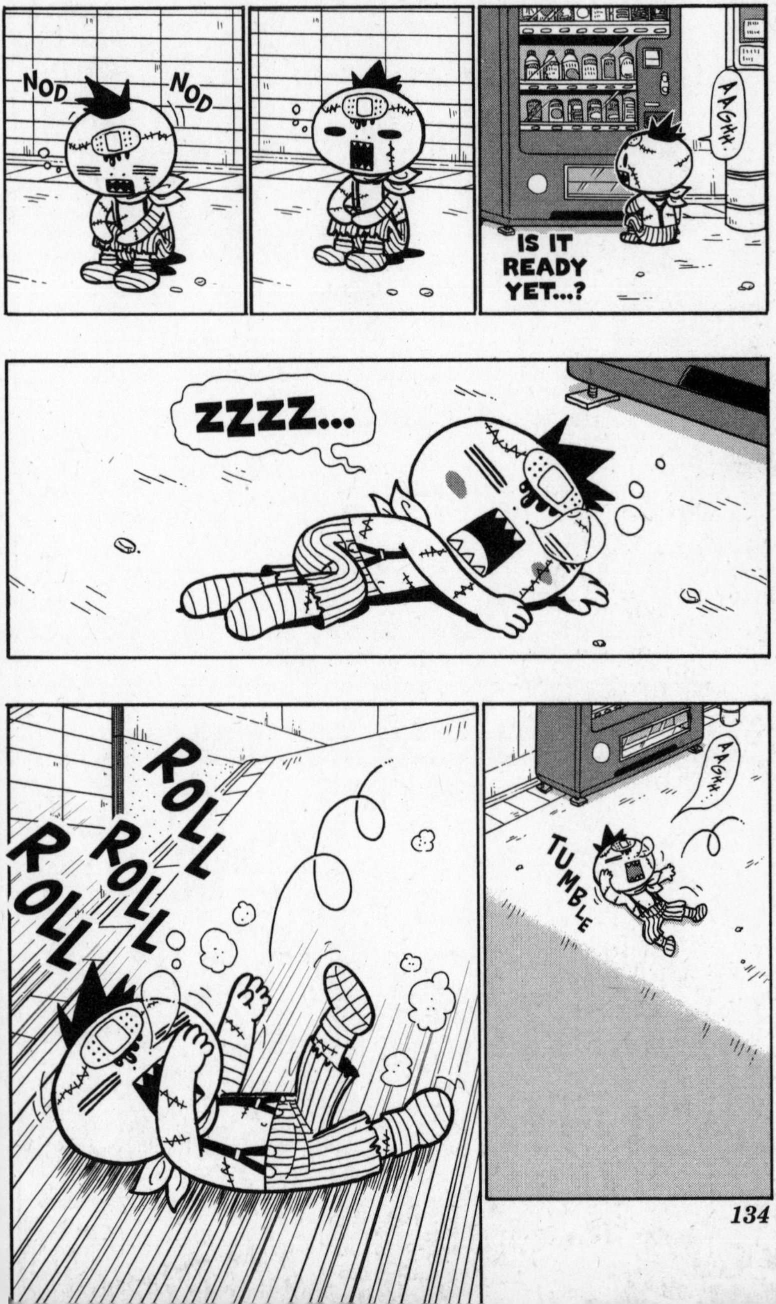
AAGHH.
IS IT READY YET...?
NOD
NOD
ZZZZ...
AAGHH...
TUMBLE
ROLL
ROLL
ROLL

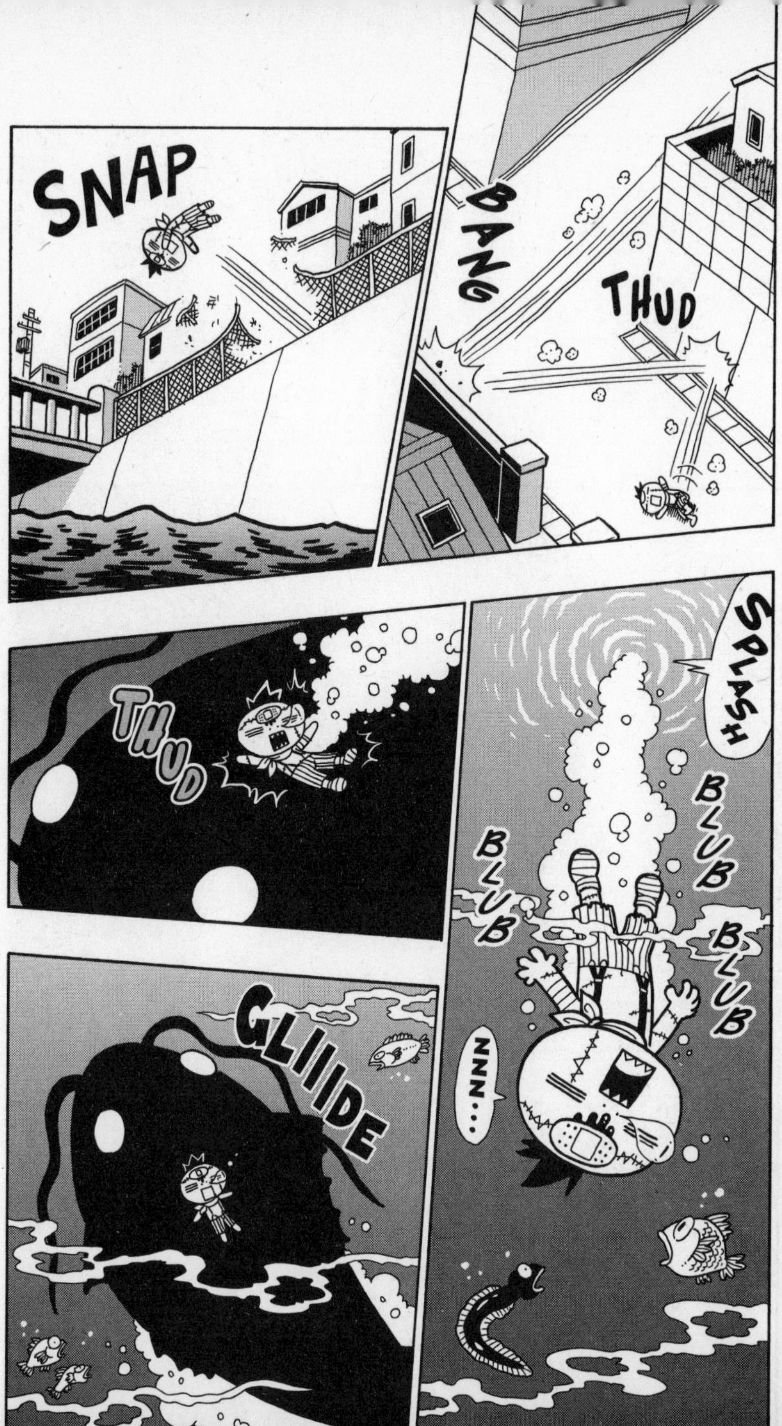
BANG
THUD
SNAP
SPLASH
BLUB
BLUB
BLUB
NNN...
THUD
GLIIIDE

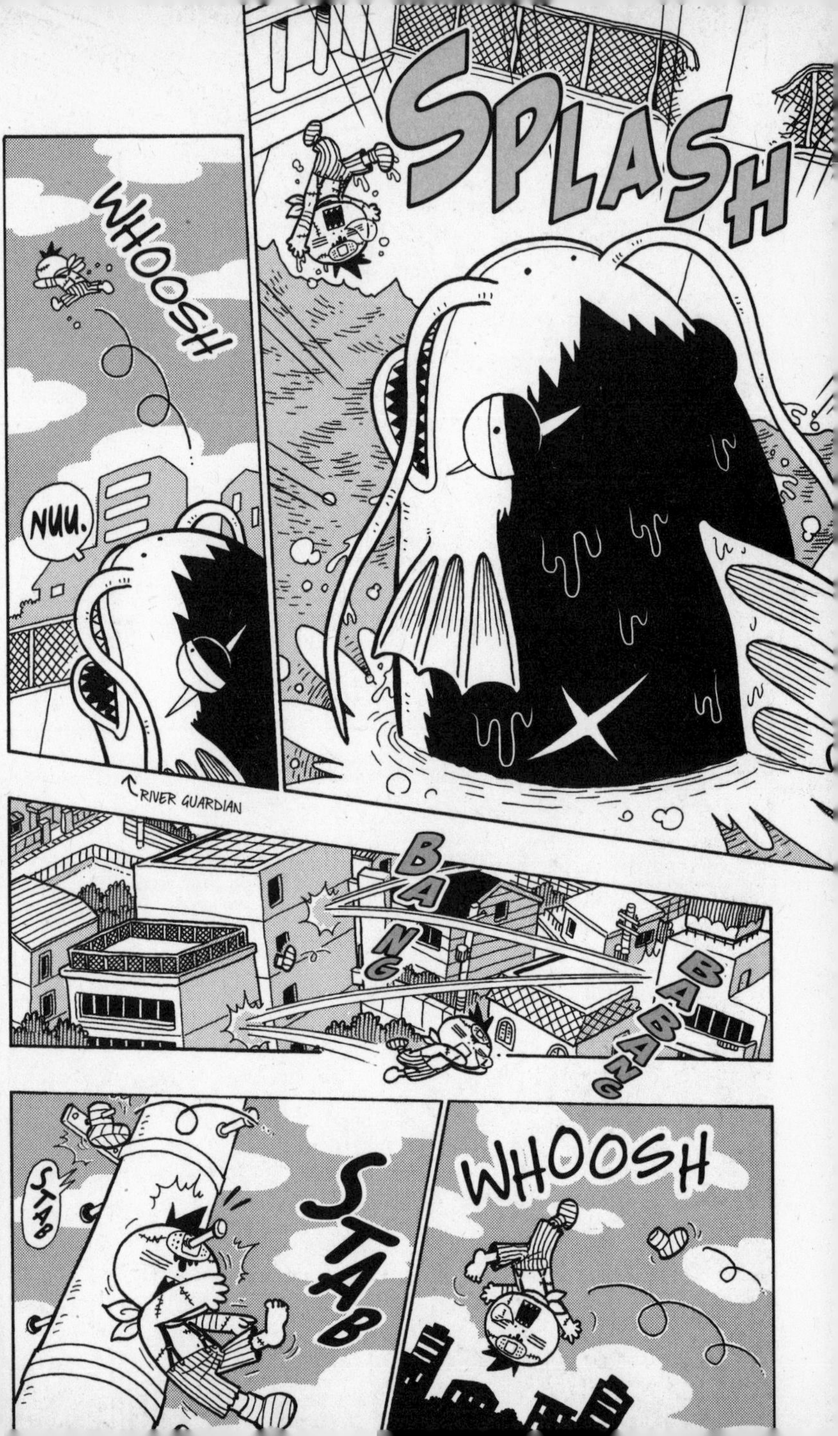
SPLASH
WHOOSH
NUU.
RIVER GUARDIAN
BANG
BABANG
WHOOSH
STAB
STAB

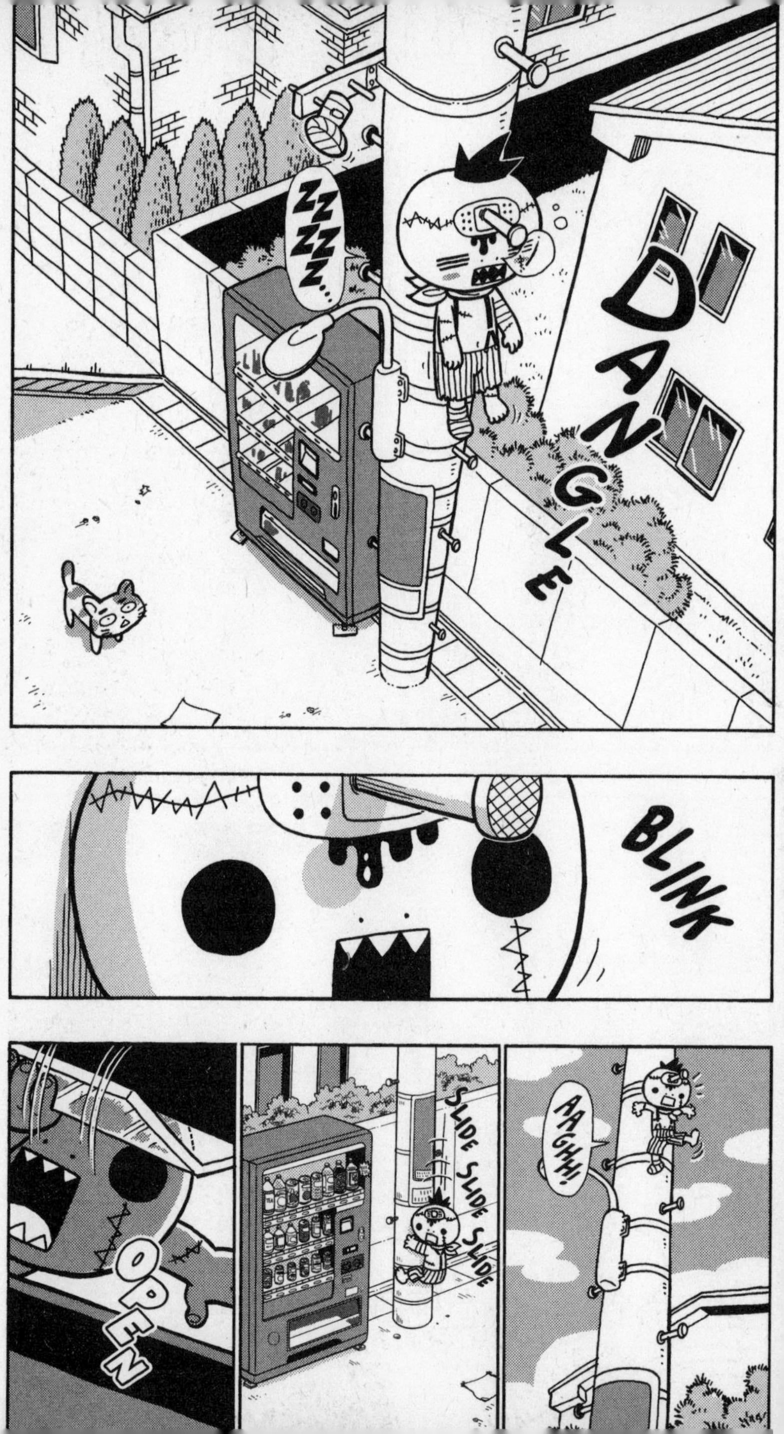
DANGLE
ZZZZZ...
BLINK
AAGHH!
SLIDE SLIDE SLIDE
OPEN

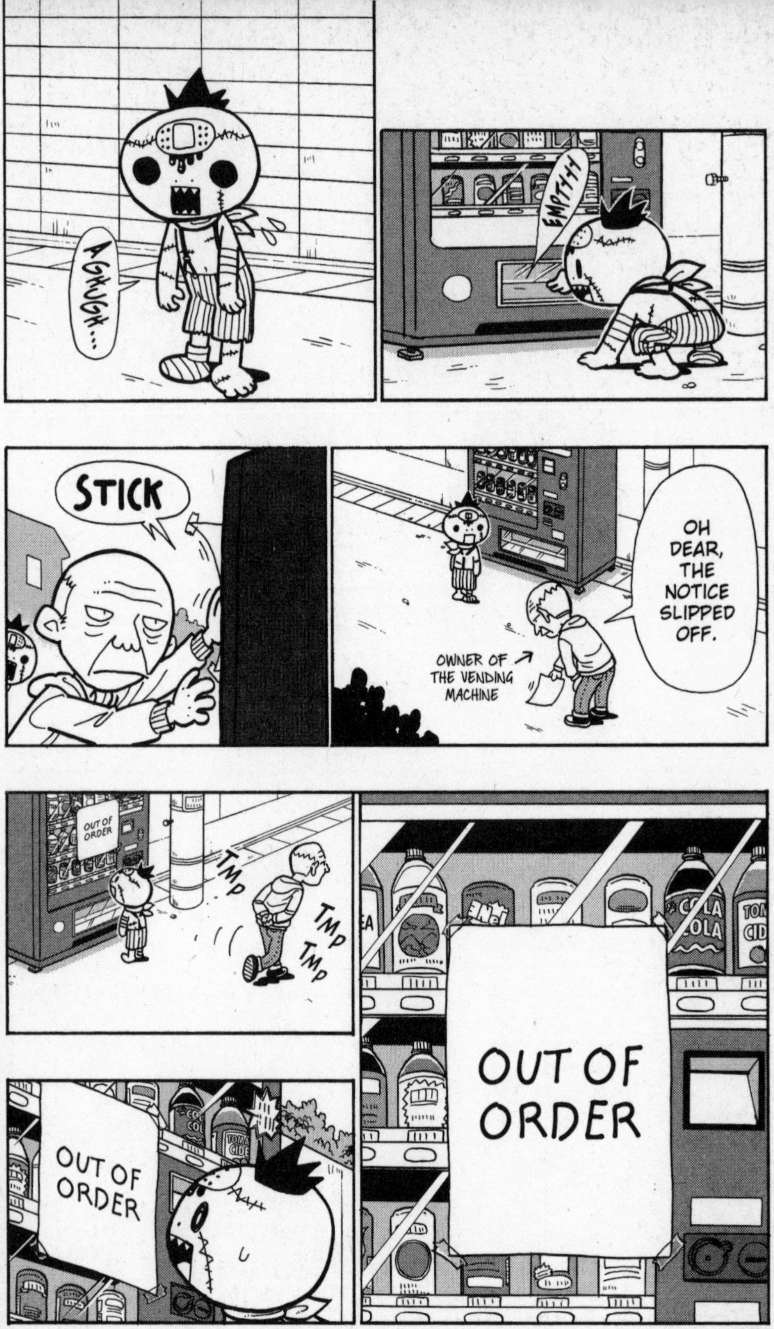
EMPTYYY
AGHUGH...
OH DEAR, THE NOTICE SLIPPED OFF.
OWNER OF THE VENDING MACHINE
STICK
COLA COLA
OUT OF ORDER
OUT OF ORDER
TMP
TMP
TMP
OUT OF ORDER

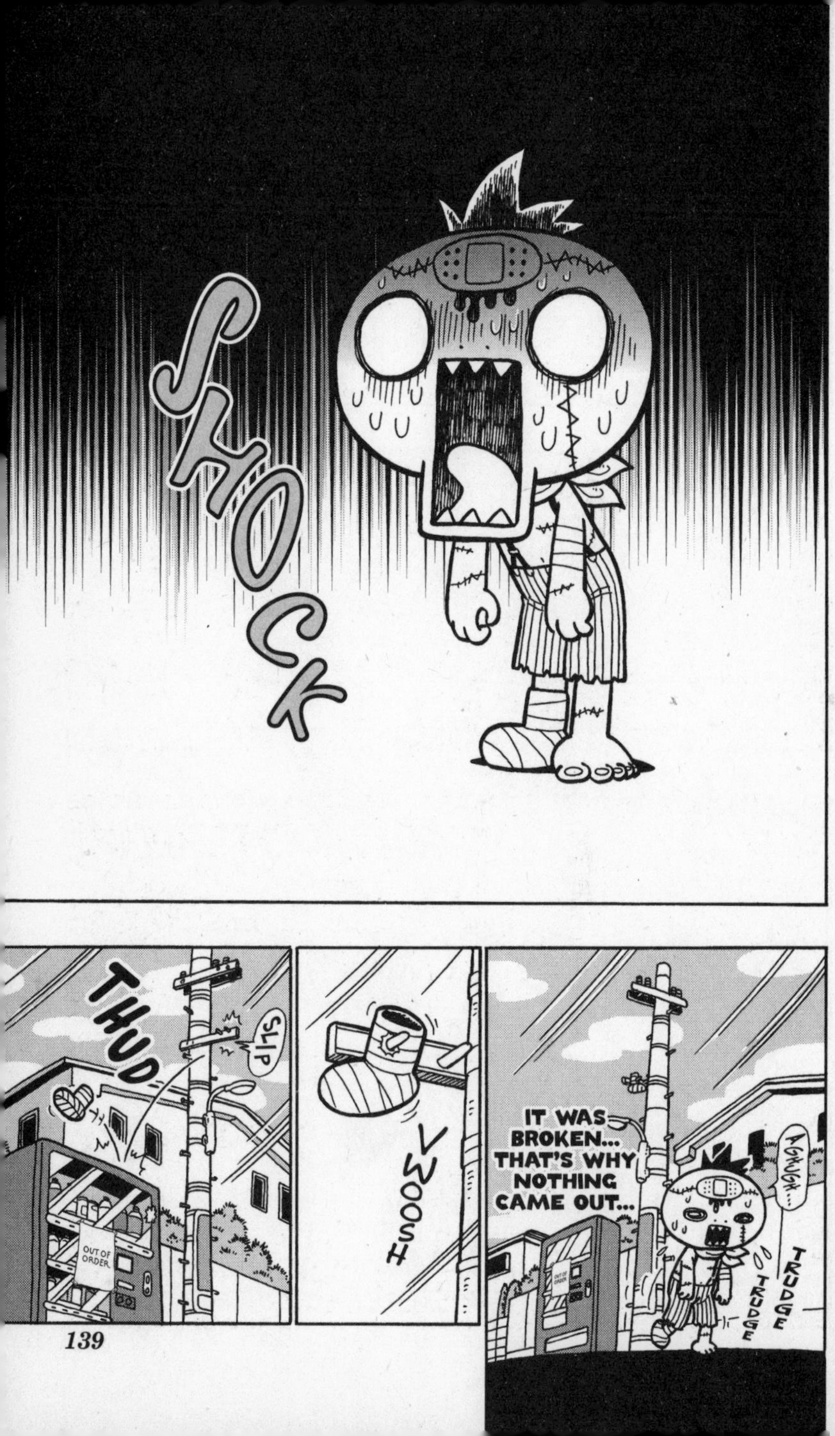
SHOCK
IT WAS BROKEN... THAT'S WHY NOTHING CAME OUT...
AGHUGH...
TRUDGE
TRUDGE
VWOOSH
THUD
SLIP
OUT OF ORDER

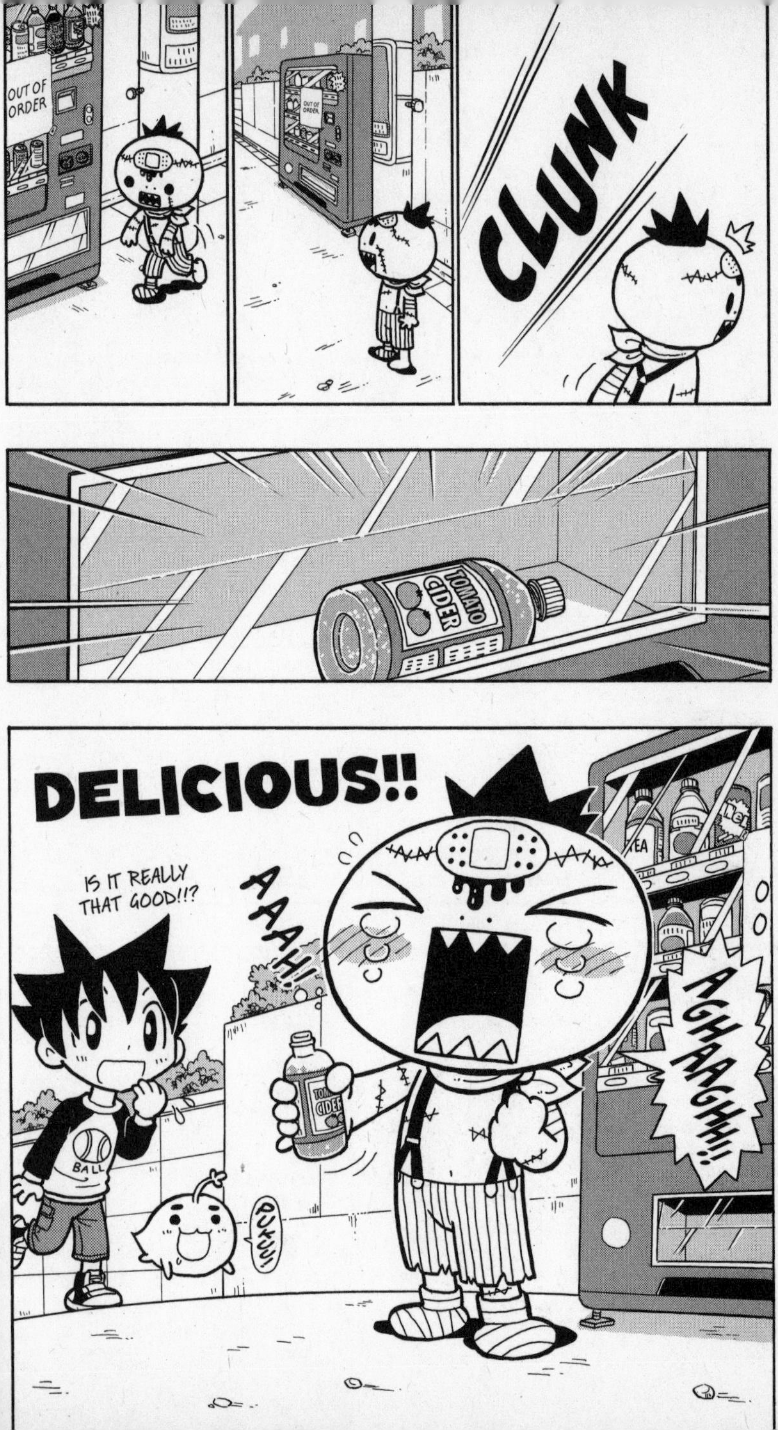
CLUNK
OUT OF ORDER
OUT OF ORDER
TOMATO CIDER
AGHAAGHH!!!
DELICIOUS!!
AAAH!!
IS IT REALLY THAT GOOD!!?
TOMATO CIDER
PUKUU!

THE RIVER GUARDIAN HAS BEEN LIVING IN SHIKABANE RIVER FOR OVER A HUNDRED YEARS.

NUU.

THE NEXT CHAPTER IS A STORY ABOUT CLEANING!!

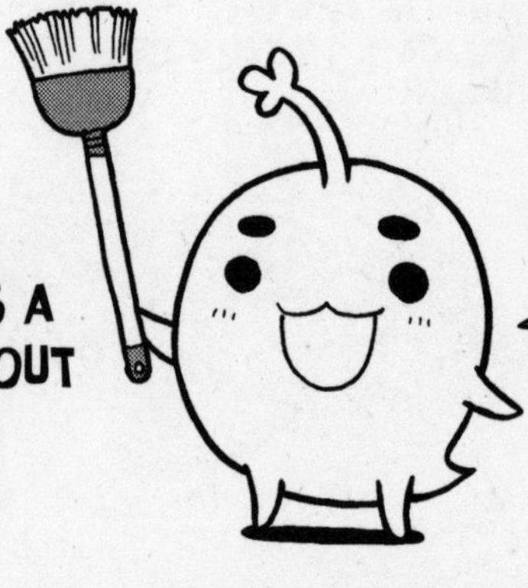
PUKUKU!

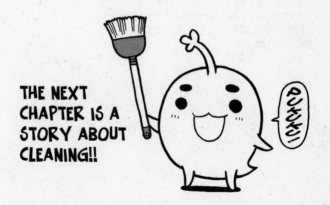

CLEANING IZ A BIG ADVENTURE!

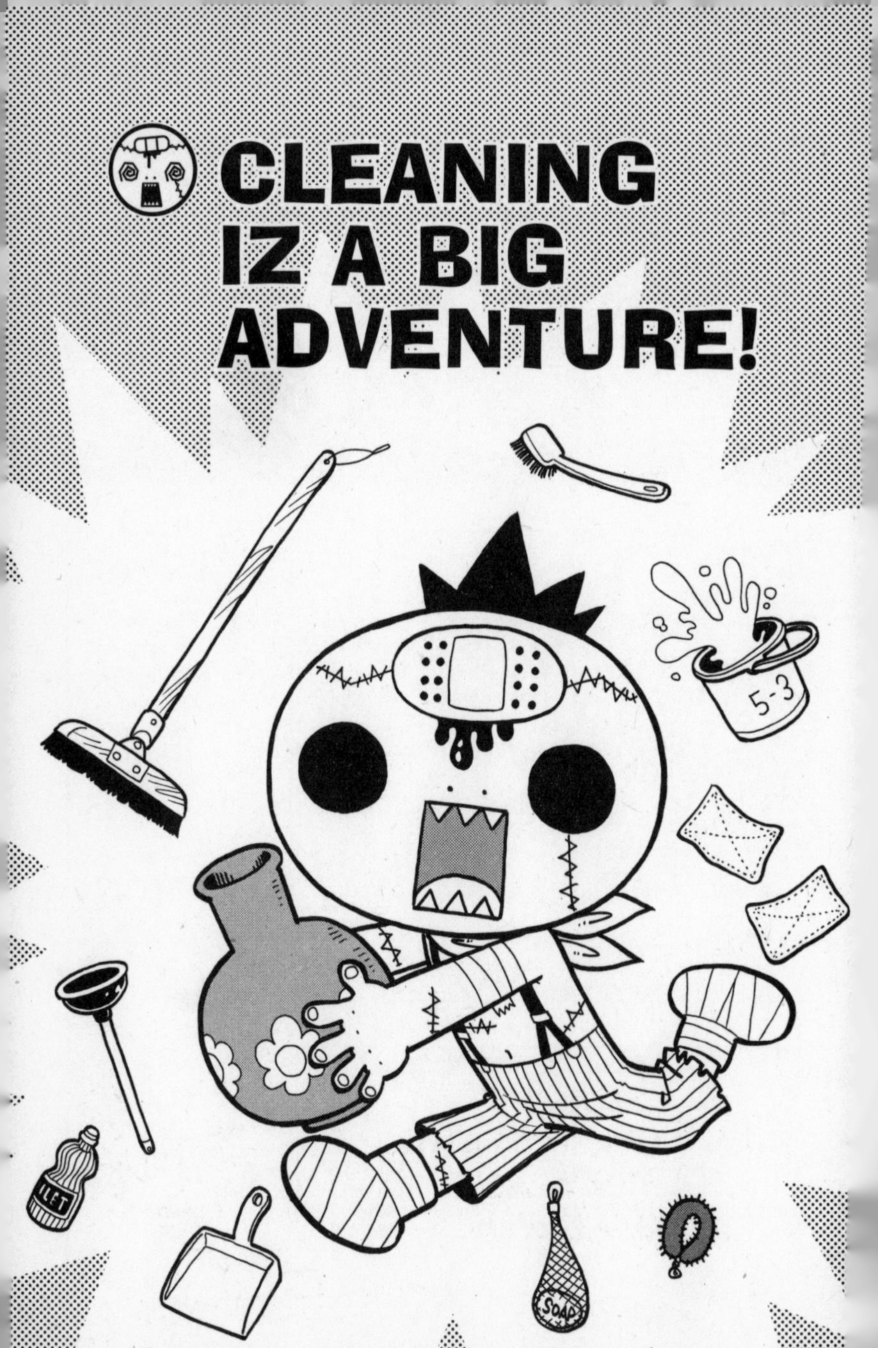
5-3
SOAP

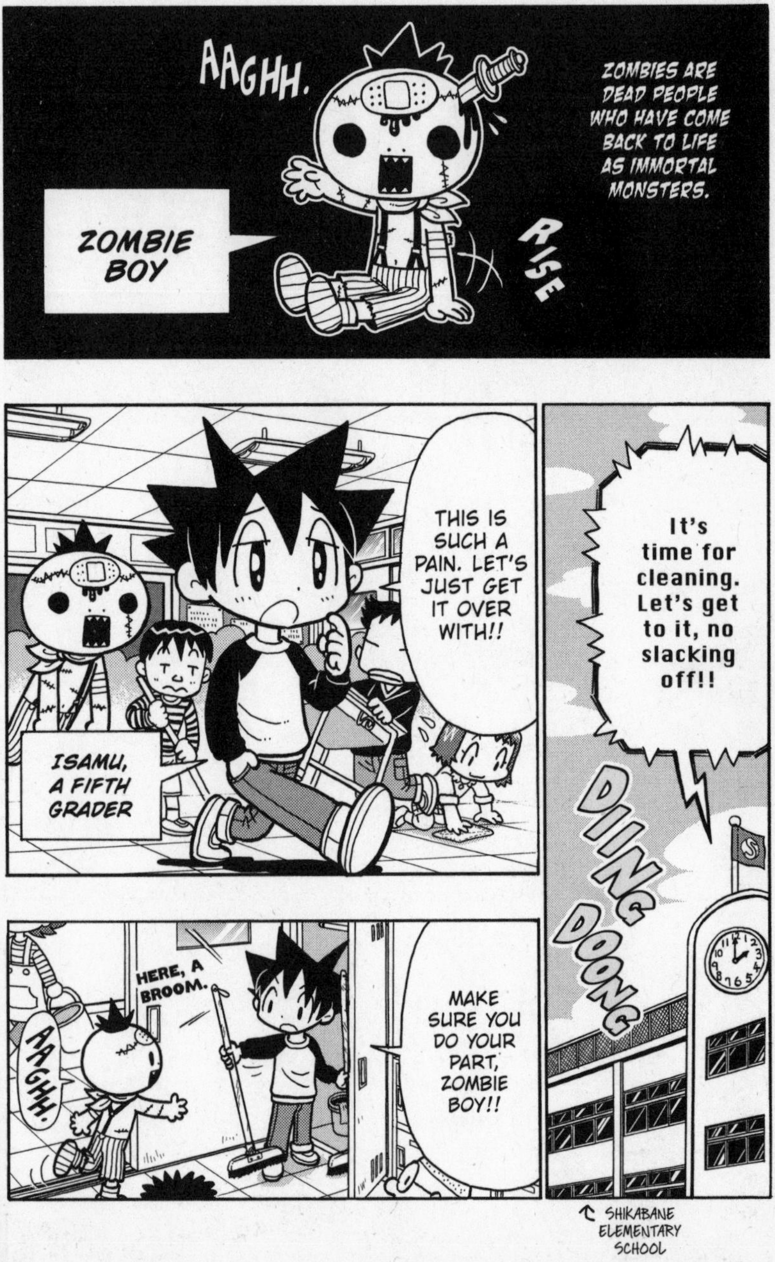
ZOMBIES ARE DEAD PEOPLE WHO HAVE COME BACK TO LIFE AS IMMORTAL MONSTERS.
AAGHH.
ZOMBIE BOY
RISE
It's time for cleaning. Let's get to it, no slacking off!!
DIING DOONG
SHIKABANE ELEMENTARY SCHOOL
THIS IS SUCH A PAIN. LET'S JUST GET IT OVER WITH!!
ISAMU, A FIFTH GRADER
MAKE SURE YOU DO YOUR PART, ZOMBIE BOY!!
HERE, A BROOM.
AAGHH.

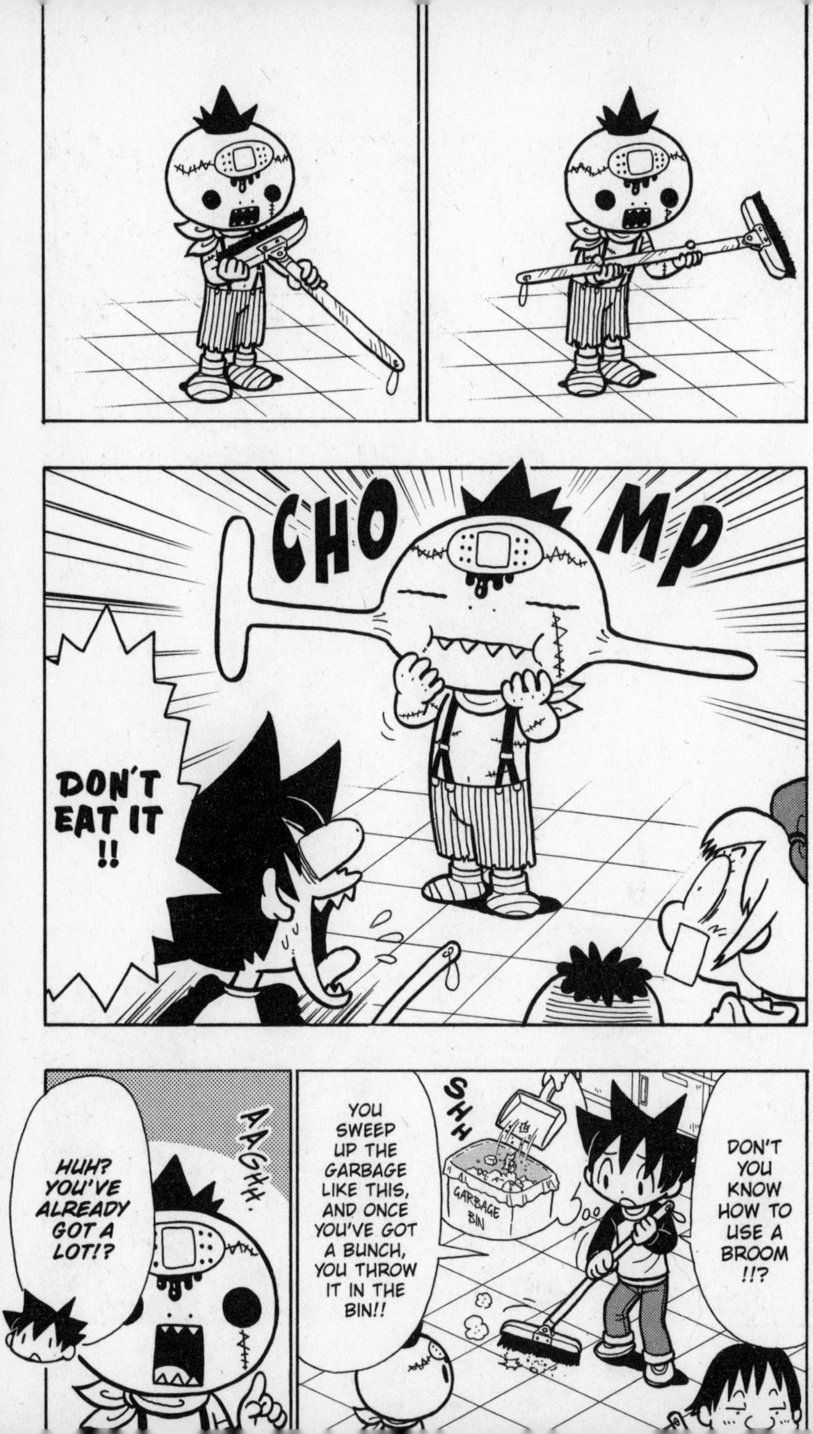
CHOMP
DON'T EAT IT!!
DON'T YOU KNOW HOW TO USE A BROOM!!?
SHH
GARBAGE BIN
YOU SWEEP UP THE GARBAGE LIKE THIS, AND ONCE YOU'VE GOT A BUNCH, YOU THROW IT IN THE BIN!!
AAGHH.
HUH? YOU'VE ALREADY GOT A LOT!?

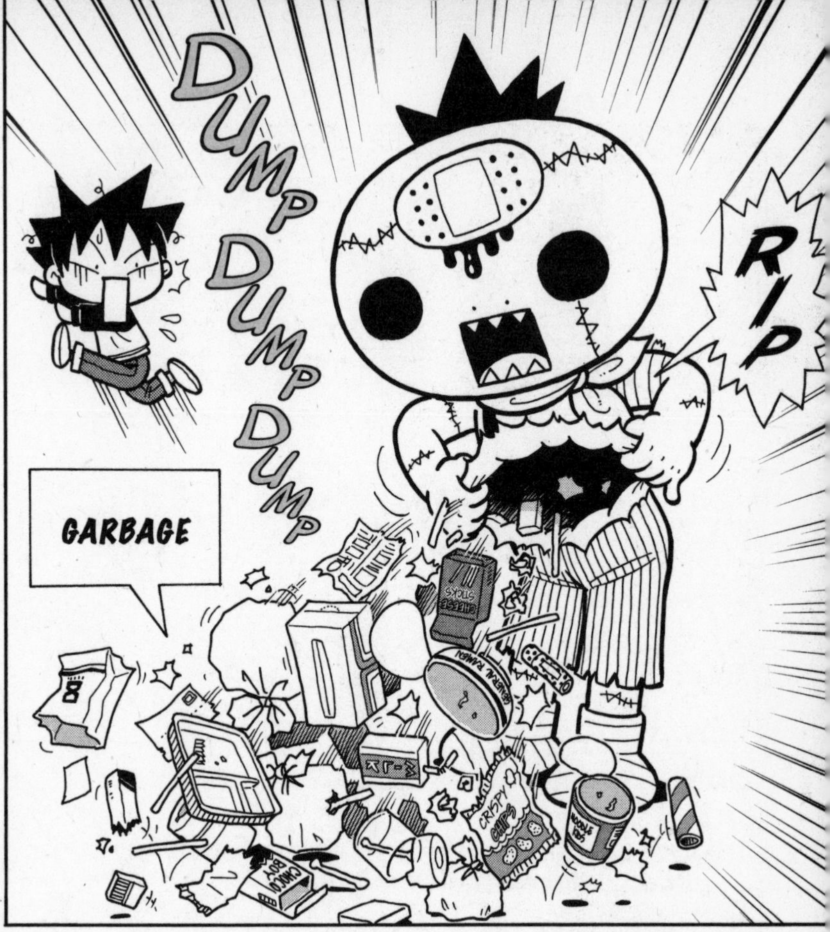
RIP
DUMP DUMP DUMP DUMP
GARBAGE
CHEESE STICKS
GENERAL RAMEN
NOODLE KIDS
CRISPY CHIPS
CHOCO BOY

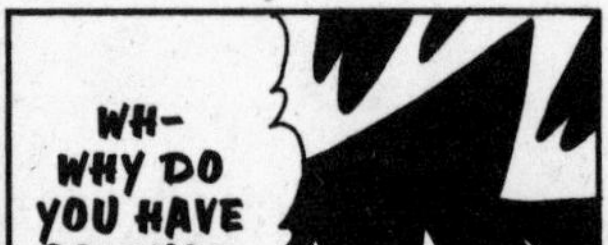
WH-WHY DO YOU HAVE SO MUCH GARBAGE IN YOUR STOMACH !!?

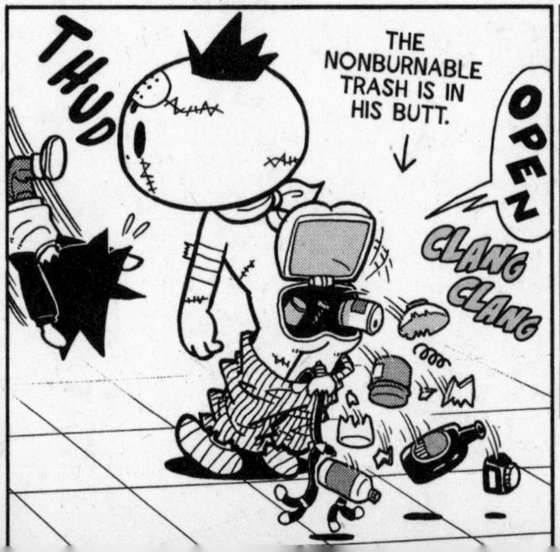
OPEN
THE NONBURNABLE TRASH IS IN HIS BUTT.
THUD
CLANG CLANG

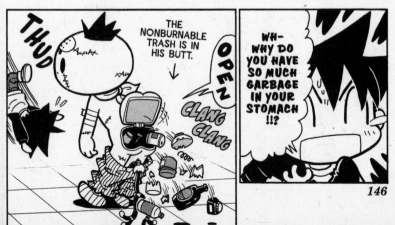

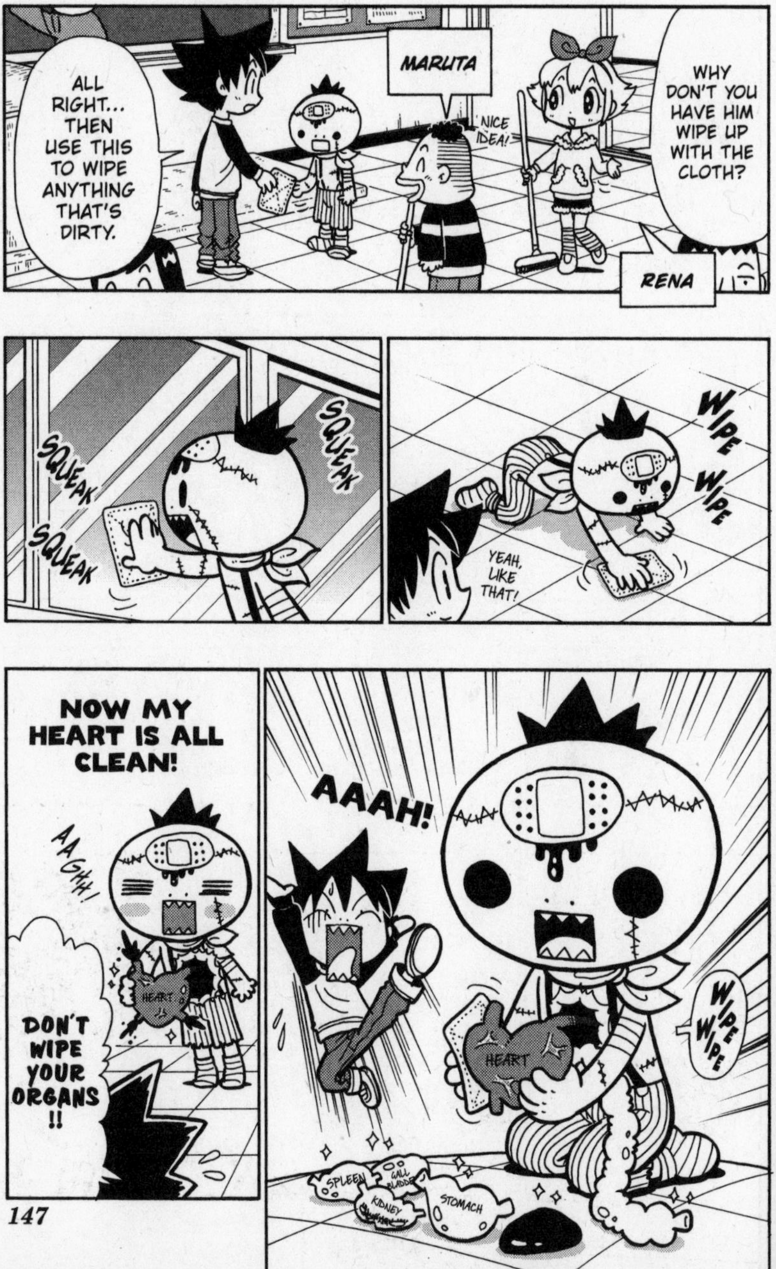
WHY DON'T YOU HAVE HIM WIPE UP WITH THE CLOTH?
RENA
MARUTA
NICE IDEA!
ALL RIGHT... THEN USE THIS TO WIPE ANYTHING THAT'S DIRTY.
WIPE WIPE
YEAH, LIKE THAT!
SQUEAK
SQUEAK
SQUEAK
AAAH!
WIPE WIPE
HEART
SPLEEN
GALL BLADDER
KIDNEY
STOMACH
NOW MY HEART IS ALL CLEAN!
AAGHH!
HEART
DON'T WIPE YOUR ORGANS!!

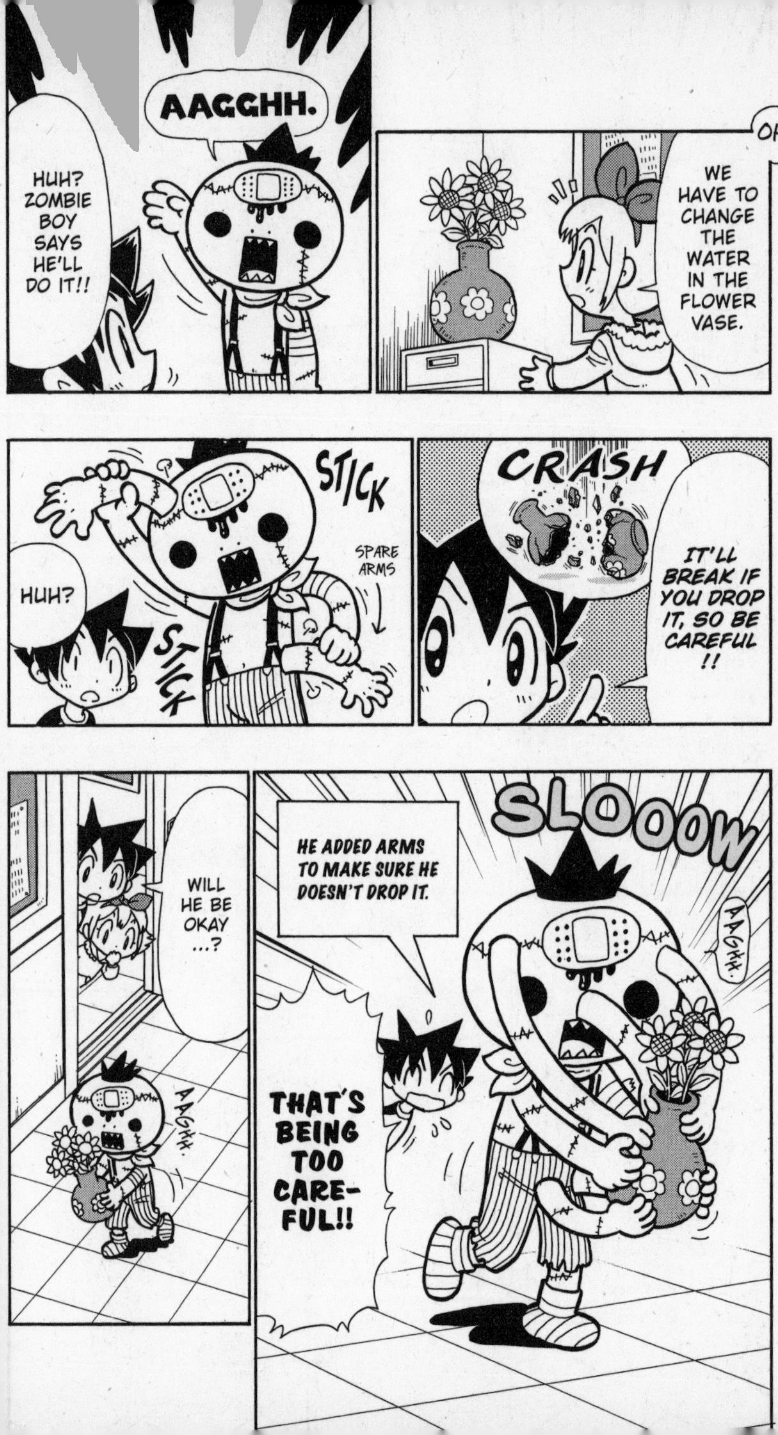
OH!
WE HAVE TO CHANGE THE WATER IN THE FLOWER VASE.
AAGGHH.
HUH? ZOMBIE BOY SAYS HE'LL DO IT!!
CRASH
IT'LL BREAK IF YOU DROP IT, SO BE CAREFUL!!
STICK
SPARE ARMS
STICK
HUH?
SLOOOW
HE ADDED ARMS TO MAKE SURE HE DOESN'T DROP IT.
AAGHH.
THAT'S BEING TOO CARE-FUL!!
WILL HE BE OKAY...?
AAGHH.

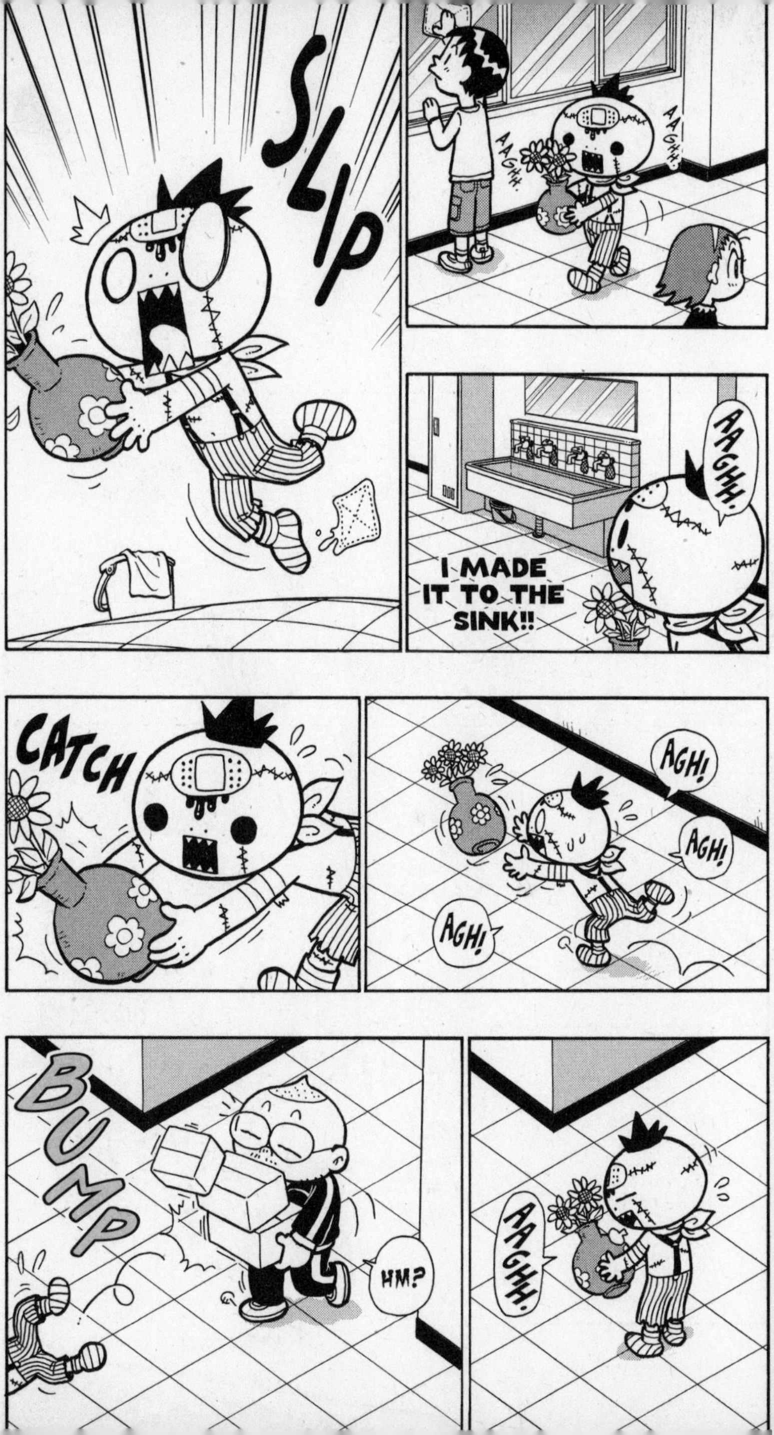
AAGHH.
AAGHH.
AAGHH.
I MADE IT TO THE SINK!!
SLIP
AGH!
AGH!
AGH!
CATCH
AAGHH.
BUMP
HM?

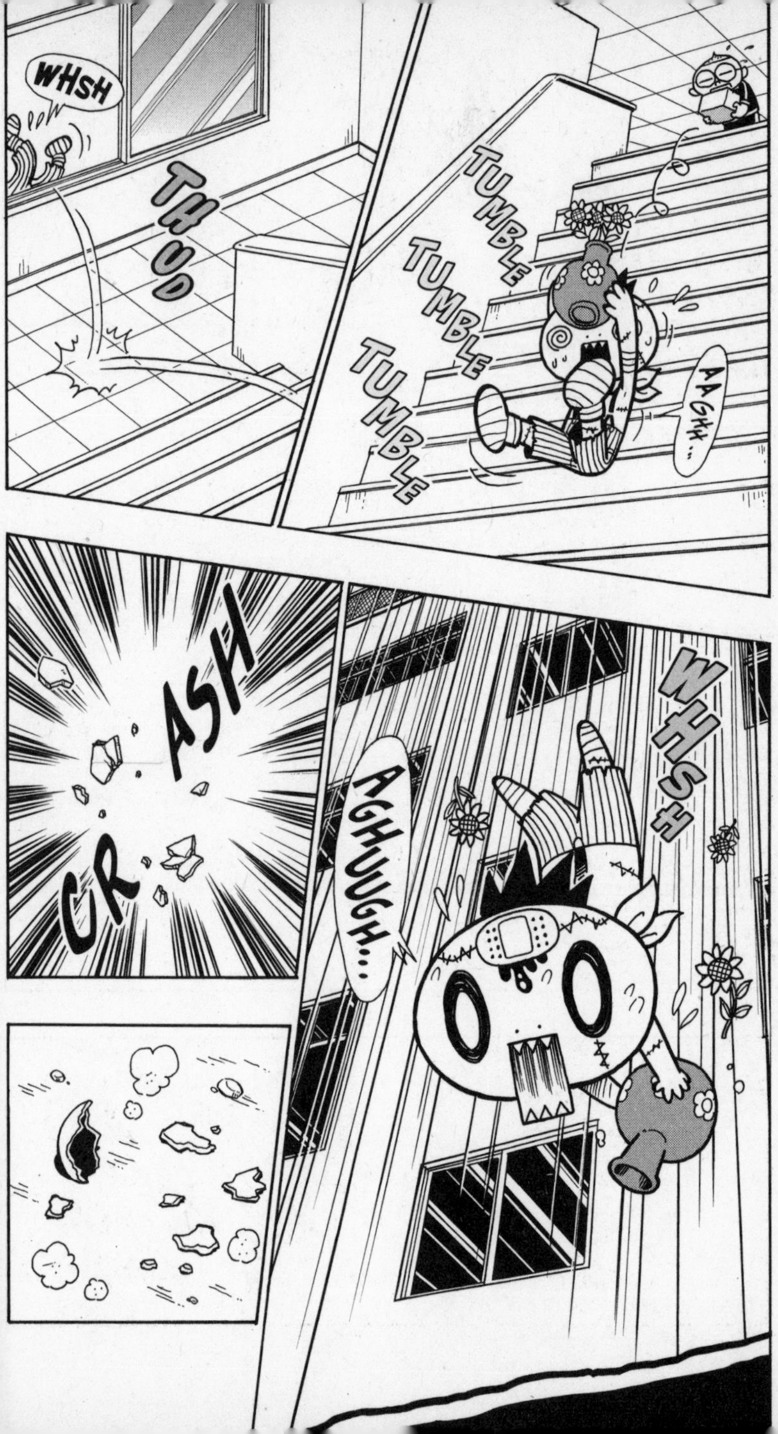
TUMBLE TUMBLE TUMBLE
AAGHK...
WHSH
THUD
WHSH
AGHUUUGH...
CRASH

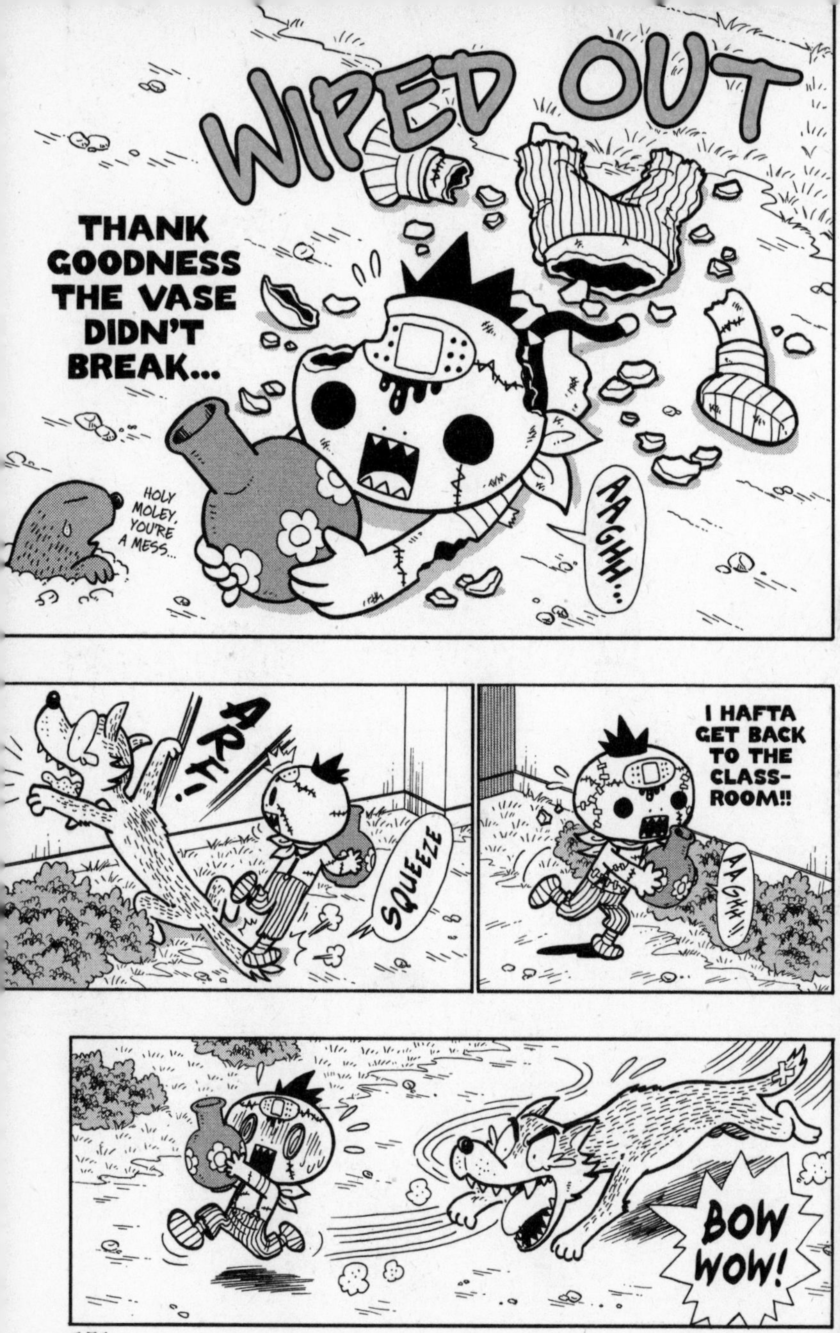
WIPED OUT
THANK GOODNESS THE VASE DIDN'T BREAK...
AAGHH...
HOLY MOLEY, YOU'RE A MESS...
I HAFTA GET BACK TO THE CLASS-ROOM!!
AAGHH!!
ARF!
SQUEEZE
BOW WOW!

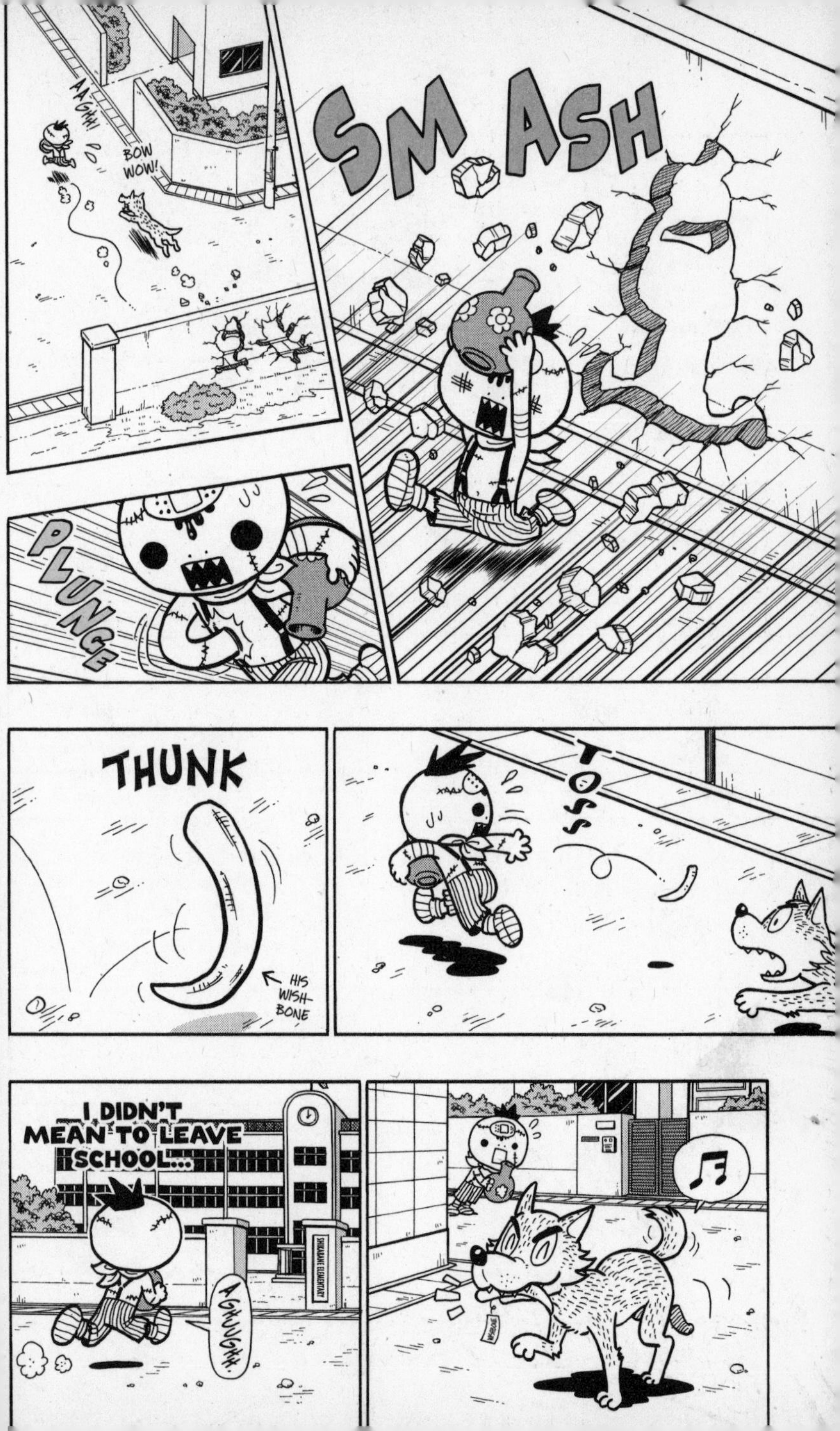
SMASH
AAGHH!
BOW WOW!
PLUNGE
TOSS
THUNK
HIS WISH-BONE
♫
I DIDN'T MEAN TO LEAVE SCHOOL...
SHIKABANE ELEMENTARY
AGHUGHH.

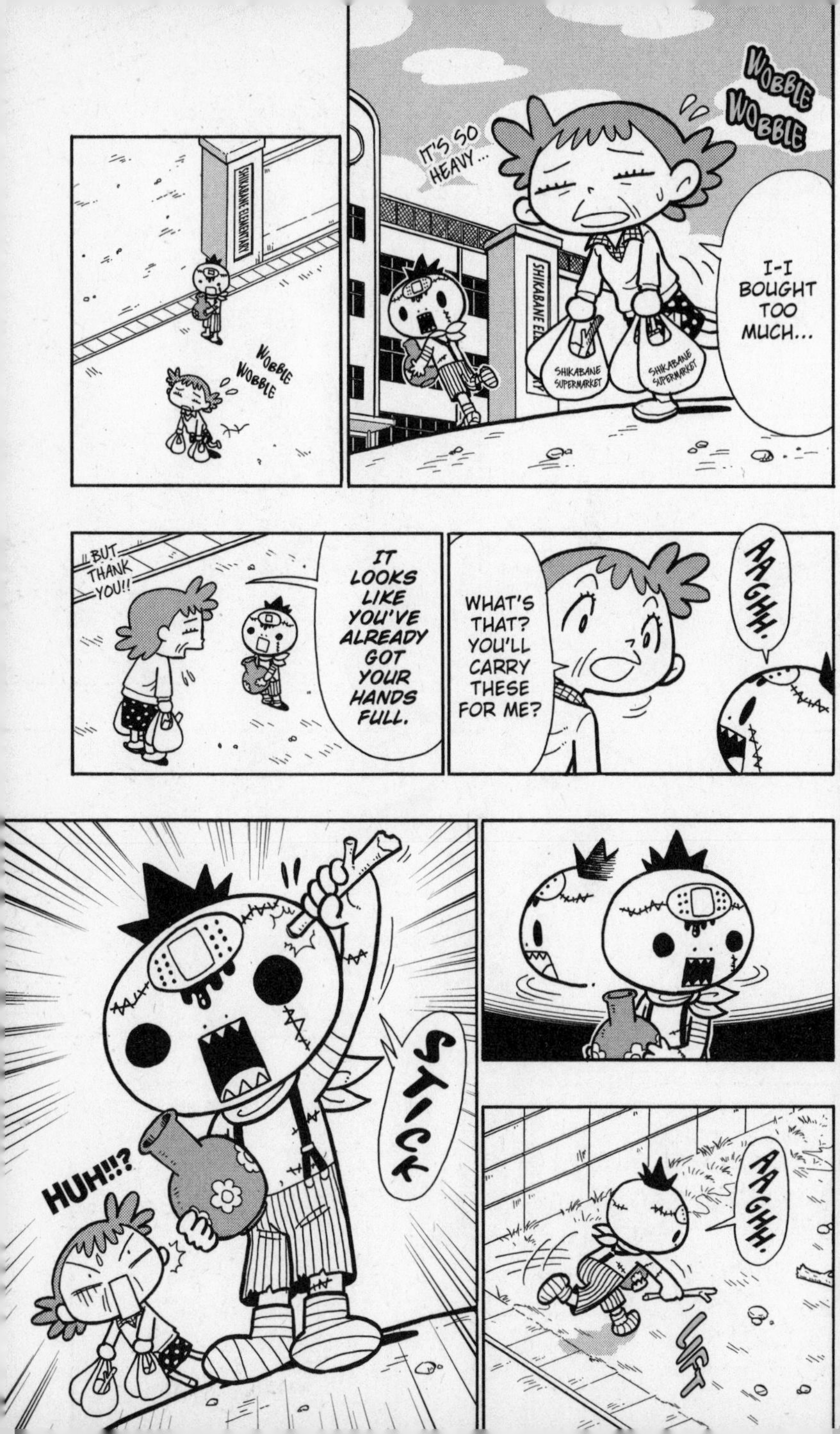
WOBBLE WOBBLE
IT'S SO HEAVY...
I-I BOUGHT TOO MUCH...
SHIKABANE SUPERMARKET
SHIKABANE SUPERMARKET
SHIKABANE ELEMENTARY
WOBBLE WOBBLE
AAGHH.
WHAT'S THAT? YOU'LL CARRY THESE FOR ME?
IT LOOKS LIKE YOU'VE ALREADY GOT YOUR HANDS FULL.
BUT THANK YOU!!
AAGHH.
STICK
HUH!!?

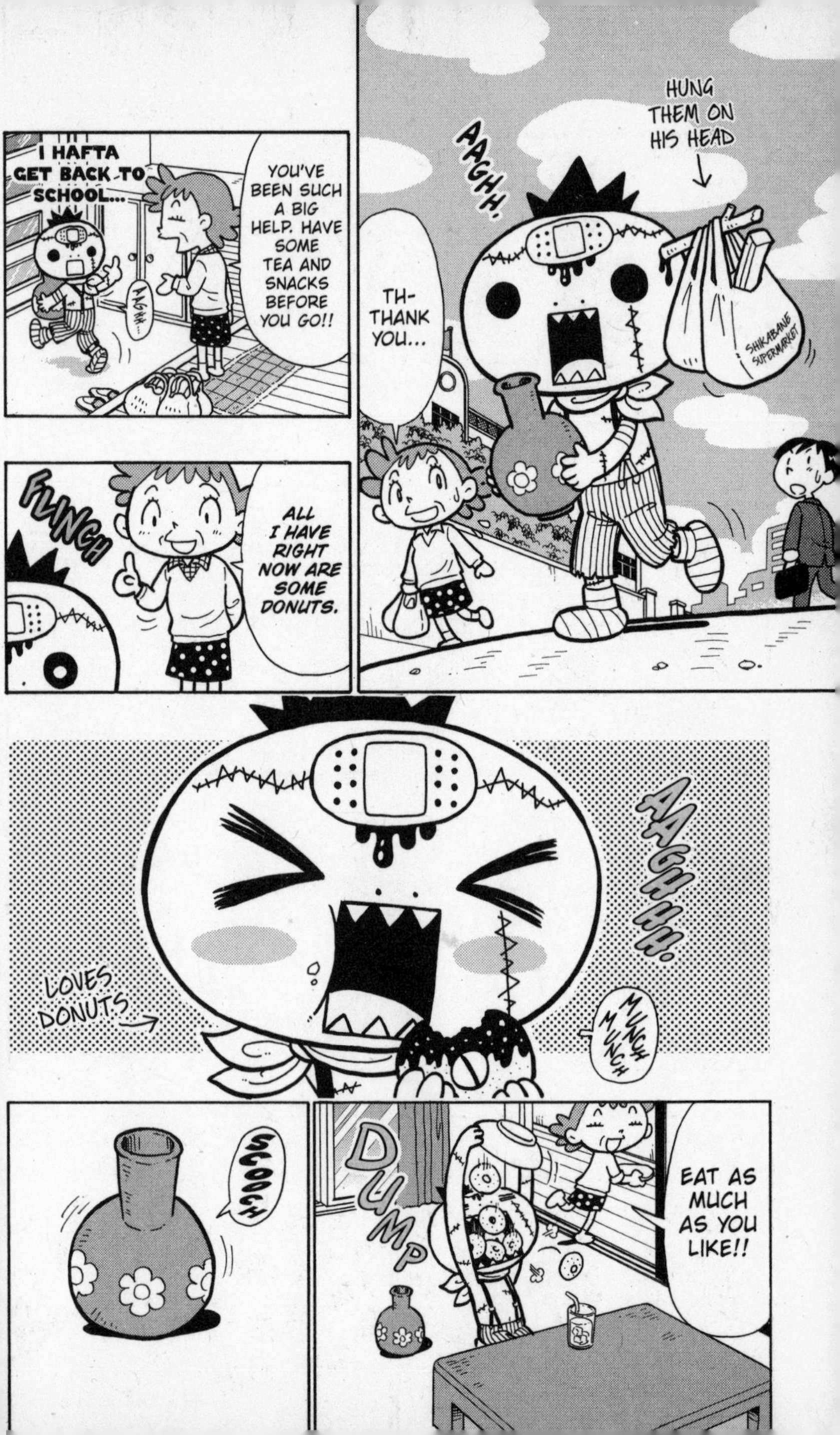
HUNG THEM ON HIS HEAD
AAGHH.
TH-THANK YOU...
SHIKABANE SUPERMARKET
YOU'VE BEEN SUCH A BIG HELP. HAVE SOME TEA AND SNACKS BEFORE YOU GO!!
I HAFTA GET BACK TO SCHOOL...
AAGHH...
ALL I HAVE RIGHT NOW ARE SOME DONUTS.
FLINCH
AAGHHHH!
MUNCH MUNCH
LOVES DONUTS
EAT AS MUCH AS YOU LIKE!!
DUMP
SCOOCH

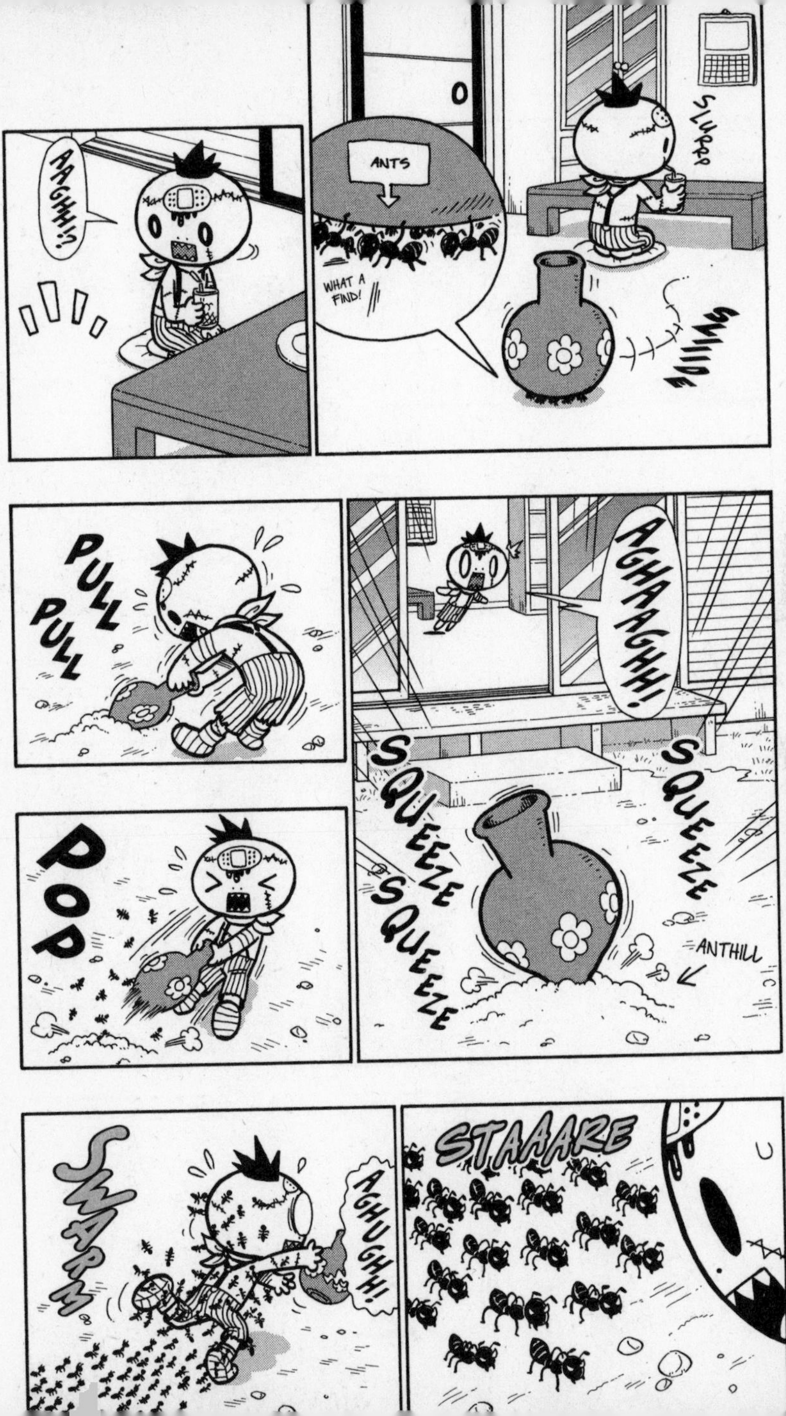
SLURRP
ANTS
WHAT A FIND!
SWIIIDE
AAGHH!?
AGHAAGHH!
SQUEEZE SQUEEZE
SQUEEZE SQUEEZE
ANTHILL
PULL PULL
POP
STAAARE
SWARM
AGHUGHH!

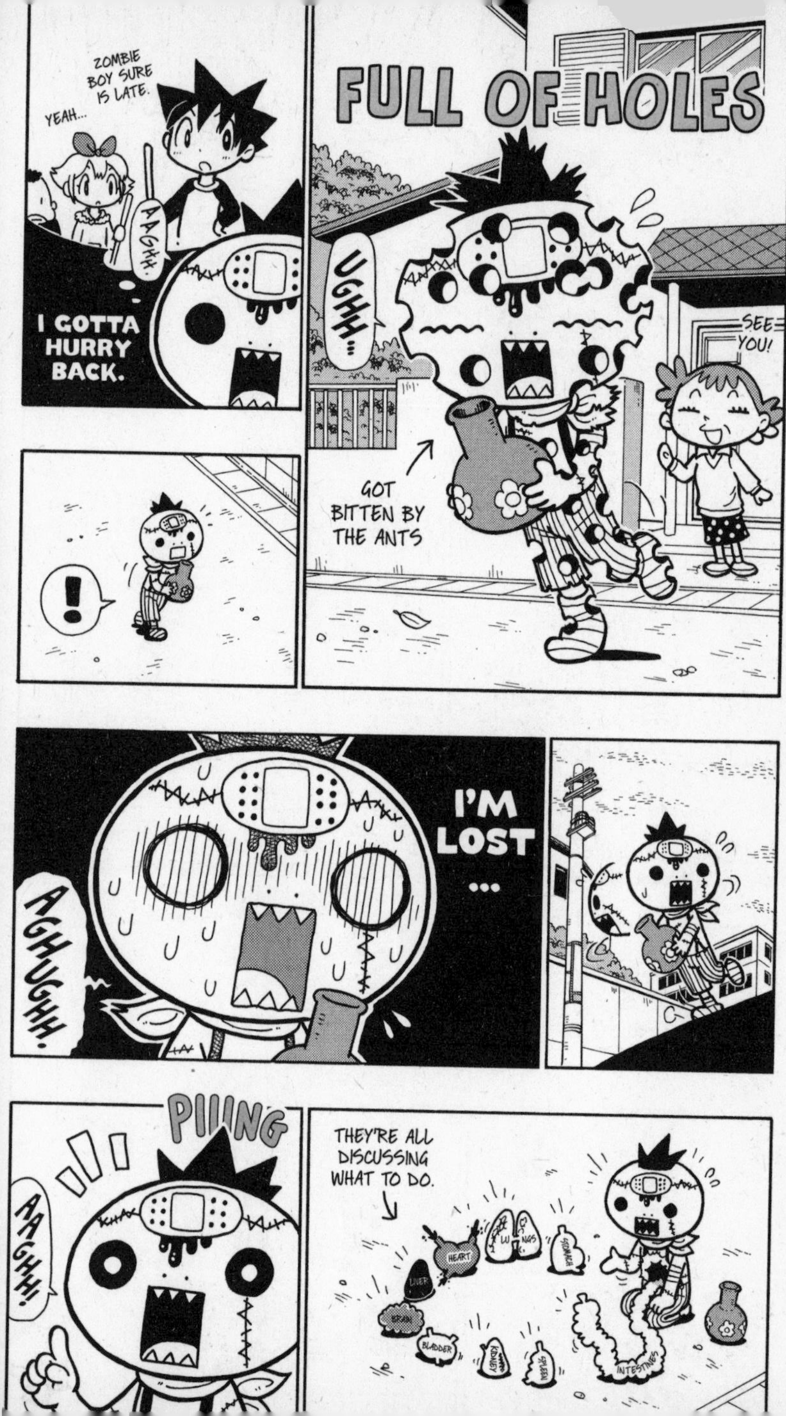
FULL OF HOLES
UGHH...
SEE YOU!
GOT BITTEN BY THE ANTS
ZOMBIE BOY SURE IS LATE.
YEAH...
AAGHH.
I GOTTA HURRY BACK.
!
I'M LOST...
AGHUGHH.
THEY'RE ALL DISCUSSING WHAT TO DO.
HEART
LUNGS
STOMACH
LIVER
BRAIN
BLADDER
KIDNEY
SPLEEN
INTESTINES
PIING
AAGHH!

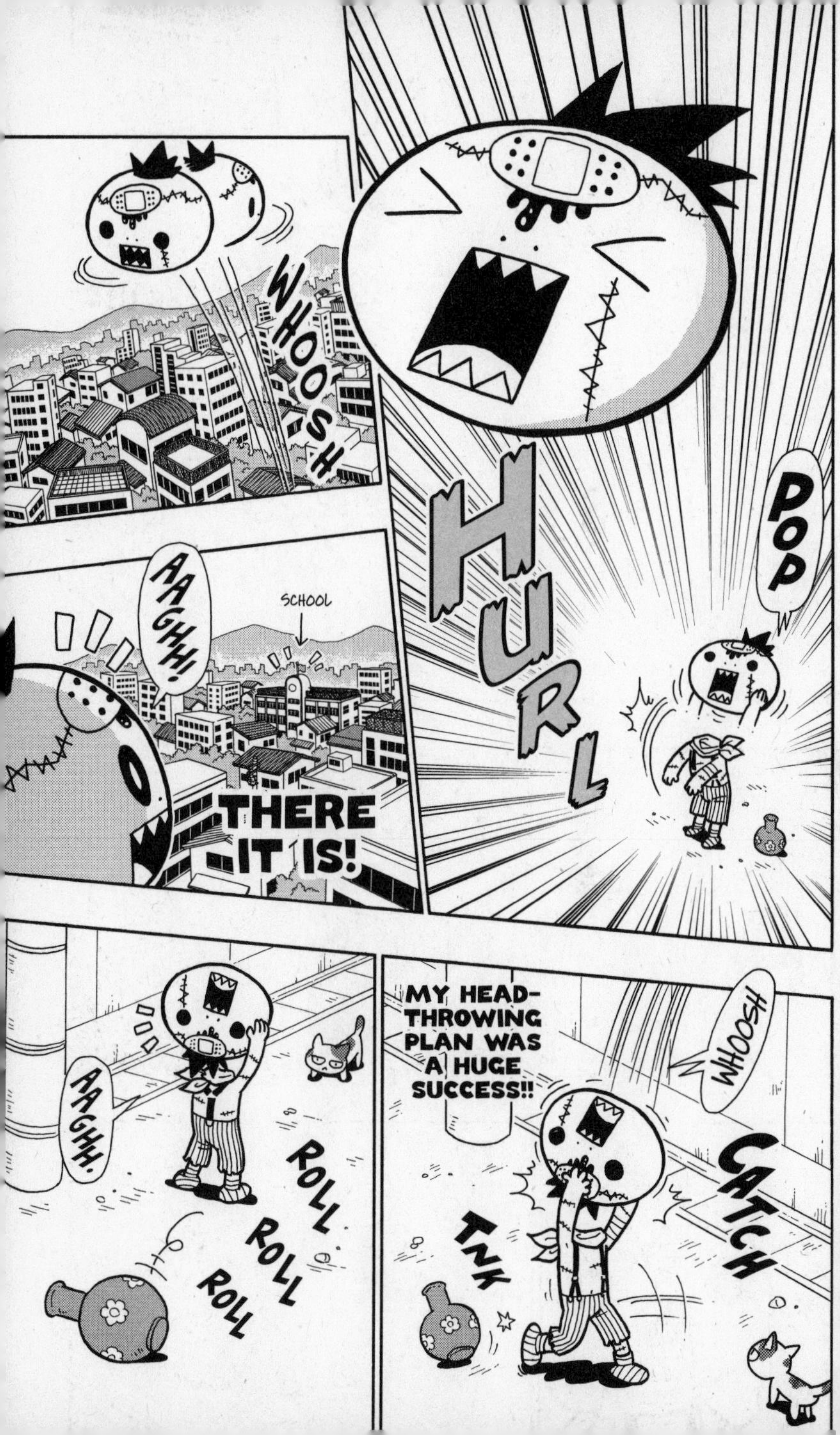
HURL
POP
WHOOSH
AAGHH!
SCHOOL
THERE IT IS!
WHOOSH
MY HEAD-THROWING PLAN WAS A HUGE SUCCESS!!
CATCH
TNK
AAGHH.
ROLL
ROLL
ROLL

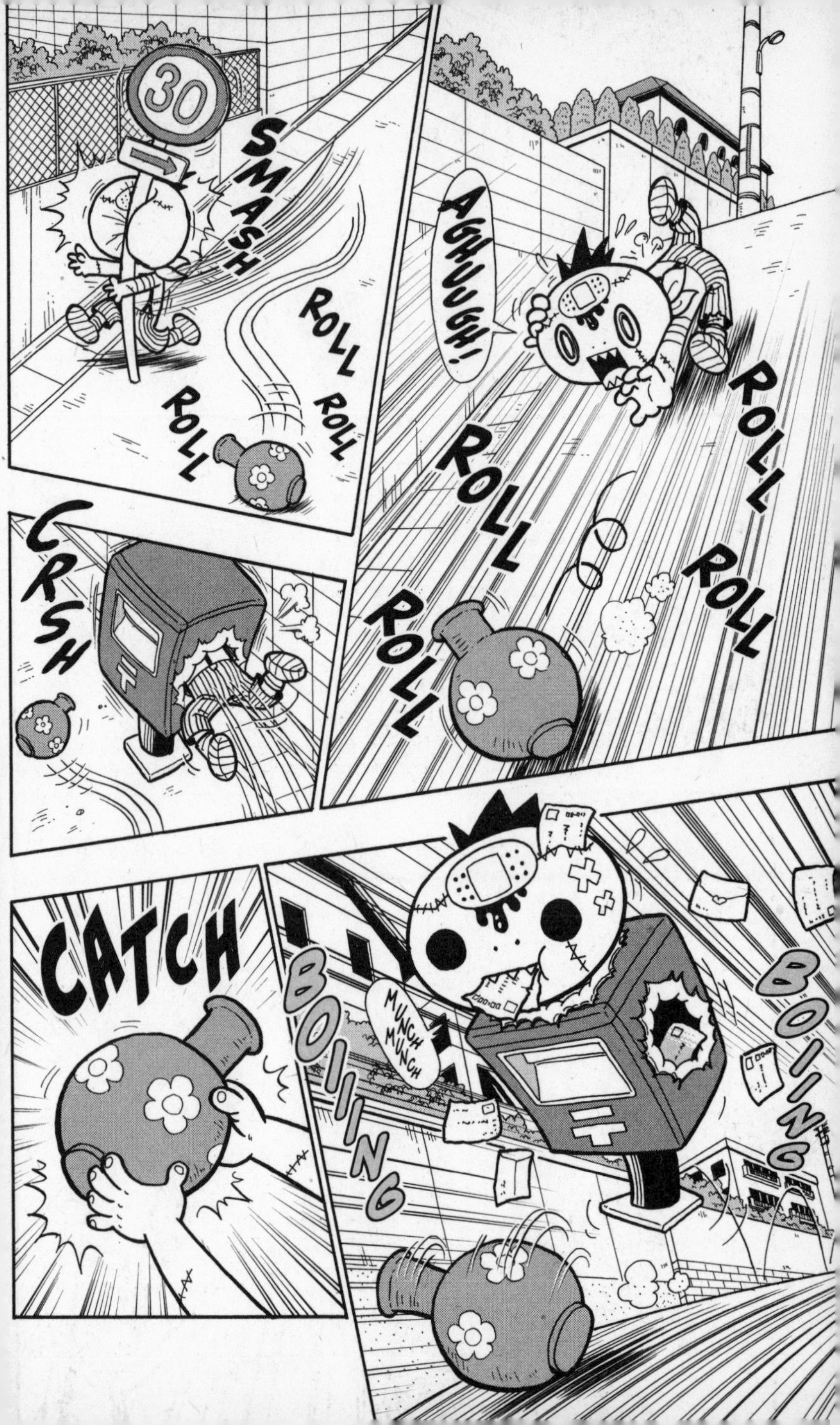
AGHUUGH!
ROLL ROLL ROLL
ROLL ROLL
SMASH
ROLL ROLL
ROLL
CRSH
BOIIING
MUNCH MUNCH
BOIIING
CATCH

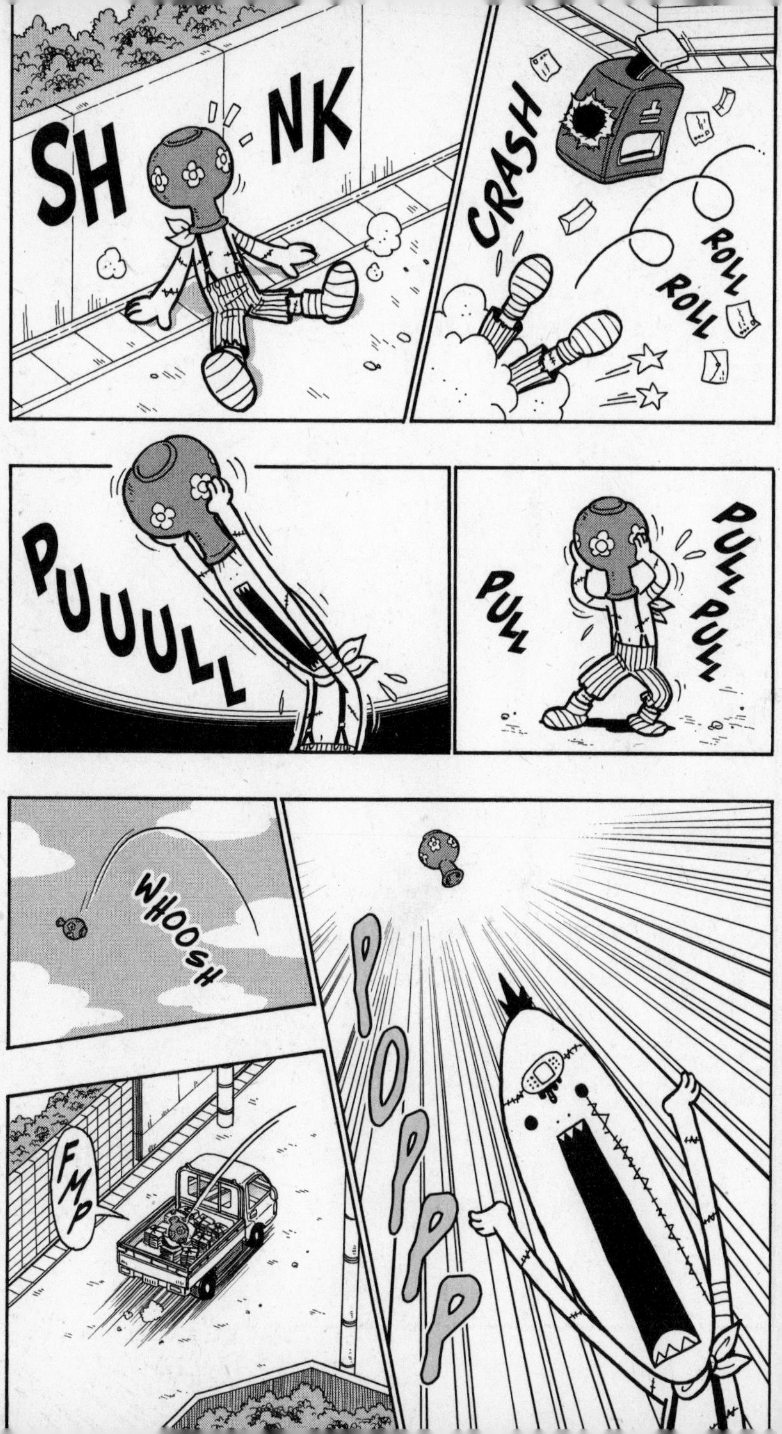
CRASH
ROLL ROLL
SH NK
PULL PULL
PULL
PUUULL
POPPP
WHOOSH
FMP

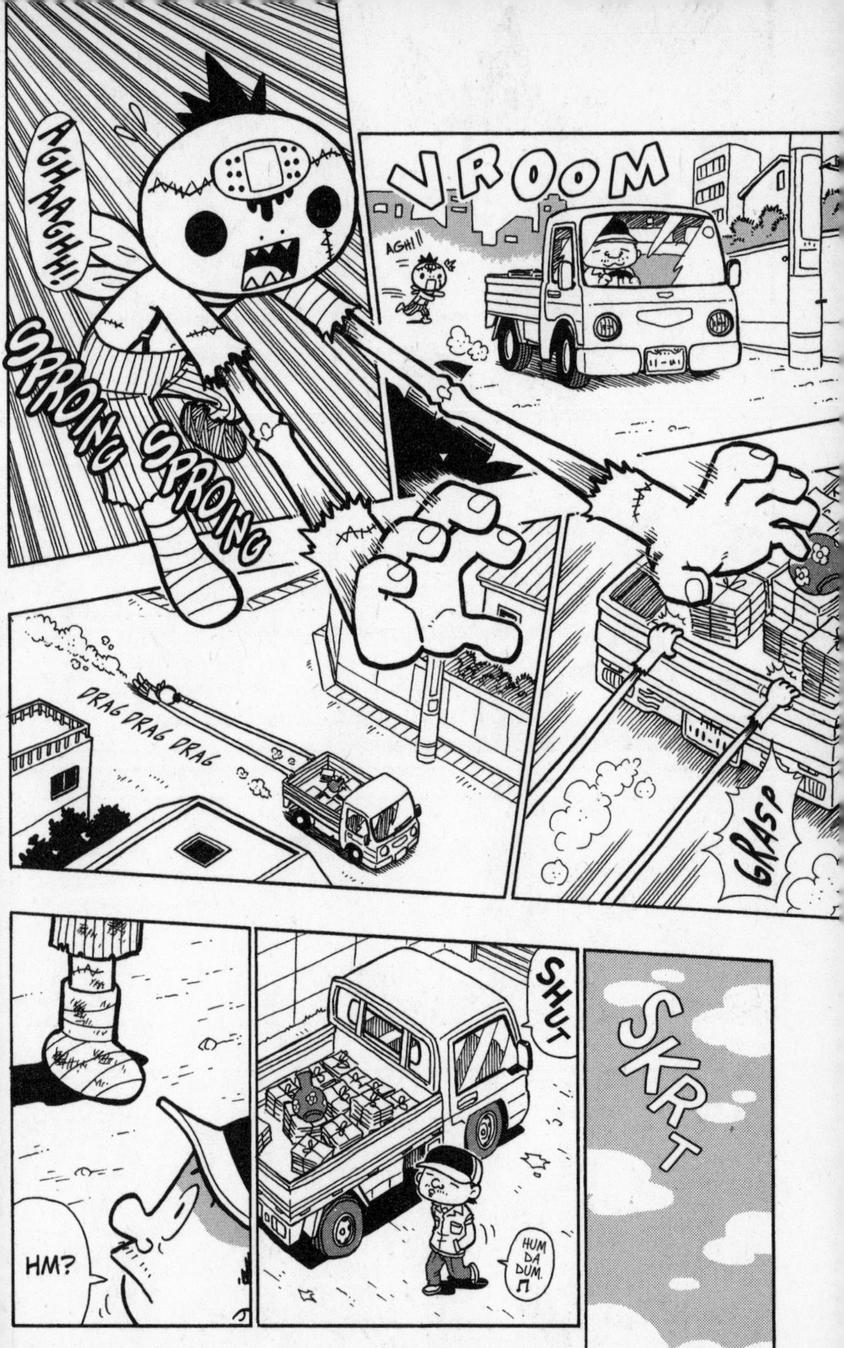
VROOM
AGH!!
AGHAAGHH!
SPROING SPROING
GRASP
DRAG DRAG DRAG
SKRT
SHUT
HUM DA DUM. ♫
HM?

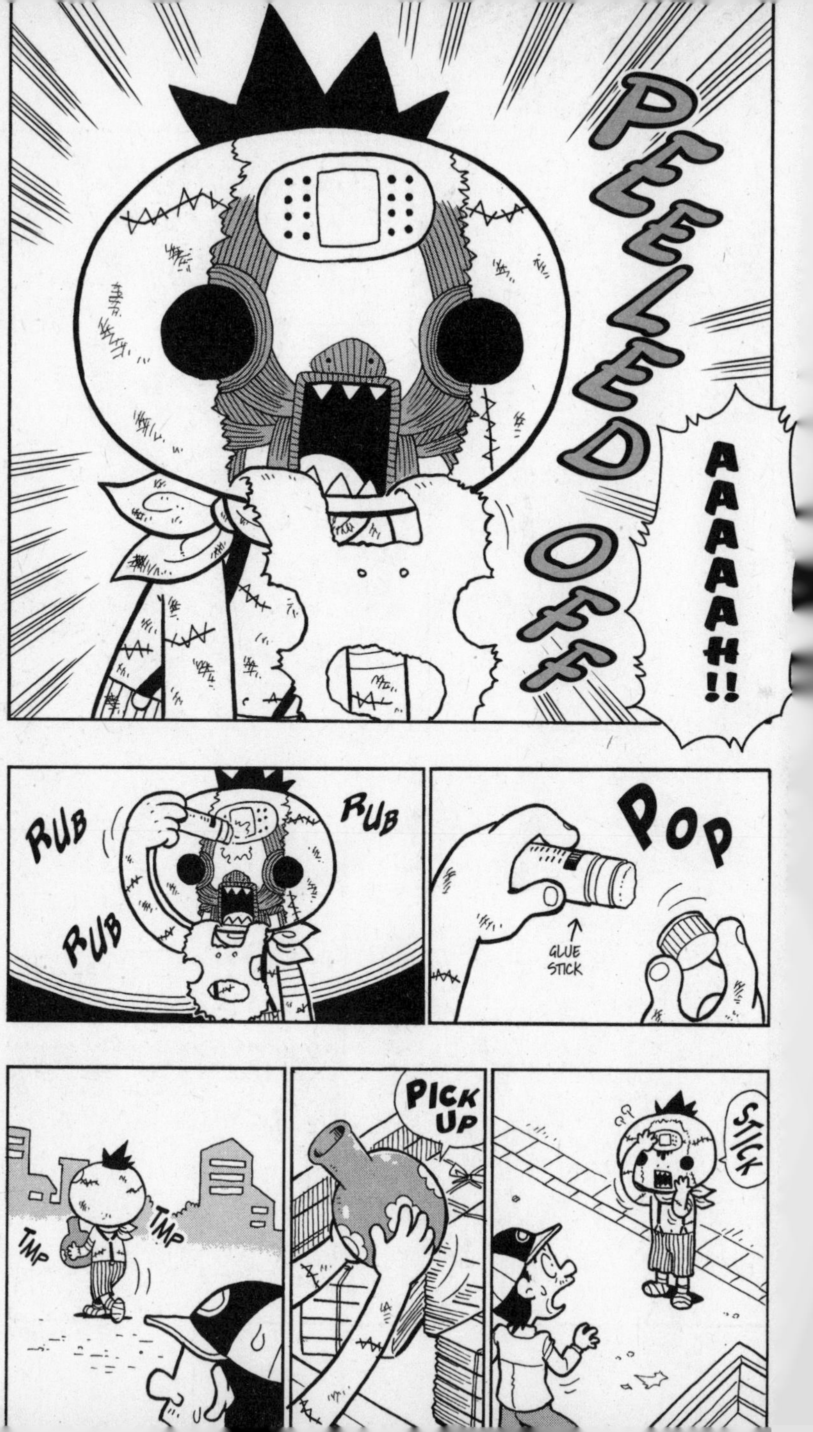
PEELED OFF
AAAAAH!!
POP
GLUE STICK
RUB
RUB
RUB
STICK
PICK UP
TMP
TMP

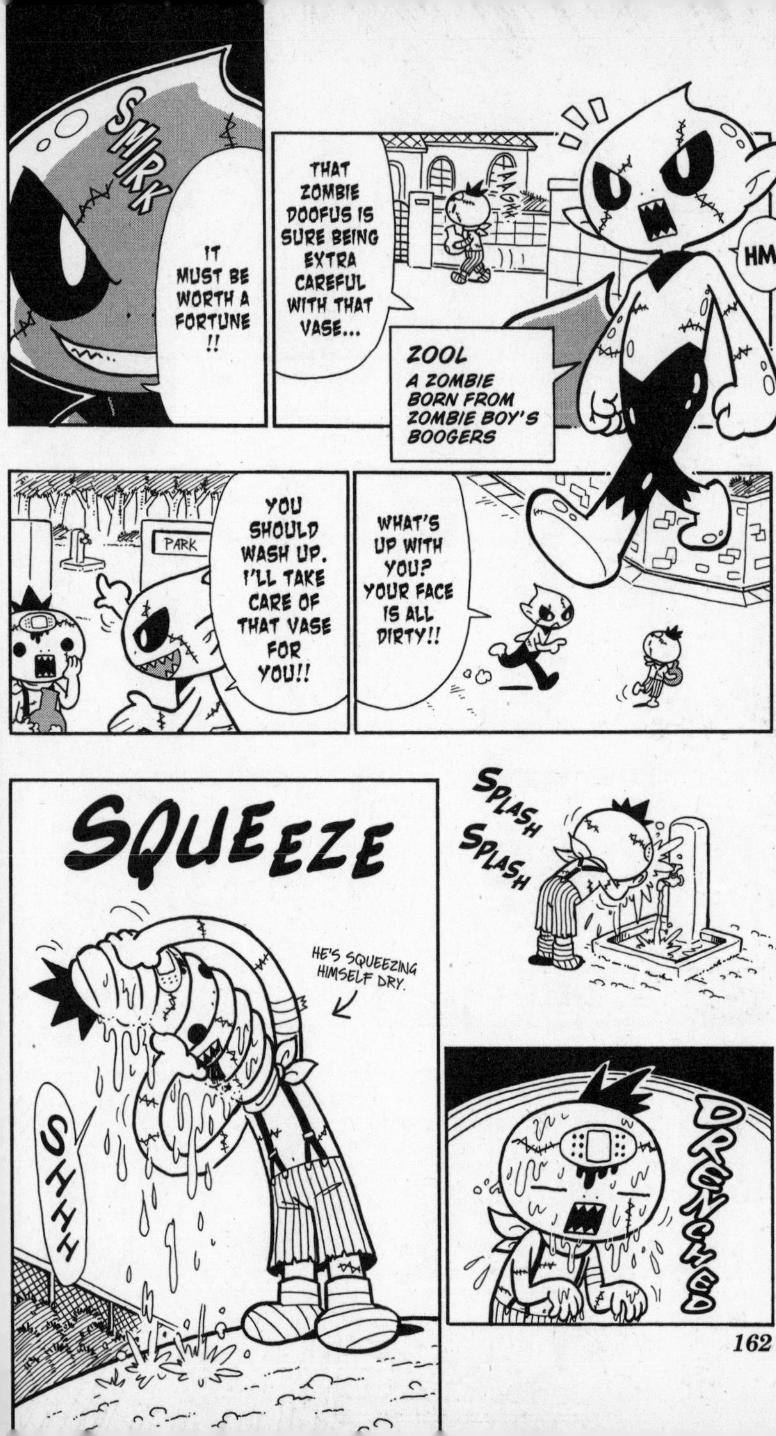
HM?
ZOOL
A ZOMBIE BORN FROM ZOMBIE BOY'S BOOGERS
THAT ZOMBIE DOOFUS IS SURE BEING EXTRA CAREFUL WITH THAT VASE...
SMIRK
IT MUST BE WORTH A FORTUNE!!
WHAT'S UP WITH YOU? YOUR FACE IS ALL DIRTY!!
YOU SHOULD WASH UP. I'LL TAKE CARE OF THAT VASE FOR YOU!!
PARK
SPLASH
SPLASH
DRENCHED
SQUEEZE
HE'S SQUEEZING HIMSELF DRY.
SHHH

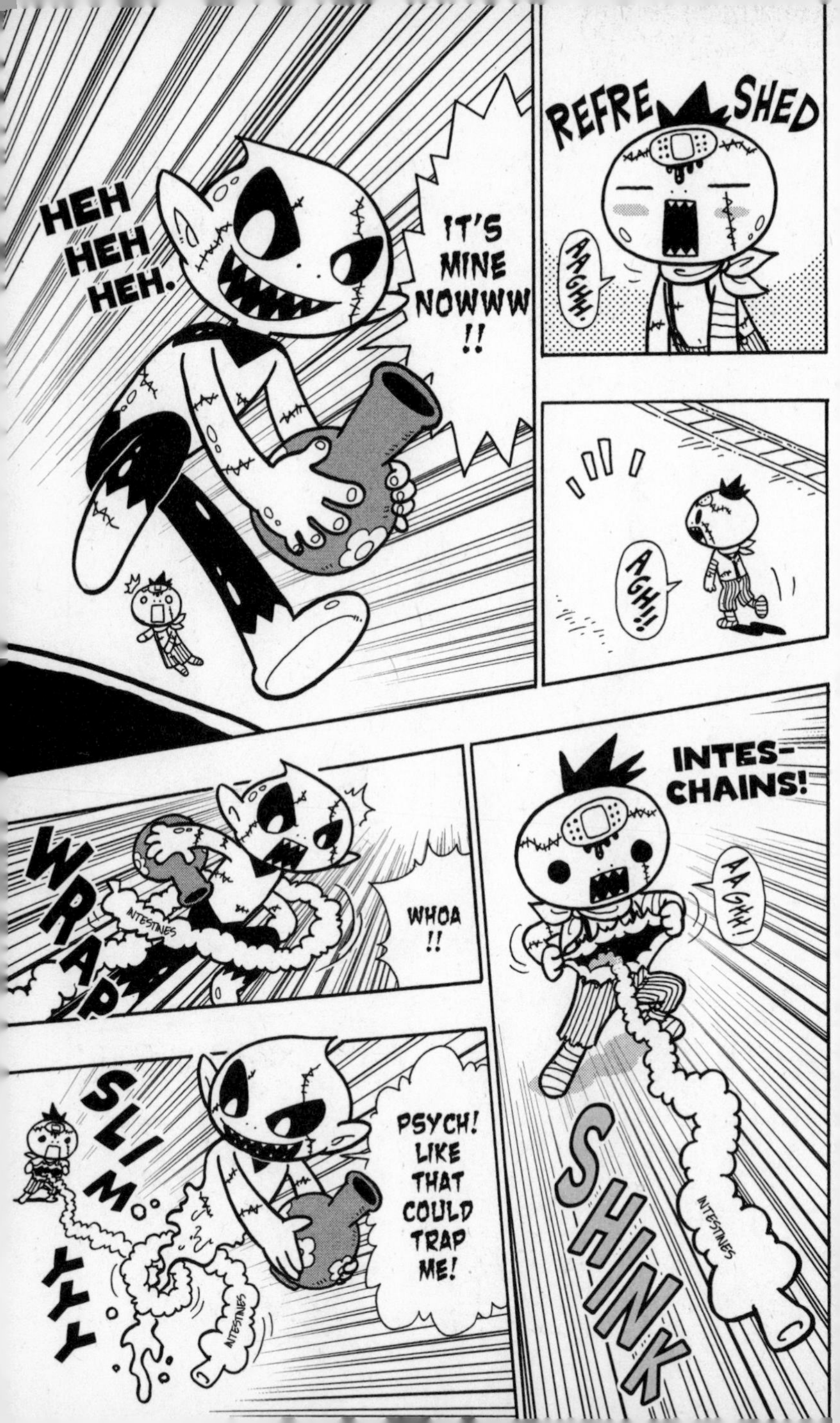
REFRE SHED
AAGHH.
AGH!!
IT'S MINE NOWWW!!
HEH HEH HEH.
INTES-CHAINS!
AAGHH!
INTESTINES
SHINK
WHOA!!
WRAP
INTESTINES
PSYCH! LIKE THAT COULD TRAP ME!
SLIM..YYY
INTESTINES

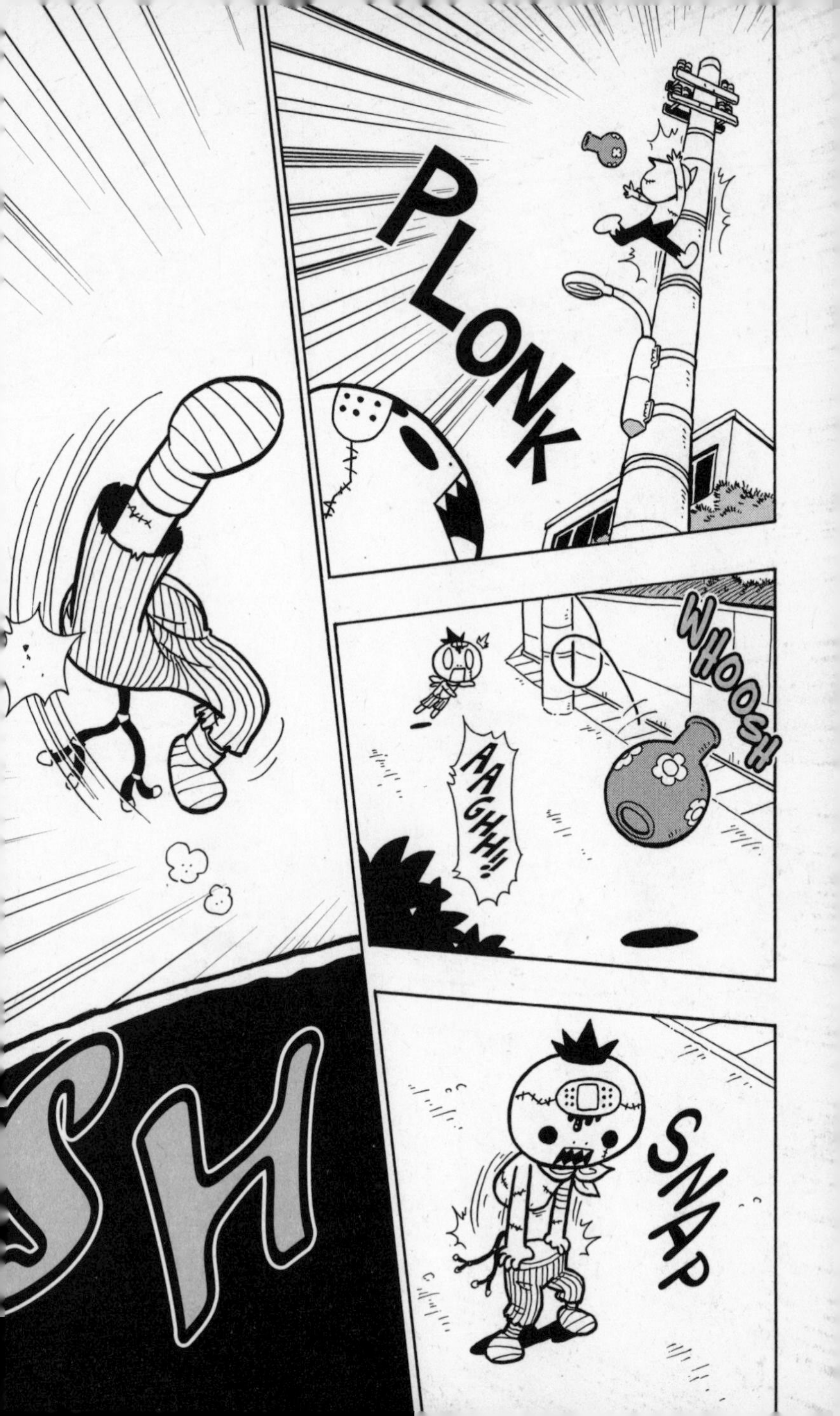
PLONK
WHOOSH
AAGHH!!
SNAP
SH

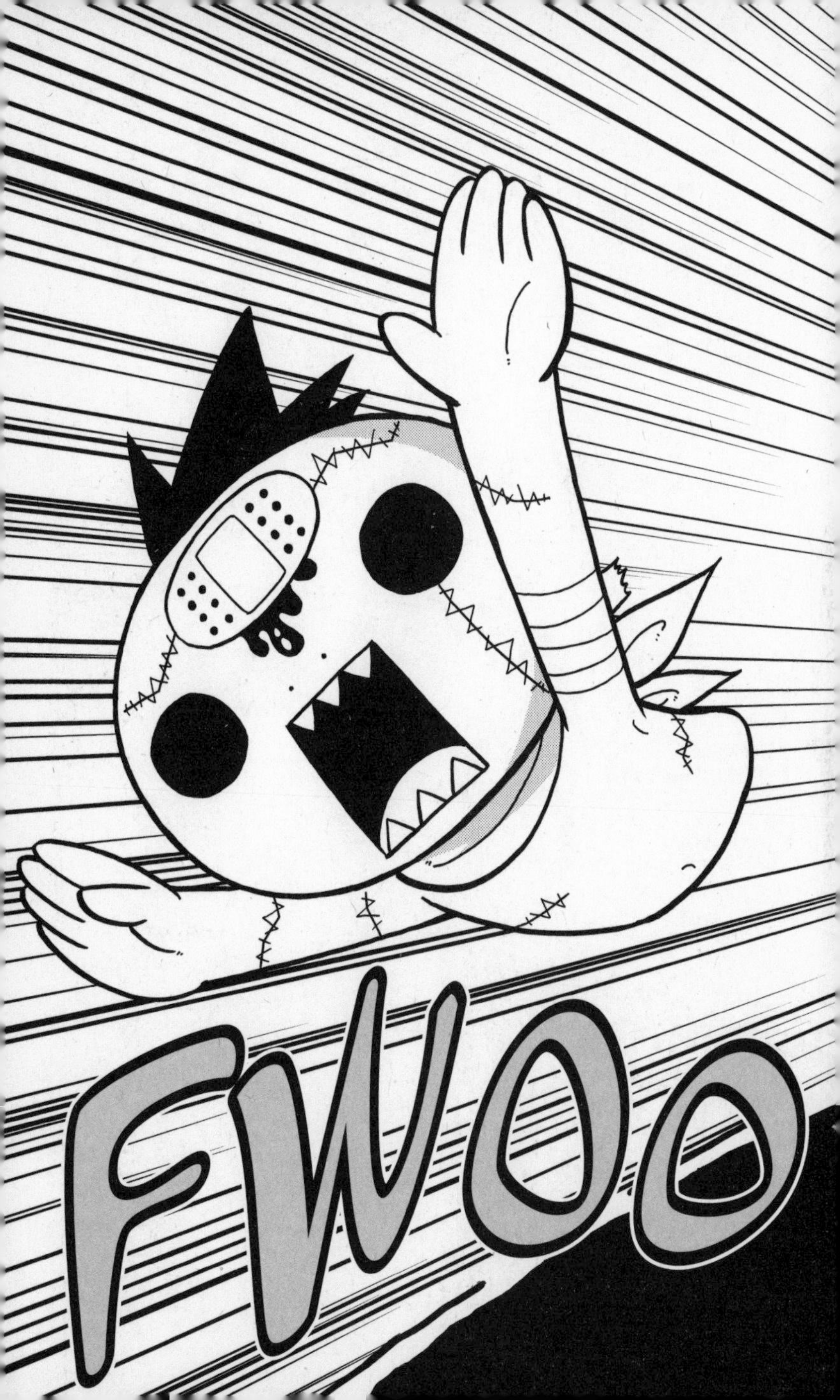
FWOO

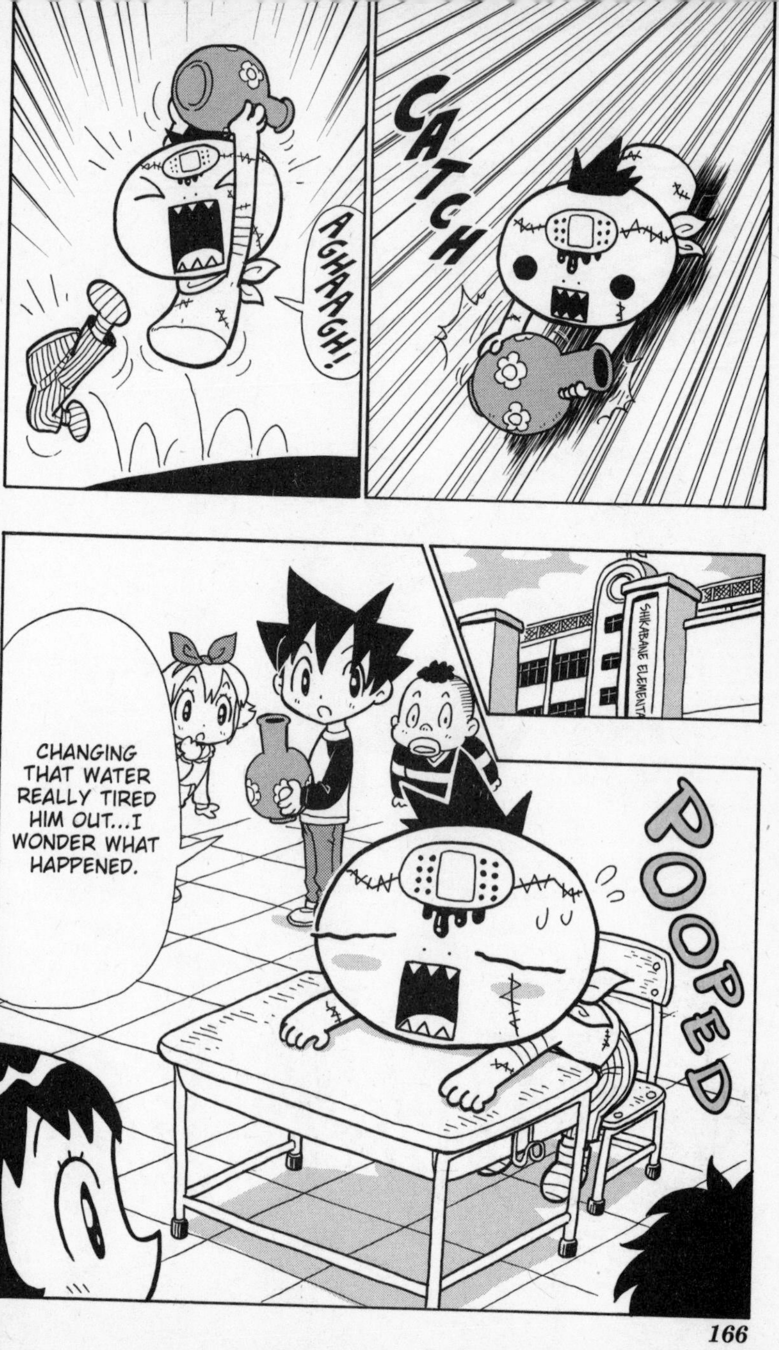
CATCH
AGHAAAGH!
SHIKABANE ELEMENTA
POOPED
CHANGING THAT WATER REALLY TIRED HIM OUT...I WONDER WHAT HAPPENED.

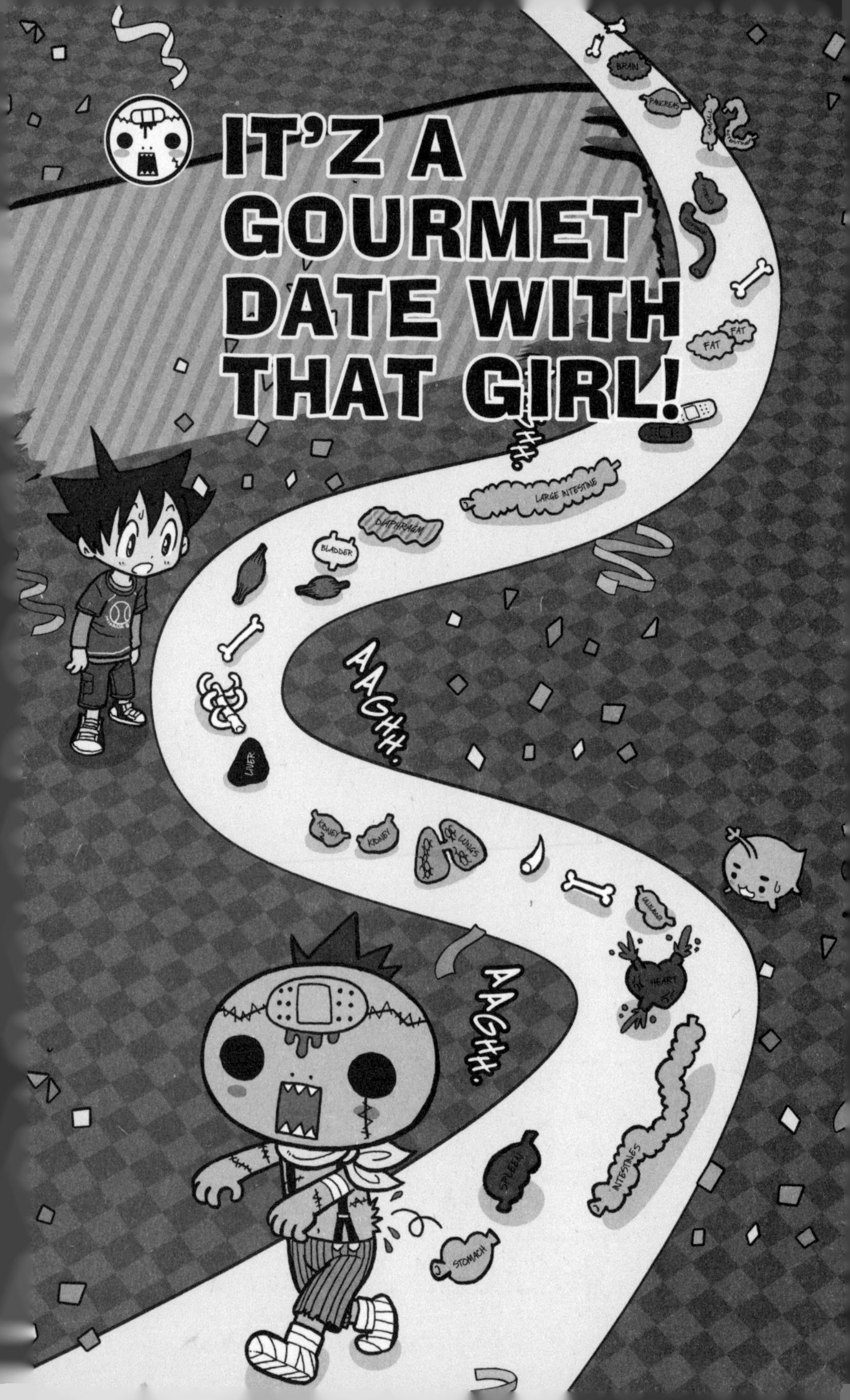
IT'Z A GOURMET DATE WITH THAT GIRL!
BRAIN
PANCREAS
FAT
FAT
LARGE INTESTINE
DIAPHRAGM
BLADDER
AAGHH.
LIVER
KIDNEY
KIDNEY
LUNGS
AAGHH.
HEART
INTESTINES
SPLEEN
STOMACH

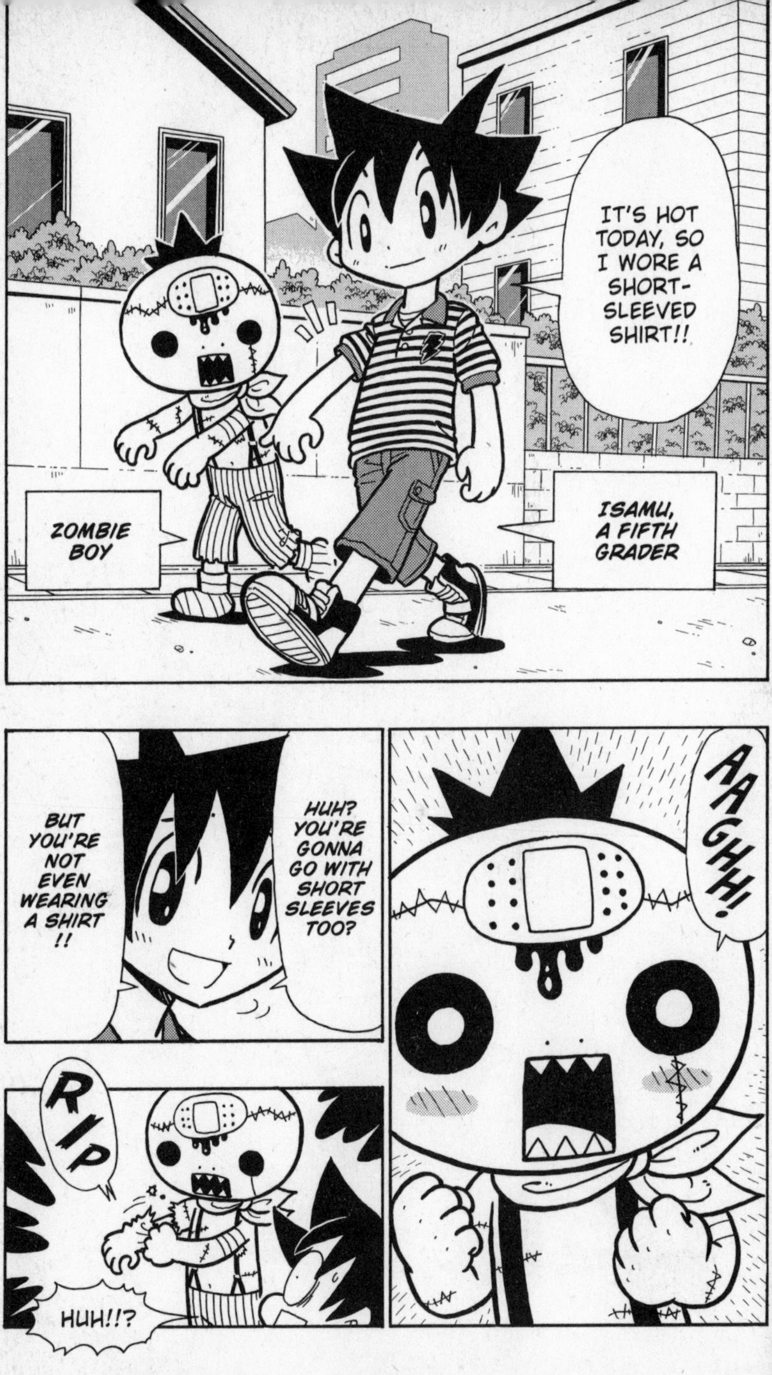
IT'S HOT TODAY, SO I WORE A SHORT-SLEEVED SHIRT!!
ISAMU, A FIFTH GRADER
ZOMBIE BOY
AAGHH!
HUH? YOU'RE GONNA GO WITH SHORT SLEEVES TOO?
BUT YOU'RE NOT EVEN WEARING A SHIRT!!
RIP
HUH!!?

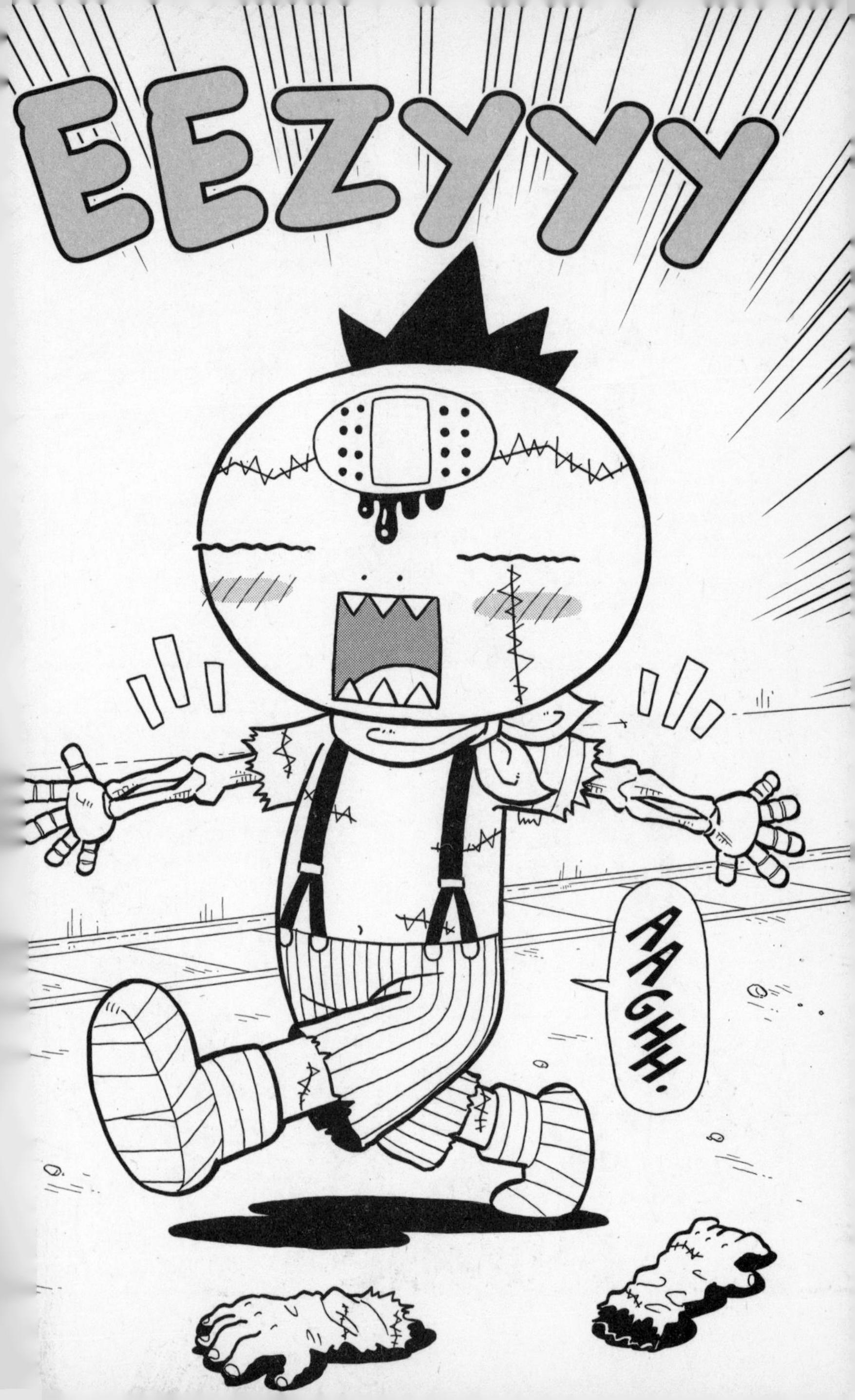
EEZYYY
AAGHH.

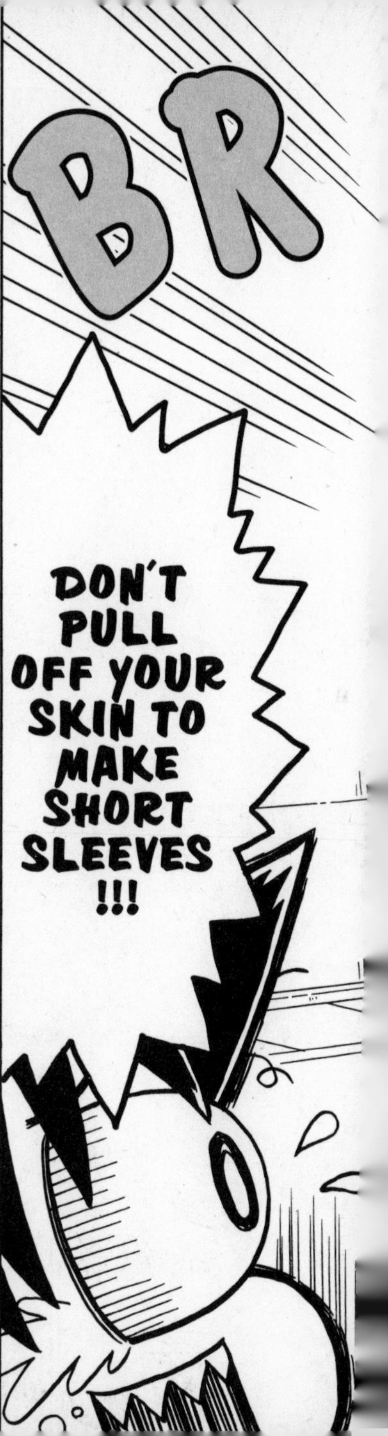
BR
DON'T PULL OFF YOUR SKIN TO MAKE SHORT SLEEVES !!!

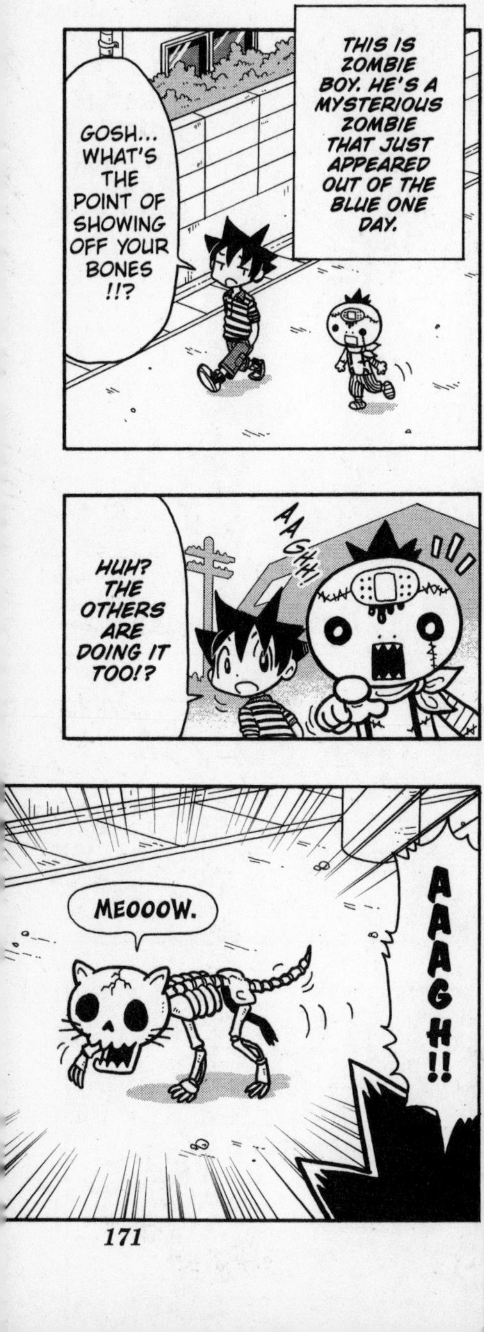
THIS IS ZOMBIE BOY. HE'S A MYSTERIOUS ZOMBIE THAT JUST APPEARED OUT OF THE BLUE ONE DAY.
GOSH... WHAT'S THE POINT OF SHOWING OFF YOUR BONES !!?
AAGHH!
HUH? THE OTHERS ARE DOING IT TOO!?
AAAAGH!!
MEOOOW.

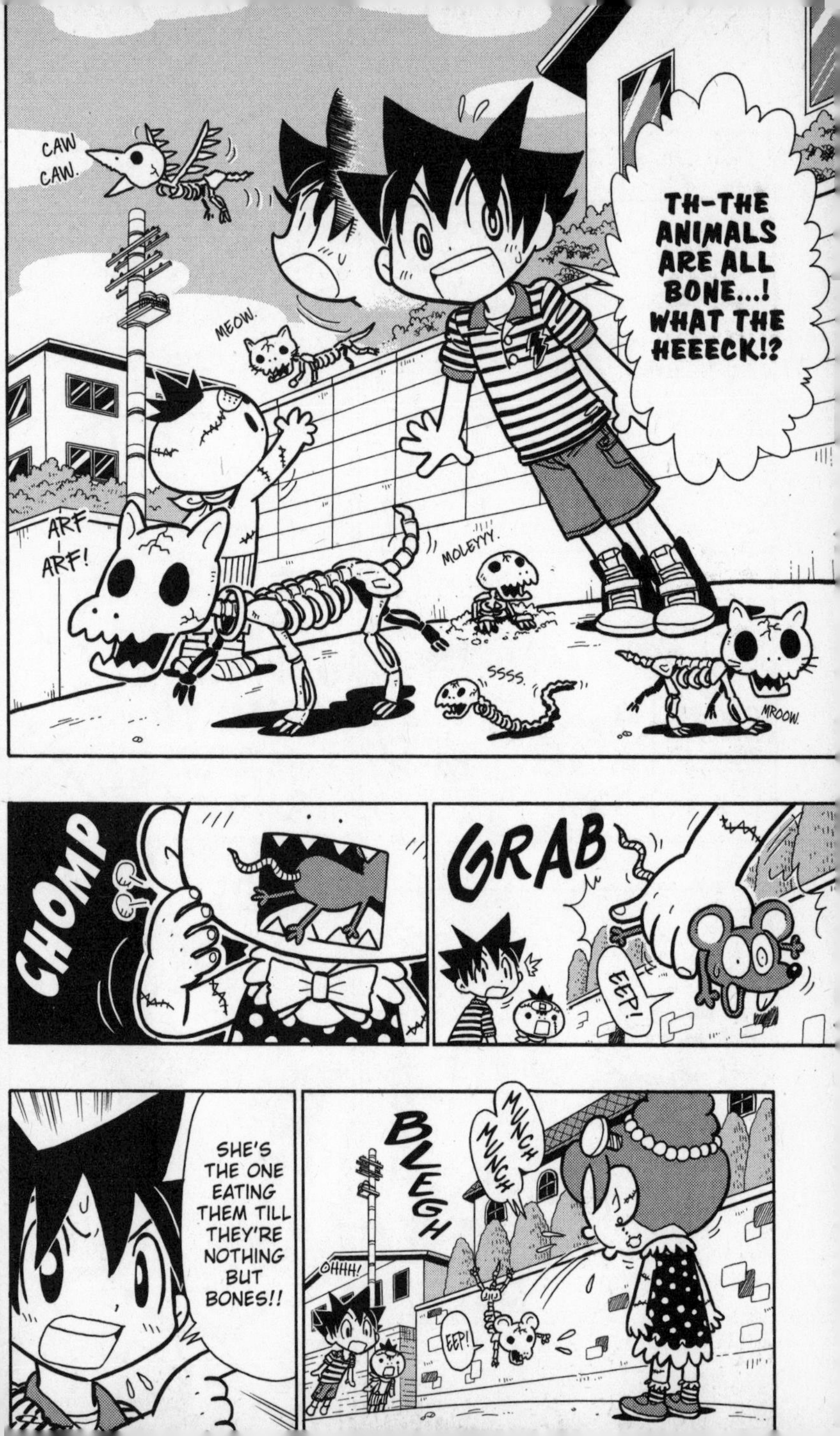
TH-THE ANIMALS ARE ALL BONE...! WHAT THE HEEECK!?
CAW CAW.
MEOW.
MOLEYYY.
ARF ARF!
MROOW.
SSSS.
GRAB
EEP!
CHOMP
MUNCH MUNCH
BLEGH
OHHH!
EEP!
SHE'S THE ONE EATING THEM TILL THEY'RE NOTHING BUT BONES!!

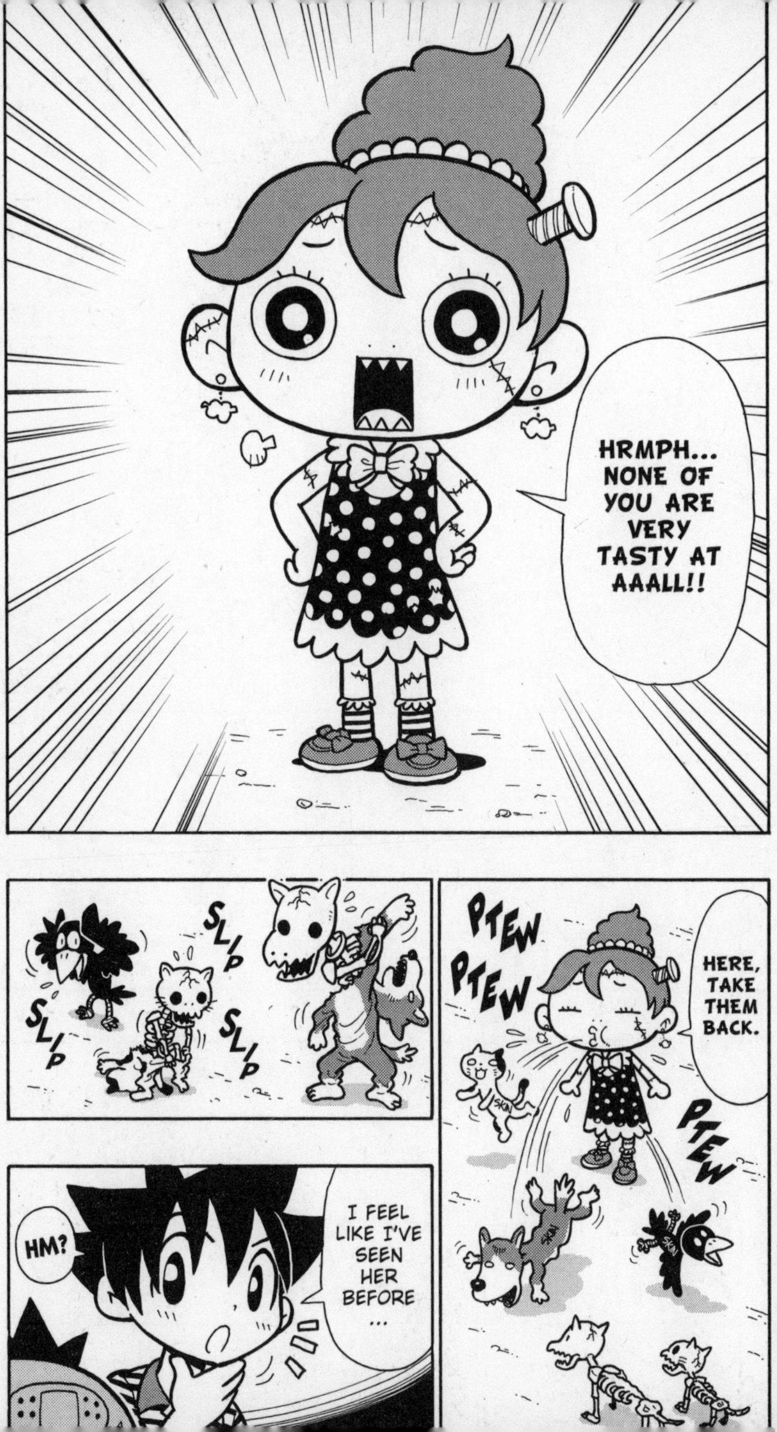
HRMPH... NONE OF YOU ARE VERY TASTY AT AAALL!!
PTEW
PTEW
HERE, TAKE THEM BACK.
SKIN
PTEW
SKIN
SKIN
SLIP
SLIP
SLIP
I FEEL LIKE I'VE SEEN HER BEFORE ...
HM?

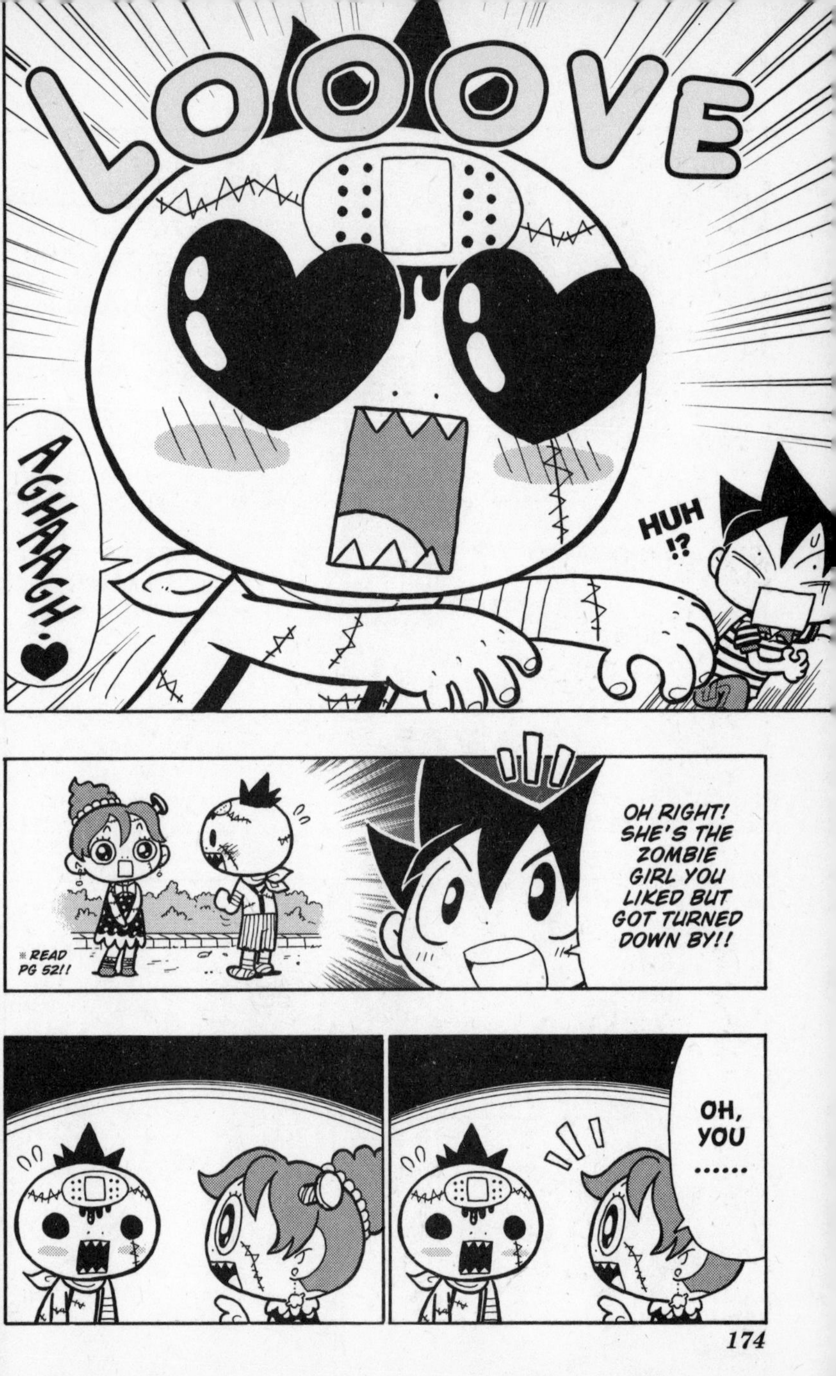
LOOOVE
HUH!?
AGHAAGH.♥
OH RIGHT! SHE'S THE ZOMBIE GIRL YOU LIKED BUT GOT TURNED DOWN BY!!
※READ PG 52!!
OH, YOU ......

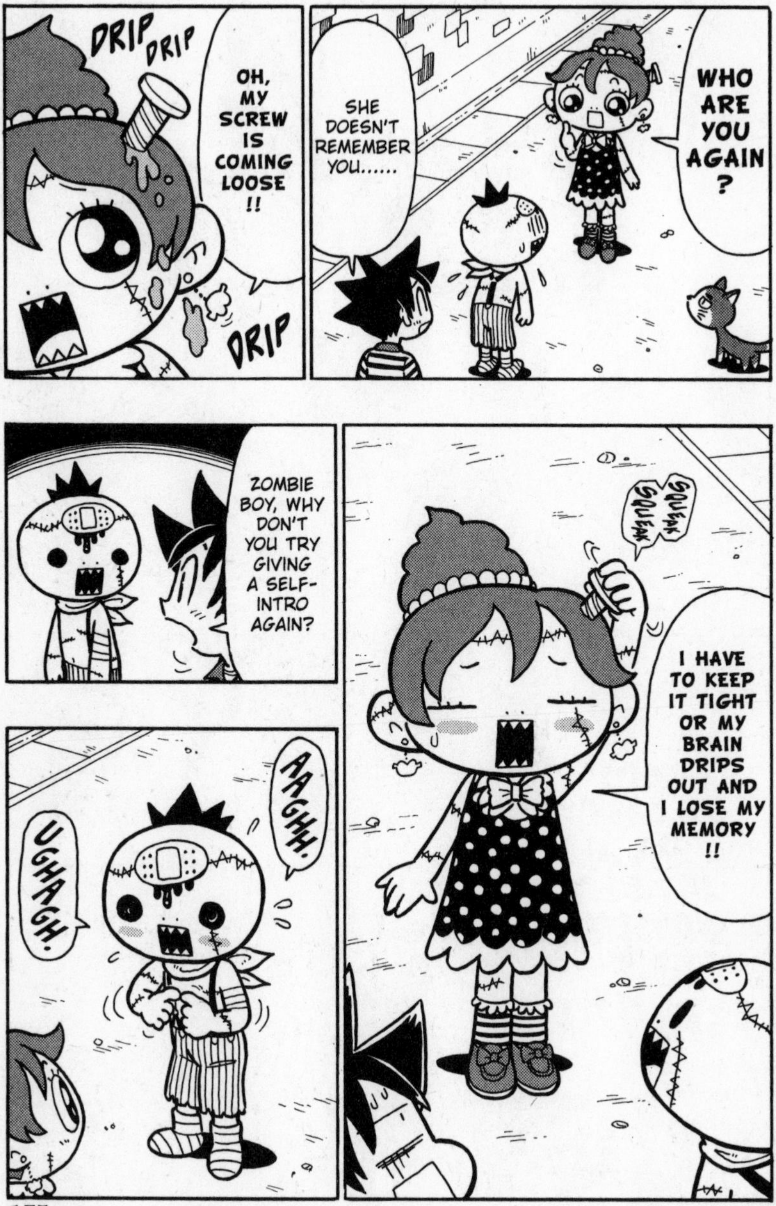
WHO ARE YOU AGAIN?
SHE DOESN'T REMEMBER YOU......
OH, MY SCREW IS COMING LOOSE!!
DRIP DRIP
DRIP
SQUEAK SQUEAK
I HAVE TO KEEP IT TIGHT OR MY BRAIN DRIPS OUT AND I LOSE MY MEMORY!!
ZOMBIE BOY, WHY DON'T YOU TRY GIVING A SELF-INTRO AGAIN?
AAGHH.
UGHAGH.

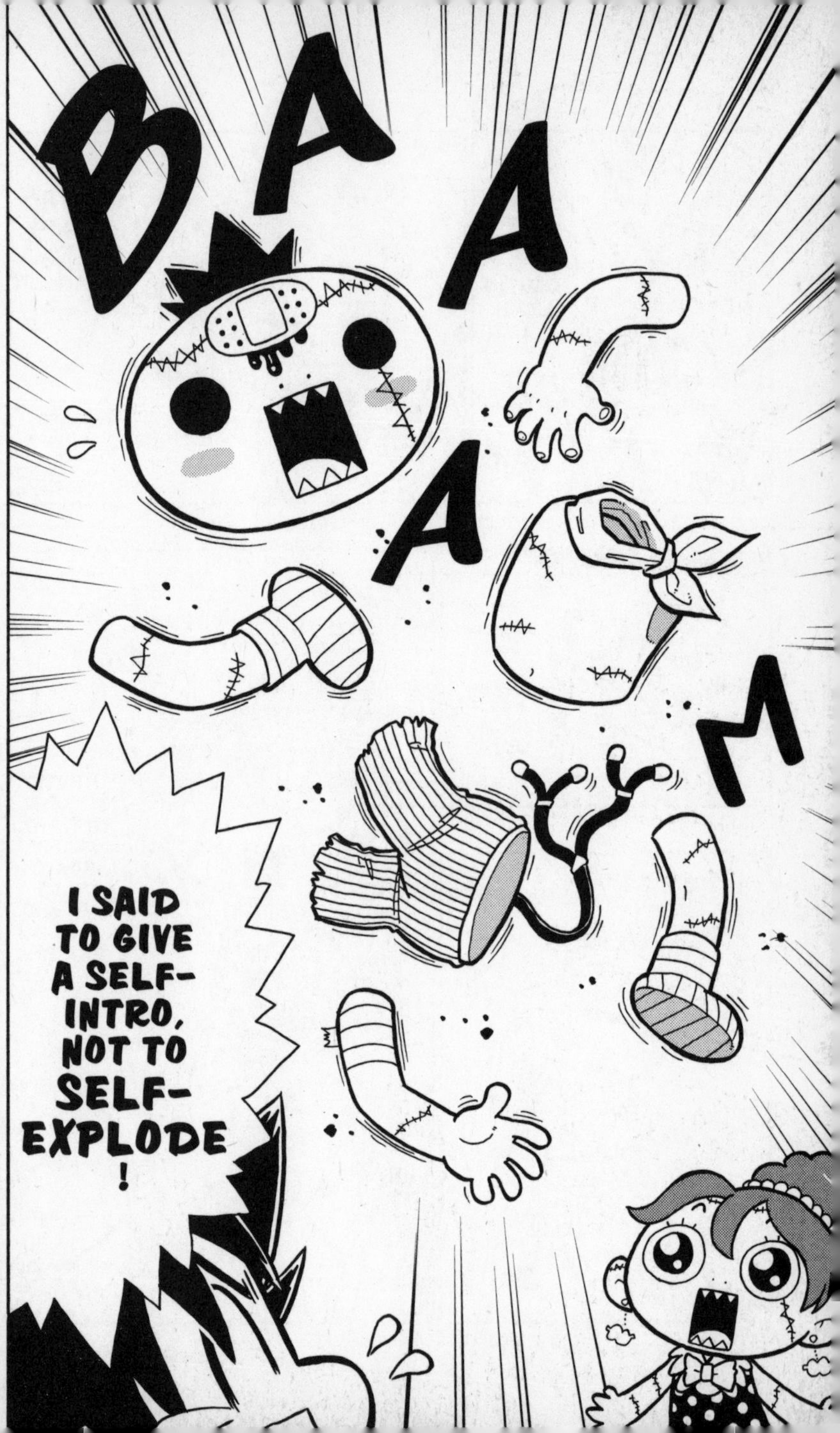
BAAAM
I SAID TO GIVE A SELF-INTRO, NOT TO SELF-EXPLODE!

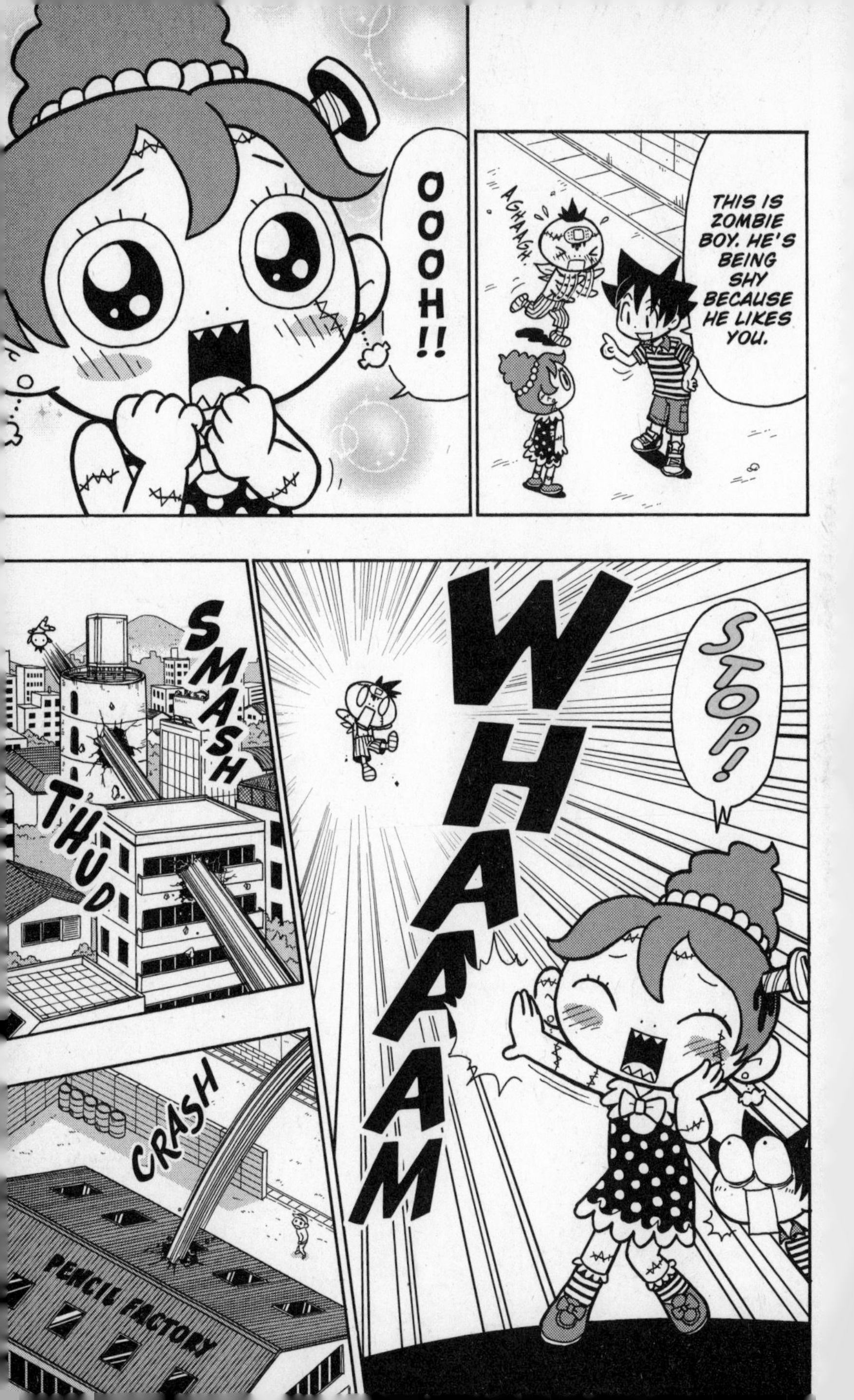
AGHAAGH
THIS IS ZOMBIE BOY. HE'S BEING SHY BECAUSE HE LIKES YOU.
OOOOH!!
STOP!
WHAAAAM
SMASH
THUD
CRASH
PENCIL FACTORY

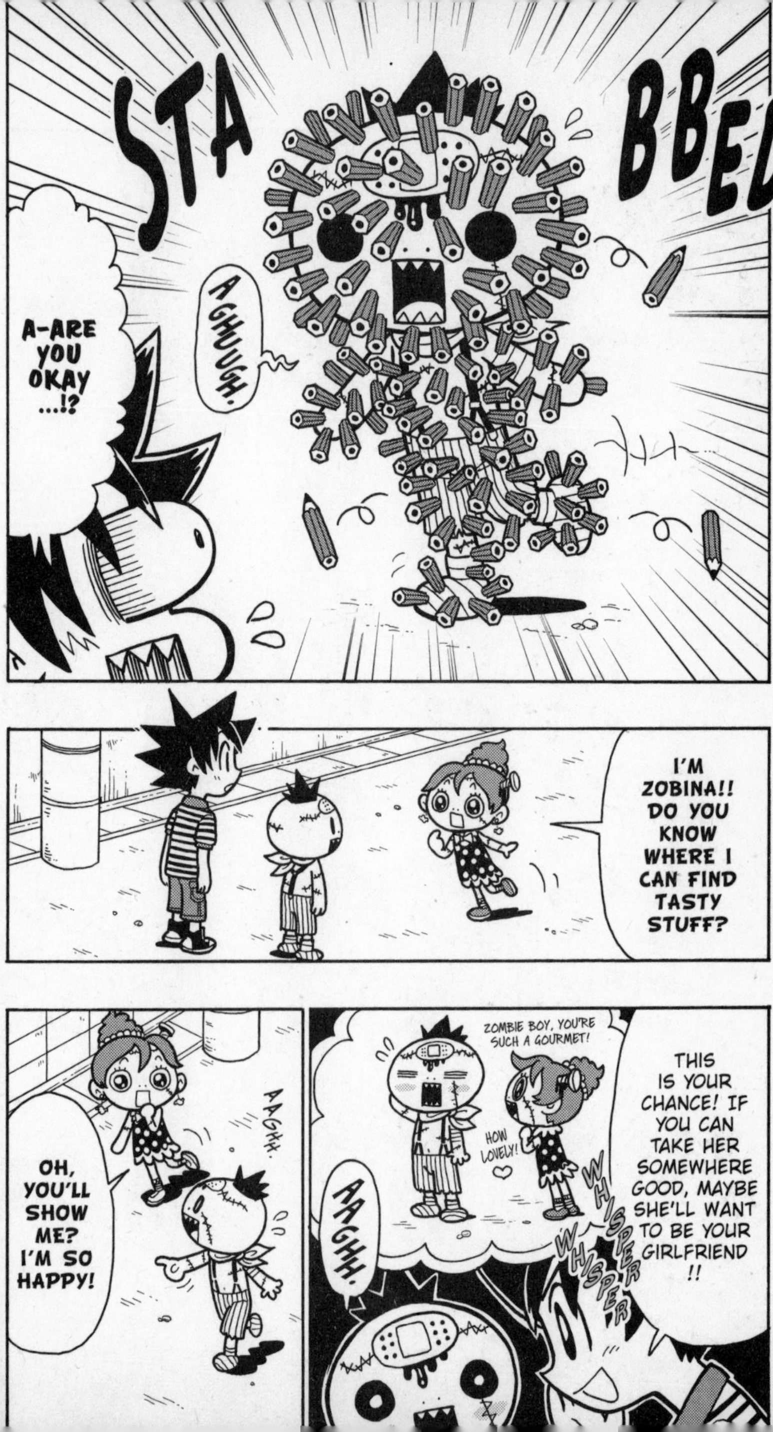
STABBED
A-GHUUGH.
A-ARE YOU OKAY ...!?
I'M ZOBINA!! DO YOU KNOW WHERE I CAN FIND TASTY STUFF?
THIS IS YOUR CHANCE! IF YOU CAN TAKE HER SOMEWHERE GOOD, MAYBE SHE'LL WANT TO BE YOUR GIRLFRIEND !!
WHISPER WHISPER
ZOMBIE BOY, YOU'RE SUCH A GOURMET!
HOW LOVELY!
AAGHH.
AAGHH.
OH, YOU'LL SHOW ME? I'M SO HAPPY!

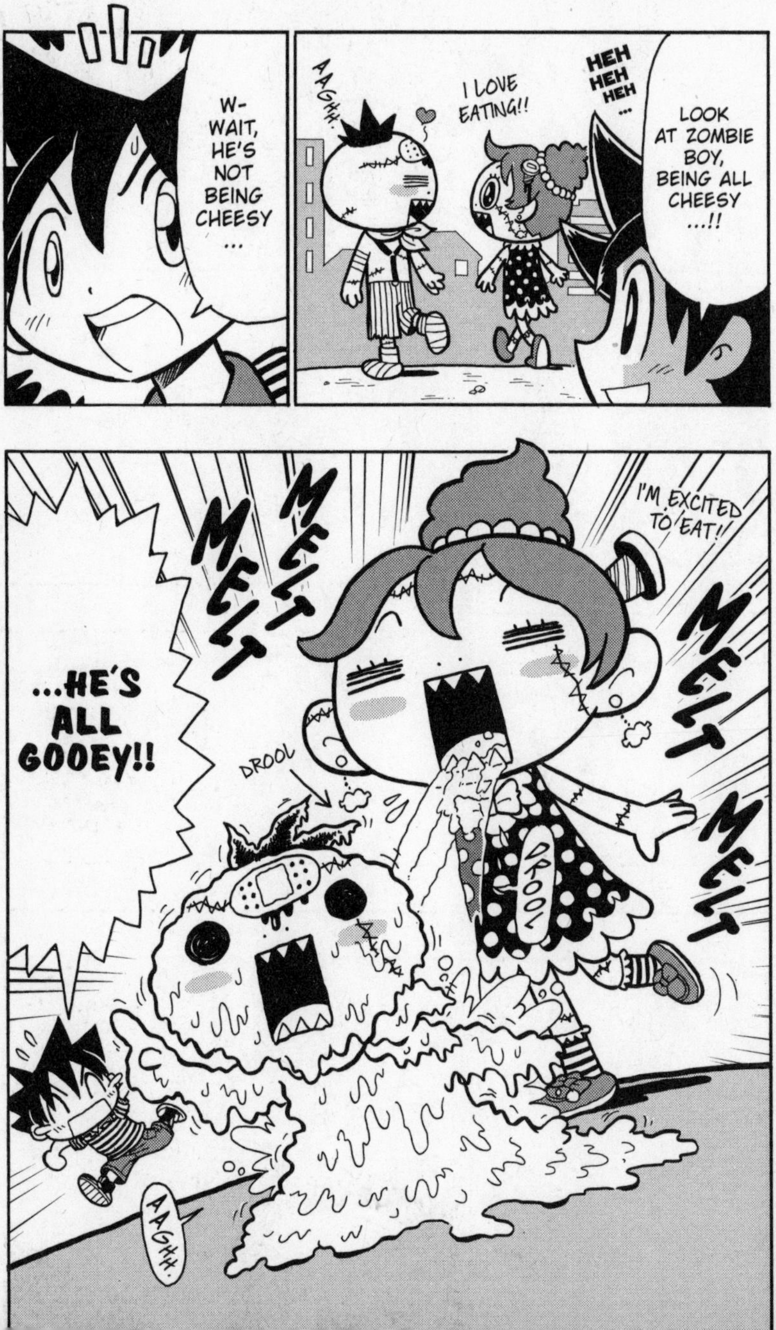

LOOK AT ZOMBIE BOY, BEING ALL CHEESY ...!!
HEH HEH HEH ...
I LOVE EATING!!
AAGHH.
W-WAIT, HE'S NOT BEING CHEESY ...
I'M EXCITED TO EAT!!
MELT MELT
MELT MELT
...HE'S ALL GOOEY!!
DROOL
DROOL
AAGHH.

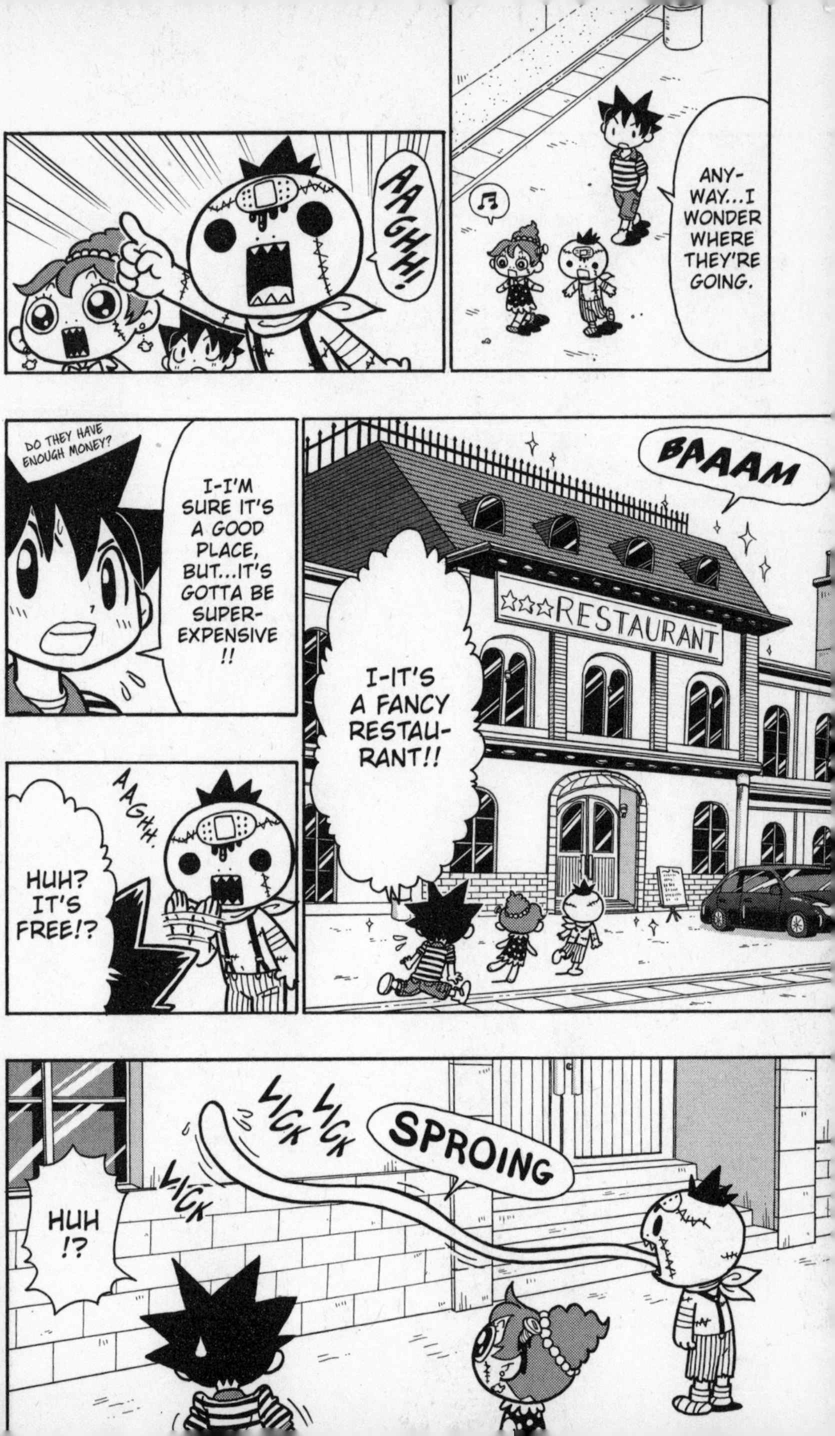
ANY-WAY...I WONDER WHERE THEY'RE GOING.
AAGHH!
BAAAM
I-IT'S A FANCY RESTAU-RANT!!
I-I'M SURE IT'S A GOOD PLACE, BUT...IT'S GOTTA BE SUPER-EXPENSIVE!!
DO THEY HAVE ENOUGH MONEY?
AAGHH.
HUH? IT'S FREE!?
SPROING
LICK LICK
LICK
HUH!?

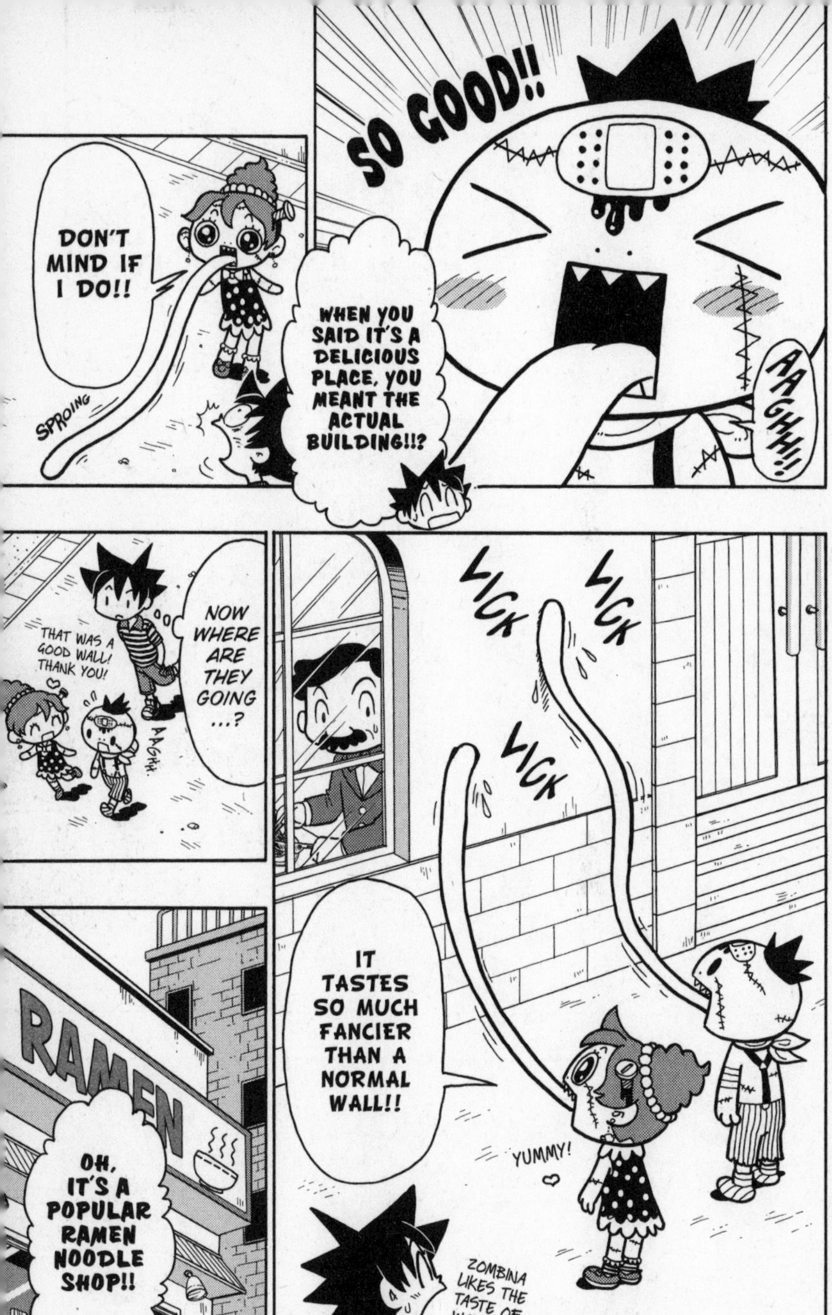
SO GOOD!!
AAGHH!!
WHEN YOU SAID IT'S A DELICIOUS PLACE, YOU MEANT THE ACTUAL BUILDING!!?
DON'T MIND IF I DO!!
SPROING
LICK
LICK
LICK
IT TASTES SO MUCH FANCIER THAN A NORMAL WALL!!
YUMMY!
ZOMBINA LIKES THE TASTE OF WALLS...?
NOW WHERE ARE THEY GOING ...?
THAT WAS A GOOD WALL! THANK YOU!
AAGHH.
RAMEN
OH, IT'S A POPULAR RAMEN NOODLE SHOP!!

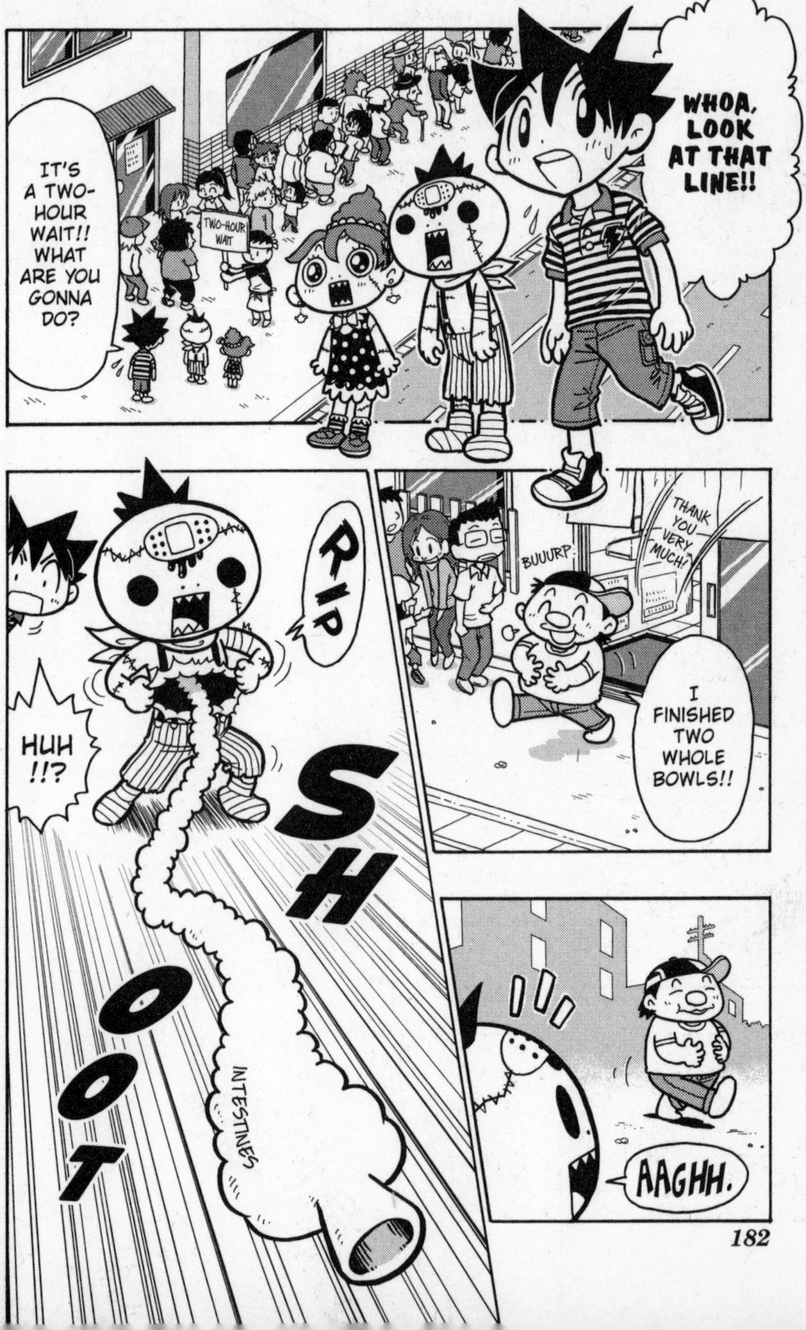
WHOA, LOOK AT THAT LINE!!
IT'S A TWO-HOUR WAIT!! WHAT ARE YOU GONNA DO?
TWO-HOUR WAIT
THANK YOU VERY MUCH!
BUUURP
I FINISHED TWO WHOLE BOWLS!!
AAGHH.
RIP
HUH!!?
SHOOOT
INTESTINES

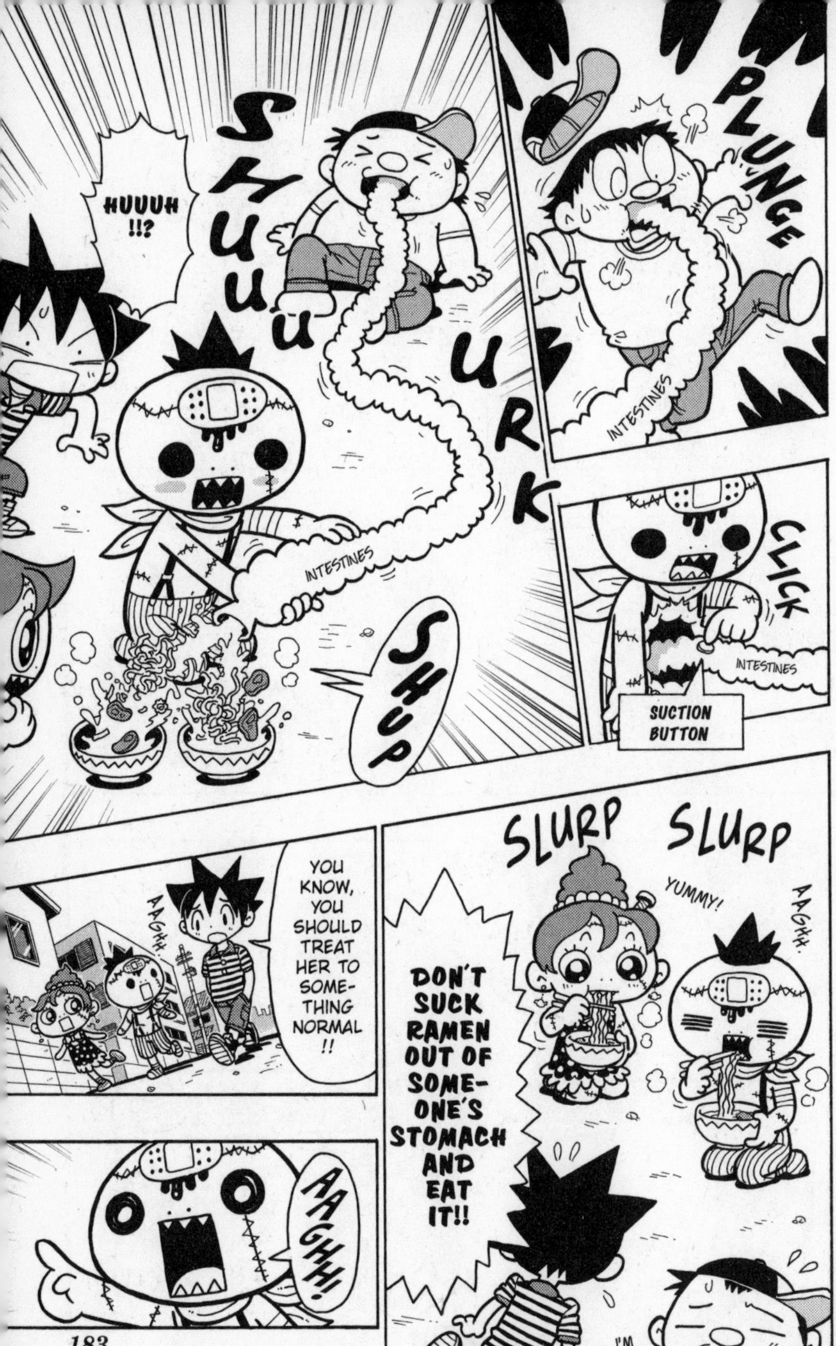
PLUNGE
INTESTINES
CLICK
INTESTINES
SUCTION BUTTON
SHUUUURK
HUUUH !!?
INTESTINES
SHUP
SLURP SLURP
YUMMY!
AAGHH.
DON'T SUCK RAMEN OUT OF SOME-ONE'S STOMACH AND EAT IT!!
I'M HUNGRY ....
YOU KNOW, YOU SHOULD TREAT HER TO SOME-THING NORMAL !!
AAGHH.
AAGHH!

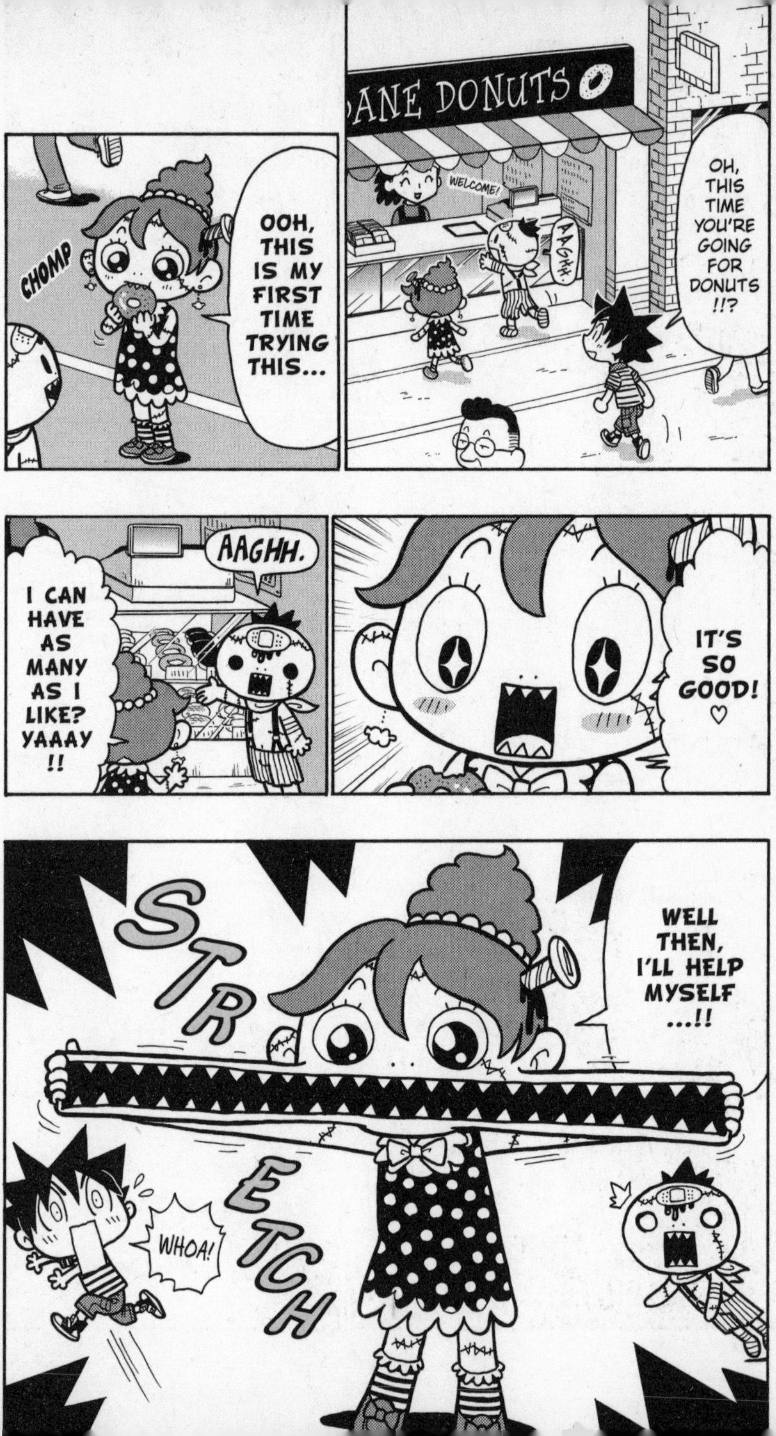
ANE DONUTS
OH, THIS TIME YOU'RE GOING FOR DONUTS !!?
WELCOME!
AAGHH.
OOH, THIS IS MY FIRST TIME TRYING THIS...
CHOMP
IT'S SO GOOD! ♡
AAGHH.
I CAN HAVE AS MANY AS I LIKE? YAAAY !!
WELL THEN, I'LL HELP MYSELF ...!!
STRETCH
WHOA!

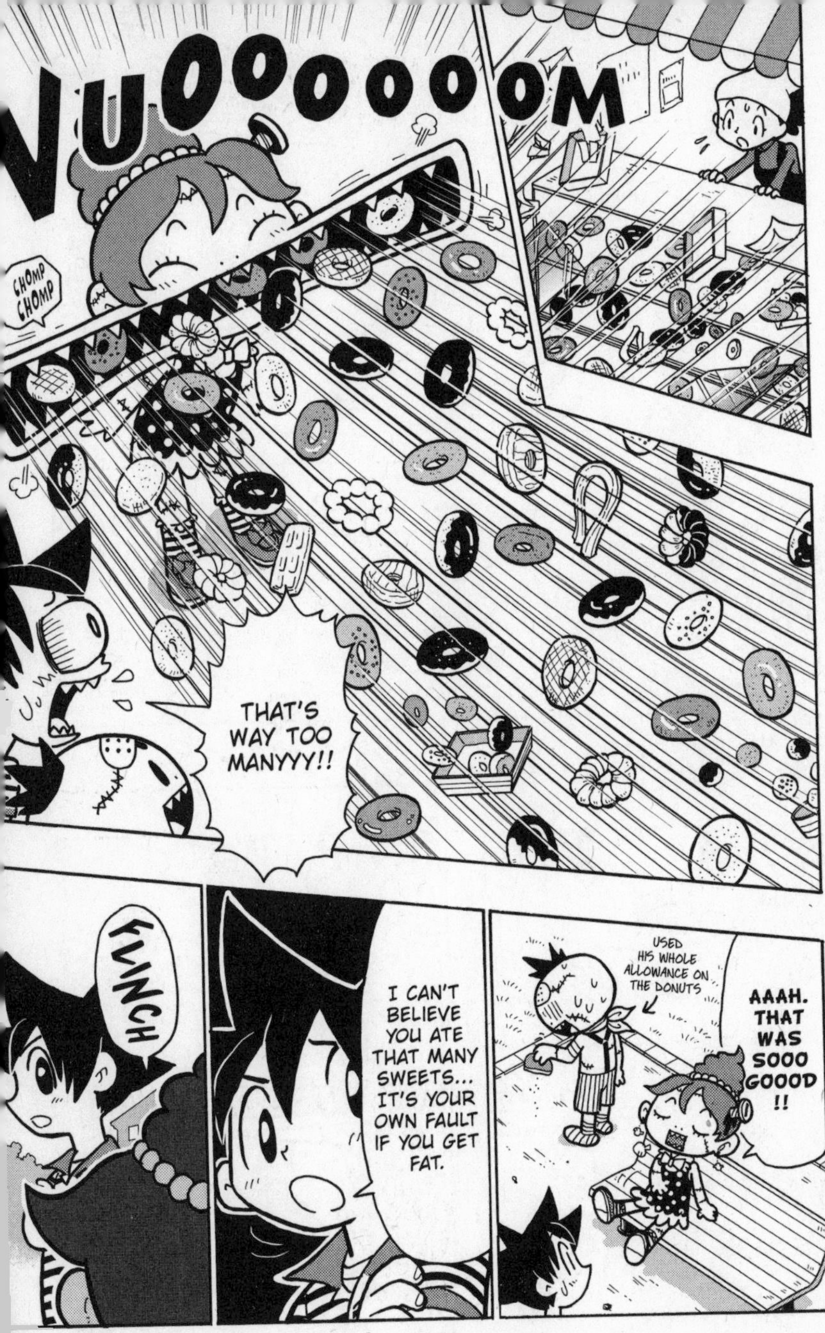
VUOOOOOOOM
CHOMP CHOMP
THAT'S WAY TOO MANYYY!!
AAAH. THAT WAS SOOO GOOOD!!
USED HIS WHOLE ALLOWANCE ON THE DONUTS
I CAN'T BELIEVE YOU ATE THAT MANY SWEETS... IT'S YOUR OWN FAULT IF YOU GET FAT.
FLINCH

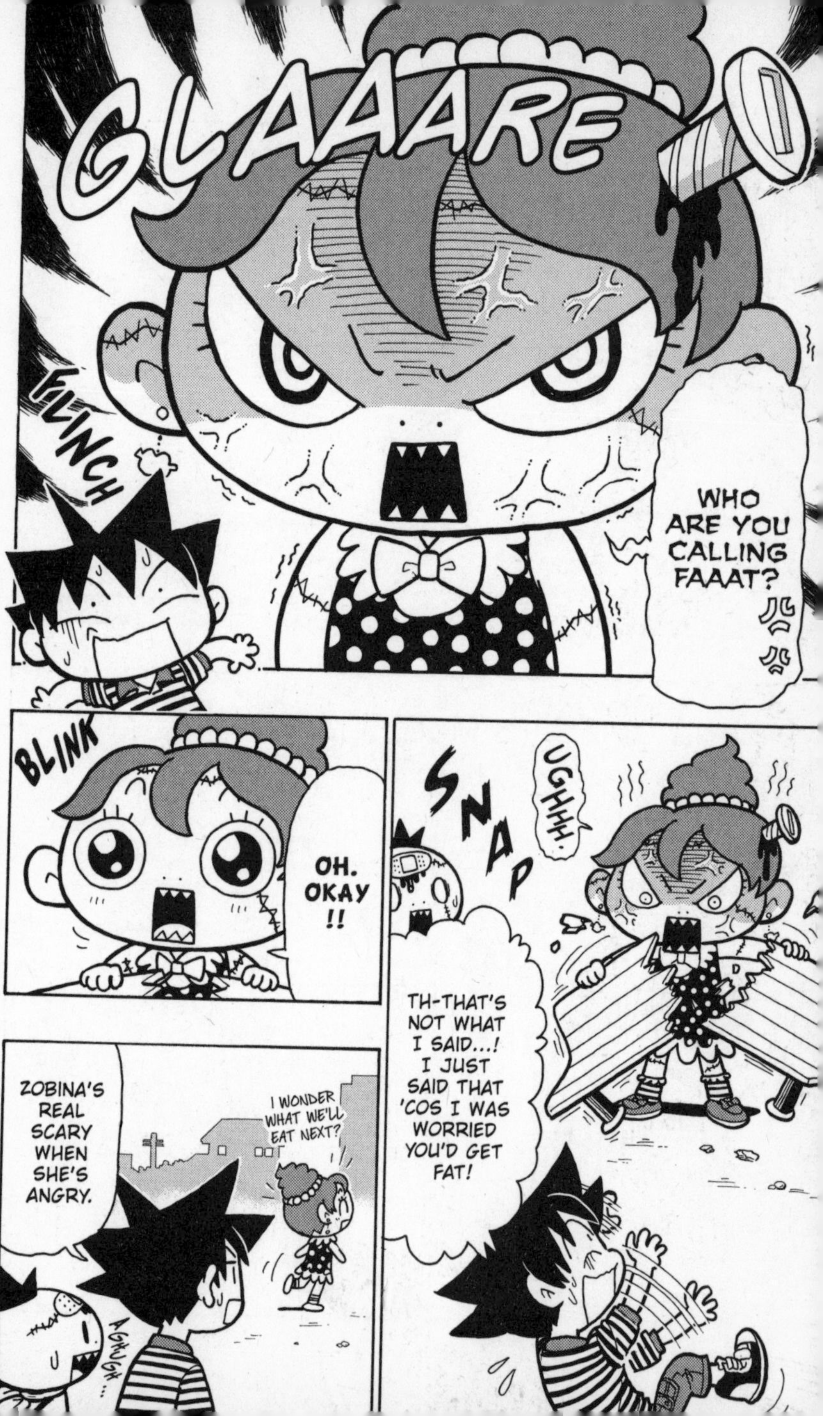
GLAAARE
FLINCH
WHO ARE YOU CALLING FAAAT?
SNAP
UGHHH.
BLINK
OH. OKAY!!
TH-THAT'S NOT WHAT I SAID...! I JUST SAID THAT 'COS I WAS WORRIED YOU'D GET FAT!
ZOBINA'S REAL SCARY WHEN SHE'S ANGRY.
I WONDER WHAT WE'LL EAT NEXT?
AGAUGH...

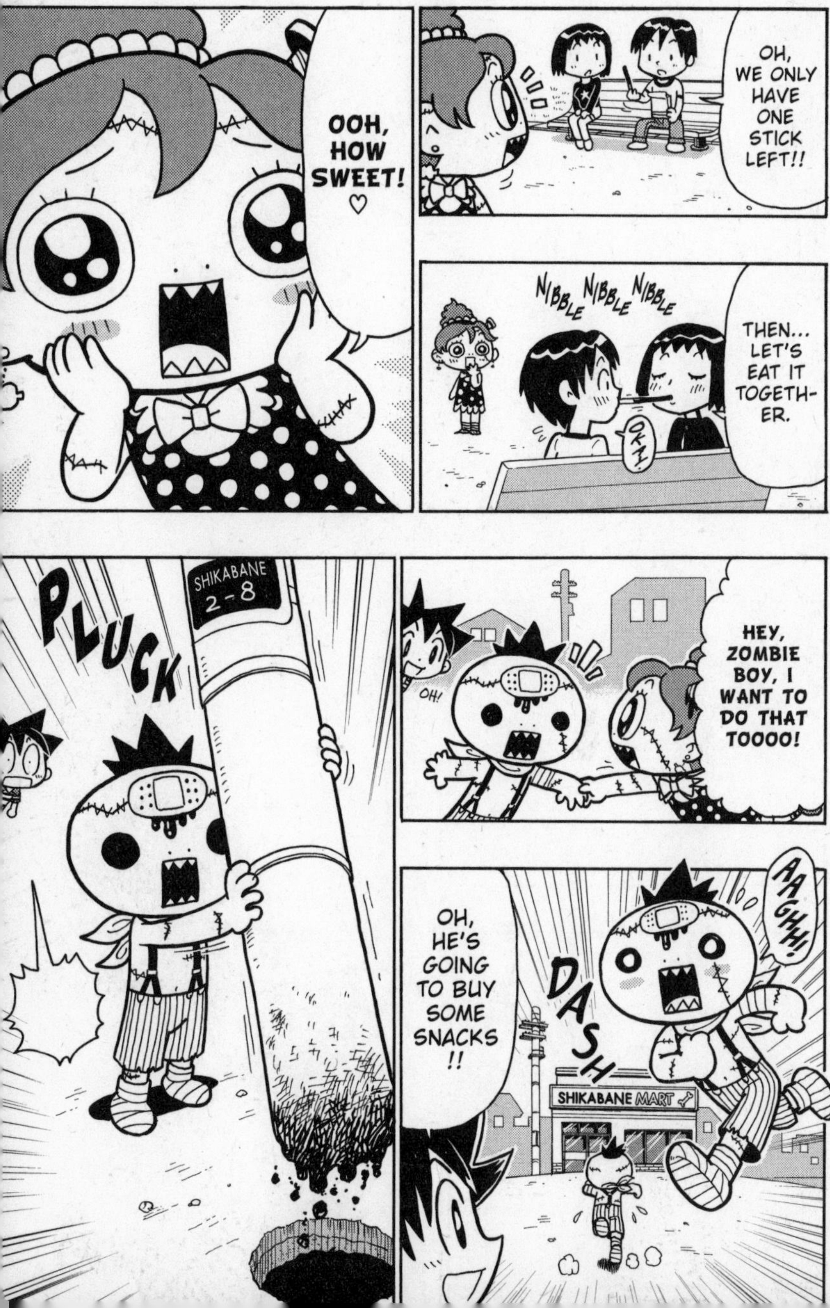
OH, WE ONLY HAVE ONE STICK LEFT!!
THEN... LET'S EAT IT TOGETH-ER.
NIBBLE NIBBLE NIBBLE
OKAY.
OOH, HOW SWEET! ♡
HEY, ZOMBIE BOY, I WANT TO DO THAT TOOOO!
OH!
AAGHH!
DASH
OH, HE'S GOING TO BUY SOME SNACKS!!
SHIKABANE MART
PLUCK
SHIKABANE 2-8

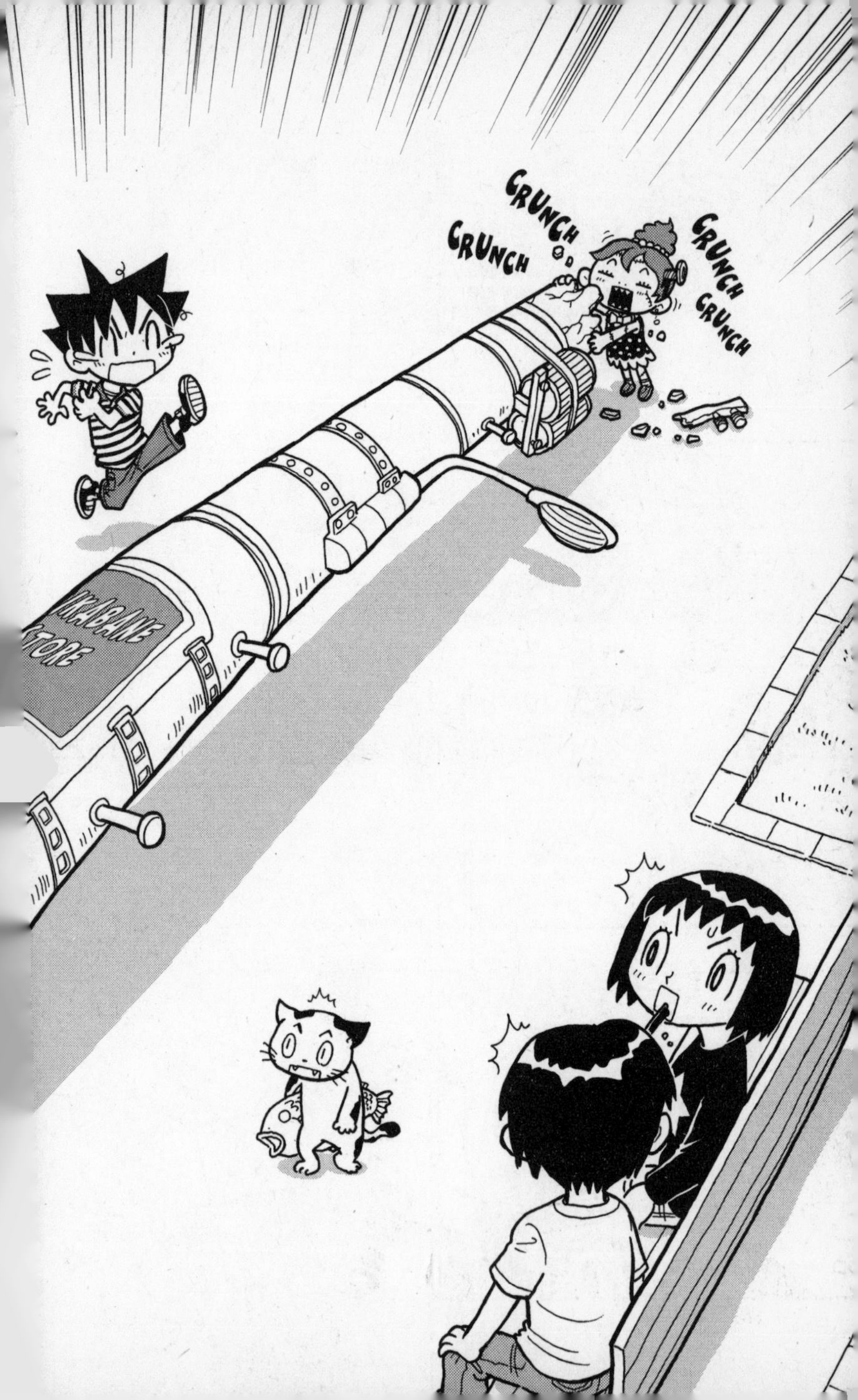
CRUNCH
CRUNCH
CRUNCH
CRUNCH

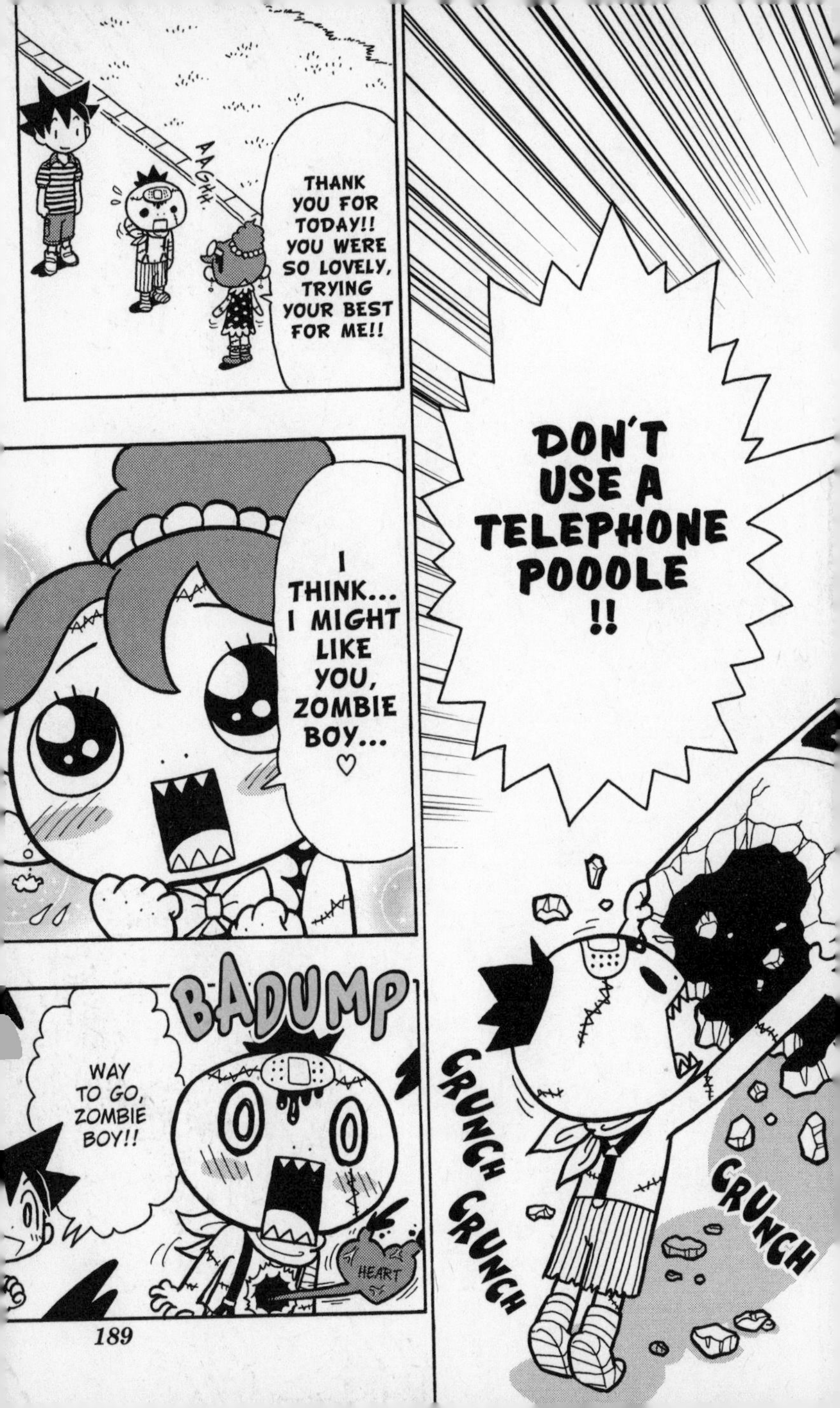
DON'T USE A TELEPHONE POOOLE!!
CRUNCH CRUNCH CRUNCH
CRUNCH
AAGHH
THANK YOU FOR TODAY!! YOU WERE SO LOVELY, TRYING YOUR BEST FOR ME!!
I THINK... I MIGHT LIKE YOU, ZOMBIE BOY... ♡
BADUMP
WAY TO GO, ZOMBIE BOY!!
HEART

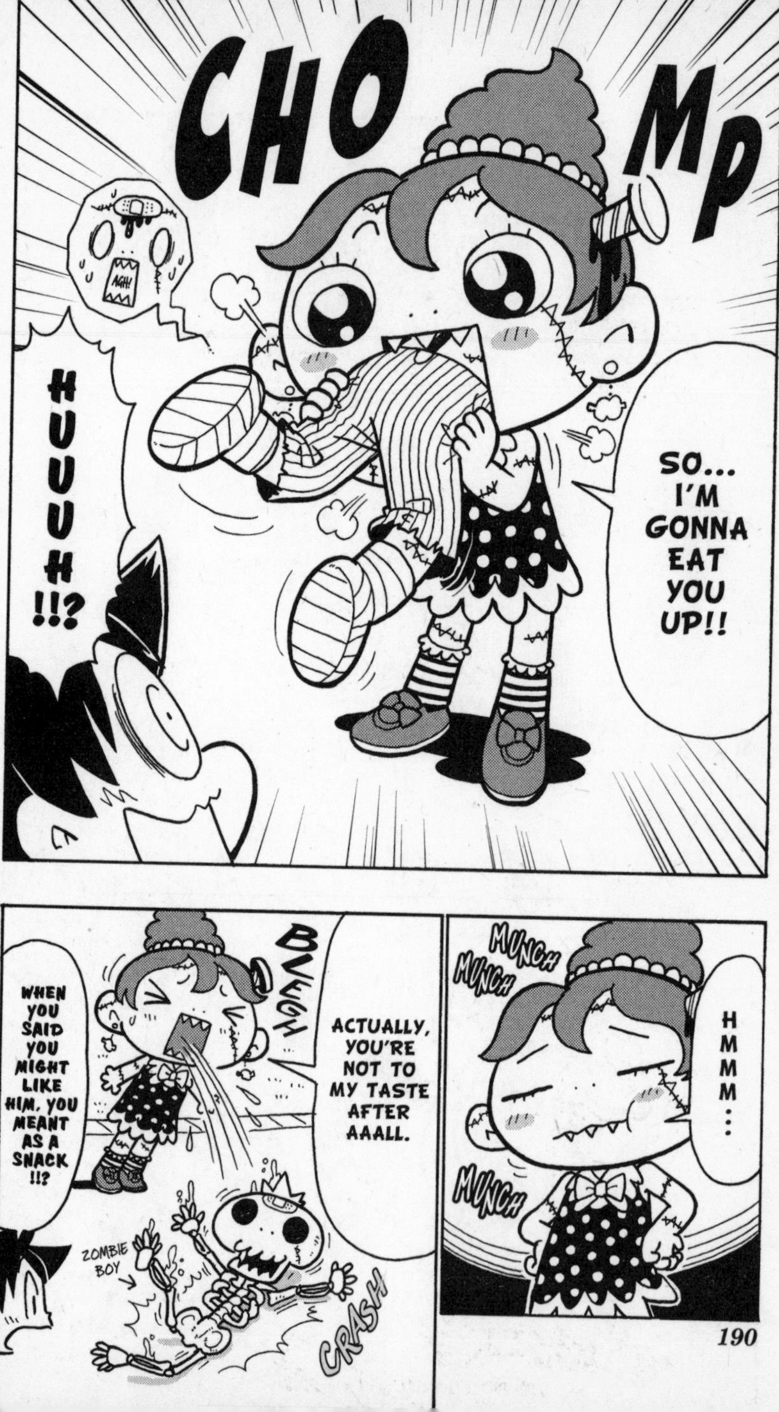
CHOMP
AGH!
SO... I'M GONNA EAT YOU UP!!
HUUUUH!!?
MUNCH
MUNCH
HMMM...
MUNCH
BLEGH
ACTUALLY, YOU'RE NOT TO MY TASTE AFTER AAALL.
WHEN YOU SAID YOU MIGHT LIKE HIM, YOU MEANT AS A SNACK!!?
ZOMBIE BOY
CRASH

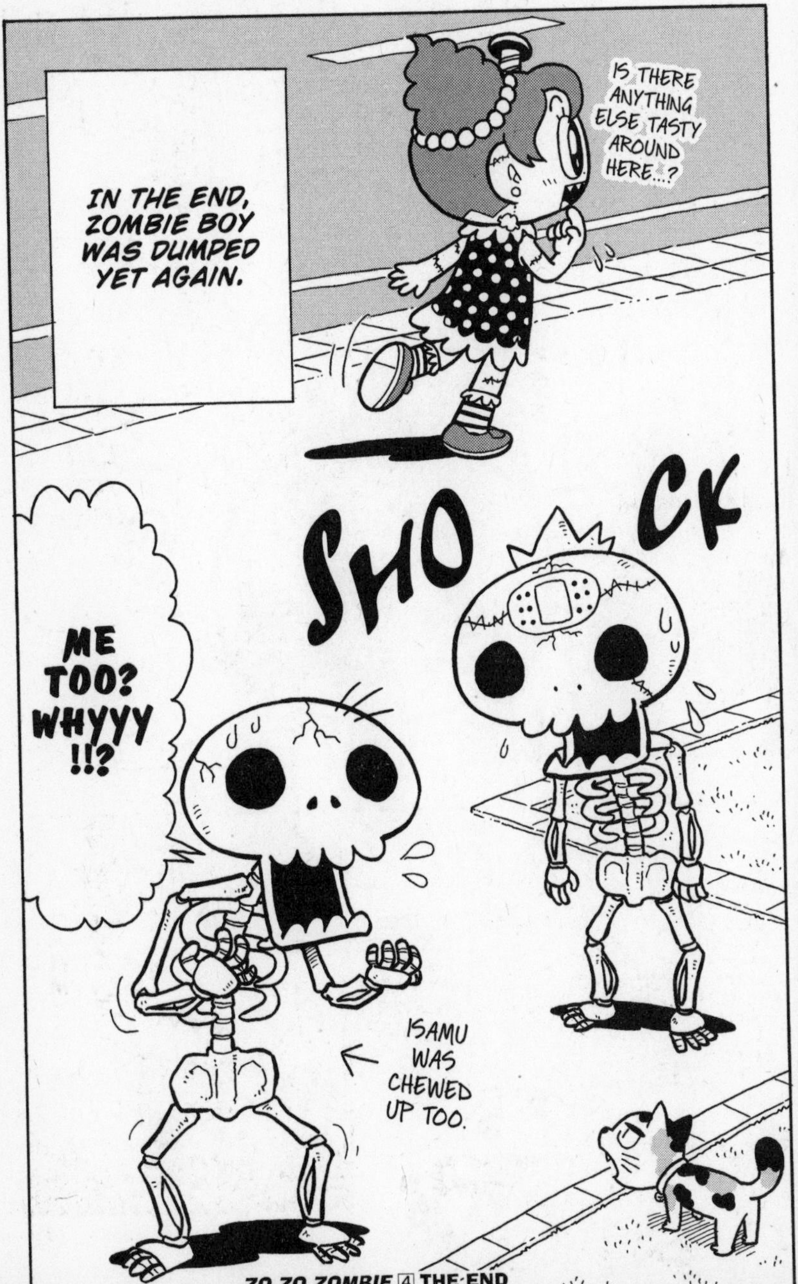
IS THERE ANYTHING ELSE TASTY AROUND HERE...?
IN THE END, ZOMBIE BOY WAS DUMPED YET AGAIN.
SHOCK
ME TOO? WHYYY!!?
ISAMU WAS CHEWED UP TOO.
ZO ZO ZOMBIE 4 THE END

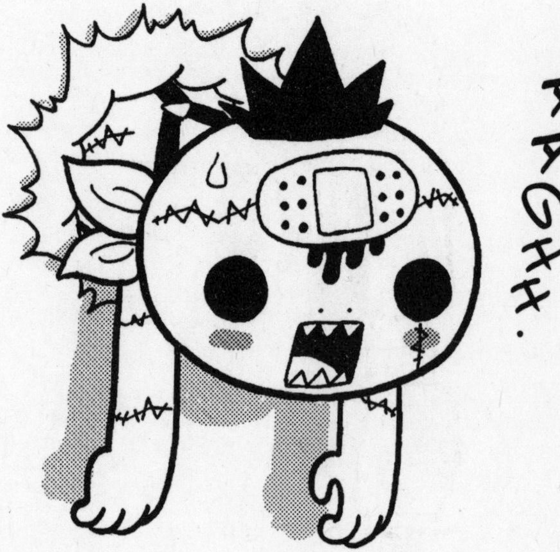
AAGHH.

ZOZO ZOMBIE 4

YASUNARI NAGATOSHI

Translation: ALEXANDRA MCCULLOUGH-GARCIA ♣ Lettering: BIANCA PISTILLO

This book is a work of fiction. Names, characters, places, and incidents are the product of the author's imagination or are used fictitiously. Any resemblance to actual events, locales, or persons, living or dead, is coincidental.

ZOZOZO ZOMBIE-KUN Vol. 4
by Yasunari NAGATOSHI
© 2013 Yasunari NAGATOSHI
All rights reserved.
Original Japanese edition published by SHOGAKUKAN.
English translation rights in the United States of America, Canada, the United Kingdom, Ireland, Australia and New Zealand arranged with SHOGAKUKAN through Tuttle-Mori Agency, Inc.

English translation © 2019 by Yen Press, LLC

Yen Press, LLC supports the right to free expression and the value of copyright. The purpose of copyright is to encourage writers and artists to produce the creative works that enrich our culture.

The scanning, uploading, and distribution of this book without permission is a theft of the author's intellectual property. If you would like permission to use material from the book (other than for review purposes), please contact the publisher. Thank you for your support of the author's rights.

JY
150 West 30th Street, 19th Floor
New York, NY 10001

Visit us at jyforkids.com ♣ facebook.com/jyforkids
twitter.com/jyforkids ♣ jyforkids.tumblr.com ♣ instagram.com/jyforkids

First JY Edition: July 2019

JY is an imprint of Yen Press, LLC.
The JY name and logo are trademarks of Yen Press, LLC.

The publisher is not responsible for websites (or their content) that are not owned by the publisher.

Library of Congress Control Number: 2018948323

ISBN: 978-1-9753-5344-5

10 9 8 7 6 5 4 3 2 1

WOR

Printed in the United States of America